DATE			

Murder at
San Simeon

Previous Books by Robert Lee Hall

THE KING EDWARD PLOT
EXIT SHERLOCK HOLMES

Murder
at
San Simeon

Robert Lee Hall

ST. MARTIN'S PRESS
NEW YORK

Library of Congress Cataloging-in-Publication Data

Hall, Robert Lee.
  Murder at San Simeon / by Robert Lee Hall.
    p. cm.
  "A Thomas Dunne book."
  ISBN 0-312-01477-5
  1. Hearst, William Randolph, 1863–1951—Fiction. I. Title.
PS3558.A3739M8   1988   87-29356
813'.54—dc19   CIP

First Edition
10 9 8 7 6 5 4 3 2 1

For
my mother

I

San
Simeon

A white froth churned upward, hissing. The explosion of tiny bubbles dispersed into a cool, buoyant calm, and the huge man lay still on the bottom, resting like some antediluvian sea monster, a protocrocodile. His sharkish eyes narrowed, evaluating. Around him stretched a grid of tiles set with masterly precision by the finest craftsmen money could buy. Ahead twined the graceful Carrara marble legs of sea nymphs summoned up by one of America's great fortunes. Above him sunlight flickered like a thousand diamonds on the water's rippling skin. Damn fine! At last, blowing and spouting like a whale, he surfaced and began to churn with slow, deliberate strokes toward the west end of the vast pool, where a tall, dignified man in a dark blue suit waited patiently with a clipboard. Reaching the white tile edge, the swimmer clung there, breathing heavily.

"You shouldn't do that, you know," the man with the clipboard said.

A fierce scowl. "I like to go down to the bottom, and I'll damn well do what I like. You worry too much, Joe."

"But the doctor . . . your heart—"

"We will *not* talk about my heart!" In a thoroughly nasty mood, the big man turned and swam sideways toward the marble steps. Streaming water, he began to drag his two hundred and thirty-six pounds of sagging flesh onto the terrace high above the sea.

An outstretched hand. "Let me help."

But the hand was swatted away. "I can do it, Joe. The day I can't get out of my own swimming pool by myself is the day you can—" Nail my coffin, the man thought, but did not say so; he hated to talk about death. "Give me that robe!"

3

Joe Willicombe held out the purple watered-silk robe, and William Randolph Hearst wrapped it around his enormous bulk.

Hearst was tall, six three. Seventy years old, he had been alive when the Battle of Gettysburg was fought, and he had seen the first railroad cross the nation. People said his rabble-rousing yellow journalism had started the Spanish-American War; history clung to his name. Decades and many fierce campaigns had passed; the *Maine* had sunk to the bottom of Havana Bay long ago, but though Hearst's once slender body had grown gross and graceless it still exuded power. Hearst shrugged back sloping shoulders. Framed by a cloudless noontime sky, his jowly face was a long oval bisected by a straight blade of nose. A shock of hair hung lank and gray across his brow, and he had ash-colored, leathery skin, from which shrewd, deep-set blue eyes glimmered like the eyes of an old iguana, smouldering with petulance. Those eyes could wither the strongest men but charmed women, who could not understand how the gallant Mr. Hearst could make anyone tremble. Hearst's voice was strangely high-pitched.

Wearing the robe like a toga, glowering, he looked like an ancient, weathered Caesar or Khan. Indeed, he had fought many battles.

He rarely forgave the men who crossed him.

This was his private fiefdom in the Santa Lucias above San Simeon Bay, two hundred miles north of Los Angeles. Trying to shake his bad mood, Hearst peered about. Taking inventory always helped. His fierce gaze went from the Spanish baroque castle at the top to the three monumental guesthouses at its feet, to the vast Neptune Pool from which he had just climbed, where marble nymphs, swans, and Venus herself, nude, wallowed in the chlorinated waves. A genuine Roman temple decorated the west end. Hearst found a flinty smile. Sixty years he had devoted to scooping up bits and pieces of Europe and the East—pillaging, his enemies called it—ever since his first trip abroad with his beloved mother at age eleven, when his father's silver fortune started him on the road of art collecting. Now even his many residences could not contain all his booty, so that his warehouses were crammed with French ceilings, Gothic stained glass, Dutch masters. Mine, he thought. An elephant trumpted from the largest private zoo in the world. Mine. Dozens of acres of landscaped grounds dotted with terraces and statues. Mine. Green hills tumbled past miles of fenced enclosures where imported llamas and zebras and wildebeests, and more dangerous animals, grazed. Mine. And beyond that shimmered the wrinkled blue Pacific, the world's largest moat. Fifty miles of coastline, more than half the size of Rhode Island. So why this lousy mood?

The old man jerked his head at Colonel Joe Willicombe, his private secretary. "Damn it, let's get to work!"

They headed up between tall cypresses. Five minutes later, they were striding over the two-thousand-year-old Pompeiian mosaic in Casa Grande's entranceway and into the Assembly Hall, a cavernous room with massive stone walls hung with Rubens tapestries. An ornate fireplace from a French chateau dominated the east end of the huge room, and life-size statues hovered in stilted attitudes, like guests frozen in the act of reaching for canapés. Hearst frowned briefly at the big central table, spread with Marion Davies' latest jigsaw puzzle.

Marion, his pretty movie-star mistress, thirty-six years his junior.

The old man felt a sharp pang. What was she up to in Hollywood? Screwing her latest leading man? Damn it, his detectives owed him a report!

Willicombe silently trailing, Hearst reached the fourteenth-century choir stalls on the far wall. One segment contained a secret panel, behind which, in one of the stone towers that burrowed up through Casa Grande, was hidden a small elevator, whose wood-paneled interior had been ripped from a medieval church confessional. Hearst loved gadgets, toys, surprises; he delighted in startling guests by popping out his secret door.

He opened the panel, and in the hidden elevator he and Willicombe rose to the third floor.

They headed directly to the study in the Gothic Suite, the brain of the far-flung empire, where every day its ruler reviewed his many newspapers, formulated policy, launched campaigns, and fired the disobedient—editors opened telegrams from the Chief with trembling hands. The room did not look like an office. Arched with

5

Gothic ribs, it more resembled a monastery chapel, a very rich monastery. Fat, leather-bound volumes stretched in rows behind leaded glass, antique music stands stood about like acolytes, and the lampshades were made of five-hundred-year-old parchment pages ripped from priceless hymnals.

Hearst trundled to the massive mahogany table in the center.

He had just plopped himself down into the baronial red leather chair at its head when his dachshund, Helena, burst into the room chasing a mouse.

"What the devil . . . !" Hearst pushed himself up.

The mouse veered around the chair; the dog negotiated the turn only halfway before Hearst collared her, yipping and wriggling. "Take her, Joe, damn it." He thrust her into Willicombe's arms. "Now, mousey . . ." The small gray-brown creature had stunned itself against a table leg and lay belly up on the stone floor, chest heaving. Hearst scooped it into his palm. Its right front paw was white. "There, there," he cooed over it as if it were a sick baby. "Still breathing. Bad Helena!"

Helena squirmed in Willicombe's arms.

Hearst strode to the door, bellowed, and a red-haired maid with a freckle-blotched face scurried in.

Hearst grabbed her hand and wrapped the mouse in it. "Don't make faces, Mary. Get this little fellow to Dr. Dilworth right now. An emergency. Tell Dilworth his name's, um, Ambrose." He snorted a laugh. "That's good, isn't it, Joe?"

The self-effacing Willicombe nodded. The acerbic columnist Ambrose Bierce had worked for Hearst for years before disappearing in Mexico.

Gingerly holding the mouse, Mary backed out.

Willicombe adjusted his glasses. "Your own doctor?" he said.

Slumping back into his chair, Hearst snorted. "I pay him plenty, he might as well earn it. Doctors, damn them. If I were younger I wouldn't have to keep them around. Get on with it, Joe."

Willicombe put Helena down, and she curled up at Hearst's feet. Poking his glasses up on his broad, bland brow, the secretary began droning reports from the ever present clipboard: messages from editors, an old lawsuit, a new Millicent Hearst charity. Hearst

6

drummed his fingers on the table. He could not help wincing at his wife's name; annoyance, guilt, a weight of obligation always accompanied it. Millicent Hearst lived a continent away in her own mansion in New York. She had raised their five sons; she devoted her life to charities. A chill politeness was all that remained between her and Hearst, but in spite of years of pleading she would not agree to divorce, and the old man had grown glumly convinced she never would. Women. Marion could be counted on for a screaming fit at the mere mention of Millicent Hearst's name.

"Charity? What sort? Another milk fund? It doesn't matter. Just tell all the New York papers to give it a big play; I want to keep that woman happy. Now, what about this lawsuit?"

"It's the fireworks thing."

"The lawyers haven't cleared that up yet? What the hell do I pay 'em for?" The litigation was decades old. It arose from a political rally in Chicago. Hearst had a childlike love of fireworks. He had sponsored a display, but something had gone wrong: a pile of rocket bombs had exploded, and a policeman had had his head blown off. Altogether eighteen people had died and nearly a hundred had been injured, and the fact that no one could decide who was at fault—the fireworks people? Hearst? the city?—had caused the thing to drag on forever. Typical, Hearst thought gloomily. People are always trying to wring something out of me.

"It's good news," Willicombe hastened to say. "The last lawsuits are close to being settled, though they'll still cost us."

But Hearst's mind had veered. He was smiling, humming. Fireworks . . . how about rockets over Casa Grande? Some weekend, for one of those big wingdings Marion loved, when forty or fifty guests were heading up the hill in the dark. That would cheer her up.

"Joe, get hold of that fireworks man in Los Angeles—Snoodles or Boodles or whatever his name is. Tell him I want to talk to him."

"Yes, sir. . . . Er, sir?"

"Out with it."

Willicombe poked at his glasses. He spoke in his graveyard baritone: "I hate to bother you with this, but . . ." With a gray look

7

he tugged a small square of paper from his clipboard and passed it to Hearst.

The old man took it warily. It was about eight by ten inches. Printed on it in anonymous block letters were six words: I AM COMING TO GET YOU.

Hearst's eyes flashed. "Another crackpot threat?" He waved the paper angrily. "Some mealymouthed malcontent is always aiming his guns at me. Why? Is it my fault the country's in a mess? You'd think I'm the only target in sight." His eyes crinkled. "Or is it because my papers always tell 'em the truth? Anyhow, the day we don't get one of these the sun won't come up. I'm surprised at you, Joe. Why pester me with this one? Alert our security men just like you always do, and call the police. If some idiot wants to to blow off steam, let him, and be damned. Besides, nothing's ever come of a single one of 'em. You know that."

"Something might. I did show this to the police. They want you to look at the drawing."

"Drawing?" Hearst peered more closely. Yes, there was a scribble in the upper right-hand corner, faint radiating pencil lines that looked like a dandelion. "So what?"

"The police wonder if you might know something about it."

"A goddamn doodle? What would I know?"

"Inspector Garcia thought it might have some sort of meaning for you. He's only doing his job, looking for clues. I'm sorry, sir. It's silly, I know." Willicombe held out his hand. "Give it back, and I'll . . ."

But Hearst did not return the paper. Usually the threats were much more specific—death, and for specific reasons, too. His leathery old thumb rubbed the anonymous sheet. Cheap newsprint. I AM COMING TO GET YOU.

He squinted at Willicombe. "How'd this arrive?"

"By mail."

"The police've already gone over it?"

"Yes."

"Fingerprints?"

"No."

"And no return address, I suppose."

"None. And the postmark was blurred."

"So it could have come from down the road?"

"Or from Afghanistan, as far as the police can say."

Hearst snorted. "Damn post office. Damn police." He looked again at the little puff of lines. Probably only a random scribble, but . . . shivering suddenly as if a memory far back had been nudged, he thrust it into his robe pocket. "I'll keep it. Tell Garcia I'll think about it; maybe I do know something after all." He began to dictate telegrams to various editors. He was adamant about the Chicago newspaper strike. "Those bandits aren't going to get a dime! Don't they know there's a depression on? Now, about Europe . . ." He always went to Europe in the summer, with Marion and the usual gaggle of hangers-on. "Germany will be the highlight. I want to talk to Hitler. Arrange it, Joe."

When Willicombe had gone Hearst sat staring at a large oil portrait on the far wall. It showed a vibrant young man with a gaze of almost fanatic idealism. Me at thirty, Hearst thought, and cursed old age. He felt more uneasy than ever; 1934 was not going well. The goddamn depression. The labor unions. The Reds.

Marion's drinking.

Hearst thumped the mahogany table so hard that Helena started awake. Absently he scratched her head while he cursed the numerous flaws in a world he could run perfectly if only he had the chance. I should be president! No, that was an old, lost issue; his many attempts had failed. He stood and began to pace, bones creaking. Was it mounting threats of ruin that ate at him? "You've got to cut back spending or go under," his financial advisors warned. Jack Neylan, his chief lawyer, was worst: "You're dropping fifteen million a year on personal expenses alone; you're heading for a crash." Hearst squeezed his hands into fists. Damn Irishman! He hated any monkey wrench in doing just what he liked; the depression might slow down ordinary people, it damn well would not stop him. But the petulance, the fury, in his cold blue eyes was tinged with fear. Could it all really be going down the drain? Desperately he reviewed his holdings: thirty newspapers; fifteen magazines; ten radio stations; seven castles, including Saint Donat's in Wales, ninety-four separate corporations, not counting the motion picture companies. Over thirty thousand people work for me: Walter Winchell, Louella

9

Parsons—even Popeye! I own fifty million worth of paintings and sculpture. Einstein and Cecil B. De Mille have eaten at my table, and I even made that fool Roosevelt president! Growing livid at this recollection, one of the great political blunders of his life, the old man felt a dangerous shortness of breath, a wild thudding in his chest. No! Cursing his mortality, damning doctors and time itself, he clamped a lid on fury.

One of his fists found the threatening note in his robe pocket. He jerked it out. I AM COMING TO GET YOU. The old man laughed.

Nobody's gotten me in seventy years.

Nobody's going to get me now.

II

You Are
Invited to
Mr. Hearst's

※ 1 ※

L ATE summer, 1934, and around Hollywood the rumor mills began to grind: Mr. Hearst might be throwing a party.

Everybody who was anybody was dying to come, because it would not be just any party. It would be one of the notorious weekends at the castle aerie on the hilltop at San Simeon, midway between the crashing Pacific surf and the San Andreas Fault. Famous faces would be a dime a dozen, and far from an America wasted by the Great Depression, pocked with Hoovervilles, creased with breadlines, another America would gather, witty and glittering, and Mr. Hearst's vast, impeccably landscaped acres would shine with the firefly gleam of celebrity: writers, politicians, movie stars. Winston Churchill had traded quips with Groucho Marx at Mr. Hearst's, and George Bernard Shaw had planted such sharp, witty barbs in Greta Garbo's famous flesh that she had fled moaning among the rhododendrons. It might happen again; something like it was sure to. What fun! Naturally everyone would adore—or pretend to adore—pretty Marion Davies, their hostess, who drank far too much and said just what she thought.

Not all the guests would be famous, of course; there were always those odd, furtive little characters whom nobody seemed to know and who were vague about their connections. Hangers-on? Friends of friends? Gangsters, some of the vetted invitees gleefully speculated, whispering again the dark, persistent, but somehow unverifiable rumors about Mr. Hearst: bribery, lechery, murder. Maybe they were just erring editors who had been ordered up for a tongue-lashing. Or Marion's strays? Dear, sweet Marion was no snob; she was always picking up strays—especially handsome young men.

In any case, there would be secret booze parties in the

guesthouses and plenty of chances for illicit sex. How could scandal touch you in so isolated a playground? Just keeping your eyes and ears open provided enough gossip for a year's knowing whispers.

So everybody who was anybody waited hopefully for the cream-colored, rag linen envelope with the embossed Hearst seal: *You are cordially invited* . . .

Meanwhile, a few people who were nobody had strong private reasons for wanting to be at Mr. Hearst's, and they were damned if they would wait for some fancy card.

❧ 2 ❧

MARION Davies was not in a good mood. Practically spitting, she dragged off her Confederate Army boots and flung them across the living room of her spacious bungalow on the MGM lot.

"G-god damn Norma Shearer! And Irving Thalberg, her b-bastard of a husband, too!"

Marion was short, only five two. Blond was in fashion for movie comediennes; Marion was very blond. Quietly fuming, she began tearing at the buttons of the gray uniform, which had been artfully muddied and bloodstained by the Metro costume department. Her stammer had been tamed for sound pictures, but it came back whenever her director called, "Cut!" "S-son of a b-bitch!" she muttered now. The picture in this case was *Operator 13*, in which she played Gale Loveless, a beautiful Union Army spy who becomes involved with handsome Confederate cavalry officer John Galliard, played by Gary Cooper.

Marion had just finished the scene in which she dressed as the enemy in order to flee to the North. She had also just received bad news: Norma Shearer was definitely getting the part of Marie Antoinette.

The last jacket button refused to pull free. "Sh-shit!" Marion ripped it off, and the brass disk thumped to the floor, landing beside a pair of shiny black shoes. An impeccably manicured hand lifted the button from the thick wool carpet and cool blue eyes examined it.

"You t-tell me, Vinny," Marion demanded. "Whattaya think of that l-lousy d-decision?"

Screenwriter Vincent X. Tashman clucked his tongue. He was lean, with sleeked-back dark hair, an aristocractic nose, an artfully groomed pencil-line mustache. The last starlet he had slept with, an ambitious redhead, had told him he reminded her of John Barrymore. Vinny acknowledged the resemblance; he was also quite aware the girl had been buttering him up. Inwardly he laughed. Too bad for her she didn't know how little pull I really have; the piranhas're already nibbling my toes. He pushed the thought aside, not liking to face the fix he was in. "It's tough breaks," he purred. "You deserve the part."

Marion grabbed a tall glass of gin from a sideboard and tossed down half of it. "Oh, that old Thalberg's a l-load of m-manure."

Vinny puffed on his imported Balkan Sobranie. "What can you expect, when he's production head? Can't W.R. do anything?"

"Popsy? Thalberg's a d-damn stone w-wall."

"Mm." A wrinkle of worry crossed Vinny's brow. If Marion's sugar daddy, William Randolph Hearst, couldn't budge Thalberg there was little hope Vinny could do it. I'll soon be peddling apples on street corners! he thought. While Marion poured herself more gin, he frowned at the coal of his cigarette. If only he had written something lately that made money, if only he could keep from punching directors who wanted to change his lines. Gloomily he sank into a swollen champagne beige armchair while Marion flounced to the spacious front window. Hearst had built the bungalow for her, but it was more like a small private resort. It had eighteen rooms. The living room alone was twenty by thirty feet, dripping with the latest art deco gewgaws, including a huge white grand piano on which Astaire and Rogers could have kicked up their heels with acres to spare. It was about four P.M. Outside in strong September sunshine the MGM front lawn sloped to the big soundstages topped by the Metro sign with its famous lion. Staring out, Marion noisily gulped more gin. Vinny tugged at the creases of his fawn slacks, crossed long legs, and while he waited for developments from Marion, idly watched a platoon of Napoleonic foot soldiers march in the direction of a giant papier-mâché Sphinx. A half dozen extras dressed in flapper garb appeared at the far edge of the lawn; a brunette who looked like Ruby Keeler hesitated, left the group and headed toward the bungalow. Vinny's heavy-lidded eyes drifted to Marion. Shimmering blond hair, full breasts, tucked-in waist, deliciously blooming hips. Hearst sure knew how to pick 'em! Even in rumpled Confederate pants and shirt she was as ripe as a peach; any man would want a taste of that. Vinny's nostrils flared as he exhaled smoke. No wonder Hearst had snatched her from the Ziegfield line, made her a star. She's got talent too, a swell commedienne, Vinny thought as he ground out his cigarette, but Thalberg's right: she could never play Marie Antoinette.

"I g-gotta hand it to W.R., he *d-does* go to bat for me," Marion said, turning. Hands on hips, she came toward Vinny, the ice clinking in her glass. "But Thalberg j-just won't b-budge. You know what I think W.R.'s g-gonna d-do? P-pull me outta here. W-Warners'd love to have me, he says. Jack Warner's just b-begging."

Vinny's eyes met hers. "You want to go?"

"D-do I have a ch-choice?"

"Do you?"

She bit her plump lower lip. "Well . . . I s-sure don't w-want to; I've m-made a lot of friends here." More firmly, as if she were trying to convince herself, "But what P-Poppa says goes," she finished.

"Naturally."

Marion stamped her bare foot. "You know what everybody c-calls me? The Most Publicly Kept W-woman in the W-world. Oh, why won't that old wife of his g-give him a d-divorce! She's a goddamn b-black w-widow, that's what she is! And this heat!" Marion dragged a hand through her blond curls. "It was a h-hundred degrees on that d-damn soundstage. An electrician f-fainted in the f-flies and nearly f-fell on me."

"How awful."

"I know it's only September, and I know it's only Southern

16

California, but I w-want snow! Why can't old Droopy Drawers give me snow?" Droopy Drawers was one of Marion's pet names for Hearst. Rubbing her glass up and down one arm, she looked dreamy, and Vinny knew that the gin, her narcotic, was calming her at last. "Gee, there was snow in Ch-Chicago," she crooned in her husky contralto. "I l-lived in Chicago once, know that? With M-Mama and Reine. Reine was my older s-sister, the f-first one of us in show business. You probably never heard of her—she's d-dead now—but gee she was lovely! I was t-ten and she was in a music hall revue. I heard the applause and just r-rushed onstage. I b-bowed. I thought the c-clapping was for me, can you beat that? Ten years old, and I've been h-hooked ever since." Her blue eyes shone. "Whatta ya think, Vinny?"

Hearst is hooked on you, Vinny thought; we're all hooked on something. "Marvelous," he said, flicking flame from a gleaming silver lighter.

"You c-come from Chicago, don't you?"

The flame stopped an inch from his cigarette. "Why, how'd you know that?"

She poked his shoulder. "What is it, s-some big s-secret?"

"Of course not." He lit up, French-inhaled, the smoke curling over his thinly mustached lip into the flaring aristocratic nostrils. "Yes, I'm from Chicago." The Illinois Home for Little Wayfarers, he thought, a bastard of a place. At least she doesn't know I shot a man there.

Vinny smiled up at her. "Chicago's swell."

"B-but I guess Hollywood is really b-better."

"Of course it is."

There was a knock on the door, and Marion made a face. "Where the hell is that Jasmine? I've g-gotta g-get out of these duds. Oh, n-nuts." Sweeping across the thick white carpet, she jerked open the door.

"Hello, Miss Davies." It was the brunette who had reminded Vinny of Ruby Keeler.

"Hi, honey. What can I d-do for you?"

"Well—" The brunette had big hazel eyes. She was young, with flushed pink cheeks and a pert little nose, and Vinny made sure to sit up straight and show his profile. "You invited me to your party, remember?"

17

Marion often threw parties after a day's shooting. "Oh, yeah, I d-did, didn't I? I didn't recognize you in that g-getup; we met in crinolines on a v-veranda in the Deep Sa-yowth, soundstage two, right? You're Gloria something, aren't you?"

"Gloria Deere."

"That's it. Well, c-come in, honey. Jasmine! Oh, hell, some drinks'll be here soon, when my m-maid gets a m-move on. 'Scuse me, I've gotta get ch-changed. Make yourself c-comfortable. This's Vinny Tashman; he wrote one of m-my m-movies."

"The good one," Vinny purred, gallantly rising, and Marion giggled as she rushed off to one of the seventeen other rooms. Suavely Vinny gripped Gloria's small damp hand and smiled into the fluttery hazel eyes. She's nervous, he thought, just an extra, one of Marion's pickups. Marion had no pretensions; she would invite anyone to one of her afternoon soirees. Vinny's opportunistic smile broadened. Maybe booze'll loosen the burnette up, he thought—right into my bed. "It's an amazing coincidence," he crooned into her upturned face, "but you're the type for a part I'm writing."

"Really?"

They chatted about that as the girl's gaze slid over the expensive furniture and bric-a-brac as if the room were a big box of chocolates that needed eating right away. Her eyes never stopped moving. "My real name's Ella Swann," she confessed. "I changed it for the movies. You're a writer. What d'you think?"

"Ella is a nice name."

"But isn't Gloria better?"

"It's more . . . noble-sounding."

She clapped her hands. "That's just what I wanted!"

Vinny heard the Midwest in her voice. "Where're you from?" he asked.

"Chicago—well, Waukegan, but I spent some time in Chicago."

Coincidence plagues us, Vinny thought. She lies a little? He laughed inside. I know plenty about lying, changing names, telling half-truths.

Gloria rubbed a greedy hand over the plush burgundy velour on a chairback. "My brother's a writer too. Sort of a, well, political writer,

18

I guess you could say." She was coy. "Actually he's a lefty, but I don't think a girl should concern herself too much with politics."

"No?" Jasmine had arrived, a slender Negro woman wearing a frilly white apron. She handed them champagne. "You're very pretty, Gloria," Vinny said, ignoring Jasmine's mocking sniff as she trotted out, twitching her behind. For reasons he was not sure of he thought about scandal. You had to be careful in Hollywood; anything went— as long as you didn't get caught. Vinny put his cosiest twinkle into his eyes. He saluted Gloria with his champagne glass. Hope my past in Chicago never catches up with me.

At that moment Clark Gable poked his head in the door, flashing the gleaming white dentures that had helped to make him famous. "Anybody home?"

"Oh, move it." Marie Dressler shoved past him. Then came slinky Jean Harlow in a sailor suit.

Harlow did a somersault near the sleek white piano.

Marion's party had begun.

𝕾 3 𝕾

WHILE Jean Harlow somersaulted, Greta Garbo paced the veranda of a Chinese hospital. Her angular face was taut with anguish, and her heavy-lidded gaze broadcast pathos. Two sloe-eyed nurses stared briefly, fearfully, before hurrying inside to patients moaning with disease. The hospital was pitifully small and inadequate, sitting in the center of a squalid village deep in the interior of Kwangtung Province, far from a main road. Outside the window, flames leapt from thatched roofs; part of the village was burning. Worse, the district was devastated by cholera, but that was not what caused the long-suffering woman to wring her hands. Herbert Marshall—to whom she had been unfaithful with George

Brent, until she saw her error of her ways and returned to Marshall, whom she really loved—had demanded that the diseased quarter be burned in order to save the rest of the populace, as a result he had been stabbed by an angry Chinese. Now her husband lay inside, perhaps dying, and she was racked with guilt.

Eloquent moans escaped the wide, thin-lipped mouth.

Garbo had made the transition from silents to sound triumphantly; *The Painted Veil* was her twenty-second picture.

"Cut!" director Richard Boleslawski called. The back-projected flames flickered out, and there was a palpable release of tension on the set in Metro's soundstage four. Garbo blinked; her wide-shouldered body sank into its customary slouch as she made her way to a chair near the big black thirty-five-millimeter camera and drooped her long-limbed body into it. Taking the cigarette that ready hands offered, she sucked on it nervously, exhaling long streams of smoke. Her glances were shy, suspicious. Her sets were always closed; no one except the most necessary personnel was allowed on them, and she grew furious if anyone, even Louis B. Mayer, tried to gawk. Apparently reassured, she let out more smoke. "Terrific, Greta," Boleslawski called. "We'll print that one."

The premier femme fatale of movies barely nodded. Along with director and extras she departed, and workmen began striking the set.

Eddie McGuffin was one of these.

Eddie had worked for Metro nearly four months. He was young, taut as a wire, strong. He had intense blue eyes that telegraphed both anger and pain, and he had a reputation as a loner, a guy with a chip on his shoulder. He had worn a mustache in Chicago but shaved it when he came to California. A shag of thick brown hair hung above a nose that was long and straight. "Your father's nose," his ma always said, but Eddie shook off those memories; his father was long dead, and as for Ma, she was convinced that that right-wing bigot who was always ranting on the radio, Father Coughlin, was God's gift to democracy.

How can you, Ma?

She also defended William Randolph Hearst; Eddie couldn't stand that.

Grunting, Eddie lifted a huge artifical palm tree onto a motorized dolly, then scrambled up to help unscrew the huge backdrop flats scheduled for the battle scenes of the Napoleonic epic on soundstage three. Tear down China today, build Waterloo tomorrow. It's crazy.

Eddie put up with it for one reason only: William Randolph Hearst.

Now, suddenly, it seemed all for nothing. Eddie was filled with despair. He had used his only connection, that girl who called herself Gloria Deere but was really Ella Swann, to get this job so he'd have a crack at the old bastard. How many times had he watched Hearst glide in a black limousine up to the fancy bungalow he'd built for his whore, Marion Davies—eighteen rooms, when millions of poor Joes and Janes didn't have a roof over their heads—while he struggled to work up his nerve? Do it! You got plerty of reason! And now, when he finally thought he was ready, when his hands itched to pick up a gun, squeeze the trigger, blow Hearst to kingdom come, came the rumors that Marion Davies was quitting MGM. Her bungalow would be taken apart and trucked across town to the Warners lot, and there would be no more Hearst.

Eddie stared out over the swarm of workmen. Like ants, he thought, and eagerly imagined a revolt, the studio burning with real flames. His fingers curled at his sides. At least I know what's what. He remembered Chicago, the Young Communist League. His life had been nothing, an empty pit, until he met them a year ago. They'd shown him the truth: oppressors and oppressed. So simple. The only way to solve the mess was to take a stand, act, fight to pull the oppressors down!

Assassination was not the official party line, but Eddie's muddled brain had mixed up personal vendetta with social goals.

He had met William Randolph Hearst once. Mr. Hearst had patted Eddie's head. Mr. Hearst had rewarded Eddie with a toy.

"Christ!" Eddie spat at the memory. A passing electrician stared at him, but Eddie glared the man down. A bell signaled the end of the shift, and pulling a cap low over his eyes, Eddie hurried out through Metro's south gate. Alone, hunched in the back of a booth, he grabbed a bite in a greasy spoon on Keystone Avenue. A guy near

21

him thumbed through *Time* magazine, Hitler on the cover goose-stepping. Hitler. Eddie shuddered. The world was going to the dogs all right, and if a man was really a man he'd do something fast.

I've gotta do something.

Eddie kept an eye on his watch. At seven he hurried out. It took him two streetcars to get from Culver City to downtown Hollywood, where he jumped off in front of Grauman's Chinese. By then it was nearly eight, the bland Southern California light fading to dusk, neon winking on. A warm breeze tumbled scraps of paper along the sidewalk. Eddie headed west on Hollywood Boulevard.

He had an appointment with a gun.

4

ONLY blocks away Otto Perkins writhed in terror.
Yellow lights screamed. Explosions bloomed in his brain, and he dropped to the floor of his shabby room in a ball, clutching his head. Strangled sounds spewed from his throat. "M-m-mama . . . !" he gasped, while his little legs, one shorter than the other, kicked furiously.

But, though small, Otto Perkins was tough. *No!* he screeched out of the well of anger that had fed him, driven him for more than twenty years, since those son-of-a-bitch days in the Illinois Home for Little Wayfarers, where the bigger orphan boys had pushed him around for laughs. His little hands made fists and the fit slowly passed; it always did, a dark wave receding. Otto Perkins found his breath; he pushed himself to his feet and clung panting to a chairback while he mopped his brow with a big white handkerchief. He squinted belligerently.

Then he remembered. He had been staring out the window of his third-floor room in this fleabag hotel, thinking as usual about revenge, sweet revenge, when it had hit him. The Temple of Cosmic

Truth was just across the street, one of those nutty L.A. religions, its sign spelled out in colored bulbs, TEMPLE OF in blue, COSMIC TRUTH in yellow. The T in TRUTH had suddenly popped, then the whole word had blown in a sharp fizz of sparks, TRUTH blacking out, hurtling down. It had been enough; a helluva lot less had set it off before, the old memory switched on and projected like some horror movie in his brain.

The fingernails of Otto Perkins's little hands bit into his palms. I'll get you, Hearst, just wait!

Otto Perkins was a dwarf, three feet, eight and a half inches tall. He always told dames he was four feet, though that was not usually the measurement they were interested in. His left shoe had a three-inch built-up heel and sole, and he went for the bottle of bourbon on the nightstand with an odd, rocking limp, as if the floor was skidding away from him. His eyes were shifty and as thin as splinters. He was somewhere between twenty-five and thirty, his face long and horselike, his head too large for his body. Bulbous and pasty, it was not a face people usually took to, but he could screw it up into a squinty imitation of cheer. That gave him a laugh. In fact he could pretend a lot of things—people were chumps! He splashed a shot into a grimy glass and stared out the window across the long, flat dreamland of Los Angeles. He smiled. Otto Perkins was not his real name. He had one, but it had been a dog's age since he had used it: when you made your way by conning the rubes, it didn't do to leave a real name behind. In fact, the string of aliases, the changing identities were sometimes more real to Otto Perkins than his own. Most people're just who they are; I'm who I *want* to be, he thought, and laughed out loud. Then the past lunged again, jabbed him, and he flinched with an almost physical pain as he recalled the foster homes that had kicked him out—"The little brat ain't nothin' but trouble!"—until he got kicked out into life.

With one abiding purpose: revenge.

The dwarf became a ball of fury. His splinter eyes narrowed to burning slits, the blue irises more clouded than usual, and for an instant his longish upper lip trembled uncontrollably.

Perkins tossed down his drink. Pouring more, he saluted Repeal, then pulled from a battered briefcase the photographs that were his

23

obsession, his reason for being in L.A., fanning them on the bed and climbing up beside them.

Chicago photographs.

Hunched there, frowning, sipping the burning liquor, Otto Perkins remembered Chicago. The snowstorm. The big, swell brownstone on Sheridan Avenue.

And he remembered the woman.

He had climbed a shaky tower of clues to get to her. That tower still might collapse and crush him; Otto Perkins knew that too well. But no cigar if you don't play the game.

I gotta play this game.

Her name was Rose McGuffin, and she had opened the door of the big brownstone six months ago and let him in, just like all the other dopes who fell for his line. How old? Sixty? But still good-looking, with reddish hair. Must've been a dish when she was young. Perkins recalled her fleeting expression of distaste as she stared down at him, a little, horsefaced guy with a game leg; he hated stares like that, but he had made himself grin to beat the band and told her in his sincerest voice that he was with National Life, her very own insurance company, just like he'd said over the phone. Flashing the official card he'd filched from the National Life office he'd sneaked into, he said he was here because of his company's very new, excellent service of photographing people's possessions so that in case there was a robbery or fire or something, everything would be accounted for and there would be no question about reimbursement.

"Of course," she said in her feathery voice, turning and gliding in an expensive lavender dress into the spacious living room, which was ten times sweller than any place Otto Perkins had ever stayed. "That sounds very good." She turned. "But why isn't my regular agent, Mr. Bleeker, taking care of this?"

"He retired," Otto Perkins said.

Momentarily her thin hands fluttered nervously at her sides. "Don't mind me," she said. "It's just my boy, Eddie. He's not back, and this storm . . . "

But at that moment Otto Perkins's splinter eyes lifted to the marble mantel, and he couldn't think about any storm. His heart thudded in his chest, his head rang. It wasn't the toy, a glass globe

24

with a miniature Alpine scene in it, that knocked him for a loop: not the other photographs either. It was the big central photograph in the fancy brass frame: William Randolph Hearst.

At the sight of it Perkins squirmed frantically inside his stunted body, and his game leg began to throb like it always did to remind him. You did this to me, Hearst! he raged inwardly. I been after you for years—but I'm not gonna twist and hurt your body like you hurt mine. I'll get you in your bloated ego, right where you live. I'll cripple you there. Everybody knows you're not lily-white, there're too many rumors for that. I've chased them a long time, banging my head against locked doors. You covered your tracks damn good, but I'm finally on to something, I feel it, and when I get my hands on it they'll hear about it in Shanghai. Your smug puss will be on the front page of every scandal sheet in the U.S.A., maybe even on the front of your own papers, and you'll pay and you'll pay. . . .

"Mr. Perkins?" Rose McGuffin said.

Perkins swallowed hard. He blinked into large, brown eyes. "Yeah," he rasped, dry-mouthed, jerking the big Rolleiflex out of his briefcase. "Let's take those pictures."

So he had them. Big deal. Now, on the sagging bed in this crummy L.A. dump, he stared down at them, his mystery, his obsession. What did they tell him? There seemed to be nothing in most of them—just a big house full of expensive things. Gullibly, Rose McGuffin had even opened desk drawers and bureau drawers so he could snap the contents, but he hadn't seen any incriminating contracts or wills or deeds. The problem was, he didn't know what he was looking for.

And yet, there was something.

Because at the end Rose McGuffin had left the living room for a couple of minutes, giving Perkins his chance to sneak a close gander at that picture on the mantel. He scurried over, perched on tiptoes. It was an eight-by-ten glossy showing the fat old bastard with a bunch of boys maybe ten or twelve years old. Wearing a dark suit, Hearst stood behind them like he owned them, and they were all—almost all—grinning fit to beat the band. There were balloons, streamers, a cake on a table to the left. Obviously a picture to celebrate something, but what? The cake was rectangular, decorated

25

like the front page of a newspaper. *Chicago Evening American*, it said. Perkins wiped a hand across his mouth. A Hearst rag all right. So what? He squinted at the faces of the boys. Just kids. Then he glanced at the other photos on the mantel and felt the first stirring of hope: the mopey-looking kid with Hearst's hand on his shoulder was in all of them. Rose McGuffin's brat, it had to be; the one she was so worried about. Something about his long glum face looked familiar, but Perkins couldn't place it.

Returning footsteps, clicking on polished parquet. Suddenly sweating, Perkins swung up the Rolleiflex, focused, snapped. Two more just to make sure: *flash, flash*. Then a step back to get the whole mantel, including the glass ball containing that little Alpine scene.

"Just finishing up," he said as Rose McGuffin came back.

"What? Oh. Yes." Her large brown eyes worried the front door. "I do wish Eddie would get home!"

"Er, this's Eddie?" Perkins gestured at the pictures on the mantel.

"Yes. My Eddie." Her feathery voice trembled.

"Nice-looking kid."

Her expression warmed. "He *is* handsome, isn't he? This is his confirmation picture, and . . ." Proudly she showed off each photograph as if she were giving a tour: her son at the circus, a school picture, a skinny kid fishing on Lake Michigan under a ragged city skyline. Perkins seethed. She's his ma, she loves him. *Would my ma have loved me?*

My ma never had much chance.

As the pictures progressed the kid grew up, became a brooding young man with a sketchy William Powell mustache. There was still something about the face . . .

"Doesn't smile much, does he?" Perkins said.

"My Eddie is a very serious boy."

"Er, what's he do?"

"Nothing. At the moment."

"Can't find work?"

"Oh, he *could*." she quickly assured him. "If he wanted. He's very smart. It's just that he has . . . unconventional ideas."

Perkins watched her small white hands grind together. What ideas? He let that go; he needed something better than this. He gulped a breath. "Say, isn't that William Randolph Hearst?" He tapped the large center photograph.

"Yes."

"Friend of yours?"

A stirring behind her eyes, a shifting, a blurring. Hiding something? But her voice was steady. "No. Eddie was a paperboy for the *Evening American*. Mr. Hearst used to give parties for the ones who sold the most papers, and that year Eddie won. He was eleven. I was very proud."

Disappointment writhed in Perkins. That's all? He peered hard at the thin, pale, pretty woman, but she was as unreadable as stone. His game leg started to ache. What if there wasn't any secret? What if this was just another closed door? Teeth on edge, he spun his gaze to the Hearst picture: Hearst, the bloated old moneybags in his rumpled suit; the boys; the table with the cake. Perkins' splinter eyes narrowed. A shiny object was half hidden behind the cake. Then he recognized it: a glass globe containing a little Alpine scene.

Just like the one on the mantel.

He picked up the one on the mantel. "This's nice."

Rose McGuffin's arm half lifted. He thought she was going to snatch it from him, but, "It is, isn't it?" was all she said, lowering her arm as if it were an artificial limb she couldn't quite control "Just please be careful."

"Sure." He tilted his head. "Sentimental value?"

"You might say so."

"Mm." It had an ornate brass base. The globe itself was about six inches in diameter. He shook it and a miniature snowstorm swirled, formed of tiny bits of glistening mica. You saw toys like it everywhere, cheap dime store junk, but Perkins was impressed by this one. The little village was carved and painted with great care, and, staring into the glass, he could almost feel the tingle of snow on his skin.

"It *is* beautiful, isn't it?" came Rose McGuffin's voice, dreamy.

"Yeah. Beautiful." He turned it over. On the brass bottom was inscribed *Karl Zimmer & Sons, Wiesbaden, 1896.* Probably meant nothing, but out of habit Perkins tucked the information in his mental file.

He shook up the little storm once more, watched it settle. He put

27

the globe back. "Swell." He met her waiting eyes. "Kind of a reward to your kid?"

"Nothing special. Mr. Hearst gave away hundreds that year. He imported them from Germany, I believe."

"He likes Germany, I read that. Likes Hitler too. You ever been to Germany?"

"Raising a boy doesn't let you travel much."

"I guess not. So your kid met Hearst. You meet him too?"

"I didn't have the privilege."

"Too bad." Perkins's mind raced: Hearst . . . her kid . . . the newsboy award . . . "Well, there's just a little more work to be done." How can I get a handle on this? his mind screamed. "A couple of papers to fill out. Routine stuff. You don't mind?"

She glanced at the door. "I suppose five minutes . . ."

They sat opposite one another, she stiff and straight in her lavender dress. He poised his pencil. "Your middle name is . . . ?"

"Ellen."

"Maiden name?"

"Forrest."

ROSE ELLEN FORREST, he printed. "And you were born in . . . ?"

"Stockbridge, Massachusetts. Don't you have all this from Mr. Bleeker?"

"Mr. Bleeker left things in kind of a mess. But don't worry about your policies, they're in good order." he asked more questions: Age? Fifty-seven. Just the one boy? Yes. And, Mr. McGuffin?

"Dead."

"Sorry to hear it."

"It happened a long time ago." Her eyes drifted to the mantel. "Poor Eddie never really knew his father."

"What'd Mr. McGuffin do?"

"He was a newspaperman."

Perkins licked suddenly dry lips. "You mean here in Chicago?"

"Yes."

His pencil refused to write. "He didn't by any chance work for Hearst too? On the *Evening American*?"

A wordless nod. Still focused on the mantel, she seemed hardly to hear him. Staring at the glass globe, or that picture of Hearst?

Damn Hearst!

28

"Uh, how did he die?"

"Train accident."

"Train . . . ?"

Her large brown eyes met his; they swirled with pain. "He fell off a train when Eddie was two. A newspaper reporter. He was a union man, trying to organize, and he fell off a train." She blinked, as if coming to. "But I don't see—is this necessary, Mr. Perkins?"

"Just asking."

"There was lots of insurance. As you see." The woman's expression became cold and bitter as she gestured to the elegant furnishings that filled the big room like displays in a museum. "Harry didn't have much, but he did have insurance. So . . ." Her voice died.

"So you've been pretty well off."

"Well off?" Tears formed in her eyes, but she squeezed them back. Her face set hard and her small chin lifted. "I don't think I want to answer any more questions just now."

"But—"

"No." Abruptly she rose. "No more questions now. You can just send me the forms to fill out."

Perkins slid out of his chair onto the expensive Persian carpet. "Sure I can, but—"

She was made of flint. "Thank you, then. Your company's new policy sounds very fine, very fair. Photographs are always good, aren't they?" Irony dripped in her tone. "They prove things, as you say." She moved toward the door. "Good-bye, Mr. Perkins." She held out her hand, and he found her grip strong and icy. Then he was helplessly outside, the door slammed behind him. The porch light clicked off like an exclamation point at the end of a command, and night sucked in around him. Snow lashed the air, but this snow, unlike the soft swirls in the glass globe, would sting and bite.

The glass globe . . .

So, six months later, the dwarf sat on the lumpy bed squinting at the photographs of Rose McGuffin's mantel. *He was a union man, trying to organize, and he fell off a train.* Her words hummed in Perkins's brain, but he still hadn't pinned down what they meant. I'm on to something, I know I am: a noose that'll hang old Hearst!

Just got to knot the rope.

Just got to make sure it's good and tight.

29

❧ 5 ❧

EDDIE McGuffin had almost reached his destination. Jumpy under neon and night, he kept his brown felt cap pulled down tight, peering from under it, feeling like a gangster, a movie gangster, Edward G. Robinson or Jimmy Cagney. The movies, he thought. Goddamn movies, nothin' real. But the crime I'm gonna commit is real. He quivered at that, a panicky blindness clouding his intense blue eyes. He darted suddenly across the street, and a big black La Salle nearly clipped him. The horn blasted; the driver leaned out and shook a fist, but Eddie hardly looked.

His angular shoulders jerked. He pictured himself crushed and bleeding under automobile tires. Maybe it would be good if I did get hit; that'd end it all right now.

No. Don't be a coward. What would Pa have thought?

At last: the Bonita Hotel. Everybody knew it was a hangout for gamblers, mobsters, racetrack touts. Nobody did anything about it, though. Payoffs, that was why. Eddie thought about his friends in the Young Communist League, the shining new world they believed in. In that world scum like this wouldn't stand a chance.

But he had business with the scum.

He entered the hotel. The lobby smelled like money. It smelled rotten to Eddie. Desk bells rang. Expensive wing-tip shoes whispered on thick carpeting. Near the elevators politicians whose faces Eddie recognized from the papers stood gabbing as cool as cucumbers with shady-looking guys in pin-striped suits, while dames in slinky dresses hovered nearby, waiting. Sly glances darted everywhere, everybody on the lookout. Nobody paid attention to Eddie, but he felt watched anyway, and he felt sweat soaking his shirt.

"Hey, kid!"

Eddie jumped. Whirling, he found himself staring down into the round leering face of Dandy Jack Pinkus.

"So, ya decided to show up after all?" Rubbery lips stretched in a grin. "Gonna rob a bank? Ha, ha! Listen." The short fat man wore a rumpled brown suit and reeked of cheap tobacco. He grabbed Eddie's elbow. "We can't do business here. C'mon out to my office." He dragged Eddie to the sidewalk. Automobile headlamps were beginning to flick on, knives of light slicing the dusk. Jack peered left, right, as if J. Edgar Hoover himself lurked with a posse of G-men. "This way." Eddie followed his waddling walk. At the corner of the hotel by an NRA poster Jack sent more darting glances in both directions before popping into an alley. Eddie plunged after him.

They went to the end, thirty feet or so. Windows above them shed a brassy light, and there were bursts of laughter. Eddie Cantor's voice chirped, "Potatoes are cheaper, tomatoes are cheaper, now's the time to fall in love . . ." Warm air blew from somewhere. Jack's grin showed yellowish teeth as he jerked a thumb at a vent. "Kitchen. Smell that chow!"

The food smells only made Eddie nauseous.

"Hey, kid, you okay?"

"S-sure."

"Swell."

Eddie focused on the lapels of the little man's coat. They were worn and greasy. Dandy Jack's name was just a joke. The guy was a punk, more scum who lived by feeding on the rotten system Eddie wanted to smash. Jack bought and sold death: guns that couldn't be traced. He could even get you a tommy-gun if the price was right.

"So . . ." Jack unreeled the word like a baited line. "I got ya that, uh, merchandise you was so anxious for."

Eddie's throat felt raw.

Jack nudged him. "Ain'tcha glad?"

"Yeah, sure."

"You oughta show it. Some thanks! I worked my ass off." Sharp eyes narrowed. "You hang around with them Reds, don'tcha?"

"How'd you know?" Eddie kicked himself. Why didn't I deny it?

With an air of self-importance, Jack rubbed his nose. "I know a lotta what goes on in this town. But I don't care, see. Politics ain't my business. Buyin' and sellin's my business. Like items like this." The round man pulled something small and dully gleaming from an inside coat pocket. He held it out, but Eddie didn't reach for it. Jack thrust it at him. "Go ahead, it won't bite ya."

Eddie took the pistol, snub-nosed, brutally ugly. He realized that he had never held a gun in his life, a real gun. Tentatively he fit his index finger around the trigger, and the gun miraculously became an extension of his hand, his arm, his will. I can kill with this! The idea thrilled and sickened him. He wanted to throw the gun away, but it was too late; the thing was already his, and abruptly he hugged it to his breast.

Jack squinted. "You're a funny duck. Here, lemme see that." He snatched back the pistol, proudly showed its features. "Colt thirty-eight revolver, a honey." He purred about its action, pointed out the filed-off serial number. "Nobody's gonna trace the thing, not to me, not to you either if you're smart." Suddenly he aimed it at Eddie, pulled the trigger: *click!*

Eddie jumped at the sharp snap of the hammer.

Jack cackled as he wiped the gun with a grimy cloth. "Finger-prints. Can't be too careful. Here, pal." Still holding it with the cloth, he handed it back. "Here's some ammo too, gratis"—he dropped a small cardboard box into Eddie's palm—"just in case you're in a big hurry, know what I mean?" His eyebrows waggled greedily. "Now, about my dough. . . ."

Eddie tucked the Colt into his breast pocket. It weighed like lead. He fumbled bills from his wallet.

"Mind if I count 'em? One, two . . . yep, right on the button: an even hundred. It's a pleasure doin' business with a guy like you. Say, how's a poor stiff come up with dough like this on such short notice?"

"Savings."

"In times like these? That's a laugh. Gotta run. So long, killer. If ya need anything else, ya know where t'find me." The fat man sauntered from the alley.

Eddie's teeth chattered. It wasn't cold here, the vent still exuded its blasts of warm, sickening air, but he was shaking uncontrollably and

32

had to lean for several moments against the grimy bricks until the world stopped reeling. Out on Hollywood Boulevard he headed back the way he had come, but he felt numbed by the black weight of the snub-nosed Colt against his breast. He passed Grauman's Chinese. Its sparkling marquee advertised a Marion Davies movie, co-starring Bing Crosby, and Eddie stood on Douglas Fairbanks's footprints and stared at posters in the unreal pinkish glow. Marion Davies, Hearst's whore. She was blond, pretty, dreamlike, and for a moment Eddie found himself lost and breathless in her creamy beauty. Then he got hold of himself. Movies were dreams all right—dreams that stole people's lives. Capitalist tools of oppression, the YCL called them. Eddie frowned. How did a girl as pretty as Marion Davies put up with that old bastard Hearst? The movie was called *Going Hollywood*, and Eddie almost laughed, because that was exactly what he had done; gone Hollywood.

To kill William Randolph Hearst.

❧ 6 ❧

S IX months I been in L.A. and getting nowhere, Otto Perkins thought. I gotta have help.

As a lean young man stood in front of Grauman's Chinese gazing at Marion Davies, Perkins grabbed up the phone and gave the clerk a number.

"New York? It'll take a minute."

"I got a minute." Sniffing, the little man clicked the receiver back on the cradle. He sneered. Bet in this dump they never make calls farther than the nearest cathouse.

The phone rang. Perkins jerked it off the hook. "Yeah?"

"Your call's through."

He sat up straight; he was about to speak to one of the most powerful men in America.

"Yes?" The man's voice was cool, clipped. It sounded far away, but the single word carried weight: I'm busy, this better be good.

"It's me, Mr. Rawlston," Perkins said, dry-mouthed.

"It is I," the man named Rawlston corrected him, "and I know who this is. Are you aware that it is nearly midnight here? Where are you calling from?"

"Los Angeles."

"You get around. And do you have something for me? Or is this the usual maybe, with the usual tiresome request for more time, more money?"

Perkins knew Rawlston hated beating around the bush. "It's a maybe, but a strong one. And, yeah, I need more dough." Drumming his fingers, he waited. Give in, you bastard; you've got to! Bart Rawlston owned newspapers, he owned magazines too; he was William Randolph Hearst's biggest competitor, and the dwarf was sure he would do anything short of murder to get something on his rival.

"All right, give me the details," Rawlston purred, and Perkins relaxed: the hook was still in the fish. He spoke for five minutes, holding back just enough to keep the publisher from trying a double cross. He knew Rawlston held back too; it was a game they played, cat and mouse.

"Mm," was all Rawlston said when Perkins was through.

"I've done what I can, but I still need some legwork."

"Legwork, or more fancy footwork?"

"I'm on to something big, I tell you. Get one of your boys to dig up as much as he can on Rose Ellen Forrest, born in Stockbridge, Massachusetts fifty-seven years ago."

"Rose Ellen Forrest?"

"And a guy who worked for Hearst in Chicago on the *Evening American*, a reporter named Harry McGuffin. He was killed falling off a train."

"A pathetic death. Is that all?"

Perkins licked his lips. "I'll need a few hundred bucks."

"You spend my money pretty freely."

"If you saw this dump of a hotel, you wouldn't say that."

A sharp laugh. "You're the ascetic type, is that it? Will five hundred do?"

"Yeah. Thanks."

"To whom shall I send it?"

The dwarf thought. He had been Otto Perkins long enough. Perkins became Pike, Otto turned to Otis. Otis Pike; he liked that; it sounded Hollywood, like some fancy producer. And wasn't a pike a fish with sharp teeth that drew blood? He gave the name. "Send it care of general delivery. I'll pick it up."

"All right, Mr. Pike, I'l do that. You're terribly zealous; I wish I knew what was really in it for you."

"Helping you out, Mr Rawlston."

Another laugh. "You lying bastard! I hope for results soon." The voice became ice. "This cannot go on forever."

There was a click, and the little man who was now Otis Pike hung up. The walls of the shabby room seemed to move in, surrounding him, and he gulped the ast of his drink. He hated depending on anyone, but he and Bart Rawlston shared the same aims, and it sure helped to be bankrolled instead of living by con games. But Rawlston was right: it could not go on. Pike longed for the end, and Rawlston was nearly fed up; Pike had heard it in the publisher's tone. Dirt, that's what I am to him, he thought. All the more reason to push things. Hearst is at that castle of his, at San Simeon. Damn it, I want to be there too!

In the meantime, chase every thread.

A siren wailed out on Sunset. Pike called a local number.

"Hello?"

"Hiya, Max." Pike gave the name by which Max knew him.

Max's Czech accent was oiled with greed. "You have some merchandise for me to dispose of?"

"Not this time. I need you to look into something. Write this down: Karl Zimmer and Sons, Wiesbaden, 1896. Got it?"

"Yes, but—"

"It's on the botton of one of those glass balls with a little town and fake snow in it, a toy. Know the kind of thing I mean?"

"I am not stupid. But I am an antique dealer, and this 'toy' is not an antique."

"Look, you know more about that kinda stuff than anybody. Just find out about it for me. I think they were imported by the hundreds, maybe fifteen, twenty years ago."

A sigh. "I shall do it. And you will pay?"

Mr. Bart Rawlston will pay, Pike thought. "Don't I always?"

"Karl Zimmer and Sons, Wiesbaden, 1896 . . ." Pike could hear the little Czech already turning the problem over in his mind. "I am not sure how long this will take. Where shall I call you?"

"I'll call you." Hanging up, Pike eased off his shoes. The one with the built-up heel gave him trouble as usual, and he cursed. A woman's laugh drifted in the night. The sound stirred him, and he leered to think how, in spite of his size and his bulbous head with its tufts of whitish hair, he had had his share of dames. I know how to get around women, I know what they like. He lifted his legs back onto the bed. Damn ugly stumps, he thought as he poured more bourbon. Bending to thumb through the photographs for the thousandth time, he paused at one of a bare-looking room. "My Eddie's room," Rose McGuffin had said. There were a couple of books on the dresser, and, grabbing his magnifying glass from the nightstand, Pike made out a title: *Das Kapital.* He snapped his fingers. "He's got unconventional ideas," she had said.

Her kid was a Red. Anything in that? Hearst hated Reds. Pike swore, remembering how he had hung around Chicago for a whole month without getting any closer to Rose McGuffin's secret. That was why he had come to L.A., to be near his enemy, to carry the battle here.

Pike heard a clattering and went to the window. Across the way a guy on a ladder was replacing the burnt out bulbs in TRUTH. A moment later the word blazed in the night. Pike grimaced. Mr. William Randolph Hearst gave your pampered little boy a present, did he, Mrs. McGuffin? Well, the old bastard gave me something too, something I never asked for, and the truth'll make him pay.

℀ 7 ℀

O NE week later a broad-shouldered man in a gray uniform squinted out through the tall black wrought-iron gates of a white stucco mansion on Laurel. The mansion was just below the famous estate that had belonged to Douglas Fairbanks and Mary Pickford. Within its walls bougainvillea clung in lush, rich clumps to the white stucco, and six acres of landscaped grounds basked in October sun. A gardener in a wide straw hat tugged weeds in a blue, shady corner. The water in the long-deserted swimming pool licked at mosaic tiles depicting dolphins while sixty-foot palm trees clacked their fronds like gossiping tongues.

Dust still devoured Oklahoma, and dispossessed farm families still caravaned west along Route 66, but no evidence of the Great Depression leaked into this exclusive, protected pocket of Beverly Hills.

The man in the gray uniform scowled. Three people in a big black touring car had stopped in the curving drive and were gaping at the house. The guard made threatening motions and, exploding with giggles, the car drove on. Probably got a map, he thought: "Home of the Stars" Go pester W. C. Fields, next block! But the burly man grinned like a cat: this job is easy street.

Lounging, lighting a cigarette, he glanced back at the house.

The second-floor balcony doors were open.

Beyond those doors lay the spacious master bedroom, the blue-tiled bath. Stepping from its large sunken tub, Charles Chaplin, known to the world as the Tramp or simply Charlie, wrapped a green striped towel about his muscled waist and angrily snatched the phone that his Filipino secretary Kono held out. At forty Chaplin had white hair. He was short but supple and practiced acrobatics every day, as he had since he had started as a boy with the Fred

Karno troupe in England. The Tramp's eloquent little mustache was nowhere in evidence—he saved that for the movies—but if it had been it would have bristled. Chaplin was furious that Kono had not put the caller off.

"Who is it?"

"Ch-Charlie! It's m-me!"

Chaplin's scowl dissolved into the puckish smile that charmed millions. The whiskey contralto, the bubbling, unselfconscious stammer: Marion Davies.

"Marion!"

Chaplin did three vigorous knee bends.

"Long time no s-see, kiddo," Marion purred.

Chaplin waved Kono off and, receiver tucked under his chin, began vigorously toweling himself. "What's the latest picture, ducks? You're calling from the studio?"

"S-studio? Th-that's a l-laugh. What studio? I mean, who knows who the h-hell I'm w-working for?"

"Righto. I heard."

"I bet even the Eskimos know it. That d-damn Th-Thalberg! He couldn't b-be b-budged about the Marie Antoinette part, so P-Popsy got h-hot under the c-collar and yanked me from Metro. I'm at Warners now."

Chaplin clucked in sympathy, but that was how Hearst was: impetuous, unpredictable—even dangerous. He recalled several dark stories; he himself had been around for one incident, when producer Thomas Ince had mystriously died after a Hearst yachting party. Heart failure, they said, but Chaplin could still smell the gunpowder. He shuddered. Louella Parsons had been there, too, with her notepad, and a bloody good thing for Hearst that she owed him her career.

"It's rotten for you. I've always thought of you as the Marie Antoinette sort—you're always losing your head."

A giggle. "Oh, you're so f-funny, you always cheer me up! I'm just *d-dying* to s-see you!"

"And I you." Stepping to the big, gilt mirror, Chaplin examined his teeth. "Er, the old boy's detectives still on your tail?"

"I g-guess so. I could just s-spit! Popsy m-makes me so goddamn mad, and then I feel sorry for him. But I *hate* being f-followed! I don't know why he does it."

"No?" Chaplin did: the extracurricular men, the booze; Hearst liked to keep tabs on his personal property. Staring into the mirror, Chaplin suddenly wondered what it was like to be old with a lively, fun-loving young mistress, and he shivered in spite of the sun coming in over the balcony.

"Anyhow, Charlie," Marion bubbled on, "I'm phoning from the r-ranch—r-ranch, ha! That may be what Popsy likes to call this old c-castle of his, but I call it the n-nuthouse. I'm going *c-crazy* up here. Jack Warner gave me a script, and I h-hate it. It's the same old silly stuff, and I want to have a p-party. I'm calling everybody. Please, Charlie—this weekend. Popsy will have a train waiting at the G-Glendale station, just like always. Lots of people've already said yes—Clark Gable and E-Bette Davis and Harpo and just about everybody. It'll be swell! The old bear is having some d-dumb old m-meeting with his money men. Some b-big financial b-blowup or other, as if h-he ever had to w-worry! But we won't let 'em spoil our fun; we'll sh-show the old b-bores. Whattaya say? B-bring a f-friend if you like, a p-pretty one. Who's the latest?"

"Paulette Goddard."

"Still r-robbing the cradle? Just k-kidding. She's a s-sweet kid. B-bring her, if you like. Do say you'll come."

Chaplin reflected. Just last April, Hearst had invited him to another party, a traveling one: his annual summer junket to Europe. I could've met Hitler; there's a balloon for deflating, he thought. But business had kept him in town. An uncharacteristic pleading note buzzed in Marion's voice, and he wondered if there was anything more than the usual giddy boredom. "Of course, I'll come, sweets. I shan't let you down."

"Oh goody! The G-Glendale station. Friday. D-don't forget."

Hanging up, Chaplin strode into the bedroom. Marion. There was something both child and woman about her that still stirred him, but their affair had had to end; she belonged to Hearst and always would, and that was that. Thinking about William Randolph Hearst, Chaplin shook his head. Sex makes fools of us all, he told himself. His valet had laid out a crisp linen suit, and he began putting it on. Beyond the broad windows, past the bougainvillea glowing with an almost incandescent light, Hollywood simmered under a sun that even in early October was like a spotlight searching every corner for scandal.

I can't stick more scandal, Chaplin thought.

Dressed, he stepped onto the balcony. In spite of the sun he felt the change in the air, a strange, warm uneasiness. Never like this in jolly old England. Earthquake weather, they call it. There're even predictions of a storm. He pooh-poohed that; the California sky only spat; that's why they made movies here. Movies. Chaplin frowned. He had not released a picture since *City Lights* in 'thirty-one; now it was 1934. Don't want people to forget me. He laughed at the improbability, but the laugh died a jittery death. The bluenoses were braying at his heels with charges of moral turpitude and bolshie sympathies. He began to pace, turning over an idea he had for a project about today's world. *Modern Times* he would call it. Too left-wing? So what. You had to stand up for what you believed. But there was a problem: sound. He had felt confident in silent movies, but sound terrified him. The Tramp just mustn't speak—that would spoil the character; but the public demanded voices. What to do?

It was bloody hard being producer, writer, director, star.

Suddenly Chaplin became the Tramp, with his jiggling walk, his twitching upper lip. He pivoted on an imaginary cane, tipped an imaginary bowler hat. His famous grin flashed for no one but himself.

A weekend at old Hearst's is just the thing. No worries. An absolutely topping way to get away from it all!

8

WALTER Winchell's staccato delivery faded from the airwaves. America had been shoveled the latest dirt from Broadway. A Sunkist commercial followed; then the sound of Ted Fio Rito's Orchestra burst out, followed by murmurs of breathless excitement: "Look, isn't that Wallace Beery?" "Oh, Dolores del Rio!" "And there's Joan Crawford!"

Crowded around the glowing yellow dials of countless radios from Portland to Tampa, from Dallas to Sioux Falls, America was whisked to the luxurious lobby of the Hollywood Hotel.

The music soared, and America was swept into the hotel's famous Orchid Room.

Harry Von Zell plugged Campbell's soup; then came the nasal voice familiar to millions: "Hel-lo from Hol-lywood. This is Louella Parsons broadcasting from the Hol-lywood Hotel in glamourous Hol-lywood, California. My guests tonight are Clark Gable and Claudette Colbert, stars of the big comedy hit of 1934, *It Happened One Night*. Looking across the room, I see many of the glittering luminaries of pictures, and later some of them will chat with us as I carry my microphone among the crowded tables. But first Dick Powell has a song for us. Dick?"

Applause.

"Thank you, Louella." Powell began warbling "Pettin' in the Park" in his bright honey tenor.

The weekly "Hollywood Hotel" radio program had begun.

There was no Orchid Room.

There was no luxurious lobby. The awed voices had been supplied by performers paid the lowest union scale to provide appropriate background noise; they stood with their scripts behind fat round microphones, while Gable and Colbert also waited docilely with their scripts—but not in the Hollywood Hotel. The hotel existed— once it had been a watering hole for many famous stars—but its glamour had faded along with its exterior, and visitors to town were uniformly disappointed that it did not live up to the glowing picture painted weekly on radio.

The director, Bill Bacher, cued Harry Von Zell with a jabbing finger as Powell's song ended to more recorded applause. In rich, mellow tones Von Zell extolled Campbell's tomato soup while Bacher's sharp eye checked that everyone was in place: the dowdy Louella, who could sink a career with a word; Gable; Colbert; the boyish Powell, silently shifting music on the stand by his mike; Fio Rito and his men.

It all took place at the CBS studios in downtown Los Angeles.

"And here are Clark Gable and Claudette Colbert," Louella intoned as if announcing the king and queen of England.

More recorded applause.

When the show was over Bacher tossed Louella her bone: "Great job! By the way, there's a call waiting for you in my office. Marion Davies."

"Do tell." Louella wore a dark blue dress decorated with huge white polka dots. Eagerly she trotted down the hall, making sure to close Bacher's door firmly before she plopped into the swivel chair by his paper-strewn desk. Automatically she jerked pad and pencil from her bag, and just as automatically, for luck, she licked the pencil point as she picked up the phone. "Marion, so *won*-derful to hear from you!" Louella's column always lavishly praised the blond star's movies and charities—she knew what would please Mr. Hearst—but the repeated phrase "Marion was never lovelier" had become a national joke.

"Louella, I'm s-so glad to reach you," Marion said breathessly. "I t-tried the *Herald* and your home, but then I remembered you w-were doing your show, and I just *had* to ask you f-first."

"First, dear? To San Simeon this weekend?"

A tiny pause. "How'd you know?"

"Clark Gable just told me you've invited him. You've invited lots of people, haven't you?"

"Have I? I g-guess I have. But I w-*wanted* to ask you first, honest.

And I would have too, only I just c-couldn't get h-hold of you. You must be s-so b-busy! How 'bout it, Louella? Cheer a girl up and s-say yes."

Louella did not answer right away; giving in too readily might make her stock go down. Her mind raced. Cute, available Dick Powell, set to star with Marion in *Page Miss Glory* for Warners, had piped up that he too would be at San Simeon. Marion's flings with her leading men were notorious, and Louella's nose for news twitched. Would little Dicky be the next fly in Marion's web? Louella smirked. The Dionne quints, Lindbergh, Dillinger, Garbo— Americans lap it all up, and I'm number one at dishing out the inside scoop.

"I'll have to cancel some very important interviews, but you can count on me, dear."

"Swell! The train'll leave Friday. W.R. and I just can't *w-wait* to s-see you. Bye."

The line clicked, but Louella sat for a moment thoughtfully tapping her pad. She had an overstuffed look, and her vague brown eyes appeared as harmless as a cow's. But Louella was shrewd; she could be lethal too, and as tenacious as a weed. Hadn't she kept her job with Mr. Hearst all these years? Didn't her byline appear daily in all his papers? Hadn't she single-handedly invented the Hollywood gossip column? Louella had not earned her preeminent place among the public gossips by being subtle or fainthearted. Besides, she liked to do well by Mr. Hearst, whom she worshipped. It could be frustrating though. Momentarily her heavily lipsticked mouth drooped like a sagging clothesline. Darn, I know plenty I never get to print! Marion and Charlie Chaplin, for example. Louella leered. Marion's like a streetcar; everybody gets to ride. Poor Mr. Hearst— no wonder he has to keep detectives on her hot little tail, she thought, flushing. Now if *I* were in Marion's place— She cut the thought off fast. After all she was a married woman. Taking out a mirror she began touching up her mouth. The lipstick did not go on straight, but she ignored that. *Dear* Mr. Hearst. She recalled the exact words with which he had acceded her demands when he lured her to his papers many years ago: "Damn it, you've got everything out of this contract except hairpins!" She also never forgot how the wonderful man had saved her life. It had been early in her career, in Chicago. She was hemmorrhaging; the doctors had diagnosed tuberculosis. But she had to work, she needed the money. It was then that Mr. Hearst's call had come, cross country: "Louella, you're fired—but on full salary, until you're completely well." At the memory, tears spilled down her puffy cheeks. How could so many people hate such a terrific guy? The public just did not know him: he was kind, fair—and he was *not* reactionary; he had good reason to attack the Communist enemies of democracy. It was a crime how even Hollywood was going Red!

Blotting her cheeks, Louella stood. People said she had gotten her job because she knew where Hearst's bodies were buried. So what if I do know things some people would like forgotten? She gathered up her bag. Could there be a story at San Simeon, an exclusive, a scoop? Louella loved scoops.

I'll be there with bells on, Marion dear, she thought as she flipped through Bill Bacher's private notes, just to keep in practice. And you can be sure this gal will keep her eyes and ears wide open.

🙚 9 🙚

VINNY Tashman had not listened to "Hollywood Hotel". All crap. And Louella Parsons was a nosy, dangerous bitch.

Besides, Vinny was very, very busy. He typed *Vincent X. Tashman* at the bottom of the letter he had just carefully composed. Pulling it from the boxlike Smith-Corona, he signed his name in the bold, artistic scrawl he had invented when he came to Hollywood. He read it over; it was good—brilliant, in fact. The flattery hid the desperate pleading.

The letter was to William Randolph Hearst, begging Hearst to let Vincent X. Tashman write Marion Davies' next screenplay.

Vinny's apartment was in the Alto Nido, on Ivar, above Holly-

44

wood Boulevard. Eucalyptus leaves shivered in the softly glowing night outside his window. Leaning back in the plush velvet chair in his mahogany-paneled study, Vinny picked up the silver lighter he would soon have to hock in order to eat and lit a slim imported cigarette. On the desk nearby sat the boxed set of target pistols with which he liked to practice.

Vinny's thin lips curled. Target pistols . . . Christ. You've come a long way off the streets of Chicago.

That made him think. Smoke curled from his nostrils. Chicago. A hard-boiled city, tough on a kid from an orphanage. But I worked my way up, on Hearst's *Evening American*. Vinny frowned. He really didn't like to remember those days. Chicago was where he had first gotten in trouble with booze. He had drunk too much; he was nasty when he drank too much. Then had come that mistake with the gun—just an accident, nobody dead, and the cops never found out. Still . . .

He shivered. Go west, young man.

Vinny had remade his identity in Hollywood.

But he still liked guns, target shooting helped him vent his frustrations. Sure had a lot of those lately. He had written a swell script for Marie Dressler, but the director had wanted to change it, and Vinny had gotten drunk and punched him and Metro had booted him out. That had been two months ago. No work since then; word had gotten around. As for Metro, they just imported more dogmeat, the likes of Dorothy Parker, Scott Fitzgerald, Ben Hecht. Vinny sneered. They chew us up and spit us out. He felt vaguely hungry, but there was nothing in the kitchenette, and as if paralysed he sat there while his cigarette went as dead as his career. The races at Caliente, I want to be at the races! He liked nursing a martini in the bar while the horses sweated for him, but even if he were there, what would he bet with?

Gloom settled over him. On credit he could last one or two more weeks.

Damn it, I need this job from Hearst!

The phone rang. He stared at it. He did not want to answer. Someone who knew how down he was? Someone who would gloat or drown him in the syrup of condescending smypathy?

With distaste, more out of boredom than anything else, Vinny lifted the receiver with a hand that had grown used to manicures every week.

"Vinny? It's Marion Davies." Her warm voice cooed that it was a damn shame about his hard luck. Then she said, "You n-need some f-fun. We're throwing a p-party this w-weekend. That's why I called. Come up, Vinny."

Villy swallowed hard. "To San Simeon?"

"Natch. It'll ch-cheer you up. W.R.'ll b-be meeting with those f-fuddy-duddy business advisers of his, but we won't let any old s-stuffed shirts s-spoil our f-fun."

Vinny controlled his glee; could he sell his idea directly to Hearst? "I'd love to come." He forced himself to make small talk about her move to Warners. "You'd have made a great Marie Antoinette!"

"Th-think so?" She sounded suddenly weary, uncertain—almost sad, but her voice perked up at the end. "Well, anyway, it's the G-Glendale train, as usual. *The Lark.* Friday. Say, maybe P-popsy can do something for you. I'll see if I can t-twist the old b-bear's arm."

Vinny could hardly believe his luck. "As a matter of fact, I *do* have an idea for a picture. It's just *made* for you."

"Swell, I n-need a good picture. Till F-Friday then, Vinny. Bye."

Vinny hung up. Lighting another cigarette, the last in the pack, he burst out laughing. Marion pulling for me; good old Marion! Too bad her latest pictures were losing money. She was good in comedy, though she flopped like a fish in serious roles. Hearst didn't see it that way, of course; he was convinced she was a great dramatic actress. He was pigheaded too, blind to any ideas but his own, and he had to be handled with kid gloves. It's him I should've punched, Vinny thought. He hated Hearst. Two years ago he had scripted a good little picture for Marion and John Mack Brown, but the old fart had rewritten some of his best scenes, turning his plot into bunk. Then Hearst had had the nerve to lecture him about how to write. Vinny despised himself for bowing and scraping: "Yes, sir; gee, thanks, sir." But now . . . Marion's willingness to go to bat for him made him flush with shame. His new screenplay was about Anne Boleyn. It was all wrong for her. But, damn it, it's right for what Hearst wants; I've got to watch out for number one! Vinny reread his letter, it still sounded good. I'll mail it tonight, he thought, it'll get to San Simeon tomorrow. Marion Davies, tragic heroine; Hearst just has to go for it.

Vinny checked himself in the bedroom mirror: crisp white shirt, slate-colored slacks, black shoes polished to a diamond shine. He stroked his thin mustache. Nobody'd ever guess how down I am. A drink at Chasen's, just one. I've got a couple of bucks left. Besides, appearances're what this town's about: eat, drink and be merry; afterward you blow out your brains.

A pink garter peeked out from under his bed. Thoughtfully, he scooped it up. It belonged to Gloria Deere, the cute little brunette he had met in Marion's bungalow. Their affair had been hot for a while, but the girl had cooled down lately. Getting fed up that I'm not making her a star? She's no dope. Talented too. She had been one of the dancers on the airplane wings in *Flying Down to Rio* with Astaire and Rogers; she'd even had a couple of lines in Marion's last at Metro. She was also good in bed; that could take an ambitious girl far. Vinny twirled the garter. Why not bring Gloria along to San Simeon? Marion wouldn't mind.

Vinny liked the idea. Humming for the first time in a long time, he tucked the letter in his inside breast pocket and took the elevator down to Ivar, where a bunch of rubes were gawking at a man in a pink bathing suit sitting on a flagpole.

❧ 10 ❧

GLORIA Deere slipped into the narrow concrete alley between the MGM executive offices and the film processing building and began adjusting her French peasant costume, to which dirt and blood-colored stain had been artfully applied for the storming-the-Bastille scene nearby. Her pert nose wrinkled. I'm going to look good in this darn old thing if it kills me!

She pulled down the blouse as far as she dared, revealing a float of plump white breasts, and struggled to tie up the skirt to show off her ankles.

At that moment Eddie McGuffin trudged by pushing a rack of hoopskirted dresses.

Gloria's hazel eyes lit; she was bursting with news she just had to tell. "Eddie, oh, Eddie! You'll never guess! I've been invited to a big party at San Simeon!"

Eddie halted. Etched by midday light, his lean head swiveled toward where she breathed excitedly in the shadows. He blinked, his whole body seeming to quiver, and Gloria got an odd, shivery feeling all over. Eddie did that to her. His dark looks attracted her, but she was a little scared of him too. Such strange, deep blue eyes. Memory fluttered in her mind, the memory of how her brother, Joe Swann, had asked her to put in a word for him. Swishing her hips à la Jean Harlow, she had persuaded one of the crew foremen to give the kid a chance. Course, she never said why. Joe lived in Chicago. He was a Red; that made Gloria nervous. Was Eddie a Communist too? She didn't pry: Gloria thought what a girl didn't know couldn't hurt her. And she certainly did not want anyone to know she was related to a Red—not these days, when the studios were kicking out anybody they thought was even pink. That was another reason she'd changed her name from Ella Swann to Gloria Deere.

Eddie slid into the shadows beside her. "San Simeon? Hearst's place?" he croaked in a funny, tight voice.

"Of course Hearst's place, silly. This man I know, a writer—he asked me." Gloria dimpled. "Oh, it'll be swell! Maybe it'll help my career. Maybe I'll meet some big shot who'll like me and make me a star. I'm so tired of not getting my big break, and—"

Eddie stood very close; Gloria found her arms locked in strong hard hands. Hot breath hit her face. "You've got to take me with you," Eddie said.

"What?" She looked at the hands gouging her flesh, then into the piercing eyes. "Take you . . . ?"

"To San Simeon."

"But—Eddie, you're hurting me."

His fingers only pressed tighter. "They let lots of people come," he hissed. "One more won't matter. You've got to do it, Gloria. *You've got to.*"

She struggled. "All right, all right!" He let her go, and she rubbed her arms. Eddie really was scary, yet she kind of liked the way he had held her and told her just what to do. She swayed provocatively, finger on her chin, just like she'd seen Bette Davis do in *Of Human Bondage.* "I s'pose if I said you were my brother . . ."

A desperate flash of smile. "Your brother; yeah, that's who I'll be. You can't say no, Gloria. You just can't."

"Sure. Everybody wants to see what the stars're like when they let their hair down. Oh, it'll be grand!" She slipped out of the alley. "I'll see what I can do. No promises, of course." There came a distant clamor, the roar of a mob. "Oh, nuts!" She shook an angry finger. "If you made me miss the crowd scene . . . !" Frantically adjusting her bosom, Gloria Deere dashed off past the papier-mâché ruins of Rome.

❦ 11 ❦

I T had been days since Otis Pike had called Bart Rawlston and Max. No news yet.

Eight P.M. Twitching with impatience, the horsefaced dwarf with one built-up shoe sat in his dumpy hotel room glowering at Louella Parsons's column in the L.A. *Herald:*

> Tempus sure do fugit. It's been just *ages* since Mr. William Randolph Hearst had a party at his fabulous estate up the coast, but he's about to throw another bash, and many of the luminaries of this fair town are invited: Clark Gable and Jean Harlow and Dick Powell and Charlie (the Tramp) Chaplin himself. There's sure to be glamour and fun, and your loyal reporter will be there too, to see and tell all.

Pike sneered at the gushy style. I've got to get invited to that party, he thought. I think I know how. But first . . .

He picked up the phone and called Max.

"So. I have been waiting for your call."

"Like hell you have. I bet you still haven't got anything on those glass balls with the snow in them. What's taking you? I'm gonna fire you, I swear, and you're not gonna collect a nickel for the time you've put in."

There was a silence. "The payment for information is the same as before?"

Pike sat up straight. "You got something?"

"Have I ever failed you? Karl Zimmer and Sons, of Wiesbaden. They manufactured many items, all of fine quality, but they were a small firm, and they did not publish catalogues. Most pieces were made to order for a very elite clientele. They specialized in intricate clocks and jewelry boxes, but they were craftsmen, masters of many skills; they could fashion whatever men of taste commissioned. I have traced the snow toys through a dealer in Stuttgart who specializes in such items. They were produced originally for a wealthy man, a politician, who made bad investments and lost his fortune in the nineties and was forced to sell everything. The toys went into auction." A tiny pause. "Does it surprise you that they were bought by Mr. William Randolph Hearst?"

"How d'you know that?"

"Public auction records. There is one other thing I know. You told me hundreds of these were imported, but they could not have been. There were only two."

"Two?"

"Specially made. Father and sons are now dead, and the firm is long out of business. But the globes are of very fine quality; they are not mass-produced. And my contact in Stuttgart—he is an expert—assures me there were only two. He has clients who would pay a great deal." Another pause. "Do you have them? Will you sell?"

"I told you, it's not like that."

"A pity. It would have rewarded us both handsomely."

"I got my reward," Pike said, and hung up. But what reward? He scowled out at an evening sky as cloudless as a studio backdrop. What's it mean? Anything? They're just toys. But the little man's instinct was stirring, tightening, screaming. *Mr. Hearst gave lots of them*

50

away; he imported them from Germany—that's what the McGuffin woman had said. Lying? Covering something up? Pike's bum foot began to ache, and with a little bark of frustration he scrambled up onto his stumps of legs and splashed bourbon into a glass.

Just two globes.

So, why had old Hearst given such a valuable present to an eleven-year-old kid? And where was the other toy?

Otis Pike snatched up the phone. He plucked at his tufts of whitish hair as he waited for the call to go through.

The icy cultivated voice came at last from New York. "I'm glad you called, Mr.—ah, Pike, isn't it, this time? That legwork you asked for has been done; it has garnered some very interesting information."

"Shoot," Pike said, nerve ends prickling.

"Rose Ellen Forrest is dead."

The dwarf pressed the phone hard against his ear. "What?"

"She died of natural causes. That is the official version at any rate. The point is," Bart Rawlston said slowly, drawing it out, "she died more than thirty years ago."

Pike blinked. "You're crazy. I talked to her in Chicago."

"Indeed?" A small laugh. 'Talking to a corpse is quite a feat. But, since you are sure you spoke to flesh and blood; whose? is the question. Let us leave that for the moment; there are a number of other conundrums to face. My man has discovered that Harry McGuffin was a reporter for William Randolph Hearst before he died falling off a train. A mail train, a local. What was a Hearst reporter doing on a mail train? Surely not chasing a story. Furthermore, there was no inquest. What shall we make of that? As for Rose Ellen Forrest, she was the daughter of an unremarkable middle-class family in Stockbridge, Massachusetts. Not much on her: a birth certificate, some school records. The family moved years ago. It was not easy to trace them, but I have connections you lack; that is why we work so well together. My man located the family just yesterday, in San Luis Obispo, two hundred miles north of Los Angeles. Is it significant that the Southern Pacific Lark stops there, the train which carries Mr. William Randolph Hearst's guests to his ostentatious pile of stone on the California coast?" A crackling

51

pause. "You can understand my renewed interest. I had almost given up on you, but I see now that in fact you may be my link to something very useful to us both. I don't like you, Mr. Pike; I prefer my employees to have real names and faces I can look at. Nonetheless, I am not backing out—not yet. Press on, at my expense. The mother died years ago of some internal ailment but Mr. Forrest remains alive. Unfortunately he is quite old, near ninety, and incoherent, wasting away in a rest home in San Luis Obispo. But he is Rose Ellen Forrest's father, no question; I shall send you the documentation. And the daughter's death certificate. She died of influenza in the selfsame San Luis Obispo, at age twenty-two." Rawlston paused again. "This Rose Ellen Forrest you talked to in Chicago—her married\name was Rose McGuffin? She was Harry McGuffin's wife?"

"So she said."

"My man confirms it. But Harry McGuffin could not have married a dead woman."

"Get to the point."

"A third party, our old friend, is playing a game, his own game; he has been playing it for years. It is a deep game, and I suspect it would cause him great embarrassment to have it uncovered." A low chuckle. "So dig on, Mr. Pike; toil in the muck. Let us hope that soon some of it will splatter Mr. William Randolph Hearst's patriotic white shirtfont. Oh, one more detail: the job Mr. Forrest came west to take; it was regional distributor for the Hearst papers. The job was offered to him by Hearst himself. A payoff? I told you there were conundrums. Solve them, please; I will be grateful—and most generous. You will be happy to learn that money is forthcoming; say, a thousand? I don't wish to stint when the well may be about to spew riches. I think that is all. Good-bye."

Darkness was sweeping in from the Pacific, a bruised purple. Outside Pike's hotel window pink, white, and blue lights winked on across the wide flat dish of Los Angeles, while from the room next door came the muffled sound of a radio: Fanny Brice as Baby Snooks. Pike dropped the receiver and poured himself another drink, but he could not keep the bottle from rattling against the glass. He turned to the bed. A piece of paper lay there beside the Parsons column: a

Hearst guest list. The Parsons column was three days old, and Pike had spent those three days scrambling to get his hands on the list, finally obtaining it from one of Parsons's secretaries who had turned out to need some fast dough. It hadn't been cheap, but it was worth it, because a name stood out, a man Pike new. A slow smile stretched the dwarf's wide mouth. Things going my way at last? He went with his odd rolling walk to the window. TEMPLE OF COSMIC TRUTH—the bulbs illuminated his long horseface in a yellowish glow. Momentarily explosions went off in his head, but for once they did not threaten to make him mad.

Downing his whiskey, Otis Pike picked up the phone once more.

❧ 12 ❧

IT was just two days until Hearst's party at San Simeon. Vinny Tashman could hardly wait—but he was also annoyed. That afternoon he had let Gloria Deere talk him into calling Marion and adding her brother to the guest list. What brother? The one in Chicago? The Red? But this seemed to be another one; she had been vague. Vinny did not want to drag along the excess baggage, but Gloria had whined and wheedled: she just wouldn't come if Eddie could not come too. But if sweetums Vinny did her this one little favor, well. . . Her voice had dripped promises.

Vinny had called Marion, who had said, "Sure, the m-more the m-merrier!"

He made himself forget it. How could the brother get in the way of anything? Besides, Vinny had promises from hot little Gloria, and he'd hold her to them too.

It was night, but still warm in his apartment. Sitting at his desk, running a hand through his dark hair, he tried to concentrate on fixing the Anne Boleyn script. It was a piece of crap—all those milords and miladies—but Hearst liked high-flown historical stuff.

Maybe he ought to leave it as it was. Christ, what if the damn guy doesn't go for it? Vinny blanched. The thought reminded him of something he'd seen this afternoon out on La Brea: Carl Lombardo peddling apples. Lombardo had been a screenwriter too, the chief idea man for that simpering, curly-haired moppet who was single-handedly keeping Fox studios out of the red. That hadn't saved him though. Lombardo had been careless. He had propositioned a Fox prop boy, the kid had raised a stink, and that had been it; a career down the drain. Anything goes Vinny thought; just don't get caught. Nobody's immune. Bad press had finished Fatty Arbuckle, and Charlie Chaplin's lefty politics and skirt-chasing weren't doing him any good with the public. Vinny got a momentary flash. How about Hearst, any skeletons in his closet? I sure could use something on the old bastard, an ace in the hole, so he'd have to buy my script. Power—it all boiled down to that. Vinny's gaze drifted to the target pistols on his desk. They had been used in *Streets of Paris*, real guns, not just props, and when he was canned he had simply walked off the lot with them. Metro owed him. His long-fingered hands caressed the dark, oiled metal. He practiced with them at a West Hollywood shooting range, and he was proud of his steady hand and cool eye.

Steady and cool when I'm sober, that is.

It was about eight P.M., velvety dark beyond the windows of the Alto Nido. His telephone rang.

He picked it up. "Yeah?"

"Hello, Vinny."

Vinny felt a chill. The voice was feathery, tickling. Someone he knew? Its moist insinuating tone made the hair at the back of his neck stand up.

"Who is this?"

"I go by Pike. Otis Pike. From Chicago. But you know me by another name." The voice told him the name.

The conversation did not last long. When it was over Vinny was sweating. His hand shook as he put down the receiver.

He had to do what the man asked, the dwarf. Just had to.

Make another call to Marion.

The night seemed to press against his window like a thick, dark blanket, smothering him, and Vinny could not sit still; he headed out. Gotta get a drink. Gotta think.

On Sunset he shied at a rattling sound. A beat-up Ford truck was creeping along in the night, its back piled with furniture: bedsprings, chairs, a small claw-footed table. Suitcases were strapped to the sides, and a battered green trunk swayed on top. Faces peered out, lost-looking: a skinny man, a woman, kids. Okies. "Mister, hey mister, c'n you tell me where—?" But Vinny had already ducked into a bar. The man peered after him. Gol darn, he thought.

The man's name was Tom Goodall; he was desperate for work. Tom Goodall's family was hungry, and Tom Goodall too had a gun.

❧ 13 ❧

EDDIE McGuffin scrambled forward with the mob. There were hundreds, thousands on the high, rocky plain, aiming for the light.

The workers of the world, united at last.

They trampled the coldhearted industrialists, the selfish capitalists, the tyrants; they stamped out hunger and inequality. Their arms were raised toward hope, and Eddie raised his arms too. Their boots made a tramping song; their voices crowed the "Internationale," and, sobbing, laughing, Eddie sang with them.

Something happened.

A roar, and the ground cracked open, and Eddie's comrades began sliding helplessly into a black abyss. There were screams, as men, women, children were sucked out of sight. Eddie stretched his arms to save them.

He shot upright in bed.

Pale morning light streamed through his grimy wondow. The walls of the dismal little room were moving. *Das Kapital* tumbled onto the frayed carpet. There was a faint rumbling, and somewhere a dog barked frantically.

Then the rumbling stopped. Shaking, Eddie ran a hand through his thatch of brown hair. An earthquake. They happened all the time, but this was the worst so far. Eddie's hotel was the San Bernardino Arms, a dump in Pinyon Canyon at the end of Vine. Sliding his lean form from the sheets, he ran water in the stained wall basin and splashed his face and arms. He jerked on a white shirt and the brown tweed trousers Ma's money had bought him in Chicago. Guilt hit him. Ma . . . no, don't think about her. It's Hearst now, and always, till the end.

But he could not help remembering his and Ma's last big scene, their fight. It was four months ago, a steamy Chicago night. He had come in from a Young Communist League meeting, and there she was, crouched by the radio, listening to Father Coughlin. "Ma, how can you listen to that hooey?" Eddie saw her shocked brown eyes all over again, as he'd been seeing them all his life.

"Don't say that. Father Coughlin is a priest."

"He's a Nazi, Ma, just like Hitler. Just like"—Eddie's gaze had caught the photograph on the mantel, —"just like goddamn Hearst."

Rose McGuffin's hand went to her heart. "Don't say that. Mr. Hearst was good to you. He's a great man."

"Great? He stuffed me with cake and handed me that glass snow thing. He patted my dumb little head. Why? 'Cause I sold lots of papers and made him some dough, that's why. He's a capitalist, Ma. He exploits the masses and gets fat off it, while people're starving in the streets."

"Oh, Eddie . . ."

Eddie turned away. "Lay off, will ya?" His hands made fists. Why did it always have to be like this? He had to get out for good. Scowling at the glass globe on the mantel, he wondered as he had a thousand times before what it would have been like if Pa had lived. Pa! I didn't even know you!

His mother had tugged his arm. "Eddie—"

"I'm leaving, Ma, he told her. "Clearing out. It's time."

A blurry panic in her eyes. "B-but . . . you don't have a job."

"I'll get one. You think I'm a baby? I gotta be on my own."

"But, where?"

"California."

Her small body seemed to shrink in the blue dress. "So far away?"

"There's work in California. Maybe I'll get a job in the movies."

"That's crazy, Eddie."

He grabbed her arms. "Don't call me crazy!"

She was crying now, sobbing, and Eddie let her go. He scared himself sometimes when the anger bubbled up, blinding him; he might hurt even her. That was another reason to get out, do what he must.

And so he had, he'd come to California. To get Hearst. Shaking, he glanced at the rumpled bed where the pistol he had bought a week ago from Dandy Jack Pinkus hid under the mattress, and a wave of nausea hit him, a pounding in the brain. He shook his head; the dizziness faded, but not the fear.

He turned on the battered radio. An announcer said people were phoning in about the quake, centered in the Santa Lucia Mountains up the coast. Near Hearst's place, he thought, yanking a tight angry knot in his tie. Russ Colombo started singing, "Prisoner of Love," and Eddie switched off the radio. He went to the reeking toilet down the dimly lit hall. Today's Thursday, he thought, back in his room, and tomorrow's Friday, and then I'll . . . His knees suddenly shook, and he sank onto the creaking bed. He picked up *Das Kapital*. The photograph of his father, his only one, his special one, was tucked inside. Blurred, it showed a compact, balding man with a bushy mustache holding a copy of the *Evening American*. Harry McGuffin. He stood beside a long row of Linotype machines in a loose-fitting suit, and his rumpled tie and easygoing air said he was a swell Joe, a regular guy; his straightforward smile said so too. Pa. But there was something sharp in his eyes; they asked Eddie questions: Who are you? What are you doing? Are you a man?

Am I?

Eddie thought about his life till now, the long line of crummy jobs that he had gotten fired from or quit, department store jobs and door-to-door jobs, peddling aluminum cookware, shoelaces, eggs. And the night school that hadn't worked out, that had only given him ideas he didn't know what to do with. The anger inside. The rented rooms, and always dragging back to Ma because the country was on the skids and he couldn't hang on to a thing.

Am I a man?

I will be, Pa, I will!

Eddie's fingers tightened on the photo. "For you," he croaked. He knew enough to want to do it. His father had tried to organize the reporters on the Chicago *Evening American*. His father had worked for Hearst, and he had died falling off a train.

Eddie grabbed his jacket and headed out. He had to buy a suit for San Simeon; he'd call in sick to Metro. On Vine Street he jammed his hands in his pockets. Hard times walked the streets. A guy passed him with a big white card on his hat: NEED A JOB, WILL TAKE ANYTHING. A breadline snaked bleakly into a warehouse.

"Hey, mister!"

Eddie turned.

A battered Ford truck had pulled up, motor wheezing, straining as if breathing its last. Suitcases were strapped to its sides, and the back was piled with furniture, an old green trunk on top. A sharp elbow poked out the window; above it, a gaunt, searching face with hollow eyes. The man had a beaky nose and a thin-lipped mouth. His jaw was grizzled, and his gray, crumpled hat looked screwed onto his head.

Eddie knew that face. It was the lost, hopeless face of America.

The man's voice sounded like dust. "C'n you tell me the way t'the coast road?" A skinny woman and three big-eyed kids peered from behind him. "Name's Goodall. Tom," the man said. "I bin lookin' for work here, but there ain't none. Thought there might be veg'tables or fruit to pick up north; oranges, peaches. I heard there was."

Eddie's head began to buzz. The sun was so bright. Dry-mouthed, he gave directions that would take Tom Goodall and his family up past San Simeon. Don't expect a handout from Hearst, Eddie thought. He yanked out a five-dollar bill. "Take this."

The man peered at it hungrily. "Aw, mister, I can't." He glanced at the wife and kids, "But mebbe . . ."

Eddie forced it into his hand. "Pay me back by helping somebody else someday." He watched the Ford chug away. Hunger, poverty—

58

why? All at once the dizziness, the nausea were on him again, and he had to lean against a brick wall to keep from falling down.

Sometimes it was just too much; sometimes he wanted to turn that gun on himself, and as he headed into Sears Roebuck, Eddie remembered two more th ngs from Chicago: how before he had charged from Ma's house he had smashed against the hearth the glass globe with the little scene in it; how with a kind of frantic glee he had ripped his Ma's precious picture of William Randloph Hearst into shreds.

❦ **14** ❧

BUT Eddie could not remember what he did not know. He could not remember how his Ma, Rose McGuffin, thin in her blue dress, with a face still delicately pretty even though she was fifty-seven and had liver-spotted hands, had, an hour after their fight, anxiously crept from her bedroom in back of the big Chicago house that she had told the dwarf was bought with Harry McGuffin's insurance money.

He's a high-strung boy, she had thought, hesitating outside her son's room. She'd fretted even when he was small. Oh, if only his father . . . But she must not think of that. Besides, she could compensate. He could easi.y stay with her, near, riding out the bad times; she had plenty of money for them both.

Money. There had been a time when she was desperate for it, and she flushed with shame at what she had done to save herself, save her son.

She had raised her hand, knocked.

No answer.

She had rushed in. He was gone, his few clothes, even his books. "Eddie!"

She ran to the living room, hoping, but he was not there either, and she halted as if slapped, shocked at what she saw: the frame of the newsboy photograph twisted on the hearth, the picture ripped to confetti on the Persian rug. Rose moaned. Her heels crunched in broken glass. Tiny curved fragments lay everywhere, mingled with the magical snow, now only flakes of mica in puddles of water— Eddie had also smashed Mr. Hearst's precious gift. Kneeling, whimpering, she picked up the brass base. The globe had been hurled so hard against the marble hearth that the intricately carved Alpine village was ruins. With shaking fingers she touched the little cumpled steeple, damaged irreparably. "Oh, Eddie . . ."

The woman staggered back to her room. She pulled her picture album from the nightstand drawer and, huddled on the bed, turned its pages as if they could protect her from the truth. Truth. The odd little insurance man's words from months ago flew into her brain: *Photographs don't lie.* But could they make up for loss? Rose fought sobs as she looked through the album; there was baby Eddie, then Eddie in a sailor outfit, a cowboy outfit. Eddie growing, Eddie gone. Tears splashed the pictures, and she remembered the dwarf again, taking pictures of everything: *flash, flash.* At least he had not flashed his big camera at this.

My secret is buried deep, she thought.

There were also photos of Mr. McGuffin, his wayward smile, his kind gaze. My husband, she thought, brushing her fingers over Harry McGuffin's face. A good man. Dead. Photographs . . . photographs.

She leapt up. In the living room she meticulously collected every scrap of the picture Eddie had ripped, and as if performing a rite that could redress old sins, she began taping Mr. Hearst back together.

❧ 15 ❧

FRIDAY.

The orange ball of sun lifted over the Sierras; its light stretched across California, warming mile by mile: Yosemite, Death Valley. Then the beams struck a huge white castle on a peak above the Pacific: Casa Grande. From the coast road it had a fairy-tale appearance, a Maxfield Parrish fantasy on its hilltop above San Simeon Bay, but it was also a fortress, isolated; only a single two-lane road climbed to it, five miles through rocky ravines and up steep brown-grass slopes, and it was surrounded by a ten-mile-long, eight-foot-high wire fence guarded by electrically operated gates. Within this fence the world's largest private collection of wild animals ran free: bison, elk, zebras, camels, giraffes; also warring yak from Tibet and fighting emu from New Zealand, beasts which could be unfriendly to interlopers.

A security force kept watch at the top.

Buried phone and telegraph wires were San Simeon's sole lifelines to the world outside the private domain William Randolph Hearst had created for himself, his art collection, Marion Davies. Should those lines be severed, should anything happen to the single road, the castle would be cut off.

Ella "Bill" Williams did not think about that. Below her window in the new wing of Casa Grande, trucks were already beginning to deliver crates of canned goods and sides of meat, and outside her half open door maids dashed to tidy rooms in the big main house, as they would be doing in the three satellite guesthouses, dusting armor and porcelain and dreamy-eyed Madonnas. Bill ignored the bustle. She had her own job to do, very delicate, politics as much as anything. There were a hundred forty-six rooms in all, and Bill had the task of assigning just the right guest to just the right one.

She sighed, sharpened three pencils, and stared at her long list. Momentarily she laughed at how no one ever turned down an invitation to San Simeon, unless he or she was out of the country or dead. Then she began sorting through a stack of three-by-five cards, each with a scribbled name and personal information. Bill was Marion's private secretary; thus she knew most of the movie people—Gable, Swanson, Powell, Chaplin—as well as Mr. Hearst's business associates: John Francis Neylan, his chief lawyer; the columnist Arthur Brisbane; Walter Winchell; Damon Runyon. Not just a party, but a big powwow this weekend, to talk about money. Bill shook her head. The rumor that Mr. Hearst was in trouble couldn't be true; the depression might've knocked the country for a loop, but it just couldn't hurt Mr. Hearst. Yet, Bill admitted, frowning, the powerful publisher had been as jumpy as a monkey lately. So had Marion, come to that. Bill set those thoughts aside, chewing an eraser. About forty guests this time, a modest gathering compared to the sixty that sometimes showed up. She would do the least important first, rooms on the fringes. Card one: Gloria Deere. She did not recognize that name. One of Marion's waifs? The girl's brother, Eddie, was coming too. Bill considered where to fit them in. Most of the hill's accommodations were double suites, two bedrooms separated by a sitting room. The farthest guesthouse, she decided, Casa del Monte. Penciling in the names, she flipped another card: Otis Pike. Frowning faintly at another unfamiliar name, Bill checked her notes. A late addition, a friend of Vincent X. Tashman, the screenwriter. I'll put them all together. She penciled the two men in opposite bedrooms in Casa del Monte.

She felt a jolt. A faint rumbling accompanied it, and her pencils and pens rattled in the Chinese celadon Mr. Hearst had given her for her birthday: earthquake. An elephant trumpeted from the private zoo, a lion roared, and chimps and baboons set up a frantic screeching, but Bill just calmly gripped the edge of her desk and waited it out. There had been more small quakes than usual lately— the San Andreas Fault was only a few miles away—but Mr. Hearst's architect, Julia Morgan, had designed everything of reinforced concrete, and it always withstood every shock. Certainly no reason to expect it wouldn't continue to do so.

When the trembling stopped Bill bit her lip. Charlie Chaplin? Where should she locate Mr. Chaplin?

The sun rose higher over Mr. Hearst's enchanted hill.

✥ 16 ✥

A S Bill went through her cards, Etta Kitt sat before the maze of switchboard wires in the communication building nearby. The telephone company had given it a special exchange to please Mr. Hearst: Hacienda One. "Hacienda One," Etta piped in her sharp, high voice. "Yes, Mr. Neylan, I'll put you right through." Rapidly she plugged John Francis Neylan's call through to Joe Willicombe's office. Etta was small, with pinched, puckish features; her thin black brows were like little pointed tents above snapping black eyes. A sly look crossed her face. Listen in? Grinning like an elf, she glanced out at the curving drive leading to Casa Grande. The telephone and telegraph rooms were in a plain single-story frame building, so hidden away among oaks that arriving guests hardly noticed it as they swept past in Mr. Hearst's shiny limousines. But I'm here, Etta thought even if they don't see. And I know things that would make most of them squirm.

You bet I'll listen in!

". . . and W.R. has just got to be persuaded he's in trouble," Neylan's brusque Irish-inflected voice was saying. "He's a hundred and a quarter million in debt, damn it. You're closest to him, Joe. I'll be there tonight, but soften him up for me, will you? He's got to listen to reason." Etta pulled off her earphones. Money talk; what a bore. Leaning back, she thoughtfully lit a cigarette. Old Hearst's rows with Marion Davies were far more interesting—and you didn't have to listen in on phone lines. They boomed out the third-story windows and made everyone wonder how long it could last. The drinking too. People said Hearst's little blonde had a bottle stashed behind every tree. Touching her frizz of black hair, Etta grinned more wickedly than ever. The hilltop phone lines would sizzle this weekend—guests making bedroom rendezvous—and she would be sure to listen. Afterward, would she dish the dirt!

Etta sank farther back, dreaming. I'll write my memoirs someday. I'll make faces turn red.

Another call, and she shot up straight. "Harpo Marx? Oh, yes, sir, Mr. Marx, I'll put you through to Miss Davies right away!"

❧ 17 ❧

COLONEL Joe Willicombe was worried.

Willicombe's office was tucked on the first floor of Casa Grande. Three telephones and several in-out boxes crammed with memos sat on the broad walnut desk before him. Willicombe was not a demonstrative man—he put down the phone as politely as if his sainted mother had just called—but silently he cursed Jack Neylan. Soften up the Chief? Who could do that? Poking at his glasses, the bulky man frowned at his main worry, the eight-by-ten scrap of paper he had been pondering when Neylan interrupted: BE THERE SOON. The damn thing was printed in the same stiff block letters of the previous dozen notes, and above the words was scrawled the same maddening symbol that appeared on all of them: little radicating lines that looked like a dandelion. A tiny sun? A porcupine? Willicombe groaned. The warnings had been arriving anonymously for the past eight months. Neither the police nor Willicombe himself had pestered the Chief since the first one, but the police were getting jumpy—the notes kept coming; could they be from some dangerous fanatic?—and Inspector Luis Garcia had insisted Willicombe prod his boss's memory again. Willicombe massaged his bald spot, where a headache was threatening to bloom. He hated the timing. There was a radio broadcast this evening, guests arriving tonight; the financial meeting, too. The Chief had enough on his mind. Of course, his bad heart always had to be considered. Sighing, Willicombe got up, consoling himself with the thought that his boss had the heart of a dinosaur—until he remembered that dinosaurs were extinct.

Have to face it, he thought. Carrying his ever present clipboard he headed out past a Botticelli *Virgin and Child,* crossed the Assembly Hall, and rose in the hidden elevator to the third floor of Casa Grande.

In the Gothic Suite he found his boss sitting at the end of the long central table, eating a boiled egg. Hearst wore a huge white napkin tucked in his vest. Looks like a big wrinkled baby, Willicombe thought with no hint of satire. He had worked for Hearst ten years; he knew his boss's childlike enthusiasms, but he also knew that in one of his murderous angers the petulant old man could equally childishly smash things so badly that he had to hire people to fix the pieces—or quietly sweep them under the rug. Willicombe made allowances; he felt genuine affection for his boss and would do anything to protect him.

Hearst's Los Angeles *Herald* was propped in front of him. His eyes twinkled as Willicombe approached on whispering shoes. "Ha, ha, I like this, Joe!" He thumped the comic page. "Little Orphan Annie says to Daddy Warbucks, 'Leapin' Lizards, who sez business is bad for the country?'" Hearst chortled. "That's the ticket—every right-thinking American ought to feel just like she does." His pouchy eyes narrowed, and he jerked out his napkin. "Joe, you have a funny, green look about the gills. What's up?"

"Just the usual reports."

"Jack Neylan had better not have been putting a bug in your ear."

"As a matter of fact—"

Hearst banged the table so hard the salt and pepper jumped. "I thought so!" He hurled the napkin down. "Damn it, you know how I hate my men powwowing behind my back. I am perfectly capable of making decisions without conspiracies in my camp. What'd he want?"

Willicombe told him.

"Damn the man! I'll give him a good dressing-down." Hearst's voice quieted. "And Joe, this weekend see he's kept as far from Marion as possible. You know they don't get along."

A discreet nod. The truth was, Neylan made Marion spit like a cat, and the feeling was mutual; Neylan hated Marion because of her influence on the Chief—and what if the old man willed his empire to her? Willicombe silently sided with Hearst's mistress. She was no dummy; she gave the Chief sensible business advice. Besides, Willicombe secretly enjoyed watching the florid-faced Neylan squirm.

The secretary kept these thoughts to himself as he reported on the ban against Mae West's pictures—"Immoral!" Hearst sputtered—and the campaign against the NRA. There was mounting trouble with reporters agitating to join the Newspaper Guild.

Hearst shook his head. "Don't I pay 'em good money? Being a newman is a profession, not a trade. The minute they give allegiance to something other than their newspaper, freedom of the press goes right down the drain."

Willicombe gave Hearst an encouraging smile. "But there's good news. That Chicago fireworks suit is finally settled. It cost us, but not as much as it might have. The bank drafts have gone out, all except to"—he scanned his clipboard—"a man named Lester C. Penworthy. He's the surviving relative. We're hunting him up now."

"Shouldn't be a long hunt with a name like Penworthy. There can't be that many Penworthys around." Hearst's jowls shook. "Money's waiting for a man, my money, and he's not scrambling for it? The country is crazy." His fingers drummed on the table. "That reminds me; are the fireworks set for tonight? I don't want anything to go wrong."

"The man from L.A. says you'll have a fine show. His crew is up in the hills now, setting up. They'll see it in San Luis Obispo, he says."

Hearst rubbed his hands. "Good!"

"Er, one last thing." Willicombe placed the warning note on the table.

Hearst bent toward it. "I've seen this before."

"You saw the first one, last spring. A dozen or so have shown up

66

since then, all with the same idea: 'getting you.' This is the latest. Sorry to bother you with it, but the police insisted. They haven't a clue who they're from, and they still hope you might be able to say something about the little drawing."

Hearst scowled. "The damn thing looks like a fur ball. 'Be there soon'—what in hell, the police think this nut is going to crash our party tonight? All right, all right; the boys in blue are useful, we want to keep them happy.' He tucked the note in his checkered vest. "Tell them I'm thinking about it. Now, get on the wire to all our editors: no shilly-shallying on foreign policy, is that clear? Roosevelt is sure to get us all knotted up with England and France if we don't act fast."

When Willicombe left, Hearst trudged out to the spacious sitting room that separated his and Marion's bedrooms. A wire cage sat on a Louis XIV writing desk just under a Della Robbia *Madonna*; in it was Ambrose the mouse, whom Hearst had saved from Helena eight months ago. "Hello, Ambrose." The mouse touched his index finger with its one white paw. "Are we pals, little mousey? Are you my very good friend?"

Hearst headed for his bedroom, the smallest bedroom of the twenty-four in Casa Grande, though its ceiling was the finest, a rare fifteenth-century work reassembled from Castle Marchino in Córdoba. A silver Florentine lamp hung from its center, and Italian primitives—a Duccio, a Segna—decorated the walls, but he took no pleasure in the room's rich detail. Jack Neylan's financial warnings kept nagging him as he peered west out a Gothic-arched window. Palm trees made a dozen ragged shapes against the morning light, and far out a faint smudge of clouds was gathering at the rim of the Pacific. A storm? Hearst scowled. Better not spoil my fireworks! He glimpsed a flash of white slacks and blouse, sun glinting on blond hair: Marion, on the tiled terrace far below. One more worry. Marion had been especially jumpy lately, drinking more than ever since her favorite niece, Pepi, had committed suicide by jumping out that third-floor hospital window, and it didn't help that her pictures had become box office poison.

Let the weekend cheer her up!

Marion vanished into the garden. What will cheer me? Hearst

thought, his old, liver-spotted fingers paddling the stone sill. A quarter of a million acres. I own it, but I also own a hundred and twenty-five million in debts. Panic shook him. I don't want to cut back, I want to go on spending! His gaze fell on the ancient Italian wellhead in the center of the South Terrace. Bought that in Verona. How long ago? Forty years? Verona . . . Tessie Powers. The Harvard Widow, they had called her, the first of many mistresses; before Marion, the woman of his life. How many women? The intervening years felt smothering, choking, and Hearst gasped, heart thudding. Damn ticker! He made himself remember: happy times gadding about Europe with Tessie and George Pancoast, his photographer—Paris, Verona, Wiesbaden. His mind touched the gay days in New York: the Ziegfeld shows; Weber and Fields; Lillian Russell, now all gone.

His mind touched Chicago too, but recoiled.

Turning from the window, his eyes fell on the dresser by the antique canopied bed. A glass globe containing a wintery Alpine scene sat there; next to it the simple box camera that was always loaded with film. Pictures; they had become his life. He had wanted to be president; he had settled for making pictures with Marion. Disgust filled him. A movie mogul, damn it, and a failure at that! He made other pictures, too—the photographs with which he measured his days. Albums of them groaned on shelves in the study, in the Gothic suite, the library, the underground vaults of Casa Grande. Seventy years old. Hearst quavered and, snatching up the camera, held it at arm's length and aimed it at himself—*click!* he laughed hollowly: No magic there. It'll just show an old man's face.

But pictures, pictures . . .

His trembling hand touched his heart. Something crinkled, and he pulled from his vest pocket the eight-by-ten scrap of paper Willicombe had shown him. He unfolded it; there was a picture there too, the odd little flurry of lines. And words: BE THERE SOON. From whom? Again memory stirred far back, but it got lost among ghosts.

Hearst tossed the paper on the dresser next to the glass globe.

Here soon? So what? I have a gun; I can take care of myself.

❧ 18 ❧

MARION Davies tripped, staggered. She saved herself by clutching a concrete column. Sagging against it, she giggled, a gay, tinkling sound. She glanced down and saw her small foot entangled in a mat of grapevines.

"S-son of a bitch," she said, without anger. She managed to pull free, but succeeded in losing her shoe. This only made her grin. Let Popsy buy me another, she thought, dragging her hand through lush blond hair, and giggled again.

She carried a half empty bottle of Booth's Gin.

Casa Grande lay southwest, ivory-colored against the intense blue afternoon sky. She was alone at the farthest curve of the mile-long pergola that wound about Orchard Hill below the Neptune Pool. The roof of the pergola was made of carved wooden crossbeams espaliered with fruit trees. All the supporting columns, hundreds of them, stood thick with grapevines, but autumn had stolen their leaves. That made Marion sad. She sniffed and drank. A strange heaviness hung in the air. It ought to be crisp and fine! It ought to make me feel good! Autumn. Wasn't it autumn in Chicago when I first stepped onto a stage? Wasn't there even some snow, just a little, feathery, drifting? Didn't I taste it on my tongue? "Silly girl," she heard her mother's voice say. But her mother was dead and this was not Chicago. Frowning she looked to the west, where the narrow coast road was a line of black macadam below the hills. Dark clouds lay banked against the horizon.

Don't spoil my party. Marion pouted.

She took another swig of gin.

Half an hour later she wandered back on the main hill. Flopping down onto an ancient Renaissance wellhead, she wrinkled her nose. This place is full of old dead junk!

Am I part of the junk?

Shivering, she rubbed her hand over the weathered stone. The wellhead was from Verona, from W.R.'s past. *He was my age when he bought it, with his old girlfriend. What was her name? Tessie something. Powell? Powers? He kept her; now he's keeping me. He dropped her. . . . Could he ever drop me?*

He wouldn't dare!

But Marion felt a moment of terror. Her dachshund, Gandhi, trotted over, and she grabbed him and hugged him so hard the little dog whimpered. A breeze toyed with her hair as she gazed at the road far below. In just hours the limousines would come in a swell parade, and Popsy's cold old house would fill with fun. *Hurry, please hurry!* There was little traffic now, black dots moving. One car slowed, stopped, and a man got out. From this far away he appeared antlike, but Marion had the funny feeling he was staring straight at her.

He remained very still by the roadside far below. Marion did not like that; she hurried indoors.

❧ 19 ❧

TOM Goodall from Oklahoma peered up under the flat of a hand. He had caught a glimpse of white, and his weathered, slitted eyes stayed fixed on that funny big house up the hill. Tom scratched his nose. *Some gol-darn rich banker's place? Owned by one o' them crooks that stole a man's land?*

Tom's battered brown hat shielded his eyes. He had on a worn cotton shirt, patched overalls, the strong heavy boots which he had worn to walk behind his plow in the proud days when he could feed his wife and kids. Then the rains had stopped coming, the corn and cotton died, and red dust took over. Nothing but oat beards and foxtails and clover burrs. Tom remembered the big winds blowing up, the dust lifting into the Oklahoma sky, the angry red sun. After a while the bankers came out and frowned at his land and thumped the sides of their cars. They said he had to get off. A hundred and eighty acres. I fed 'em with it, but when I couldn't pay they grabbed it back. A bunch of farmers tried to hang the judge that gave the order, but they landed behind bars. Even the Reds showed up; they said they'd help, but it was all hot air; they couldn't save the land. Then the farm sale, and it all went—team and wagon, harnesses, carts, seeders, hoes. No more'n a hundred for the lot. Handbills everywhere said TOP DOLLAR FOR FRUIT PICKERS IN CALIFORNIA, so Tom had packed his family onto Route 66, but the Ford had broken down outside Albuquerque. Thirty-eight bucks for some crook to fix it, and the rest had gone for gas and food. I come, Tom thought with helpless fury. Where's my job?

He turned to look at his family inside the Ford. The kids licked dry lips, waiting. Ellen just sat there. Tom felt hollow inside. She don't believe in me anymore; she don't believe in nothin'. Did I do wrong? That fiver that guy in Los Angeles give me—maybe I shoulda spent it on food instead of on gas and oil to get where I might find me a job. Now the Ford wouldn't go. He had heard her throw a rod. She was dead as a doornail, and they were done for, and he was a failure, not even a man.

Ellen was sobbing, a dry sputter. Her shoulders moved, her body heaved, but no tears came. The kids started to cry too, and Tom could hardly stand it.

He glared at that rich bastard's castle up the hill. You owe us little guys! he thought. What're we supposed to do?

It was then that he remembered his gun.

71

III

Getting There
Is Half the Fun

※ 1 ※

THE taxi purred east on Santa Monica Boulevard. Behind it late afternoon light was lengthening over the low, flat, pale, stuccoed dreamland of Hollywood. The sky was porcelain blue, so fragile-looking it seemed ready to crack.

The taxi's radio was on, broadcasting William Randolph Hearst's high-pitched voice to America:

> We must beware of the Communist bear menacing us inside our borders. Rule by the proletariat is rule by the least capable and the least conscientious element of the nation; it is rule by the mob, government by ignorance and avarice, dictatorship by tyranny and terrorism. It is a failure in Russia. It is a growing danger here. I know, my friends, that you welcome the truth. I can only say I am proud that this free country of ours permits me to . . .

The taxi veered north, found Glendale Boulevard, headed for the Southern Pacific station. The San Fernando Mountains were a pink-gray haze. NBC chimes sounded, then Major Bowes came on. A little girl's voice began singing "On the Good Ship Lollipop," and the driver switched off the radio. He had a large, veined nose. "They all wanta be Shirley Temple," he drawled over his shoulder. "I'm not crazy about Hearst, but he sure knows what he's talkin' about when he raps them Reds."

"Shut up," Eddie McGuffin muttered from the back seat. "What d'you know about Reds?"

"Well, excuse me for livin'!"

"Now, you just hush, Eddie." Gloria Deere sat next to him. She squeezed his hand, but he only stiffened.

"If things were done the Communist way," he said, "the country wouldn't be in this mess. Hearst, ha! You think he'd spend a nickel to save your starving ma?"

The cabby hooted. "Lay off, buddy. Hearst is a bum, but he pays for breadlines all over the place. Who do the Reds feed? Gimme that old guy any day, and if you don't like it you can get out and walk."

Eddie lurched forward, but Gloria dragged him back. "Stop it, I said." He collapsed glumly, and she sighed in relief. Orange groves slid by to the right. "My brother doesn't mean it. Please drive on."

The cabby grunted, and Eddie glared out the window. Gloria's large hazel eyes fixed on the rock-hard line of his jaw. He seemed ready to pop. Oh, why'd I let him talk me into this? My brother, Eddie Deere—what if someone finds out I lied? My chances in Hollywood'll go up in smoke. But it's too late now, I'm in too deep; just got to make the best of it. Gloria bit her pretty lower lip while the taxi pressed on through the afternoon. Burma Shave signs flicked by; then a big white board announced GLENDALE.

All the time Eddie's hands knotted and unknotted in his lap. Pa— for you!

The pistol was ready, in his bag in the trunk.

❦ 2 ❦

THEY pulled up at the Glendale station just at 5:10. Over the station roof the sky was developing a pink polish above the dark clouds that had been massing all day. Eddie and Gloria stepped from the taxi into an electric bustle. Red-capped Negro porters rushed to and fro, brows sheened with sweat as they struggled with mounds of luggage, and there were famous faces everywhere, the Hollywood people and the newspaper people, standing in groups, gesturing and tapping cigarettes. A gay explosive murmur filled the air. Across the platform the Southern Pacific Lark was shiny, poised as if to fly, and Gloria forgot Eddie. The sleek train thrilled her, and she could not help gasping as a honey blond in champagne-colored satin clicked by on high heels, followed by a groaning porter pulling bags on a cart. The woman balanced a huge fox fur on slim elegant shoulders as casually as if it were air. 'Carole Lombard," Gloria breathed.

"So what," Eddie muttered.

"You didn't see *Twentieth Century*? She's a big star."

Eddie sulked. He wanted to be above it all, but he felt intimidated as he watched Lombard join a glamorous circle rippling with laughter: Gloria Swanson, Dick Powell, the dapper Adolphe Menjou. His stomach knotted.

Gloria pinched his arm. "Now you be good. Don't you dare spoil my weekend! And if you tell me one more time how Communists hate movies I'll just scream."

"I'll behave. I can stick to a deal. Let's get our bags."

The wiry little cabdriver helped them lift three suitcases and a cosmetic case and Eddie's single scuffed leather bag from the trunk. Gloria handed him money.

"A good thing you Reds've got dames to pay the bills." The cabbie slammed his door. "Say hello to Hearst." Cackling, he drove off.

"The bastard," Eddie said.

"That's okay, you'll pay me like you said. Oh, hello, Vinny."

A tall, slender man in a light linen suit had strolled up. He wore a gleaming white shirt, a blue checked scarf tucked in at the throat, and he was smoking a lavender-tinted cigarette. "Hiya, gorgeous." He pecked Gloria's cheek. "You look like a million." He gave Eddie a heavy-lidded look. "So, this's the famous brother."

"Er, Vinny Tashman, my brother Eddie. Vinny's a screenwriter, Eddie."

"Um." Eddie made himself shake Vinny's hand.

Vinny regarded them. "You don't look like brother and sister."

"Oh, we are." Flushing, Gloria locked her arm tightly in Eddie's. "Vinny, can you get us a porter?"

"I'll carry my own bag," Eddie said.

Vinny made a face. "Don't be silly. Whattaya think these people are for?" He snapped his fingers, and a redcap hurried over. The porter reached for Eddie's bag, but he snatched it away, scowling.

"I said I'd do it myself."

Vinny peered at him. "Suit yourself. Whattaya got in that thing,

77

anyway, booze?" A quick laugh. "That's smart. Old W.R. is tight with his booze."

"It's none of your business what I carry in my bag," Eddie snapped.

"Don't get hot under the collar." Vinny winked at Gloria. "Your brother been sleeping on doorknobs?"

"Eddie, please." Gloria piped a jittery little laugh. "It's just that he's not used to so many famous people around."

"I thought you said he worked at Metro."

Eddie stepped between them. "I do, and I can talk for myself. All these swells don't impress me one bit."

Vinny blew smoke in Eddie's face. "You got a chip on your shoulder? I don't get it. Gloria told me you were dying to come along. I guess you just didn't know what you were letting yourself in for. Well, you're gonna have a very unimpressive weekend, because that's who Hearst and Marion Davies invite—swells." He looked Eddie up and down. "Mostly swells, anyway." He took Gloria's arm. "I need to speak to you for a minute, babe. Alone."

She shrugged free. "Not now, Vinny."

Vinny frowned, but the frown quickly turned to a grin. "Harpo!"

A short, balding man halted nearby. He had a round face and a wide mobile mouth. In his brown plaid suit he looked more like a postal clerk than a star, and he was smoking a fat cigar. "Yeah?"

"It's me. Vinny Tashman." Vinny stuck out his hand.

"Vinny . . . ?"

"You remember. Vincent X. Tashman. I worked on some of that *Animal Crackers* dialogue."

Harpo's round eyes blinked. "You did?" He stared at Vinny's hand. "Uh, yeah, I guess you did." He shook the hand. "Gladda see you again." His gleaming eyes fixed on Gloria, and his mouth widened in the famous puckish grin. "Who's the pretty lady?" His eyebrows waggled madly.

"Gloria Deere. Gloria, Harpo Marx."

"Lovely!" Harpo lifted Gloria's hand to his lips, smacked it, and fluttered his lashes.

"Oh, Mr. Marx!"

Harpo looked inquiringly at Eddie.

Vinny sneered. "This mug's her brother. Eddie. Eddie was just telling us how swells don't impress him."

"Hell, they don't impress me either." Harpo pumped Eddie's hand. "You're heading up to Hearst's too? You play poker? We'll get a game going. I get along with guys that hate stuffed shirts. Well, so long— uh, Vinny, Eddie, Miss Deere." He strolled off trailing cigar smoke.

"He's so cute!" Gloria squealed. "I didn't recognize him without the wig and that old hat and coat."

"He didn't recognize the famous Vincent X. Tashman, either," Eddie said.

Vinny scowled. Eddie wanted to punch him, but just then he noticed a tiny, pale man in a gray pin-striped suit watching them. The dwarf wore a broad-brimmed fedora. Eddie watched Vinny's gaze find the dwarf, and Eddie did not miss the fear and hatred that flared in Vinny's eyes.

The little man came over. He had a rolling, hobbled walk, and Eddie noticed that he wore a thick-soled built-up shoe on his left foot.

"Hello, Vinny," the dwarf said, beaming. He had a long, horseface, a wide, lopsided mouth. His complexion was dead pale, as if sunlight never found its way under his hat brim. He sported a red carnation. "I said I'd wear a flower so you'd be sure to recognize me. Do you recognize me, Vinny?"

"You didn't need the flower," Vinny muttered.

The dwarf laughed. He looked at Eddie and Gloria. "Who're your friends?"

"This's Gloria Deere. And her brother, Eddie."

"Pleased to meet you." The man had a soft voice—too soft; it hid something sharp and hard. His hand clung unpleasantly to Eddie's as they shook, and slitted gray eyes squinted up. "Don't I know you, Eddie?"

"No."

"Sure we never met? Forget it." The dwarf kept grinning. He rocked on his heels. "My name's Otis Pike. Vinny and I knew one another a long time ago. In Chicago. We were kids, but we haven't forgotten, have we, Vinny?

"No."

A nod. "People don't forget, even if they want to; that's what I think. You sure we don't know one another, Eddie? I guess not. Vinny asked me up to Mr. Hearst's. Nice of him after all these years isn't it? I'd like to talk for a while, Vinny. Catch up. Excuse us?"

"Certainly," Gloria said.

"Let's . . ." Otis Pike gestured down the platform.

"You're the boss," Vinny said between his teeth.

Pike cackled. "The boss! The boss!"

"See you on the train, gorgeous." Vinny looked sour. "And buy your brother a stiff drink—he needs one."

"What a funny little man," Gloria said, watching them walk off. She bunched her fists. "Oh, Eddie, you're being just *terrible*!" But at that moment a platinum blonde with bee-stung lips wriggled from a taxi, and Gloria's anger dissolved. "Oh, look! Jean Harlow!"

🪬 3 🪬

"**B**EEN a long time, hasn't it, Vinny?" Otis Pike said when they were out of earshot.

"Not long enough."

"Don't complain. I'm not asking to be pals. We're doing one another a favor, that's all. It's business. Vincent X. Tashman—that's cute. You weren't Vincent X. Tashman when I knew you. You were little Vinny P. Tashman, the brat, the bully. You bullied me sometimes, Vinny. Remember?"

"That was a long time ago."

"Bullies always want to forget. But the guys that get picked on don't forget—and sometimes they get theirs back. What's the X supposed to stand for?"

"Xavier."

Pike snorted. "You have a helluva nerve. I guess that sort of thing goes over in Hollywood, the little lie. The big one too. You know anything about big lies, Vinny?"

"I know your name's not Otis Pike."

"It is now. Call me Otis, Vinny, or I'm afraid I'll have to give you a hard time. Remember, I know what happened in Chicago. You still play with guns?"

"Sometimes."

"Don't play with them this weekend. I'm not after you, understand?"

Vinny stopped. He looked at Otis Pike closely for the first time, into the thin, splinter eyes he had hoped never to see again. Their cold glint frightened him. "Who?" he asked.

"Bigger fish," Pike said from under his white fedora. "Much bigger than you." His grin spread even wider. "Introduce me to some movie stars, Vinny. I want to meet some stars."

❧ 4 ❧

THE Lark's engine hissed steam. A whistle screamed, and a very pink man in a very dark suit trotted about urging everyone onto the train. He bustled up to Eddie and Gloria. "You're with Mr. Hearst's party?" He squinted at a list. "Edward and Gloria Deere. Yes," he checked their names off. "Please board. The last three cars, they're specially reserved. Ask for anything you like—food, drink. This's your first time?" He waggled a finger. "Let me give you some advice: don't drink too much and you just might be invited back." He beamed at a man standing behind them. "Oh, Mr. Chaplin, how nice!"

Gloria turned to find Charlie Chaplin's brown eyes fixed on her. Chaplin sent her a gleaming smile, and her heart flip-flopped in her chest. She felt her cheeks go scarlet, but she had the presence of mind to flash him her sultriest Dolores del Rio stare before Eddie tugged her away.

"Who's the girl?" Chaplin asked thoughtfully as they headed off.

"Gloria Deere," the pink man said. "A bit player, I believe. No one important. The man's her brother. Mr. Chaplin, you really *must* board. The Southern Pacific will not wait, even for you."

Chaplin kept his smile as he headed for the train. Gloria Deere. Decidedly a possibility. Glad I didn't bring Paulette along after all.

❦ 5 ❧

LOUELLA Parsons had already found a vantage point, a strategically placed window seat, facing the platform, where she could watch everyone board. Her husband, Harry "Docky" Martin, sat next to her on the plush red velvet with which the Southern Pacific had upholstered Mr. Hearst's special cars. Docky read the latest issue of *Time*, J. P. Morgan glowering from the cover. Louella kept her eyes peeled. Jean Harlow, Clark Gable, Joel McCrea. I've come a long way from small town, America, she thought, savoring her success. She focused on Eddie and Gloria. Who was the brunette? An up-and-coming starlet? The young man with her, he was tall and lean. Not bad-looking. But that suit! As cheap as they came, and he didn't know how to wear it either. But there was something about him that held her. He looked tense, stormy, yet it was more than that: Louella thought she knew him. Her tongue flicked her lips. Where've I . . . . ? But she couldn't remember, and she decided it was her imagination. Still, there might be a story there. She touched her mouse-brown hair. Her instinct tingled. An unprintable story? She wriggled and giggled. That had never kept her from prying.

"Yes, dear?" Docky said at her little laugh.

"Oh, read your old *Time.*" She tapped him affectionately. Dear man! When her first marriage failed she had been lucky to find Docky, unglamorous but dependable. Louella got back to work. Leslie Howard strolled into view. He looked elegant and harmless— but he was a notorious skirt chaser. Then there was brittle Dorothy Parker, laughing nastily at something. And that handsome new young limey, Cary Grant, who had made *I'm No Angel* with Mae West. Then there was a dwarf. Louella sat forward, frowning. The hobbling little man was walking with Vinny Tashman. Vinny. He was on the skids, but Marion had invited him anyway. Had he and Marion ever . . . ? Louella fidgeted with frustration: it was unfair that God had gifted her with instinct but had held out on mindreading! Her eyes narrowed at the dwarf. He wore a wide-brimmed white fedora that hid his face, as if he didn't want to be seen; his jaw was long and pale. He gave her the creeps. Who was he? Who had invited him? Vinny Tashman seemed on edge in his company.

Louella jotted rapid notes on her pad. She had her work cut out.

❧ 6 ❧

EDDIE and Gloria reached the next to last car. Climbing aboard they found themselves in a mad crush of people hugging and kissing and clinking cocktail glasses. Champagne bubbled at a small bar at one end, while a five-man combo played "Life Is Just a Bowl of Cherries" in a jazzy, gay rhythm.

Gloria clapped. "Oh, doesn't Mr. Hearst know how to do things!"

"You ain't seen nothin' yet," a tenor voice said, and she looked up into Dick Powell's twinkling eyes. Powell saluted with his glass and moved on.

"Oh, Eddie!"

"Anybody with plenty of dough could do this," Eddie muttered as they pushed through the crowd. "Farmers're starving."

Gloria groaned. "Mr. Hearst's money is giving these bartenders and porters and conductors and even those men in the band a job, Mr. Smartypants. Why'd you want to come anyway, if you can't have any fun?"

Suddenly Vinny Tashman was at their side. "Your brother giving you a bad time?" he asked smoothly. "Follow me. I'll find us places."

Cigarette smoke filled the club car, and the chatter rose to a near deafening level. From outside came the blast of a second whistle, then the train gave a lurch, and Gloria almost toppled. Taking her arm, Vinny led them through the connecting passage, Otis Pike trailing in his white fedora. Eddie felt the dwarf staring at him. "What's eating you?" he snapped, but the dwarf only smiled. Eddie clung tightly to his bag.

The next car had fewer people in it, but they were just as glamorous, chatting up a storm. The Lark began to move, the platform and the exhausted-looking porters sliding away to the left. Gloria wanted to hear everything. There was conversation about Babe Ruth's last season with the Yankees, Bonnie and Clyde being mowed down by tommy guns; movie talk as well: who had what part, who had seen who with whom at the Trocadero or the Cocoanut Grove. Vinny pointed out people: "Walter Winchell. Damon Runyon. Frances Marion and Herman Mankiewicz; they're screenwriters. That's Adela Rogers St. Johns, the reporter. Hedda Hopper has been in some of Marion's movies. Good God, even Walter Howey!" Vinny lowered his voice. "He's editor of the Chicago *Herald-Examiner*. They call him the Iceman. I worked for him when I was in Chicago. He has a glass eye; it's the friendly one. The man with the pushed-in face is Arthur Brisbane, Hearst's chief columnist and mouthpiece, a specialist in the pithy platitude. Ah, here are some seats."

He indicated two facing banquettes. Gloria hated to sit down; she wouldn't be able to see nearly as well. She glimpsed the dancer Irene Castle, Marie Dressler, Basil Rathbone, others she had seen on the

84

Metro lot. She gasped. Louella Parsons seemed to be looking right at her. Oh, put me in your column, Louella! Make me a household word!

Vinny drew her in beside him, and Eddie sat next to her on the outside, clutching his bag. Otis Pike scrambled onto the seat opposite Eddie. Pike's short dangling legs and odd, long, smoothly shaven face made him look like a sinister doll. A birdlike balding man in a neat dark suit already occupied the window seat on Pike's side. He peered at them through round, thick glasses. "Hello." He stuck out a hand. "Willis Snipe. Set designer. Warners. Are you in the movies?"

"I write for them," Vinny said.

"I'm an actress," Gloria informed him, touching her brunette curls.

"Really? What studio?"

Gloria primped. "I just can't decide."

Snipe grinned proudly. "I may do the sets for Marion Davies' first for Warners. It's with Dick Powell and Claude Raines—a Napoleonic thing, but a comedy. Isn't that a laugh? The movies are crazy, but I don't care; I just do my job. The great thing is, I've been invited to see Mr. Hearst's house at San Simeon. I'm thrilled about that! I studied architecture before I came to movies. Do you know Mr. Hearst's architect, Julia Morgan? She's one of the best. I've heard so much about Casa Grande. It's a real castle. Mr. Hearst *is* a little medieval, don't you think?" He turned red. "Oh, I don't mean in any bad sense, but—well, you know. That strange house of his, that big strange house . . ." Willis Snipe suddenly mopped his face and withdrew like a turtle, and for a moment they all stared at citrus groves speeding by in the dying light.

The train hooted, curving northwest. "Anybody for a drink?" Vinny asked.

"A champagne cocktail," Gloria said.

"Nothing," Eddie murmured.

"Bourbon whiskey for me," Pike said. Watching Vinny snap his fingers at the white-coated waiter, he sneered. Mr. Fancy Dan has come a long way from that Chicago orphanage—look at that dopey mustache! Pike wanted to laugh. Then, glancing down the aisle, he glimpsed a lumpy woman with a round, pasty face. Louella Parsons. She was watching them, and Pike's eyes narrowed. What's on the old bat's mind? Pike beamed at her deliberately, and she reddened and ducked her head. Parsons is supposed to have all of Hollywood's deep dark secrets crammed under her bonnet, he thought, and she's worked for Hearst for years. Maybe she knows what I'm after, the real scam about that miracle dame, Rose Ellen Forrest, who died and came back to life.

Pike's gaze slid to Eddie Deere. Why do I know this mug? He's as jumpy as a flea on a griddle. Something to hide? Pike's game leg began to ache. There's more than meets the eye, he thought.

Their drinks arrived, clinking on a tray. The waiter passed them around. Outside the windows the sky shaded into the dark bruised purple of dusk while the club car door kept sliding open and closed, admitting bursts of music as people came and went. Wearing a spidery smile, Gloria Swanson stood not ten feet away, tapping a tall man's chest with the end of a long ebony cigarette holder. The man had a cleft chin and spoke with an English accent.

"Gee, who's that?" Gloria whispered.

"His name's Archie Leach," Vinny said. "He goes by Cary Grant."

"Handsome!" Gloria giggled as she sampled her champagne. "I've never met Mr. Hearst," she said eagerly. "What's he like?"

"Nobody knows," Otis Pike said. He shrugged. "Isn't that what people say?"

"People say a lot of things," Vinny replied. "You know the Ince story?"

"I've heard it," Pike said, softly.

"Oh, tell!" Gloria squealed.

Vinny crossed his legs and lit one of his lavender cigarettes. "It happened a while back. Hearst had a party on his big yacht, the *Oneida*. Marion Davies was there, of course, and Charlie Chaplin, Louella Parsons, several others. Not a party as big as this one. Something went wrong. Afterward the papers said the producer Thomas Ince took sick on the sail—some sort of stomach trouble—and died pretty soon after. Word leaked out that liquor was on board, but this was Prohibition; if word had spread it would've cost

Hearst a load of bad publicity—something he hates, especially where Marion is concerned. But there was worse: witnesses said that when Ince was taken off the yacht there was a bullet hole smack in the middle of his forehead. Yet no charges were ever filed."

"Goodness!" Gloria exclaimed.

Vinny puffed a smoke ring. "See what I mean? What's true about Hearst and what isn't? People just naturally gossip about him. Rumors still hang on that the whole thing was a blowup over Marion. Ince was good-looking; he was a tomcat too, and his dear little wife wasn't along on the trip. Other people say the fight was with Chaplin; Hearst meant to put a hole in him and shot Ince by mistake. Oh, there're lots more stories. About women, for example." Vinny laughed. "If old Hearst had fathered all the illegitimate bastards he's supposed to, we'd have to annex Mexico as a playroom."

"There's the Fallon trial too," Pike said. "Hearst almost got accused of fathering twins by 'an unnamed film actress.'"

"So you're a student of Hearst," Vinny said.

Pike folded his stubby arms. "Not really. A lot of it was in the papers a dozen years back. Everybody must've read it."

"Still, you have a remarkable memory," Willis Snipe breathed.

Pike smiled thinly. "I don't forget much."

The Lark hooted again. All of a sudden the hairs prickled at the back of Pike's neck. He swiveled in his seat.

Louella Parsons stood right at his elbow.

She wore a loud print dress, and her flat nasal voice made Pike cringe. "Hello, Vinny. No, don't get up. You were all talking about Mr. Hearst behind his back; I heard you." She clucked her tongue. "That's not nice. Such a *won*-derful man! He saved my life once, you know."

"I've heard." Vinny introduced everyone.

"You'll find Mr. Hearst so helpful to work for; he can give such good advice!" Louella said to Willis Snipe. She turned to Gloria. "I knew I'd seen you before. You were with Marion and Gary Cooper in *Operation Thirteen*, weren't you? Marion was never lovelier in that one. And Mr. Deere, are you in pictures too?"

"On the stage crew. At Metro," Eddie muttered.

"Everyone is important in our industry, even those behind the scenes," Louella pronounced. Eddie's face still nagged at her memory, but maybe she had only known someone who looked like him. "And Mr. Pike, what do you do?"

"I'm in life insurance."

"How interesting. I couldn't help seeing you and Vinny board together. Are you old friends?"

"You might say so. We were kids together. In Chicago."

"I worked in Chicago once. I didn't like it. Do you still live there?"

Pike smiled up at her. "I live all over. We insurance men have to travel."

"I see. Well"—Louella fussed with the froth of lace at her throat—"I must visit lots of other people, but we'll chat again, won't we? After all, we have the whole weekend. Ta-ta." The loud print dress sailed away.

The train rocked and clicked. Outside, black inland hills seemed to shift and rear in the growing darkness. Their second round of drinks arrived, and Gloria buried her nose in the fizzing bubbles. The connecting door now stood open. Near it, Jean Harlow and Charlie Chaplin danced a fandango in the aisle, dipping, swaying, Chaplin clenching a rose fiercely, comically in his teeth, while Harpo and ash blond Bette Davis and Clark Gable, grinning, clapped their hands to the rhythm. Gloria felt Chaplin's warm gaze brush her, and, emboldened by the champagne, she fluttered her fingers at him. He fluttered back and did a mock swoon. She giggled, and the train seemed to swim in a golden champagne fizz.

Everyone watched the dance except Vinny, who sank into a funk and pretended to drink. He felt like getting thoroughly snookered, but he didn't dare. He wanted to get everything out of this weekend, Gloria included, but it was a helluva start. He hated having to drag along her touchy brother, and he didn't like the way Charlie Chaplin was making eyes at his dish.

Then there was so-called Otis Pike.

Vinny's gaze went to the dwarf's long pale face beneath his fedora. The little bastard. How'd he find out about that guy I shot in Chicago? Vinny began to sweat. For Christ's sake, it was an accident! And what the hell made him pop up like this after all these years?

Vinny cursed, but he could only cross his fingers and hope the little rat had been telling the truth when he said he was after bigger fish. Hearst? Just don't queer my deal! Vinny pictured the target pistols in his luggage. I'll use them if I have to, he thought, but this time I'll watch the booze. I'm not gonna shoot anybody unless it's on purpose.

The man Vinny had identified as the screenwriter Herman Mankiewicz suddenly poked his head up from the seat behind Gloria, his destroyed-looking eyes glimmering alcoholically. "I heard you askin' about ol' W.R.," he slurred. "Well . . . Hearst come, Hearst served—thass the ol' bastard for ya." Saluting with his glass, Mankiewicz dropped from view like a slowly sinking ship.

❧ 7 ❧

THE Lark pulled into the San Luis Obispo station shortly before nine. A fleet of boxy black limousines waited under a row of yellow lamps. While porters and drivers transferred luggage, Mr. William Randolph Hearst's guests stretched their legs on the long platform. The heat of Indian summer licked the air. Cicadas chirped. Insects ticked against the lights.

The night seemed to take a breath.

Then the dark sky flickered. "Lightning . . ." But the gay laughter, fed by booze and high spirits, kept its slightly hysterical edge. There was a jockeying for cars: who would go up with whom?

Gloria felt tipsy. She wanted to ride with Charlie Chaplin, to find herself pressed against him in the dark, but Vinny led her apart to a big black Daimler. Eddie trudged after them, Pike close on his heels. "And where are you from, Mr. Deere?" the dwarf asked.

"Same place as my sister."

"And where is that?"

"Ask her." Eddie halted. "Mind your business, see? You want me to

89

get nosy too? Just how come your so-called friend, Tashman, hates you?"

Pike blinked up into angry blue eyes. Something made him think of Chicago, but alarm chased the idea away. "Vinny doesn't hate me," he said, forcing a smile.

"Ha!" Eddie stalked off.

Pike rubbed his long jaw and his game leg throbbed even more. Eddie Deere was trouble. Lightning sputtered again, a far-off flicker. Vinny, Gloria and Eddie had already lined up in back of the Daimler, but there was a jump seat, and the dwarf perched on that, facing them.

Abruptly the front door snapped open and Herman Mankiewicz clambered in. "'Lo there." He waggled a silver hip flash. "Jus' ask. Plenny for ev'ryone." Taking a long swig, he flopped around, facing front.

"Occupational disease," Vinny murmured, "of screenwriters."

"But you don't have it?" Pike gave him a glittering look.

Vinny met the look. "I watch my step. We *all* oughta watch our step."

There were seventeen limousines. The first two pulled away; theirs followed smoothly. Otis Pike peered out at San Luis Obispo. A nowhere burg. The nearly deserted main street consisted of a drugstore, a grocery, a five-and-dime, a barber, Betty's Beauty Shoppe; a lanky man in a cowboy hat sauntered along kicking a can. But Pike was interested. Somewhere in town was a rest home, where Rose Ellen Forrest's old dad was waiting for death. Taking his secrets with him too, damn him! Pike scowled under his hat brim. Old Forrest . . . distributor for Hearst's papers . . . influenza . . . daughter dead at twenty-two . . . another woman with her name. Why? Pike's fingers curled. I'll find out! He had brought along a very special camera. He also had in his bag all the photographs he had snapped at Rose McGuffin's house, as well as the information Rawlston had sent, including birth certificates: Rose Ellen Forrest's, Harry McGuffin's, their kid's. There was something there, some clue, a spark that would blow Hearst up like a bomb, he only needed the match to light the fuse. The Daimler purred out of town. He tried to relax. I'm safe—except for Vinny, who knows who I really am. Cut it out, he told himself. You've got plenty on that phony; he won't dare open his yap. Pike turned and gazed past the black-capped driver. The coastal range lifted around the gently swaying car, swallowed it. Night. All at once a gas station loomed around a bend, a sudden blaze of light, and bright flashes went off in Otis Pike's brain.

Terrified, he began to sweat.

Gloria dreamed of Charlie Chaplin's cute, sweet smile.

Aware of her leg against his, Vinny smoked. Hearst, buy my screenplay!

Eddie McGuffin clutched his bag. He felt strangled inside the ill-fitting Sears Roebuck suit he had bought for his big moment. He felt suspended on a high, rickety bridge above an awful chasm, frigid winds blowing, and each shaky step, each mile the Daimler ate up, led only to death.

My own?

Grim, trembling, he toyed with the idea of martyrdom.

The air smelled of the end of summer: dust, insects, dry grass. The road continued to lift through the Santa Lucias, seventeen sets of headlights veering right, left, probing the inky curves. The cream of Hollywood and the American press, heading to see Mr. Hearst. At last, past the San Andreas Fault, the Pacific slid into view over a rise, a sheet of crinkled foil under a brass-colored moon. Descending, the caravan found the coast highway and began to wriggle north through black deserted acres.

"We're on Hearst land now," Vinny announced.

Gloria eagerly peered out. "Oh! Where's his mansion?"

"Relax, babe; it's a long way. The big boss owns fifty miles of coast. But you're in his private little country all right, and he's king of the castle."

"Hearst isn't king of anything!" Eddie snapped. "He's a leech on society!"

"Christ," Vinny muttered, and even Herman Mankiewicz mumbled in his drunken stupor.

"Oh, Eddie," Gloria moaned.

Eddie glared. "Well, he is! A capitalist exploiter of the masses!"

"You sound like a Red, Mr. Deere," Otis Pike's soft voice fluttered.

A headlight hit Eddie's face, white and strained. "So what if I am?"

Pike stirred. "Mr. Hearst hates Communists. Shouldn't you watch what you say?"

"Yeah, kid." Vinny chuckled, blowing smoke. "Or else the king of the castle might decide to chop off your head."

Eddie swallowed hard and slumped back. Pike tried to find his face in the dark, but it was gone now, mingled with the shadows. Pike was suddenly tense. That book on Eddie McGuffin's dresser: *Das Kapital*. No, he told himself, breathing hard, it's got to be coincidence. Chicago is two thousand miles away, and this is Eddie Deere, not Eddie McGuffin.

Still . . .

Silvery waves lifted and crashed in the moonlight to their left. "Maybe we'll make a movie at Hearst's," Vinny murmured in the dark.

"Honest?" Gloria said.

"One of his home movie specials," Vinny went on. "He writes the scripts and hands out the parts, and directs 'em too. He's been doing it for years, since before his big house was built, when the place was just Camp Hill and people went up by mule. I don't know who ever looks at them after they're done. He probably keeps them, tucked away in his nooks and crannies. I bet he's got more nooks and crannies than anybody else in the world."

Pike smiled in the dark. Nooks, crannies, pictures, evidence. Hearst was supposed to have hundreds of old photo albums. Stored where?

"We ought to see the castle soon," Vinny said. There was a glimmer of lights up the dark slopes to their right, but something else drew their attention. Headlights picked it out: loaded with furniture and suitcases, a battered Ford truck tilted like the abandoned carcass of some huge animal at the side of the road. White faces briefly flickered as they sped past: a thin woman, some kids. "Okies," Gloria murmured, touching her lips. The scarecrow shape of a man showed too, frantically waving, but not one car stopped.

"Hey!" Eddie grabbed the driver's shoulder. "They need help!"

The driver barely turned his squarish head. "Can't stop, sir. Mr. Hearst's orders."

"Told you we were on the king's land," Vinny said, "and on the king's land the king makes the rules."

Eddie sank back. The curve of a small bay appeared to the left. "San Simeon Bay," the driver announced. Opposite, to the east, the Santa Lucias climbed in ever steeper rises, and there, at the top, lit by floodlights, showed the pearlescent twin towers of a huge house dwarfed by distance. "Mr. Hearst's place," the driver said. "Only five more miles to go."

The caravan turned right onto a narrow two-lane road. Beams picked out bold, black letters: PRIVATE PROPERTY, NO TRESPASSING. Noting fingers of fog creeping among the hills, Pike shivered. Vinny stubbed out his cigarette in the ashtray. In her excitement Gloria gripped his arm.

Hearst! Eddie thought in fear and fury, and he could almost feel the cold steel of the pistol through his bag.

The limousines went a quarter of a mile, then halted one by one at a gate set in a tall wire-mesh fence. Spilling light, a small wooden building sat beside the gate, two men checking each car as it entered. One carried a clipboard, the other wore a pistol. "Hiya, Billy," the clipboard man said to their driver. With a smile he peered into the back. "Evening, folks. Names, please?" They gave them, and he checked them off. "The gentleman sleeping in the front?"

"Herman Mankiewicz," Vinny informed him.

Mankiewicz jerked awake. "Uh, yes, dear?"

The gate man patted the side of the car. "Have a pleasant stay," he said, and waved them on. ANIMALS HAVE THE RIGHT OF WAY, announced a sign just inside the gate. BEWARE OF BUFFALO!

"I was in Buffalo once," Mankiewicz slurred, tilting his head back for a long drink.

They were on a grassy coastal plain, huge packing crates looming on the dark fields about them. "What's in those?" Gloria asked.

"Part of W.R.'s collection," Vinny said. "Things he hasn't uncrated yet. They say there's a whole Spanish convent in some of those boxes, every stone numbered."

"Boxes . . . stones . . ." Mankiewicz softly muttered.

The road rose sharply; the line of cars began to climb through California maple, live oak. A pungent bay-laurel smell filled the air.

They entered a draw. The two limousines ahead of them dipped and vanished around a curve; momentarily they seemed alone.

Abruptly, four strangely spotted sticks sprouted in the middle of the road, and the car banged to a halt.

"Oopsy-daisy!" Mankiewicz yelped.

"Omigosh!" Gloria could hardly believe her eyes: the sticks were the legs of a giraffe.

The beast stood chewing at a treetop, its jaws lazily moving, huge eyes staring. Cackling in delight, Mankiewicz leaned out the window and waggled his flask. "Here, giraffe, wanna drinkee?"

"Honk," Vinny said.

"Can't," the driver drawled. "Mr. Hearst's orders. He doesn't like his pets to get nervous."

Mist hid among the trees, wreathing the giraffe's long neck. After a moment the animal ambled agreeably into the dark. "Wasn't he just the *cutest* thing?" Gloria squealed. Then she screamed: not three feet away an ostrich was glaring at her. Its beak jabbed viciously through the car window and she drew back, banging her head. "Ooh . . ." The beak had brushed her hair; she clung to Vinny, whimpering.

The ostrich bounded off.

Vinny stroked Gloria's shoulder. "Let's get out of here."

The driver put the car in gear. "Better put up your windows," he advised, "and make sure you don't wander off the hill alone, day or night. Mr. Hearst is good to his animals, but some of 'em can be mean."

"Not as mean as people," said Otis Pike. The caravan climbed on. Headlights picked out zebras among scrub; the squarish, lowered head of a water buffalo with fiercely glaring eyes. Other forms, unidentifiable, flitted and stirred in the gloom, while fingers of fog began to crawl across the road.

The throbbing in Gloria's head subsided. She did not like the fog; she also did not like the black pools of shadow where the roadbank fell away on either side of them as if huge hands had scooped out the night. She shivered. But the great house was like a beacon, flashing into view around curves, growing larger as they rose to meet it, a glimmering jewel. "Gee . . ." Her heart fluttered in her breast. "Gee . . ."

❧ 8 ❧

IN the limousine behind them Carole Lombard sat wrapped in
her fox fur by a window. In front Harpo lounged, smoking his
cigar, while next to him Joel McCrea hummed a western tune.
Louella Parsons had the other window seat in back. She snuggled
tight against Docky, who sucked placidly on his pipe. Louella had
been to San Simeon many times, but the prospect of a Hearst
weekend always thrilled her. The line of cars curved this way and
that, up, up.

There was a bump.

Louella stirred. "Did you feel that?"

Docky took his pipe out of his mouth. "What, dear?"

She squeezed his arm. "Oh, you big lug, you never notice
anything."

"It was just a little jolt," Joel McCrea said in his easy way.

Louella made a face at the back of his head. She peered out. They
were on a rise, San Simeon Bay glinting far below. In the distance
clouds were beginning to blot out the stars. Louella frowned,
glimpsing something: a dark shadow, a gash or cut in the road where
their car had lurched. It was at a hairpin curve, visible only for an
instant, and if she hadn't looked back just then she would have
missed it. She recalled the earthquake that morning. Had it damaged
the road?

She leaned forward to tell their driver it ought to be looked into
but never said the words, because just then the sky exploded with
light.

95

9

"OH!" Gloria clapped her hands. Pink, yellow, and blue rockets were bursting overhead, a spectacular blur of color. There were whines, whistles, pops. Streamers crisscrossed; rockets skeeted, rainbowed, showered. The fireworks splashed the sky, drowning night, causing the hills to flicker wierdly, to rear and shift. Casa Grande flickered with them, as if it were not real but projected like a movie on the mountaintop and might wink out at any moment. A flock of deer scattered across a knoll. Was that an elephant trumpeting?

"Hearst says hello in a big way, doesn't he," Vinny said, pulling out a cigarette, "for a guy who doesn't want his pets to get nervous."

Otis Pike screamed.

Everyone stared at him.

The dwarf's little legs were kicking, and his hands clawed in an attempt to cover his eyes and ears at once. "Stop it, stop it!" he gibbered.

They were helpless as he writhed, and his cries panicked Eddie, who wanted to shout too, to leap from the car, be swallowed by the night. Vinny burnt his fingers on his match. Gloria's wide eyes glistened. The fireworks ceased; the steep slopes sank into darkness, but Pike continued to moan.

"Your fren' drinks too much," Mankiewicz said.

Gloria clucked her tongue. "Poor little guy." Something about Pike repelled her, but she reached out and patted his hand. "Are you all right?"

"Y-yes . . . sorry." His fingers pulled away from her touch. "I just . . . just don't like bright lights." He choked a laugh. "Even a flashbulb scares me."

Vinny watched him. "Yeah . . . ?"

96

Pike mopped his face under the wide-brimmed fedora as the line of limousines continued up. Then the road leveled, and shortly they were passing through a tall gate. Their headlights stabbed down a long straight stretch, where the tangle of brush gave way to handsome plantings of fruit trees and oleanders. Bougainvillea was espaliered on a low stone fence.

And at last the big floodlit Spanish colonial mansion burst into sight around the last curve, looming: Casa Grande, with its three monstrous guesthouses and the Neptune Pool sleeping at its feet.

"Golly!" Gloria breathed.

Mankiewicz raised his flask. "'In Xanadu did Kubla Kahn a stately pleasure dome decree . . . !'" Twisting around, he winked. "I been here b'fore. You ain't seen nothin' yet."

❧ 10 ❧

WILLIAM Randolph Hearst watched his guests draw near. He stood under the stars on the Celestial Bridge linking the twin Celestial Suites high up on Casa Grande. Rearing stone lions punctuated the stone balustrade, and the massive twin bell towers loomed above him right and left. The fireworks had pleased the kid in him, and he smiled. Damn fine! But his smile sank to a scowl at the inky blot at the rim of the sea: clouds. He had wanted to organize one of his famous picnics in the hills; now maybe he couldn't. He peered at the approaching cars, a winking ribbon of headlights.

A pale form appeared at the south doorway, white cloth fluttering. "P-Popsy, you'll c-catch your d-death. You g-get in here right now!" Marion hurried out. "Brr. Aren't you ch-chilly?"

"No. And don't talk about death." He clutched her close.

She snuggled. "I just don't w-want Popsy to c-catch c-cold."

"Did you enjoy the fireworks?"

She bit a thumb. "L-loved 'em!"

Hearst sniffed discretely. No reek of booze, thank God. He hugged her tight. Sweet Marion! Sometimes he thought she drank to get away from him. But she needs me, I know! I'm a fool, he thought, his lined jowly face buried in her silken hair, reflecting on the thirty-six years separating their ages, but I love her. She's sure to be happy now that company's here, gossip, games, gags. Will she get into mischief this time? The old question wearied him. Younger men were coming, handsome men. And Marion liked young handsome men.

Hearst sighed. Nothing's ever perfect, he thought, and for some reason he recalled the note Willicombe had brought: BE THERE SOON. The notes had been arriving for months, Joe had said. A joke? A real threat?

The publisher's pouchy blue eyes turned cold, narrowing as the first limousines rolled up below.

❧ 11 ❧

"OH, it's just like a great big movie set!" Gloria exclaimed, stepping out onto a wide, red-tiled terrace. The whole hill was terraced, rising through levels and gardens to the looming central house. Paths wound away into shadow north, south, uphill, down. Light twinkled from glass globes on the heads of stone statues, and nearby an ancient Roman sarcophagus nestled in a flowery niche. To the left a four-thousand-year-old Egyptian god gazed blank-eyed from a stairway.

"Hearst's edifice complex," Herman Mankiewicz yammered from the front seat, but Gloria hardly heard. She wanted to take in everything: the big house, the gardens, the rich and famous emerging like fireflies from their black cocoons into the fragrant night air. Her eager gaze climbed Casa Grande's floodlit white facade to the high stone bridge spanning the bell towers. Two figures stood up there, tiny in the distance, one bulky, one slender, dressed in white. Hearst and Marion, golly! Gloria saw Eddie's hot blue eyes watching them, Vinny's too, creepy Otis Pike peering up from under his hat. Gloria shivered, though she did not know why. Silly men! Not one of them looked like he planned to have a good time.

All the limousines had drawn up by now, and people were being led away by butlers and maids to their assigned rooms. Herman Mankiewicz spilled out of the car. "Jehovah couldn't afford th' taxes," he muttered, staggering. A butler took him firmly in tow. Shortly a red-haired maid rushed up, plain and flat-nosed, her face blotched with freckles. Breathlessly nervous, she blinked at them. "Mr. and Miss Deere? Mr. Tashman? Mr. Pike?"

"How'd you know our names?" Pike asked.

"They telephone from the gate who's in which car. They keep track of just *everything* up here. My name's Mary. I'm to show you to your rooms." A flustered half curtsy. "Follow me, please. The men will bring your bags."

She led them downhill, north. Their driver watched them go. Billy Buller was his name, a stocky man with thick dark hair. Lounging against the Daimler, he snorted. Funny ducks—but the brunette was a dish. Buller's face was handsome in a heavy, squarish way: straight black brows over black eyes, an arrogant slash of mouth. Billy massaged his big hands. Time for a drink. With Etta. Course, it'd have to be on the sly—Hearst didn't like fraternization—but the old man's watchdogs hadn't caught them yet. What rubes those guards were! If they ever had to really keep an eye on things they'd fall on their faces. Billy expected more than a drink; he'd get it too, but first he'd tell Etta about that boozing Mankiewicz and the screaming dwarf. Gossip always made her hot.

Billy chuckled as he lit a Lucky Strike. Old man Hearst sure invited some lulus.

A tall butler had taken charge of Louella and Docky, but Louella paused to watch Gloria, Eddie, Vinny and Otis Pike troop by. Her eyes narrowed. I still want to know all about these people. "Jean!" she cried as Jean Harlow wriggled over in peach-colored satin.

99

"Hiya, honey!"

They avidly kissed cheeks. "How ever did I miss you on the train?" Louella had already forgotten the bump in the road.

In the floodlit gardens splashes of vivid green stood out amid blue-black shadows. Following the maid, Gloria floated on air. The impressive aquamarine expanse of the Neptune Pool glimmered below, and she gasped. Past stone balustrades fog continued to thicken and creep, a sinister rising tide, but she ignored it; she forgot that awful ostrich. Up here was safe, a dream, Hollywood heaven! She glimpsed funny Marie Dressler trundling across the terrace. Clark Gable without his wife—hadn't Louella's last column hinted they were on the skids?—Carole Lombard in her fox fur with Dick Powell cracking jokes. Charlie Chaplin—where was cute Charlie? Then she saw him, a butler leading him toward the main house. He did not look back, and Gloria bit her lip. She longed for one more sweet smile—but there was plenty of time for that.

A tiny mouse zipped across her path, but she only giggled.

The mouse had one white paw.

Otis Pike was several paces ahead of Gloria, his eye on the skinny maid; he wanted to talk to her. He glanced back; the others trailed far enough behind that they wouldn't hear. His leg still ached, but hobbling, almost tripping, he caught up.

"Your name's Mary?" he asked. "Mary what?"

The girl started at his words. "O'Grady," she squeaked in her reedy voice.

"A pretty name."

"Really?"

Pike beamed at her. She reddened and looked away, and hope glimmered in the little man. Can she be had? Dressed in a black uniform, she was flat-chested, hardly a looker. But, then, neither am I, Pike thought. We're a pair, he told himself, leering, and I need an ally up here. One with a set of keys.

"What's it like working for William Randolph Hearst?" he asked in a bright, friendly voice.

Trailing, Eddie watched them, hardly seeing. He felt more out of place than ever, trapped. That big house, the gardens like a maze, all the Hollywood swells who probably thought he was dirt. And

Hearst, the capitalist monster up there in his castle, looking down and sneering. Eddie still clutched his bag. He sweated in his ill-fitting suit.

Just ahead Vinny strolled next to Gloria in apparent nonchalance. But Vinny was not relaxed. Hundreds of thousands of bucks, he thought bitterly, taking in white marble statues and hand-painted tiles and a real ancient Roman temple that must have cost an arm and a leg to get up the hill from Italy. Hearst probably didn't even feel it. And I'm hocking cigarette lighters to buy lunch. I want a spread like this, damn it! I deserve one!

Vinny thought of booze. He wiped a hand across his mouth. Whoa. One step at a time. I've gotta sell Anne Boleyn.

Descending a curving path, they stopped in the U-shaped courtyard of a handsome white stucco building with a red tile roof and ornate brass grillwork. Gloria was surprised at how completely the gaiety of the main terrace had been left behind; they were alone in deep shadow, palm fronds rustling overhead. "Casa del Monte," the maid told them in her thin little tremolo. "I'll show you your rooms." There were two entrances. She led Eddie and Gloria through the left door while Vinny and Pike waited outside.

The dwarf's eyes glittered. "The Deere dame's cute," he said. "That brother of hers, what d'you know about him."

"He's got a chip on his shoulder."

A lewd smile. "You have plans for the sister?"

"Tell me your plans first."

"No dice. I hold the high cards. Just keep that in mind, Vincent X. Tashman."

Vinny's right hand bunched. He wanted to slug Pike, just like when they were kids, but he ground the fist into his palm. Pike's pale jaw gleamed like ivory in the gloom. He said nothing more, and Vinny was glad when the maid came back. She took them in the right-hand door, an elaborate chandelier blazing up to reveal a spacious foyer smothered in oriental carpets, old oak, gleaming brass. Pike made a mental note: Casa del Monte was H-shaped; the Deeres were in the west leg, he and Vinny in the east. The foyer opened to the right onto a large sitting room with fireplace and overstuffed sofas; the bedrooms, each with a private bath, were at

·either end of this. Vinny had the one nearest Casa Grande. The maid took him to it. His door clicked shut, and she came back shyly to Pike. He smiled at her. The light in the sitting room was soft and orange. "I meant it when I said Mary O'Grady is a pretty name," he said.

"I hate my name!" She flushed under her freckles. "You really like it? I'll show you your room."

The dwarf's room was dominated by a huge canopied bed. Tall windows showed dark hills, a glimpse of sea.

Mary stood by the door fussing with her hands, not meeting his eyes. "Your bags will be here soon. Breakfast is any time after seven; just come up to Casa Grande. Mr. Hearst likes most things informal."

"So do I. You live on the hill, Mary?"

"Yes, sir."

"Where?"

"In the south wing of the main house. The servants' wing."

"You sleep there?"

"I have a room there, yes sir. A little room."

Pike moved near. "You sleep alone?" he asked huskily.

The maid swallowed hard. "Oh, sir . . . of course I do," she answered, backing away. "Er, I have to go now; I have work to do."

"No. Not yet." He grasped her hand, and she stared down at his hand holding hers but did not pull away. Pike watched goose bumps spread up her bony white arm, and triumph filled him. I may be a dwarf with a bum foot, but I can handle the dames. "You have pretty hands too, Mary," murmured the little man with the built-up shoe, "and pretty hair. I like red hair." He reached up and touched her stiff curls. She was trembling. He did not want to scare her; he let her go. Her large brown eyes met his, uncertain, desperate, and he gave her a sad, longing look. "I'd like to know you better, Mary. Come to me when your work's done. Will you do that, please? Just for a chat. I'm a lonely man, and it would make me very happy."

"I shouldn't, sir." She grabbed the door handle. "I simply can't." She looked near tears. "B-but I *do* understand about being lonely; oh, I *do*." Her staring brown eyes blazed. "It's so awful to be alone! Yes, sir, I will—I'll try, I mean. I'll try to come if I can."

❧ 12 ❧

HALF an hour later the hill lay silent in the night. The floodlights had been turned off, but the globes on the heads of the tall stone statues still shone on the terraces, the gentle steps, the maze of curving paths and gardens. The seven Hearst limousines were in their garages; the rest, rented, had purred off downhill.

A dark form crept along the terraces: Billy Buller. From his room above the garages he snuck from shadow to shadow, knowing just which paths to take to avoid Hearst's paid eyes, the security men who would stop the dopes too dumb to avoid getting caught and send them back to their rooms. Billy glanced up at Casa Grande. Third-story lights were on, Hearst working late. Seventy years old—how'd he do it? They said he spread his newspapers on the floor and turned the pages with his toes. Billy laughed at that. The fog had reached the hilltop, tendrils of mist sliding across the tiles. All at once Billy heard soft footsteps, and he ducked behind a marble statue of Adam and Eve just as a thin pale figure came into view at the top of some steps. Billy's black brows knit. He recognized her: Mary O'Grady, the skinny red-haired maid with a face that could stampede cattle. Moonlight hit her; she looked scared as a rabbit. What was up?

She darted toward Casa del Monte, and Billy's broad mouth twisted. So, she's gonna get hers, too? With the dwarf?

Billy laughed nastily. It happened all the time on the hill. To each his own.

Five minutes later he was rapping softly on the window of the telephone office in the wooden building by the main drive.

Etta Kitt jumped up from her switchboard to let him in. "Oh, you big goof!"

"Hi, babe." Grabbing her, Billy fastened his mouth on hers. Thirty seconds later he pulled away grinning. "Guess who I just saw sneaking around?"

Etta's face lit up. "Tell!" she cried, and Billy knew it was going to be a good night.

❧ 13 ❧

CHARLIE Chaplin's room was on the second floor of Casa Grande, at the back, the Doge's Suite. The wilderness of the Santa Lucias lay black outside his windows, miles of nothing, which he did not like to look at. Della Robbia Madonnas gleamed on the walls, but Chaplin ignored the priceless antiques. He sat in one of the big, soft chairs that filled the house, drumming his fingers. I want some jolly good fun! he thought. He was annoyed with Hearst for treating his guests like patrons in a hotel. Because they had arrived late, they had been shown straight to their rooms; greetings and socializing were supposed to wait for tomorrow.

Not bloody likely, Chaplin thought, jumping up. I'm going to make plans right now!

He picked up the phone.

❧ 14 ❧

ALONE in his room in Casa del Monte, slumped on a big
Spanish bed, Eddie McGuffin, a.k.a. Eddie Deere, stared
bleakly at old paintings and fringed carpet and carved wood
inlaid with ivory. It's a goddamn museum! Feeling adrift, he was
desperate for an anchor. His scuffed leather bag lay open beside him,
and he dove into it for the snub-nosed Colt. Frantically he checked
it: well oiled, bullets in the magazine, one in the chamber; but it too
felt alien. I've never even fired it, he thought and felt more helpless
than ever.

Can I kill a man?

Eddie's brown stock of hair hung over his brow. His knobby hands
started to shake, and he wanted to laugh, but hysteria strangled in
his throat.

Pa, dead, he thought.

Yet the pistol was comforting. Holding it against his cheek,
smelling its dry, dead odor, he lay down on the bed and switched off
the lamp, and the darkness of the alien place enfolded him. I got
here, didn't I? he thought, grasping for some glimmer of hope. I've
come this far. I can make a better world.

But he felt very cold, and, suddenly shaking, he drew his knees to
his chest and began to sob.

🙦 15 🙤

VINNY Tashman tiptoed into the west suite of Casa del Monte. He hesitated in the dimly lit sitting room. Which bedroom was Gloria's? Taking a chance, he knocked on the north door, and her voice came to him through the oak.

"Who is it?"

"Vinny."

A long silence. "I want to sleep, Vinny. Go 'way."

"But—"

"Honestly, Vinny. We'll talk tomorrow."

Vinny opened his mouth, closed it. *Bitch*, he thought, retreating. As he stepped out the west door into tendrils of fog, he thought he saw something, a hint of movement among bushes at the far end of the courtyard. Red hair? That skinny maid? He decided he was seeing things.

I better get something out of this weekend, he thought as he slammed back into his wing of the guesthouse.

🙦 16 🙤

IN a frilly pink nightie Gloria slipped under cool crisp sheets. She smiled at the ornate wooden bedposts that stood at attention around her. How grand! She had never slept in such a swell bed. Had it once belonged to a duke? But, snuggling down, she began to fuss. Darn, I don't want to spend my weekend fighting off

106

Vinny! she thought. What a sap I was to get involved with him; he's nobody. And Eddie—that mug. At least he isn't after me too. She chewed her lip. Is there something wrong with me—or is Eddie the kind of boy that doesn't like girls? She was mad at him, but she couldn't help feeling sorry for him too. He seemed all mixed up. What was eating him? Sniffing, she rolled over. Just let him be good and not embarrass me!

The bedside telephone rang, and eagerly she grabbed it. "Yes?"

"Cheerio, love!"

"Who's this?" But she knew, and her heart flip-flopped.

"An ardent admirer, love," came the bright British-accented voice.

"Oh, Mr. Chaplin!" she squealed.

❧ 17 ❧

IN the telephone office, Etta Kitt pulled Billy Buller near her earpiece. "Get a load of this."

Listening to the soft sly suggestions Charlie Chaplin was making to Gloria Deere, Billy leered. "Gives me ideas." His hands reached for Etta's small hard breasts.

❧ 18 ❧

OTIS Pike sat in his bedroom facing hills and sea.
Before him on an Italian marble desk were spread large
sheets of blue paper covered with spidery white lines:
architectural plans of Hearst's estate at San Simeon. The dwarf had
gotten them months ago from the county planning bureau, just in
case, but they were discouraging. There was more than he could
take in: the big main house, three guesthouses, a half dozen
outbuildings and greenhouses. Casa Grande alone contained over
one hundred rooms, including basements and vaults: thirty-seven
bedrooms, fourteen sitting rooms, forty-one bathrooms, plus the
Assembly Hall and the Refectory and the library and the movie
theater and the kitchens and numerous elevator shafts and circular
staircases boring up through it all. You could get lost in there, Pike
thought, tugging at his tufts of whitish hair. And he didn't know
what he was looking for, damn it.

Lightning flashed far out to sea. He jumped, and a clammy
coldness swept over him. Stay away, storm!

Hell, I've got good reason to be jumpy, he thought. Still, he felt
like a chump for yelling his head off in the limousine.

A knock came at his door.

Pike hid the drawings. He opened the door.

Mary O'Grady looked washed out and so scared that it seemed a
boo! would make her run. She knotted and unknotted her hands. "I
came, sir. But just for a while."

Pike smiled. "A while will be enough." Gently he led her to the
two chairs he had carefully arranged by the bed. She was nearly a
foot taller than he, but soon that wouldn't matter. "We'll just talk a
little, get acquainted," he said softly, holding her hand. "Now, tell me
all about life with Mr. Hearst."

❧ 19 ❧

ON the third floor of Casa Grande, William Randolph
Hearst stood by the mouse cage, furious. Its door was
open; Ambrose was gone. Who had been so careless?
Some maid?

She'll pay!

Willicombe had gone downstairs to send off the postmidnight
telegrams. The big house was silent. Hearst peeked into the Gothic
Suite's south bedroom. Moonlight touched Marion's blond curls,
spread on soft silk. Her chest rose and fell smoothly. Satisfied, the
old man lumbered to his room. His valet had laid out nightclothes as
usual, and he changed into a long striped nightshirt and slippers
while Helena watched him from a red tasseled cushion on a chair.
Patting the dachshund's head, Hearst went to the window. He liked
to look out before sleeping, to survey his domain: the tiled terraces,
the guesthouses, the cliffs and long slope to the sea. The fog was a
ghostly tide, rising, and Hearst turned away uneasily. His eyes fell
on the glass globe on his dresser. The note came to mind again,
nagging, and he checked the top dresser drawer: the pistol was in
place under some shirts.

He shut the drawer. Foolish! But better to be safe than sorry. I
wasn't so skittish when I was young. Do the old think they have
more to lose than the young? Sadness overwhelmed him. They don't
think, they *know*, he decided, sinking with labored breath into the
six-hundred-year-old canopied bed. I've done all I can, he thought.

❧ 20 ❧

FAR downhill, Tom Goodall fed his family the last of the bread and salt meat he had hoarded. The children chewed hard, staring; his wife sat stiff in the front seat as if she were dead. Damn those fancy black cars that wouldn't stop and help a man! Damn those fireworks too! The fog surrounded the Ford—no such thing as fog in Oklahoma—and Tom Goodall shivered. He was scared. And mad. Listening to the sea wash in and out, he thought he'd go crazy. They're havin' a party up there, and there's no town in sight, and we're starvin'. It ain't fair!

Abruptly Tom pulled his hunting pistol from its case in the back of the Ford. He jammed it in his belt.

I'll save my family one way or another! he thought.

❧ 21 ❧

MEANWHILE Ambrose the mouse scurried downhill toward his old burrow under the road.

His burrow was where Louella had felt that bump.

Eddie fell asleep hugging his gun.

Heaving and grunting, Otis Pike listened to Mary O'Grady's soft, sharp cries. She'll do what I want, he thought.

* * *

In her room nearby Gloria dreamed of Charlie Chaplin, while Vinny Tashman tossed and turned, longing to get drunk.

The fog swallowed Casa Grande's lofty twin towers. A lion coughed loudly in the zoo, and next to Docky, gently snoring, Louella dreamed that pale lopsided little men were creeping up on her with murder on their minds.

IV

Hide and Seek
On The Hill

🙚 1 🙙

S UN slanted west over the southern California coast.
Tom Goodall jerked awake at a cawing sound. Wiping a
hand over his grizzled jaw, he blinked out the Ford's window
at a big black crow on a Burma Shave sign.

The crow cocked its head, lifted shiny wings, sailed off.

Sure wish I could fly, Tom thought. He felt stiff. Looking at his
wife and kids, asleep on one another in the seat beside him, he
remembered his plan. Lifting little Jenny's head from his lap, he slid
out onto the gravel shoulder. Mist fleeced the lower meadows, but
the hills were clear and bright with morning light.

Black thunderheads hung offshore. The big house waited.

Tom checked his long-barreled Smith & Wesson, then he went
around the Ford and touched his wife's shoulder through the
window.

Her eyelids lifted.

"I'm gittin' us some food," he said. She looked scared, but it was
too late for scared. Clamping his hat on tight, he turned and
stomped across long dewy grass toward the hills.

2

MARY O'Grady sat up in bed. Someone was banging on her door.

"Mary O'Grady, you get up!"

Mary stared at the clock. Blessed Virgin! After six! She should've been on duty ten minutes ago.

Scrambling out onto cold maroon tiles, she splashed water on her face but paused at the mirror above the basin in her small, plain room. With trembling fingers she touched her freckled cheek, as if she had never seen it before.

Oh, Mr. Pike! she thought, bony chest heaving.

Pulling on her uniform, she scurried out into the bustle of servants preparing the big house for breakfast.

3

IN the Doge's Suite Charlie Chaplin did thirty deep knee bends before trotting to shower in the cavernous marble bath, humming "Who's Your Little Whoosis?" as he shaved. Picturing Gloria Deere, he stroked an imaginary mustache. "My room or yours . . . ?" he whispered in his most seductive voice, and laughed. You dog! Back in the spacious bedroom he glanced out the window. He did not like the lonely, twisted look of the Santa Lucias, but there was plenty of sun. Tennis? There were some excellent courts built above the indoor Roman Pool. He put on casual whites.

116

Thank God old Hearst liked things easygoing—to a point, he thought. The only problem would be skirting the moral watchdogs after dark, but he could manage that. Pressing the curved brass door handle, Chaplin stepped out of his room.

He stopped dead, scratching his head.

A long, deserted hallway lined with tapestries and armor led in either direction. How to get downstairs?

He cursed. Casa Grande was a bloody rabbit warren. He had been here many times before but he always got lost.

❦ 4 ❦

I N Casa del Monte Gloria Deere woke, stretched. Stroking the richly embroidered coverlet, she felt like a princess.

She hugged her knees. Does Charlie really go for me? World-famous Charlie Chaplin? The memory of his voice on the phone made her squirm.

❦ 5 ❦

E DDIE had been up before dawn. Nightmares had wakened him: trains howling through fog, animals growling, Hearst's ugly puss sneering. Now he sat staring bleakly through leaded glass up at Casa Grande. But he remembered other dreams too, sweet ones, of slender blond Marion Davies. After that glimpse of her on the balcony last night, white scarf blowing, he couldn't get the pretty face he had seen on movie posters and in the Hearst papers out of his mind. In those dreams he had been her hero. Help! she had called, reaching out soft slender arms only to him.

I'll save you from Hearst! he had cried.

The lean young man grabbed his head. It throbbed with a white, fierce pain.

When? he thought. That's the question.

He leapt up, fists bunched. I'm gonna talk to Hearst before I do it! He's gonna get a piece of my mind!

🙞 6 🙜

V INNY Tashman smoked furiously. In a blue silk robe he sat scribbling notes for his screenplay before heading up to breakfast. He reread the dialogue. Still all those damn milords; he could not seem to get rid of them, but it wasn't *too* awful. Maybe Marion could play Anne Boleyn after all. Vinny crumpled up the paper. Who'm I kidding? That's nuts! How can I do it to her? He tossed down his pen. I'm desperate, that's how. Emitting nervous puffs of smoke, he squinted up at Casa Grande.

Did W.R. get my letter? Has Marion put in a good word?

7

I N the bedroom opposite Vinny's, Otis Pike pulled the heavy black shoe with the built-up heel onto his twisted left foot. Kneeling, he slid notes, photographs, and documents from the locked briefcase under the rumpled canopied bed and perched at the desk by the north window. He poured over the papers for the thousandth time. Nothing, except the old tingling feeling that something was there that he just wasn't seeing. What, damn it? Smirking, he thought about last night. Mary O'Grady. The skinny dame was a talker; she probably didn't have anyone to spill things to. All he had done was give her an ear, and she had yammered away about anything he asked. Most of it was useless, but he had perked up when she talked about the basement vaults below Casa Grande: wine cellars and meat lockers and closets of party costumes, but other rooms too. "They're full of stuff he's collected for years. Photo albums. Letters. Personal things," she had said. The dwarf's long face screwed up into a wicked mask. Got to get a gander at those "personal things!"

Sighing, Pike hid the pictures and documents back in the briefcase. Breakfast time. He put on a dust-gray suit. Stepping outside under the rustling palms, he peered up at the white looming front of Casa Grande. The clue that'll finish old Hearst is there, I know it is!

The pale little man headed up the hill, his ruined past screaming in his brain.

🙠 8 🙡

"**I**SN'T it just *swell!*" Gloria had run into Eddie, and together they climbed through lush gardens toward the broad terrace fronting the grand big house. Gardeners were out clipping hedges. The morning air had a delicious bite.

"It's all built on the bodies of oppressed workers," Eddie muttered.

"Oh, you're too young to be such an old poop."

Herman Mankiewicz groped into view looking as gray as week-old steak. "Cast call," he said, gesturing vaguely uphill.

Crossing a huge terrace with a fountain, they followed the dissipated man through massive iron gates into Casa Grande. A Pompeiian mosaic decorated the entrance floor. "People actually *died* on this thing," Mankiewicz murmured. "Welcome to Hearst's!"

They entered a magnificent room. "Ooo," Gloria breathed. It was easily a hundred feet long, thirty high. The ornate ceiling was carved wood. Ancient Italian choir stalls lined the walls, and straight ahead rose a sixteen-foot-high French Renaissance fireplace topped with marble busts. Eddie glowered at the massive stone, huge tapestries, dark wood tables and gleaming silver and felt more weighed down than ever, crushed. How could you win against this?

"Hearst's five-and-dime," Mankiewicz said, plowing toward a door to the right of the massive fireplace. Others were heading there too—Dorothy Parker, Bette Davis, Adolphe Menjou in natty tweeds. Louella Parsons was on the arm of a solid, pleasant-looking man smoking a pipe. Her husband? Gloria wondered. Louella waved gaily, and Gloria flushed with pleasure, though there was a greedy glint in the columnist's eye that she did not quite like.

Vinny touched her arm. "Sleep well?" Reluctantly Gloria faced him. His sharp brows were inquiringly arched, and he wore a blue

120

blazer with a peach-colored ascot tucked neatly into the open neck of his crisp white shirt. Gloria did not like his piney after-shave.

"Except for that lion roaring," she told him. She tried not to pout. How'm I gonna shake Vinny?

"I heard it too," Otis Pike said. He had slipped up behind them so quietly that Gloria jumped The little man winked at her. "If I were you, honey, I'd watch out for wolves." Vinny scowled at him, but Pike only smiled. The top of his head was dotted with wisps of whitish hair that made him look creepier than ever, Gloria thought.

Pike squinted up at Eddie. "And how are you this fine morning, Mr. Deere?"

"Just lay off," Eddie grumbled.

They heard a *psst!* and discovered the set designer Willis Snipe across the room, beckoning excitedly from the left side of the fireplace. To reach him they had to thread their way around overstuffed chairs and sofas and a huge mahogany table spread with a half finished jigsaw puzzle of a snowy Alpine scene. Snipe was jiggling with excitement. "It's fascinating, and I just had to show *somebody!*" He pointed at a section of choir stall. "Mr. Hearst's secret door!"

Gloria was doubtful. "Looks like some old monk's chair to me."

"Oh, it *is* a monk's chair, but it's a door too. You'll see. It's hinged, and at precisely seven thirty tonight Mr. Hearst will emerge through it. There's a circular stone staircase in back, and in the center of that is an elevator that goes up to his private rooms. The house is quite odd. It's like a hotel in a way, with the public rooms downstairs, but the funny thing is, there's no visual or spatial connection with the guest rooms and private rooms upstairs. No foyer, no grand staircase, only six winding stairwells and elevators. Standing down here, you have no architectural clue that there's anything above or below. And the stairs and elevators are hidden in towers that can't be seen from the ground-floor rooms. Upstairs is just as confusing. I'm in one of the third-floor bedrooms, and it took me twenty minutes to find my way down here."

"You need a map, you mean?" said Otis Pike.

Snipe beamed. "Exactly. A map."

"Or a guide?"

"Ha, ha, yes, a guide!"

Pike stepped to the choir stall. He touched the gleaming old wood. "Does Mr. Hearst keep his secret door locked?"

"Not that I know."

Vinny watched him. "Let's cut the chitchat," he said curtly. "Breakfast is waiting."

They walked past the gaping fireplace and through the door to its right. A room of no less baronial magnificence confronted them: the Refectory, marble-floored, immensely long. Another ornate antique ceiling hung thirty feet overhead, and just below that, between Gothic clerestory windows, bright Siennese banners floated in the morning light. There were more choir stalls, and tapestries lined the walls, while a polished wooden refectory table punctuated with enormous silver candlesticks stretched forty feet down the center.

"Oh, I just want to *die!*" Gloria gushed.

Laughing, chatting, the rich and famous carried plates of food from portable steam tables at the far end of the room.

"See?" Willis Snipe rubbed his hands. "When you open a door you never know what you'll find."

"It must make for interesting weekends," Vinny said, but his eyes were searching for Marion. Up this early? He had to find out about his screenplay. Taking Gloria's arm, he led her toward the food, and they all filled blue-patterned Japanese plates from the assortment of eggs, chops, kippers, potatoes, toast, fruit, and jam presided over by bustling butlers.

Cary Grant brushed Gloria's arm. "Pardon me."

Dick Powell helped her to bacon. "Having a good time, kid?"

"Are you at Metro? You can't be at Metro," Gloria Swanson breathed into her face before stalking off with a glinting smile.

Jean Harlow nudged Gloria's ribs. "Don't mind the Ice Queen, sweetie. Her career's taking a nosedive, and she's out for blood."

Gloria swallowed. All these stars! She was speechless, able only to gape at Harlow's shining platinum hair. Was it really that color naturally, as they said?

Harlow wriggled off with Leslie Howard, and Gloria let Vinny steer her to a place at the long table, but her mind was on Charlie Chaplin.

122

Mary O'Grady came from the direction of the kitchen carrying a tray of toast. Glimpsing Otis Pike, she swung suddenly around and hit Herman Mankiewicz *crack!* on the nose.

Mankiewicz staggered. "Bless you, m'dear!"

"Oh . . . oh . . ." Bursting into tears, Mary wheeled and fled from the room, but few people noticed. There were a dozen or so already seated at the long table, more wandering in all the time, and who cared about some maid with the heebie-jeebies? Silverware busily clinked while laughter flew up to the carved ceiling.

Vinny slid out one of the heavy Italianate chairs for Gloria. Settling, she kept looking everywhere. "Is Mr. Hearst here? Marion?"

"Probably still sleeping."

"Sleeping it *off,* you mean," Eddie grumbled, plopping down opposite them.

Vinny smiled meanly. "You should watch your mouth, know that, kid?"

"Don't call me kid!" Eddie's fists bunched, and he looked as if he were about to take a swing across the table.

Otis Pike slid into the chair next to him. "You should do what Vinny says. Vinny's a tough customer. He made a big stink in Chicago."

"Oh, tell us all about it!" Gloria urged.

"Mr. Pike isn't telling anything," Vinny snapped.

Pike's long jaw came barely to the table edge. He tucked a big white napkin in his collar. "Can we expect our famous host to join us for breakfast?" he asked pleasantly.

"Hearst ought to hide from shame," Eddie muttered.

"Now you just stop it." Gloria turned to Vinny. "Is it true he pops out that secret door right on time, like a cuckoo clock?"

Vinny sawed at a chop. "So I hear. The rule is, be in the Assembly Hall at seven. Hearst shows up at seven thirty. Dinner at eight, then a movie in his private theater."

"Let's hope he shows one of mine," said a British-accented voice. "Cheerio, love!" Charlie Chaplin stood at Gloria's elbow, wearing white tennis clothes. Balancing a plate in his left hand as if he were about to juggle with it, he made a sweeping bow. "May this lowly weed plant himself beside you, lovely flower?"

Gloria felt like fainting. "Please do."

Chaplin settled to her left. He smiled expectantly around the table.

Gloria found her voice. "Uh, Mr. Chaplin, this's my brother, Eddie. And Mr. Pike. And Vinny Tashman. Vinny writes screenplays."

"You and Chaplin are friends?" Vinny growled.

Chaplin was airy. "We're telephone chums." He cut into a mound of eggs. "Vinny Tashman . . . didn't Metro sack you for punching Vance Milgrim? What cheek! But it was a bully thing to do. The man's a tartar—he wouldn't know a good script if they printed it for him in braille. Are you in the movies too, Mr. Pike?"

"No."

"Very wise. They play hell with your life. You have to be so careful."

"Of what?"

"Everything." Chaplin laughed. "Art, politics, women."

Gloria giggled.

"Of scandal too?" Pike asked.

Chaplin looked thoughtful. "I prefer to call it bad publicity."

"I've heard about you and women," Vinny said. "You have a lousy reputation."

"Oh, but I had a ripping time getting it!" Chaplin regarded Eddie. "You have a smashing sister, Mr. Deere."

"Is it true you're a Communist?" Eddie asked.

"Crikey, not so loud!" Chaplin bobbed his head at Louella Parsons, just down the table. "Especially when that vulture is anywhere within a fortnight. I'm for the common man, let's put it that way, shall we? I'm writing a movie about how people are crushed by industrial society. *Modern Times*, I call it."

"How can you eat at Hearst's table?" Eddie demanded.

Chaplin looked at him. "Oh dear." He dabbed the corners of his mouth. "We're *both* eating at it, you know."

Eddie flinched.

"My brother has funny ideas," Gloria put in quickly.

"But nobody ever laughs," Vinny said.

Chaplin only smiled. "I daresay people think I have funny ideas too." All at once Gloria felt his hand on her knee under the table, and he leaned close. "I say, do you play tennis, Miss Deere?"

"No-o," she got out in a shivering tremolo.

"Pity." The comedian's hand slid to the inside of her thigh. "What games *do* you play?"

"Parcheesi," she squeaked.

"I *love* Parcheesi!" Chaplin crowed.

Gloria leapt up. "Er, I need more eggs." She rushed off with her plate.

Chaplin shrugged and went on eating. "I have that effect on some women."

"N-not on m-me, s-sweety." Slender white arms slid around his neck, and a dimpled face framed by honey-blond hair nestled on his left shoulder: Marion Davies.

Eddie's mouth went dry. Marion was more radiant than he had dreamed, more vivid than any movie poster, and he felt suddenly choked and breathless. She wore white flared slacks and a low-cut loose-fitting blouse that showed her breasts as she bent forward. She smooched Chaplin's cheek, and Eddie felt a hot angry wave of jealousy—of this man and Hearst and anyone who touched her.

Chaplin grinned at her over his shoulder. "Still pretty as a picture!"

She planted her hands on her hips. "What p-picture? Wh-Whistler's M-Mother?" She laughed, a gay, free sound. "Hiya, Vinny."

Vinny scraped back his chair. "Hello, Marion. Nice to see you." He lowered his voice. "Uh, I need to talk to you. In private."

Her pert nose wrinkled. "Serious stuff, huh? It's too g-goddamn early to b-be serious. We'll t-talk later. Right now l-little Marion n-needs a drinkee. Orange juice, of course." Blowing a curl off her forehead, she cocked her head at Pike. "Who's the short stack?"

"Otis Pike," Vinny said. "You said I could bring him along."

Pike stood. "Hello, Miss Davies."

Marion rolled her eyes at the dwarf. "H-honey, you n-need some v-vitamins!" Her gaze found Eddie, and she looked at him a long time, her white brow puckered. "I kn-know you, don't I?"

"No."

"You sure? I know a helluva l-lot of m-men." She was frowning in puzzlement. "What's your n-name?"

"Eddie Deere."

"Oo, you're a d-dear, all r-right. B-but you look a l-little sad." Leaning across the table, she touched his cheek. "Why so s-sad, sad boy? I'm sad too sometimes, know that?" She giggled. "Maybe we can be sad t-together. Kiss Marion hello, sad boy." She offered her mouth.

Her breath smelled of liquor, and feeling half-drowned in her deep blue eyes, Eddie sat frozen, helpless.

"No k-kiss?" Marion straightened, but her voice stayed soft. "Y-you owe me one, k-kid." A wink. "I'll be s-sure and c-collect."

"She will, too," Chaplin said.

Gloria came back. "Oh, hello, Miss Davies. Thank you *so* much for inviting me."

"Call me M-Marion. Don't m-mention it; the m-more the m-merrier. Say, I'm organizing a little t-tour of P-Popsy's junk shop for the n-new kids on the b-block and anybody else who w-wants to t-tag along. Interested?"

Everybody nodded.

"Swell. See you after breakfast."

🕸 9 🕸

DOWNHILL Gil Hapworth double-checked his list with a knife-sharpened pencil. Yep, everybody had showed last night. Sliding the paper in a slot in his office file, the paunchy, sandy-looking man stepped out the gatehouse door and squinted against the sun, shading his eyes with his hand. A herd of Montana black buffalo grazed just behind the strong eight-foot-high metal fence that stretched as far as he could see north and south. Nice morning—but those clouds. He frowned. Big and black, they lay less than a mile away, sliding in from the Pacific. *Pacific* meant peaceful, but when storms whipped in things could get nasty.

126

What the hell, I'll just shut my windows.

Dooley Smith came galloping along the road that wound uphill, raising dust. "Hey, d'ja see him?"

"Who?"

"Some guy. He climbed the fence. I saw him—leastways I think I did. It was awful far away, but I'd swear—"

Hapworth narrowed his eyes. "You'd swear to Mr. Hearst?"

Dooley stopped short. "Uh . . ." He hung his head.

Hapworth rubbed his jaw. Call uphill, just in case? No. Dooley only had thirty-two cards in his deck, just enough brains to shovel the right amount of feed to the zebras each day. Besides, if any bird was dumb enough to climb the fence he had a big surprise coming; Mr. Hearst's animals were used to being left alone, and they didn't take kindly to visitors.

Sheepishly Dooley peeked at Gil from under his mop of hazel hair. Better not tell'm the guy was packin' a gun, he thought.

❧ 10 ❧

IN his room above the garages Billy Buller lounged on his unmade bed and thought about Etta Kitt. A hot number! She had even put scratches on his back last night. Chuckling, Billy lit a cigarette and blew smoke at the ceiling. Not a bad job, working for old Hearst. I'm on call all the time, but there ain't much to do. He had a room all his own, and for the time being, until something better came along, he had Etta too.

Yeah, it was swell.

But Billy felt restless. Grunting, he rose and pulled his binoculars from a drawer, taking them to the window. Spying gave him something to do.

The bulky driver had to laugh. All the help did it, kept their eyes peeled, their ears wide open. Hell, you had to pass the time somehow in this nowhere place sixty miles from the nearest town. Billy's lenses swept the hillsides, searching for animals screwing; he liked to watch that.

Maybe some people? He'd seen that too, once or twice.

Hey, there was some guy inside the fence, heading uphill! Billy's black brows knit. Can't be a Hearst man; they're s'posed to steer clear of that part; it's for the animals. What's the big idea? The guy was way down, at least three miles. Suddenly one of the huge cape bulls charged, and Buller roared with laughter as the guy hotfooted it toward a stand of oaks. He disappeared among the trees, the bull at his heels, and Billy watched a long time, but neither one came out. What a joke! Maybe the guy was stuck up a tree, or worse, but Billy didn't make a move to send help. Let the chump take care of himself. He shifted his binocs to the towering black clouds. Comin' in, he thought; looks mean.

Sure hope old Hearst don't ask me to drive downhill in that.

🙞 11 🙜

J OE Willicombe stared for a long, still moment at the eight-by-ten sheet of paper that Mary O'Grady had just handed him. He lifted his eyes to the girl's freckle-blotched face. "Where did you find this?"

Her Adam's apple jumped. "Under one of the big candlesticks on the table in the Refectory, sir. A bit of it was sticking out, that's how I noticed."

"So someone wanted it found," Willicombe murmured, as much to himself as to the maid. He read it again: HEARST, I'M HERE. The familiar little drawing decorated the upper right hand corner, an ominous flurry of lines.

He and Mary stood apart in an alcove of the morning room at the rear of Casa Grande. Nearby, the last of the breakfast crew pushed the portable steam tables back to the kitchen in the south wing. Adjusting his owlish glasses, the secretary examined the girl. She was thin, homely. Her eyes stayed on the carpet; she twisted and untwisted her hands. She had worked here how long? Eight months? A year? Twenty years old, a hard worker who wanted to please. Willicombe felt suddenly sorry for her. Had she reached the peak of her life, a lowly maid who would rise no higher? Momentarily he wondered about all the servants: did they harbor dreams, or did the enormity of the living fantasy in which they worked crush dreams? "Just who ate breakfast by that particular candlestick?" he asked.

"No one, sir. It's the farthest away from the serving area."

But everyone coming in from the Assembly Hall would have passed it, Willicombe thought. "And you didn't notice anyone putting this there?"

"No. I . . . I had an accident. I was out of the room for a time."

Willicombe pursed his lips. By now all the guests had eaten breakfast; all had walked by that particular candlestick at least twice, once on the way in and again as they left; any of them could have slipped the message there. For that matter, he realized grimly, so could any of two dozen Hearst employees. Damn. More than a hundred people on the hill—a hundred suspects?

"Mary, you're not to say anything about this to anyone. It's probably only a joke." He forced a smile. "You know how Mr. Hearst's friends like to joke. But if you hear of anyone who saw someone leave this note, come tell me right away, understand?"

"I will, sir."

"Thank you, Mary."

The girl scurried off, and Willicombe stood for long moments staring at the wrinkled Santa Lucias, bleak and forbidding even in sunlight. We're too damn alone up here, he thought. I'll call the police, I'll alert our security men. But the police were in San Luis Obispo, many miles away, and there were only three security guards to keep watch over hundreds of rooms and acres of gardens. The chief's splendid isolation could be a weapon used against him. Uneasily Willicombe trudged to his office. *A joke, these messages are only a joke!*—but he didn't believe that.

He dreaded reporting to the Chief.

❧ 12 ❧

"R-RIGHT this way, l-ladeez and gentlemen!"
In sparkling sunshine Marion Davies led her postbreak-fast tour downhill to a large squat building on the northeast slope. She banged through tall metal doors, and they found themselves in a cavernous blue and gold tiled room where Carrara marble statues lined a long, brilliant rectangle of water. "Our s-second p-pool, the R-Roman one. Popsy l-likes to p-play Caesar."

Intricate mosaics decorated everything. Her entourage oohed and ahed: Gloria, Eddie, Vinny, Otis Pike squinting out of his little sliver eyes. There were also Herman Mankiewicz, Louella Parsons, Willis Snipe, Damon Runyon. Hands in the pockets of his baggy pants, Joel McCrea chewed a toothpick. Hedda Hopper peered out wryly from under a wide-brimmed straw hat. The bulbous-browed colum-nist Arthur Brisbane trundled next to last, followed by an angry-looking man with a black bar of moustache, whom no one seemed to know.

This was Mama Marion's Morning Tour, as she called it. Other guests had gone horseback riding or to play croquet or tennis; there had been no sign of William Randolph Hearst.

They skirted the pool, footsteps echoing, voices volleying. "It's like Grauman's Chinese!" Gloria breathed.

"But flooded," Herman Mankiewicz cracked, "for a picture that's all wet."

The diving platform was built like an altar. Joel McCrea grinned around his toothpick. "Human sacrifices?"

Marion tapped his arm. "Oh, we only s-sacrifice v-virgins."

"Imported," Hedda Hopper put in. "Rare fruit."

Vinny anxiously touched Marion's elbow. "Marion, sweetheart, when can we talk?"

"Not now, honey." She hurried on, and Vinny ground his teeth.

Eddie trudged silently. He could not take his eyes off Marion. Her floating blond hair, her rose-petal cheeks, her dimples and free, jaunty body proclaimed a gaiety that pulled him like a magnet . . . He tried to fight it. *This mess of a world has got to be fixed!* She had added a tiny hat with a little yellow feather to her outfit of white slacks and blouse. She was a golden vision, and his heart ached. *And I'm going to shoot the man who keeps her?* The idea of facing Hearst filled him with terror.

Sunlight splashed the gardens, though there was a chill where overhanging oaks cast deep blue shadows. Exiting the Roman Pool, Marion led them down a curving path. The hill slid to their right into a wicked tangle of manzanita, and Gloria peered down the sickeningly steep slope at glinting rock far below. "Er, that earthquake yesterday," she said, voice quavering, "is it safe up here?"

"Don't worry," Marion said. "P-Popsy has an ironclad c-contract with G-God."

The *thwack* of tennis balls came to them. There were courts built on top of the building housing the Roman Pool, and squinting back against the sun they glimpsed Charlie Chaplin, Dick Powell, Jean Harlow, Carole Lombard, dashing about in a game of mixed doubles. Chaplin waved and clowned, and Gloria got goose bumps remembering his hand on her leg. When she turned she found Marion's blue eyes examining her.

"T-take my advice: w-watch out for Charlie. He's good for a laugh—but l-laughs don't l-last long around here." A surprising bittersweet smile. "It's j-just advice, sweetie. You d-do what you want; p-people always d-do."

They descended another path, past stucco walls crowded with purple bougainvillea. "There's a b-bunch of old r-rooms and things under these terraces," Marion told them.

Otis Pike had been silent. "Old rooms?" he asked abruptly in his feathery voice.

"Yeah. P-Popsy is n-never s-satisfied. He keeps building and he just p-piles more on top of what was there before. M-must be a r-rat's nest underneath, b-but I've never seen. You c-can g-get to some of it from inside the house, b-but who w-would want to?"

131

Willis Snipe vigorously polished his glasses. "Fascinating!" he said.

They headed on. Sticking near Gloria, Louella Parsons wore a purple and white checked dress. She knew San Simeon well but had tagged along on Marion's tour to keep an eye on the cast of characters. Not being able to pin people down galled her. That little man, Pike—she shuddered—Universal should sign him for its next monster picture! Something was eating Vinny Tashman; she could tell. What? Gloria Deere—pretty. Maybe I should stick a note about her in my column; then if her career goes anyplace, I can say I told you so. Louella squinted her puffy eyes at Eddie, scuffing along with his hands in his pockets. A Gloomy Gus. Something about him still nagged her. Louella saw things most people didn't; she had already noted that his eyes were blue; Gloria's were hazel. Brother and sister? Her nose for news twitched so hard she almost sneezed.

Marion's dachshund, Gandhi, trotted up, and the women fawned over him, while the men stood apart by a marble statue of two nude wrestlers in a glade.

Damon Runyon turned to the fuming little man with the black moustache. "I don't believe we've met."

"Lewis Summerbee," the man growled. As if he had only been waiting for the chance, he exploded: "Hearst!" He glared at Willis Snipe. "Fascinating? Ha! So were Genghis Kahn and Jack the Ripper!"

Arthur Brisbane's enormous frontal lobes throbbed dangerously. "I take it you have some complaint against our host?"

But Summerbee was not daunted. "You bet I do. I'm a subeditor on the San Francisco *Examiner*." A bitter laugh. "I actually used to be *proud* to work for Hearst, can you believe it? But he was a crusader then; he exposed corruption, the bosses, the machines; he fought for the little man. Not anymore. Now he just wants to foist a lot of wacky ideas on the public, turn them into a mob. Well, I won't put up with it! I'm here to be fired, I suppose. I've been here three days, and he refuses to see me. That secretary of his keeps putting me off, but if he thinks he's going to wear me down and send me back like a whipped dog, he's nuts."

"Who's nuts?" Louella asked stiffly. The women were back.

Marion rolled her eyes. "It's g-gotta be Popsy."

Louella shook a finger at Summerbee. "It's not nice to make rude comments behind Mr. Hearst's back. After all, we're his guests."

Eddie had been growing more and more frustrated and furious. "Hearst is a goddamn *fascist!*" he blurted.

They all turned to stare, while a breeze flicked at dying leaves.

Louella clutched her breasts. "Mr. Hearst is a great man!" she declared.

Eddie glared at her. "He's rich, if that's what you mean. But did he earn it? He inherited it all, every dime."

"Oh, Eddie," Gloria moaned.

Eddie kicked viciously at a stone. "Leave me alone. It's a free country, even up here, and I'll say what I think."

"Of c-course you w-will." Marion stepped close to him. "B-but don't get in a p-pet. P-Popsy's no f-fascist. You j-just d-don't understand him. He has his own ideas, and a l-lot of them are r-right. He b-believes America is the greatest country in the world. W-we all b-believe that, d-don't we?"

"I don't," Eddie muttered.

"Yeah, tell us all about Russia," Vinny sneered.

"You h-hush." Marion pushed Eddie's shock of brown hair up on his brow. She peered in his face. "You're a f-funny k-kid. You hate old D-Droopy Drawers? Don't. Sure, he h-has his f-faults. And he l-likes things his way. But he's a g-good m-man. You may not b-believe it, b-but it's t-true. We fight sometimes, but I l-love him—even if we can't be m-married."

Eddie stared helplessly. Under her hat the breeze rippled her blond curls. He was entranced by her creamy skin, her dimples and blue, blue eyes. Tell me you love *me!* he thought, jerking away in misery, trembling and wanting to sink into the ground.

Marion bubbled sudden laughter. "Aren't we the d-dopes? L-let's go see the monkeys!"

They followed her down tiled steps. Someone ought to warn the Chief about that young man! Louella thought. Eddie trailed behind, and Otis Pike turned to glance at his gloomy face. Eddie McGuffin—Eddie Deere? Naw, I'm crazy.

When'll I get Marion by herself? Vinny wondered.

They descended between tall cypresses to the Neptune Pool, an

133

oval of sparkling turquoise water jutting out over the sea. The Greco-Roman temple at its far rim glowed with mellow autumn light. Marion pirouetted at pool's edge. "Anybody n-need a bath?"

A handsome, grinning face broke the lapping water at her feet: Clark Gable. He flashed his white teeth. "Come on in, the water's fine!" he said, heading off with long-muscled strokes.

Harpo sat in baggy shorts at the far end smoking a cigar and chatting to Adela Rogers St. Johns, who lounged in sunglasses on a flowered chaise. Bette Davis promenaded with Leslie Howard under a blue parasol. Three or four others gazed at the view over the curving stone balustrade.

"Oh, it's just swell!" Gloria exclaimed.

But Marion was frowning out to sea. "Shit, look at those g-goddamn c-clouds. I don't want it to r-rain on my p-party."

"Tell Popsy to telegraph God," Herman Mankiewicz yapped.

Marion led them southwest toward the zoo. In five minutes they had reached the complex of concrete enclosures and cages among rustling eucalyptus. An elephant's trunk poked at her over a heavy wire fence, and she patted it. "S-sorry, forgot my p-peanuts." She dimpled. "Isn't he just the c-cutest thing?"

A sudden breeze scattered more leaves. The clouds were moving rapidly now, filling the sky. A last flicker of sunlight winked through a thick gray mass, then shadows swept over the hill. Frowning at the gloom, Marion gave one more pat to the elephant. "Oh, l-let's hurry. These are the p-panther cages. And n-next . . ." She trotted on.

"Miss Parsons." It was Otis Pike's soft voice.

Louella looked back at the dwarf. "Yes?" She halted, though she did not want to. The others were just ahead, then they vanished around a bend, and she was alone under agitated gray skies with the odd little man. Pike didn't move, just stood there smiling faintly. Eucalyptus leaves shivered in more windy gusts; the panthers paced and snarled. Ordinarily Louella loved any chance for a confidence, and there was plenty she wanted to worm out of Pike, but she did not like the way his piggy eyes fastened on her face.

"How well do you know Mr. Hearst?" he asked.

"I've worked for him many years. Why?"

Pike stepped nearer. "But how well do you know him?"

"He's a wonderful man!"

"Even Miss Davies admits he has his faults."

"He may have, but—"

Stubby fingers flicked impatiently. "I know. You'd do anything for him. You told us that."

Louella drew herself up. "I owe him my life."

"Really? Maybe other people owe him something too."

"What do you mean?"

"A woman like you . . . everybody says you know where the bodies are buried." The eyes slitted even more. "Are there bodies? Do you know where they're buried?"

Louella felt her breath come in gasps. "That's none of your business. Who are you to ask questions like that, anyway?"

A shrug. "Only an insurance salesman, a nobody. But my job makes me very interested in life and death and buried bodies. There are lots of rumors about your boss and bodies. That Thomas Ince story, for instance." The panthers paced and hissed. "Did Hearst shoot Ince?" Pike made a gun of his thumb and forefinger and pointed it in her face. "*Bang!* He's a good shot, isn't he? Loves animals? I heard he used to pick off sea gulls from the bow of his yacht."

Louella was trembling. "You're crazy."

Pike shook his head. "Just curious. We're a pair, know that? I like to know things about people, just like you do."

Louella opened her mouth, closed it. "Oh!" she huffed in indignation, and turned and marched away.

"Miss Parsons seems upset."

The voice was deep, solemn, and Pike jerked around to discover a tall, portly man in a dark blue suit peering at him only four feet away. The man wore glasses; he carried a clipboard. About sixty? Looks like a penguin, Pike thought.

"Willicombe," the man said coolly. "Joe Willicombe." He held out a large flat hand, and Pike shook it. "Mr. Hearst's private secretary."

"I know."

"Oh?"

"I've heard of you."

A faint smile. "I try very hard not to be heard of." Poking at his

135

glasses, Willicombe gazed off down the path. "What's wrong with Miss Parsons?"

"The cats must've scared her. Personally, they don't scare me."

"You and she were having a chat."

"Sort of."

"Forgive me, there are so many guests. What is your name?"

"Otis Pike."

"Ah, yes, Mr. Tashman's friend." Willicombe made a mark on his clipboard.

"Checking up on us all?"

"The hill is a big place. Mr. Hearst doesn't want anyone to get lost. People do, you know—but there's always a way to find out where you are." A tree branch stretched out over the path, and Willicombe plucked a telephone receiver from a nest of leaves.

"Whattaya know," Pike said.

"New guests are usually surprised. There are over three hundred telephones up here, not counting the ones in the rooms. You can find one almost anywhere, if you look hard enough. Mr. Hearst hides them in trees or behind rocks. He doesn't like to spoil the landscaping."

"I guess he can afford it."

"He does what he likes."

"So I hear." Pike examined the phone. "There's no dial."

"You don't need one. All the lines connect through Hacienda One—that's our private exchange. When you pick up a phone the central switchboard answers and you ask whatever you want. 'Where am I?' Seems to be the most common question." Willicombe spoke into the receiver. "It's all right. This's Joe Willicombe. I'm just showing a guest how the system works." He put the phone back. "Well, must be off. Work to be done. Have a pleasant stay, Mr. Pike."

When the tall man was gone, Pike cursed. How much had he heard?

13

WILLICOMBE rounded a bend. Stopping, he gazed about to make sure he was not observed, then peered through a narrow parting in a thick growth of laurel. He could see Pike, but Pike could not see him. Willicombe knew all the best vantage points; that was how he had eavesdropped on Pike's conversation with Louella Parsons—a grilling, was more like it. What was the dwarf's game? Willicombe watched the little man mop his brow before scurrying after Marion Davies' party. He moved fast in spite of his game leg, like an animal, a ferret or a weasel, and the secretary frowned. He circled Pike's name on his list.

I too would do anything for the Chief, he thought, glancing up at the black clouds that were clamping down on the hill like a lid.

14

LEAVES flew through the air in a rising wind. Marion's tour was gathered in front of the baboon cage as Pike hobbled up. Agitated by the coming storm, the baboons were leaping frantically from perch to perch, screeching and gibbering, showing their ugly red behinds.

"I heard one of these fellows would as soon bite off your nose as look at you," Joel McCrea was saying. He tugged a lock of hair. "Sure am glad they're behind bars."

137

Suddenly a baboon flung a handful of dung. It spattered Louella's dress.

"Oh!" She gaped in horror at the brown, runny filth dripping down her purple and white front. "Oh, oh, oh . . ."

Pike pulled out his handkerchief. "Let me help."

She stared at him, "Don't you touch me!" she shrieked, and fled wailing up the path.

"Oh, sh-shit," Marion murmured watching her. "If it isn't one th-thing it's another." She grabbed Eddie's hand. "C-come on, help out." She led him off after Louella.

"She seems to like your brother," Vinny said to Gloria, silently cursing Marion for getting away.

"I don't see why she shouldn't like him," Gloria sniffed. "He's a perfectly nice boy."

Herman Mankiewicz jiggled with laughter. "Haw, haw, haw! Monkeys who dish the dirt better than Louella! Haw!"

At that moment rain began to fall.

✂ 15 ✂

A MBROSE felt the first drops of rain. The small brown mouse with one white paw darted into the dark space under the hairpin curve in the road; he had made it home in time.

He rested for a moment. It had been a long journey down from the big house where the man had locked him in a cage, and he had had to hide from owls, so it had taken him all night and part of the morning to get here. His home had once been a ground squirrel's burrow; the squirrel had dug deep under the road, a warren of tunnels. He had been followed by a fox who had enlarged things, but the fox had run off because of the cars that rumbled back and forth all the time. The smell of the other animals had gradually seeped away, and Ambrose had added his own tiny tunnels. In fact he had been in the process of finishing one when fine pickings called him up the hill. He had not disliked the man who had saved him from the dog and fed him and stroked his fur, but he preferred being free.

His sides stopped heaving. He felt hungry but did not care to forage in the wet. Winding his way up to the tunnel he had been digging, he began to claw, dislodging dirt, pushing it back.

Under the road, at the hairpin curve.

At the edge of the steep ravine.

🙦 16 🙧

TOM Goodall clung to the lowest branch of a big maple. A dozen feet under him a cape bull snorted and pawed at dead leaves.

Tom had sat there more than an hour. "Git, darn you!" he yelled. "My wife and kids need food!" The bull just glared, and licking dry lips, Tom fingered the long-barreled pistol he had tucked in his belt. Kill the bull? He did not like shooting animals.

And what if I waste all my shots?

He laughed, a desperate wail. What do I need to save bullets for? I ain't gonna shoot nobody. The laugh turned to fury. Folks oughta help folks! How come them cars didn't stop last night?

Rain began to tick on the maple's curled brown leaves. Gosh darn, Tom thought, peering up. Then the sky let loose, and in moments he was soaked and shivering. Ellen! The kids! Pulling the gun from his belt, he sighted down its barrel at the patch of skull between the bull's sharp horns.

Don't want to kill him, but—

Suddenly he slipped on the rain-slick branch. Grabbing to save himself, he dropped his gun.

As he fell he saw a telephone receiver tumble from the leaves.

17

ETTA Kitt stared at her switchboard.

"Help . . . up a tree . . . there's a goldarn bull . . . *help* . . ."

The line went dead.

Somebody's screwy, Etta said to herself, her sharp brows dancing, or one of the guests is playing a joke. On a chart she checked the location of the call. She frowned: it was remote, a couple of miles downhill, at a phone that wasn't much used, even by the ranch hands. Staring out at the rain, Etta drummed her fingers. Not likely any guest would be there among the wild animals. Somebody really in trouble?

She decided to report it.

She punched in a line to Joe Willicombe's office.

18

"THIS way, h-hon." Marion Davies led Eddie into a white gazebo on a little rise. It was cosy, private. Leafless vines wound up to thick wooden beams; the rain could not get in. Zebras grazed on the slope just below, and there was a view all the way down to San Simeon Bay, iron-colored under an angry sky.

"I h-hate this rain, d-don't you?" Pulling off her hat, Marion shook her shining blond curls.

"I thought we were going to help Miss Parsons."

140

"Oh, l-let her h-help herself. She's a b-big g-girl."

"But—"

"I w-wanted to be alone with you, g-get it? Hasn't a g-girl ever w-wanted to be alone with you before?"

"I guess."

Marion sidled near, smiling. "You kn-know what happens n-now, don't you?"

"No."

Her voice grew husky. "You p-put your arms around me and we k-kiss." She shut her eyes.

Eddie did not kiss her. "You said you loved Hearst."

The eyes drifted open, puzzled. "I h-have met you before, h-haven't I? But m-maybe it was j-just in my dreams; maybe I met a tall, handsome, s-sad boy like you in my dreams. Sure, I l-love Popsy. I love my little d-dachsy. I love g-gin and p-pretty clothes." She placed her hands on his chest. "M-maybe I l-love you too, a little. So what?"

"You don't know me."

She looked away. The rain crashed about them, and she bit her lip. "S-sometimes when you kn-know people too w-well, you don't l-love them like you sh-should." Her blue eyes met his again. "Besides, kn-knowing isn't l-loving: loving is loving. You have a l-lot to l-learn, and I'm a good t-teacher, so—"

Rising on tiptoe, Marion Davies pressed her mouth against his.

Eddie let her kiss him. Soft lips. A supple, slender body so close it seemed to melt into his. He heard a small sound in her throat, felt her hunger. He felt his own. Their hungers met, fed.

Eddie jerked away, panting. Hard brown vines scraped his back. "I can't," he said, shaking.

"You d-don't like me?"

"I do like you."

She slid her hands in the pockets of her white slacks. Her voice grew very quiet. "You've g-got a g-gun, haven't you?"

So. She had felt it in his coat. "So what?" he demanded.

She laughed. "L-listen kid, it's not a c-cigarette lighter, it's a g-gun. Fess up. Why?"

"I'm afraid," he blurted.

"P-poor b-baby. Of what?"

He was silent.

"That's okay. M-Marion understands. Everybody's af-afraid some-time or other. B-But you sh-shouldn't've brought a g-gun. It's n-not n-nice. P-Popsy doesn't allow g-guns. I r-really ought to t-tell him."

Eddie panicked. "Don't. Please."

"P-promise to p-put it right away? Nobody's g-gonna hurt you up here. M-Marion'll p-protect you."

"I promise." He felt ashamed of the lie.

"G-good." Shivering, she looked out at the rain. "I'm afraid too, but I d-don't carry a g-gun," she told him, her expression bleak. "I d-drink. C'mon." Wearing a bright, forced smile, she took his arm. "Let's s-see if a l-little booze can warm up my s-sad, s-scared boy."

❧ 19 ❧

W ILLIAM Randolph Hearst entered the elevator, pressed the Down button, and descended four floors from the Gothic Suite, past the Assembly Hall to Casa Grande's underground vaults.

He stepped out, alone in a whispering silence. Lit by dim brownish light, concrete corridors yawned away in all directions, and a dank chill pressed at him. Turn on bright bulbs? He reached for the switch but pulled back his hand. No. The semidarkness suited his mood; it suited secret acts. Why did I come down? Voices called me, that's why. Uneasily he began to thread his way among stacked shelves and boxes of things he had saved for years, decades, half a century; down corridor after corridor of them, into room after shadowed room, until his past began to close in on him. The further he plunged into the maze of reinforced concrete tunnels, the further back in time he went. He passed more than a dozen rooms of statues and paintings and old carved stone. He began to run his hand along shelves. There under glass was his yellowed first edition of the *Examiner*, March 4, 1887. Next, a photograph of Tessie Powers. Then mementos of his young manhood at Harvard. He smiled without humor. I was a dud student—but, oh, I had my fun! There was plenty of evidence of that: Champagne Charlie grinning from a shelf. Charlie had been his pet crocodile, whom he had had stuffed after the poor animal died of drink. Then there was the chamber pot with the Harvard president's name on the inside. He had given it to the president as a gift, but it was the last straw; he had promptly gotten canned. How Mother had cried! He trudged on into his dusty past. At last his boyhood loomed: his red and green polka dot rocking horse; the sled his mother had given him when she took him to the Sierras to see snow for the very first time; the puppet theater he had played with in the big San Francisco house while his father ran silver mines far away. There were photo albums too, hundreds.

The old man stopped. He pulled from a side pocket the note Willicombe had shown him only an hour ago: HEARST I'M HERE, with its familiar ominous flurry of lines. Hearst's breath came fast; the paper crackled faintly under his fingers.

This is it, isn't it? This is why I punish myself down here.

❧ 20 ❧

R AIN continued to fall. Noon drew near. Mr. Pinkerton, the head butler, lifted the large brass cowbell from the antique anvil, which had in medieval days resounded with the blows of armor-making, stepped out Casa Grande's portal into the streaming wet, and vigorously clanked it before scurrying back to shelter, softly cursing.

Gloria Deere and Louella Parsons were already safe and dry on a flowered sofa in the Assembly Hall. "A cowbell to call people to lunch?" Gloria giggled.

Louella waggled her fingers at Marie Dressler, who looked like a tugboat groaning into port. "Hello, dear."

Marie rasped a gruff greeting and plowed on.

Louella had recovered most of her dignity; she had changed from the soiled dress into one on which large magenta orchids blared amid jungle green. "Isn't it funny?" she said to Gloria. "W.R. is *so* sentimental. He used to camp up here with his father and then with his wife and his five boys before there were any buildings at all. It's still the Ranch to him, and he likes to have reminders, like the cowbell, of the good old days of roughing it. You'll see, we'll have paper napkins for lunch, as if it was a picnic. And there'll be catsup and mustard bottles right alongside the expensive silver."

"Will he come down?" Gazing at the carved ceiling, Gloria imagined the great man stirring somewhere up there like God in heaven.

Louella touched her mouse-brown hair. "If he does I'll introduce you." She had questions for Gloria, but first she surveyed the room. At the far end Docky played poker with Harpo, Damon Runyon, and Cary Grant. Clark Gable and Carole Lombard sat on opposite sides of the big jigsaw puzzle, frowning. They had never gotten along since Lombard had presented Gable with a smoked ham at the end of their only picture. Marie Dressler warmed her backside by the monstrous fireplace. Having deliberately plopped down next to Gloria, Louella decided it was time to dig some dirt. "Just tell me *all* about yourself, my dear, and about your handsome brother too."

But at that moment Herman Mankiewicz rolled up to them, his bleared eyes proclaiming that he had been holding a private gin bash. "Chawmin' dress," he slurred to Louella. "Calla lillies?" He thrust an elbow at Gloria. "May I escort you in to lunch?"

Giggling, Gloria rose. "Love to! Er, d'you think there are any parts for me in any of your scripts?"

Louella's silver smile melted to brass. For some moments people had been scurrying in under dripping black umbrellas, which they tossed on the mosaic in the entranceway. Chatting and brushing off stray raindrops, they began moving toward the Refectory doors by the fireplace: angular Basil Rathbone, the trim reporter Adela Rogers

144

St. Johns, Gloria Swanson wearing an arsenic smile. Jean Harlow wisecracked to Dick Powell, who burst into "Singin' in the Rain."

All at once Charlie Chaplin bobbed up at Gloria's side. "Got lost upstairs again and nearly missed lunch." He winked. "Happy I didn't miss you. May I?" Unlinking her arm from Mankiewicz's, he wound it around his own. "You'll never miss her, old chap. My God, I'm famished!" He breezed her through the door.

Lunch was served buffet style, the steam tables once more in place at the far end of the long room, and as Louella had predicted catsup and mustard bottles were much in evidence. As she and Charlie carried plates down the line of food, Gloria kept her eye out for Mr. Hearst. Was that him? Nudging Charlie, she pointed at a tall owlish man wearing glasses.

"Hearst? Hardly. But you're close. It's Joe Willicombe, the old man's private secretary. Looks frightfully glum, doesn't he? Not like old Joe to be so morose. Grilled salmon, m'dear?"

Joe Willicombe was indeed glum. Standing at a strategically chosen vantage point near the far passage to the morning room, he watched the guests troop in. Invaders, he thought sourly. They slept in Mr. Hearst's beds, swam in his pools; they trod on his flower beds and gobbled his food—and one of them sent threatening notes. Had the notes been threats, exactly? Maybe not, but the implication was there. Willicombe's eyes found the far candlestick, where the latest one had been dropped. Would another appear when lunch was through? The red-haired maid darted past carrying pots of tea. She ducked her head. A guilty look? Willicombe chided himself. The poor, homely girl isn't capable of plots. I'm just too damn on edge.

Louella joined the end of the food line. Feeling a hand on her arm, she turned to find Otis Pike leering up at her, and goose bumps rose on her back. "You get away from me," she snapped.

The dwarf looked contrite, his head momentarily bowed so that Louella stared right down on his horrible tufts of hair. "I gave you a bad time out by the panthers. I wanted to say I'm sorry."

"Well . . ." Louella almost gave in. "No," she said, lifting her chin. "I simply don't want to talk to you." Yet she regretted her haste. Awful as he was, she wanted very much to talk to Otis Pike.

Pike wanted to talk to her too, but he only shrugged and made his wide mouth smile, though his leg had begun to ache. What if the old bat knows something? But there were other ways. Catching Mary O'Grady's eye, he nodded slyly; they had an appointment.

Mary nodded back, this time without breaking anyone's nose—and turned to find Joe Willicombe's gaze fixed on her. Coloring, head down, she scurried past him, her heart leaping at the thought of the madness she planned with Otis Pike. Can I do it? she asked herself.

Pike picked up a plate. Rain dashed against the clerestory windows between the Siennese banners, but happy, witty chatter drowned the sound. Marion fluttered in in salmon pink slacks and blouse, a blue sailor's knot at her throat, and the gay glaze of her eyes said she had downed one or two before lunch. What'd she and the Deere kid done with their time? Pike wondered. Charlie Chaplin and Gloria found seats. "That red-faced Irishman's Jack Neylan, Hearst's head lawyer," Charlie pointed out. Marion cut Neylan dead. "Well, I'll be," Gloria said. Nearby Arthur Brisbane intoned against the NRA—"It's steering this country to the brink of disaster!"—while Cary Grant chatted to Hedda Hopper about being a struggling young actor in England and Willis Snipe goggled ecstatically at the architecture.

Eddie sat with little food on his plate. Marion rounded the table; Vinny Tashman half rose to offer a chair, but she swept past as if she had not seen him, and his face purpled when she dropped into the vacant seat next to Eddie.

Other people noticed as well—few of the in crowd missed anything—and secret, knowing glances flew about: Hearst's mistress had her line out again.

Herman Mankiewicz coughed laughter like a cold engine starting up.

Gloria Swanson's head darted like a cockatoo's.

Harpo described poker strategy to ash blond Bette Davis, whose big eyes rolled with amusement.

Damn it, I *know* Eddie Deere, Louella thought, drumming her red-painted nails. "Don't smoke your pipe at lunch, dear!" she reprimanded Docky. Scraping back her chair, she headed for Joe Willicombe.

His eyes puckered warily at sight of her. "Hello, Louella. Enjoying yourself?"

"Oh, I always do at Mr. Hearst's!" They surveyed the room. "Is the Chief coming down?" Louella asked.

"He might. Then again he might not. He's got a lot on his mind."

"Finances?"

"Money is always a big subject."

"But—"

"You know the Chief has a hand in everything."

Louella made a face; Joe was a damn cool cucumber. Her instinct buzzed, but she stuck to what she had come for. "That Gloria Deere is a pretty girl, isn't she?"

"The brunette with Mr. Chaplin? Very."

"You think she has a career ahead of her?"

"That's your domain, Louella."

"She's pushy, I'll say that for her, and that never hurts. But her brother—what a sad sack! Know anything about him?"

"Nothing."

A pause. "How about that little man, Pike?"

Willicombe met her eyes. "Mr. Tashman's friend?"

"He gives me the jitters!"

"Does he?"

"Just look at him!" Louella licked heavily lipsticked lips.

"I don't know anything about him either," Willicombe said.

"You know what room he's in, don't you?"

"Yes."

"Well . . . ?"

"He's in Casa del Monte. Why?"

Louella laughed as if it were all a joke. "So I can stay away from it," she said, striding off.

Willicombe echoed her laugh, but he remained uneasy. He had glimpsed the brief exchange between Louella and Pike; he had also observed what he thought was a flicker of glances between Pike and Mary O'Grady.

The secretary clenched his hands behind his back. What's going on?

At that moment William Randolph Hearst entered the Refectory.

147

Pike sat near Vinny; he saw the publisher at once, a massive gray-looking man in a suit that hung like an untailored bolt of cloth on deeply sloping shoulders. Lines like scars cut his long sharp face. A shock of iron gray hair hung across his brow, and he wore a red string tie, western style. Pausing by the stone fireplace, his quiet, staring presence took over the room, and conversation ebbed. Bastard! Pike thought, but felt a chill of fear. Hearst's blue eyes had remarkable power; they seemed to search, pierce every corner of the Refectory, and Pike shivered as they grazed him.

Does he know who I am?

No. Can't.

We meet at last, Pike thought, clenching his jaw.

Jumping up, flying to the old man, Marion pecked his cheek, and Hearst's ice melted to an adoring gaze. "Popsy's h-here! L-look, everyone! P-Popsy!" She trundled him forward as if he were a half-wit. "Now, you j-just *have* to m-meet everyone n-new," and she began to drag him around the table.

Not me; not yet, Pike thought.

Sliding from his chair, he slipped behind the table, glad for once to be small, easily overlooked.

But Willicombe saw him scurry out through the morning room.

Itching for a story, Louella saw too.

🎐 21 🎐

OUTSIDE, palm trees flapped like flailing hands. Rain whipped San Simeon in sullen slanting waves, but the mouse with one white paw was barely aware of the storm. In loamy dark, Ambrose continued to dig under the road just downhill, unaware that water was pouring into the tunnels behind and below him, dissolving them to mud.

Mud that began to slip toward the edge of the steep ravine.

🙠 22 🙢

VERY far downhill, at ocean's edge, rain drummed on the roof of a stranded Ford truck. Inside, huddled with her children, a thin shivering woman bit her knuckles. Oh, I should've stopped him! Ellen Goodall thought, picturing poor Tom, soaked, maybe in trouble. That temper of his . . .

Lord, keep him safe!

🙠 23 🙢

AS his wife prayed for him, Tom Goodall came to.

He was lying on his back in soggy leaves. Rain slapped his face. Blinking, groaning, the rangy man struggled up. He felt for broken bones. Then he remembered the bull. He scratched his chin. Run off, I guess. That phone? He stared up at the tree he had fallen from. A receiver dangled overhead, and his weathered eyes traced an electric line from the ground to the branch.

They're nuts around here!

Tom blinked. Bit of a headache but nothin's broke. He grinned without humor: my hat didn't even fall off.

Tom squared his shoulders. Wet, cold—and mad—he scooped up his long-barreled pistol and plunged uphill.

24

MARION led Hearst down the long table.

"Hello, W.R.," Louella said adoringly.

"You look wonderful!" Hearst said.

"Remember me, Mr. Hearst?" Vinny Tashman leapt up to pump the old man's hand.

Hearst's eyes were vague. "Er . . ." he said.

Marion hurried him along. "And th-this's Eddie D-Deere," she said brightly.

Rain flung itself at the high windows. Eddie rose slowly, his face drained. His hand knocked over a glass of water. The dampness spread on the tablecloth but Hearst seemed not to notice. He peered into Eddie's face and something flickered in his sharp blue eyes.

"Eddie . . . ?" he said in his high-pitched voice.

Oh, jeepers, Gloria thought, watching her fake brother's jaw begin to twitch, he'll say something dumb and my career'll wash right up on the rocks!

25

OTIS Pike cursed his game leg. It throbbed with sharp jabs of pain, but he kept clumping doggedly along the north perimeter of Casa Grande. Damn the rain too. He had had to creep out through the morning room, and it was a helluva long way around to the front of the house; by the time he reached the broad main terrace he was soaked.

Ducking inside, he paused in the vestibule among the discarded umbrellas to peek into the Assembly Hall. Good. It was peopled only by massive, silent furniture, no busybody servants in sight, all the guests in the next room at lunch. Hurrying to the antique choir stalls left of the fireplace, he reached out—Gimme luck!—and expelled a *whoosh* of satisfaction at the tiny click and give of the wood. The hidden door Willis Snipe had described was not locked; it swung open, revealing a circular concrete staircase.

In the center of the stairs was a small elevator car.

Pike was about to pop in when a growling sound made him whirl. A dachshund stood six feet away baring its teeth.

"Hush!" the dwarf hissed, lashing out with his good leg, and the dog scampered under the jigsaw puzzle table.

Pike mopped his brow. Flinging a last rapid glance about the Assembly Hall, he pulled the hidden door shut and stepped into the elevator. It was paneled in old wood, more of Hearst's booty. "So far, so good." Pike examined four ivory buttons in a brass panel, the bottom one labeled BASEMENT. Save that for later, with that dopey maid. Next came ASSEMBLY HALL, then FLOOR TWO, FLOOR THREE.

The architectural drawings had taught Pike what he needed to know. He pressed FLOOR THREE: Hearst's private apartments.

Whirring to life, the elevator lifted him upward.

❧ 26 ❧

GLORIA leapt up. "I'm Eddie's sister, Gloria," she gasped. "I and Eddie are *so* happy to meet you, Mr. Hearst. So glad Marion invited us." She stood between the massive old man and Eddie. "We're just enjoying ourselves so much," she babbled. "You have a *swell* house. And the view. And the animals, and the swimming pools, and, well . . ." She stared at the lined face peering at her, searching for more words, wanting to keep Eddie from opening his mouth and ruining everything by blatting about Reds and fascists, but she had simply run out. Oh, help! she thought, feeling as if she might just faint.

"I'm happy you're enjoying yourself, Miss Deere," Hearst said with a ponderous bow.

"Oh, we *are!*" she panted gratefully.

"Everybody is, P-Popsy," Marion said, moving Hearst along to the next guest.

Hearst cast one last curious glance back at Eddie; his cold eyes glinted. Weakly Gloria sank into her chair and dragged Eddie down beside her. *"You just be good!"* she whispered, but Eddie had buried his face in his hands, his shoulders shaking. Crying? Gloria draped an arm about him. "There, there. What's wrong?" He really was a mixed up boy.

Louella watched them with a hard, set face, but Vinny saw only Hearst. Marion leads him around by the nose. She can really help me, she can!

Joe Willicombe saw none of it; he had vanished from the room.

❧ 27 ❧

THE elevator stopped at the third floor. Pike was terrified. What'll they do if they catch me? But he had come too far and wanted this too much to turn tail now.

Stepping from the elevator, he found himself just where the drawings had predicted, in a small lobby. There were the usual oriental carpets, armorial tapestries, madonnas, brass fixtures, and lampshades made of old vellum hymnal pages. A massive suit of armor seemed to glare at him. Hearst, stay away till I get what I want! Left was the study. Pike stepped into it, his tiny eyes narrowed. So this is the command post. The storm was muffled; silence drummed in the air. The long rib-arched room, with its hand-painted vaults, leaded-glass bookcases, and marble fireplace in-furiated the dwarf. People die, but this old bastard lives on like a king! Is this where he hides it, his precious secret? Can I find it and smash him? Pike's fingers itched to tear the place apart, but he stuck to his plan: start in the bedroom.

Retracing his path, he mounted three steps into a large private sitting room. The view through Gothic stone arches showed a gray, rain-washed vista falling away to a crawling sea: Hearst's fifty miles of coastline. He owns it all, Pike thought and found a smile. I'm gonna take it away.

Marion Davies' suite was north. Pike turned in the opposite direction, past the private bath and closets, into Hearst's bedroom.

It was smaller than Pike had expected, but all the stuff in it was first rate, from the tent-shaped carved ceiling to the canopied bed with corkscrew posts. So close! Pike thought, and fear momentarily rattled his twisted frame. Clammy sweat burst out on his brow and he started to shake, but he controlled himself. Take it one step at a time. Kneeling, he unscrewed the heel from his built-up shoe.

The heel contained a camera, miniature but efficient; Pike had tested it many times. His waxen features set hard as his eyes began to search. Let's find something good . . .

An old woman's photograph hung by the bed: Phoebe Apperson Hearst. Her eyes glowed with adoring love for her only son, and Pike struggled with a burning jealousy. He blinked it away. Next to Mrs. Hearst's picture was some fancy lettering under glass. He stretched on tiptoe to read it.

> If thou wouldst have me paint
> The home to which, could love fulfill its prayers,
> This hand would lead thee, listen . . .
> A marble palace lifting to eternal summer
> Its marble walls, from out a glossy bower
> Of coolist foliage musical with birds . . .
> And when night came . . . the prefumed light
> Stole through the mists of alabaster lamps,
> And every air was heavy with the sighs
> Of orange groves and music from sweet lutes,
> And murmurs of low fountains that gush forth
> In the midst of roses!—Dost thou like the picture?

153

Pike sneered. A palace? More like a mausoleum. No, I don't like the picture.

He turned aside.

Then he saw it, sitting on the dresser on the other side of the bed: the toy, the glass globe containing the little Alpine village.

The dwarf's brow bunched; his white tufts of hair bristled. The thing was on Rose McGuffin's mantel eight months ago. How'd it get here?

Chicago, snowy Chicago . . .

Then he understood. Scurrying around the bed, he lifted the globe with trembling fingers and turned it over to peer under the brass base. *Karl Zimmer & Sons, Wiesbaden.* Yes!

Two. There are only two, Max had said; this had to be the other one.

The mystery of it seared the little man. Why did Rose McGuffin, who stole the identity of a dead woman, have one of them? And why did William Randolph Hearst keep the other on his dresser where he would see it every day?

Pike felt caught in a web. He righted the globe, and its artificial snow glittered, swirled; it transfixed him, and as he stared into the snow he remembered the mantel, the photograph of Hearst and her newsboy son, Eddie. But Eddie would not be a newsboy now; the spoiled brat would be grown. The dwarf's mind groped toward an answer, and he felt it near, tickling, just out of reach. It had to do with those papers Rawlston had sent him; with Rose Ellen Forrest; with Harry McGuffin who died falling off a train. And Wiesbaden. He gripped the globe tighter. Why Wiesbaden?

In his mind, Pike saw Hearst's hated face, and the secret was in that face too.

Pike reached out to possess it.

"What are you doing here?" came a stern, angry voice, and the little man dropped the globe.

❧ 28 ❧

"**O**H, p-poop!" Marion dragged her fingers through her blond hair. "When's this old r-rain going to stop? Can't you s-stop the r-rain?"

"I'm afraid not," said William Randolph Hearst.

"Then what g-good are you?"

Marion spoke too loudly, and sitting next to her among guests at the long refectory table Hearst gave her a pained look. "You've been drinking, haven't you?"

She twisted in her chair. "Here? Ha! It's as d-dry as a b-bone up here! Who can g-get a d-drink? You think I'm t-tight? You're the one who's tight, l-locking up the b-booze. . . ."

Guests near them conspicuously averted their gazes. Clark Gable fingered his mustache; Dorothy Parker made faces at Damon Runyon, who appeared strangled between embarrassment and laughter. Rolling his pale-lashed eyes, Leslie Howard did Romeo pining for Juliet.

"I'm only thinking of your health," Hearst said.

"D-don't b-bother. I'm y-young and healthy—which is more than I can say for y-you." Marion bit her lip. "Oh, gee, s-sorry Popsy. Really. I didn't m-mean it. F-Forgive me?" She clutched at his arm. "Oh, s-say you do."

"I do," Hearst said, but his expression was thunderous.

Marion flashed a bright, desperate smile. "This d-damn old w-weather—it's enough to d-drown d-ducks! Oh, l-let's b-be ducks!" She leapt up, laughing almost hysterically, and everyone stared.

At that moment Eddie wanted more than ever to carry Marion away from all this.

She waggled a finger. "Now, d-don't go 'way. I'm going to g-get the d-duck suits." Scampering from the room, she dashed back moments later lugging a pile of yellow rain slickers and rain hats. "We're g-going to be y-yellow ducks. Marion's going to be the m-mama duck, and the rest of you will be b-baby d-ducks. S-see? We'll play f-follow the d-ducky. Who wants to p-play follow the d-ducky?"

Charlie Chaplin jumped up, quacking and duck-walking, and relieved laughter spurted around the table. He shrugged into a yellow slicker. "Number-one son," he announced in a strangled duck voice, and, giggling, Gloria rushed to grab the next slicker.

Vinny grabbed the third.

Wearing a black look, William Randolph Hearst rose and stalked from the room.

29

JOE Willicombe scooped up the glass globe. It had not broken, and the secretary replaced it on the dresser.

He scowled down at Pike.

"I asked what you were doing here, sir."

Pike had immediately slumped down onto the red and blue oriental carpet. He fiddled with his heel. "Trying to fix my shoe," he said. "It's not easy being a cripple." The toes of the secretary's polished black shoes were only a foot away. "There," Pike said at last, standing and testing the heel. He hoped his smile was nonchalant. "It does that sometimes."

"This is Mr. Hearst's bedroom. His private bedroom."

"Is it? Then you ought to have signs."

"How did you get up here?"

"Elevator. I didn't walk up with a leg like this."

"Mr. Hearst's private elevator?"

"I didn't know it was private."

"How did you know it was there?"

Pike shrugged, patting his lapels. "Somebody showed us. Lots of people seem to know—it's no secret. This morning Miss Davies told us guests had the run of the place. I was just poking around. Anything wrong with that?"

"What were you doing with the glass globe?"

"Looking at it. Doesn't Mr. Hearst put out all this stuff to be looked at?"

"Why look up here?"

"It's raining outside."

"It's lunchtime."

"I finished eating. Where's your clipboard? Don't you want to check off my name? Okay, okay." Pike headed for the door. "If places are off limits," he said over his shoulder, "you ought to lock them up. But I don't want to cause trouble; I promise to stay miles from here."

Hands in pockets, he hobbled out, but under his jacket his shirt was soaked with sweat.

Willicombe waited until he heard the elevator start down, then in a very bad mood he descended to the ground floor and headed for his office, where telephone and telegraph lines led to all parts of the world. He found one of his three phones jangling. He made a grab across the broad oak desk, but the phone stopped ringing. He angrily adjusted his glasses. If it's important they'll call back.

Sitting, Willicombe picked up another line.

He intended to find out all he could about poor crippled Otis Pike.

❦ 30 ❧

AT her switchboard Etta Kitt blew a frustrated puff of smoke. She had tried seven times to get through to Joe Willicombe, but no one ever answered. She jerked out the plug. To hell with it; let that guy down the hill take care of himself!

Water poured off the eaves outside her window. Etta leaned back. Anticipating the night ahead, all those busy calls and sneaky appointments under cover of dark and storm, the wiry little woman tapped a tooth. Her puckish grin flashed. I'm wasted here. I oughta work for Parsons!

❧ 31 ❦

"QUACK, quack," Marion said.

"And triple quack," Charlie Chaplin echoed.

The line of eight yellow-slickered "ducks" moved downhill in the whipping rain, Marion in the lead. "Now, children, we're all g-going to look at the f-flowers."

"Are flowers good to eat?" Chaplin quacked at her heels.

"Are they good t'drink, thass what I wanna know," Herman Mankiewicz demanded.

Mama Marion pinched his scarlet cheeks. "Oochie, oochie! We'll f-find some nice gin flowers for l-little Herman—but only if he's a g-good baby d-ducky."

"Oh, a goo'duck, a goo'duck!" Mankiewicz jabbered.

"What's in there?" Gloria asked as they passed a low frame building tucked away among dripping oaks.

"The t-telephone and t-telegraph offices."

"I don't see any wires," Louella said.

"They're underground. Popsy d-doesn't like the n-nasty things showing; they s-spoil his v-view."

"He likes to be blind about lots of things, doesn't he?" Eddie muttered.

Marion tsk-tsked. "Is Eddie being a b-bad little d-ducky again? Later, when we're alone, Mama will g-give you m-medicine for that; Marion's special t-tonic. Here we go!" She turned right, and after a moment of scrambling and sliding over wet leaves they came to five long greenhouses. "F-follow the l-leader." She led them into the nearest glass-paned building.

Inside was warm and steamy, lush with plants. Overhead lights provided artificial sun, and spring and summer flowers bloomed out of season in bright splashes of red, yellow, purple.

"Oh, Marion," Louella exclaimed, "you've never taken me here before!"

Wearing coveralls and big rubber boots, a wizened little man who looked like a dead twig shambled over. Marion hugged him. "Th-this's Nigel Keep, Popsy's head g-gardener. Nigel's an old dear, and he's a g-genius with p-plants."

"Hardly a genius," Keep murmured.

"No? Just l-look at these orchids."

Keep shoved one hand in a baggy coverall pocket. "Well, Mr. Hearst likes flowers at all times of the year, so we do our best."

"That's a wicked-looking pair of shears," Vinny said.

Keep glanced at the black-handled cutters he held. "Plants need trimming back. It helps them grow."

Louella touched the sharp blades. "Ooo!" She shivered. "I'm glad I'm not a rose!"

"You're not even a weed, m'dear," Mankiewicz said. He swayed in Keep's direction. "Any gin plants, perchance?" he asked.

Rain drummed like rifle fire on the overhead panes. Marion strolled off, humming, along one of the narrow gravel paths, and Vinny caught up with her. "I've been trying to talk to you all day."

She fluttered her lashes. "Have you?"

"D'you know if W.R. got my letter? Have you talked to him about my movie idea?"

Marion examined some small pink pansies. "S-sweet, aren't they. You suppose flowers h-hurt when you c-cut them?" Her eyes were deeply sad. "I *d-did* say I'd talk to Popsy, didn't I? You think I h-hurt him terribly by what I said at lunch? I don't m-mean to hurt him, but . . . oh, damn, if only he'd m-marry me!" She wrinkled her nose. "S-sorry. Your movie? God knows, I n-need a good m-movie. Now, you j-just t-tell me all about it."

"It's *perfect* for you," Vinny said eagerly. He described the plot. It sounded silly even to him, overblown, but he pumped it up as much as he could, with all the flourishes he could think of. He talked for five minutes.

Marion tilted her head doubtfully. "Anne B-Boleyn? You really think—"

"Of course I do."

"Anne Boleyn?" came an insinuating voice, and Louella popped out from behind an orange tree.

Marion turned to her. "Vinny thinks I ought to p-play Anne Boleyn."

Louella thrust a rubbery smile in Marion's face. "You'd be *won-* derful, dear!"

"W-would I?"

"You can play *anything!*"

Suddenly Marion laughed and clapped her hands: down the path Charlie Chaplin was hanging monkeylike from a tree branch, hooting and scratching. "Quack, quack!" Marion exclaimed, darting off to round up her other stray duckies.

Vinny started after her—he still hadn't gotten what he wanted— but Louella clamped his arm firmly in hers. Coyly she patted Vinny's hand. "You really think Anne Boleyn is right for Marion? Never mind." Her tongue flicked like a snake's. "What I *really* want to know about is your little friend, Pike, and I expect you to give me the exclusive scoop. Remember, Louella can do good things for you—or she can sink you like a rock, and no one will even notice the bubbles."

Twenty minutes later Marion's duckies emerged at the Neptune Pool. Its beauty was considerably diminished by the storm: rain swept in gusts over the oval expanse of water. But that hadn't deterred everyone. Wearing a baggy red swimsuit, Harpo lay on his back on a rubber raft, paddling about as his big cigar puffed smoke. A large striped umbrella protected the cigar from the rain.

Harpo bugged his eyes at them. "Choo-choo!"

"Oh, it's a s-swell party after all, it is!" Marion exclaimed.

Shivering with cold, Louella was in a snit. She had dug almost nothing out of Vinny about that horrible Pike, except that they had lived in the same orphanage in Chicago. Why had the dwarf snuck out at lunch, as if he did not want to meet Mr. Hearst? What was Vinny hiding? Glancing around, she saw that Vinny had slipped away, and her brow puckered. Where had he gone?

Well, I've got things to do, too, Louella thought.

All eyes were on Harpo, and the plump determined woman took the opportunity to creep off into the storm.

❧ 32 ❧

MARY O'Grady started. "You gave me a fright!"

"I said I'd be here." Pike had found her right where she had said she'd be, just off the billiard room in the out-of-the-way corridor leading to the movie theater. A terra-cotta madonna beamed from a niche above the console keyboard where the carillon bells were played. The dwarf smiled his sappiest smile up into Mary's homely freckled face. She was twisting her hands; that worried him. She's jumpy; don't let the dumb dame back out now.

Suddenly she bent and pecked his cheek. "Thank you, oh, thank you for last night!"

"I should thank *you*," Pike said.

161

"I just never . . . It was my first time, and—"

"Sure." He held her thin hand. "You still want to help me?"

"If you need me to. I *want* you to need me. And afterward?"

"We'll leave together. You and me, Mary."

"Oh, Otis! And it doesn't matter to me that you're— I mean—"

"Small? And my leg? And my foot?" Pike had to bite down hard to hold on to his smile. "Nice of you, Mary. You're a swell girl. Now just lead the way, like you said."

🙦 33 🙤

"I'LL b-be d-damned!" Hands on hips, Marion Davies gazed around the Neptune Pool in wide-eyed dismay. First Vinny, then Louella, and now Charlie Chaplin and Gloria Deere had vanished without saying boo. "Where're m-my duckies?"

"Here's one, quack, quack." Herman Mankiewicz sat with his legs dangling in the water, trousers rolled up. But he had neglected to take off either his gartered maroon socks or brown brogans, and both were now waterlogged. Rain dumped on him in buckets.

"You'll c-catch your *d-death!*" Marion exclaimed.

"Nope. I'm pickled." Loudly, tunelessly, he began humming "Little Annie Laurie" while Harpo choo-chooed past beneath his striped umbrella. Together they set up a howling discordant chorus.

"Capitalist decadence," Eddie muttered under his dripping yellow rain hat.

Marion made a face at him. She lifted her arms to the storm. "Capitalist fun, whee!" She thrust her face in his. "My other d-duckies've all r-run away; it's just you and m-me. Want to have a l-little f-fun?"

"You belong to Hearst. He owns you like everything else."

She shook her finger under his chin. "Mister, I own myself, so d-don't you d-dare—"

162

"I love you!" Eddie blurted. He hung his head.

"Well . . ." Marion said softly amid the crashing rain. She came so close that their hat brims touched. "P-poor kid. D-don't take things s-so s-seriously—ha! Who am I to talk? I t-take things seriously too. Maybe that's why we c-click. Just don't l-love me; it wouldn't work. Loving h-hurts. You're a R-Red, aren't you? Just l-love your idea, that's the t-ticket. Say, you r-really *are* a c-cute k-kid. I'm sure we've m-met before. She ran a finger slyly along his chin. "We c-could have our own f-fun, hm? A kiss, a cuddle? We w-wouldn't hurt anyone. I l-like who I l-like, and I m-make whoopie with whoever I want. You've gotta understand that."

Eddie stared at her helplessly. "You have so much . . . freedom."

"Freedom, ha! Women are n-never f-free. Not like men." She dragged him across the tiles to the edge of the terrace. "See all that? It's my prison. It's b-better than b-bars."

Eddie looked out, down. Storm-swept cliffs plunged, dissolved to hills, flattened to the gauzy coastal plain fronting the sea. He frowned. "Who's that?"

"Where?"

"There." Squinting, he pointed, but the tiny figure vanished into a eucalyptus grove. Eddie blinked the damp from his lashes. "I thought I saw a man. Coming uphill."

"In this weather? D-don't be s-silly." Marion hugged his arm. "W.R. owns all of it, all except that m-mountaintop way off there."

"You're wrong. I own the mountain too."

They turned. Wearing a tentlike yellow rain slicker and wide-brimmed rain hat, William Randolph Hearst stood framed by the Greco-Roman temple. Just behind him, in modest brown rainwear, stood a small, pinched-looking woman with a birdlike head and sharp amused eyes.

"Popsy!" Marion cried, unabashed. "This's Eddie, you m-met'm at l-lunch. Eddie, this's Julia M-Morgan, P-Popsy's architect. He tells her what to b-build, and she b-builds it."

"It's not quite as simple as that," the birdlike woman said in a voice like dust.

"I l-like to make them simple," Marion said.

"You sometimes complicate them unnecessarily," Hearst said, his eyes fixed belligerantly on Eddie.

Marion clucked her tongue. "Now, Popsy . . ." Rubbing against him, she pulled the yellow collar up around his chin. "D-don't want m-my old b-bear to c-catch c-cold." She tapped his nose. "What is b-bad m-man doing out in n-nasty old r-rain?"

"Looking at my property."

"Mr. Hearst is thinking of making some changes," Julia Morgan put in.

"Popsy's just n-never satisfied," Marion said to Eddie, who could not tear his eyes from the old man's brooding gaze.

Can I really shoot him?

Marion grabbed Eddie's arm. "Oh, you always want to w-work, work, work," she snapped at Hearst. "I'm going to t-take this innocent child right away before you r-ruin him. But you're to come in as s-soon as p-possible and have a n-nice warm b-bath. Bye!" Marion pulled Eddie from the terrace.

Hearst's eyes followed them; he saw Eddie glare back.

"That young man doesn't like you," Julia Morgan observed amid the hissing rain.

"But he likes her," Hearst grumbled, clenching his fists. "Damn it, who is he?"

❧ 34 ❧

"SO this is your little room," Charlie Chaplin said.

"For now," Gloria said, dimpling.

They grinned like mad. Thunder rolled outside Case del Monte. Simultaneously they pulled off their yellow slickers and dropped them where they stood. "Let's call it *our* room," Chaplin said, winking. "Now . . . does this little key lock this little door? Why, it does—splendid!" He began slipping off his trousers.

"Oh, Mr. Chaplin!" Gloria exclaimed.

"Call me Charlie."

"Oh, Charlie!"

Finishing with his pants, the comedian reached for his shorts. "The grand unveiling!" He jerked them down, and Gloria's mouth made an O: everything she had heard about the Tramp was true.

🎀 35 🎀

"T HIS way," Mary O'Grady said, creeping along a narrow deserted passage.

Following, Otis Pike barely saw Rembrant's glowing *Saint Luke*, the Gobelins tapestry, the angular Chinese bronze serving vessel on its pedestal. "No one will see us?" he asked.

"Don't even think it. Oh, it's just *terrible* what Mr. Hearst did to you, practically stealing your mother's heirlooms!"

"Terrible," Pike agreed, sticking to the maid's heels. For five minutes they had passed no one; Mary was leading the dwarf into a part of the house he had not seen. He had fed the gullible girl a line, and she had swallowed it whole. His dear old dad had been employed by Hearst, he had said. "Hearst worked him to death. We were very poor. My mother was forced to sell her valuable heirlooms at auction—it was awful. I cried and cried but Hearst didn't care; he just grabbed them up for a song. They can't mean much to him, but they have sentimental value for me. I only want what's mine."

"You mean to *steal* them?" Mary had gasped.

"Course not. I only want to know where they are—that's the first step. I hear Hearst keeps catalogues of everything: photographs, descriptions, locations. Can you—would you help me find those books?"

"I don't know," Mary had said, scraping her hands over her bony chest. "Mr. Hearst has been good to me, but . . . yes," she had finally agreed.

Dames, Pike thought as they crept along; they'd fall for anything. Mary halted by a Gothic-arched stone doorway in the rear of the north wing. A whispering silence surrounded them. "Has Hearst ever mentioned a woman named rose McGuffin?" Pike asked.

"I don't think so. Why?"

"Er, it's my mother's maiden name. This is it?"

"Near." Mary glanced up and down the corridor. "It's roundabout, but it's way off from the servants' wing, and no guests are staying in this part of the house." She pulled a key from the pocket of her white apron. "I had to steal this. Oh, just look, my hand is shaking!" She led the way through the door into a circular tower, and with softly scuffing sounds they started down cold gray stone steps. "There are six sets of stairs; these are the least used." Her whisper set up ghostly echoes in the deepening dark. When they reached the musty-smelling bottom, she used the key to open a heavy door faced with metal.

Chill air blew at them. "These are the vaults," Mary said.

❧ 36 ❧

"MR. Tashman?"

Vinny whirled. Hoping to get something on that little rat, Otis Pike, he had been stealing across Casa del Monte's east sitting room toward the dwarf's door. Now, awkwardly, he found himself staring into the doughy face of a tall, balding man dripping rain.

"I didn't mean to startle you," the man said.

"Uh, you didn't."

"No?" The man glanced at Pike's closed door. He wore round spectacles and carried a clipboard: Joe Willicombe, Hearst's private secretary.

Vinny shook the large, flat hand which Willicombe coolly held out. He licked dry lips. "Er, something wrong?"

"Not really. Do you mind?" Willicombe slipped off his raincoat and hung it on a peg. His glasses glinted. "You wrote a movie for Miss Davies once, didn't you? How's the screenwriting business?"

"Never better."

"Really? Nice to hear it." He gazed about as if he had never seen the room. "Let me come to the point. Your friend, Mr. Pike—we'd like to know more about him. For our records."

"Records?"

"Yes. Mr. Hearst is a newspaperman. It makes him happy to have the scoop on everyone."

Vinny flinched at the echo of Louella's words. He lit a cigarette but could not keep his fingers from shaking. "Why don't you ask Pike in person?'

"I can't seem to find him just now. You *will* cooperate, won't you? Especially considering that it was at your request he was invited?"

Vinny gulped. "Why not? Sure."

"Good." Smiling and settling firmly on the sofa, Willicombe poised a gold pen over his clipboard. "Oh, please sit too; this may take a little time. Now. You and Mr. Pike are dear old friends, right?"

37

PIKE sensed the whole massive bulk of Casa Grande above them, a crushing weight, and for a moment he felt suffocated. His breath fluttered; his leg punished him with pain. He hated cramped dark places, and in a panic he recalled how the bigger, stronger boys in the orphanage had once locked him in a closet for half a day. Even after they had let him out he screamed. He mopped his sweating brow.

"Are you all right?"

The dwarf managed a weak smile. "Never better." He looked about. The thought that Hearst's secret might be here lit a flame in him. Upstairs was spacious and richly furnished; here a maze of austere concrete corridors stretched into dimly lit distances. Ceiling-high shelves and packing crates loomed among the shadows. I was right to get help, Pike thought; those houseplans didn't show any of this.

"The catalogues?" he said to the skinny red-haired maid.

"This way."

She led him in a direction he thought was north but might be east, past crates and boxes piled high. No guards down here? Hearst must think it's safe. Pike shivered at the memory of that fat flunky, Willicombe, and his clipboard. Weaseled out of that by the skin of my teeth, the dwarf thought, but I've got to watch my step with the nosy secretary. That toy on Hearst's dresser, the glass globe with the snow inside. A memento? Of what? It's the best clue yet; it proves for sure I'm on to something. But Pike was annoyed with himself. Get the dust out of your eyes! Rose Ellen Forrest McGuffin and a dead father and a newsboy Hearst had given a toy to, and the same toy here—I ought to be figuring how they add up. Wiesbaden . . . Hearst admired Germany, he had visited Hitler this past summer. Was that it, some political scandal? The damn publisher was notorious for funny politics.

There was a scurrying sound, and Mary pressed back against him.

"It's just mice," he said as the squeaking creatures darted under a crate.

"I hate mice." Mary quavered. "Funny how Mr. Hearst likes them. He even made a pet of one for a while." She led on, pointing. "That direction's the wine cellar. And that way's the cold storage room. And that's the costume room—Mr. Hearst just loves costume parties. I've been down lots of times to bring things up; that's how I know the way." They had taken two—or was it three?—turns in the dimness. Pike tried to memorize each step. "I think this's it," Mary said at last.

"You don't know for sure?" He snatched her left arm.

Her amber eyes flickered. "You're hurting me."

"Damn it, I *need* you to know."

"Yes, this is it. See? There're the catalogues."

Pike looked through a rectangular opening into a room roughly twelve feet square lined with shelves holding hundreds of tall thick books. Releasing Mary, he rushed past her so fast that he almost tripped on his built-up heel. He grabbed an album at random and eagerly flipped pages. His heart sank. It was filled with pictures of ornately decorated Mexican saddles, along with lists: costs, sizes, weights, descriptions, purchase dates, numbers that corresponded to storage and display places in Los Angeles, New York, Saint Donat's Castle in Wales. Mexican saddles in Wales? Crazy. And useless. Pike jammed the book back and grabbed another. It was a catalogue of Afghan carpets. The next was Turkish carpets, the next Iraqui. The little man whirled on Mary. "The *family* picture albums," he demanded, "the *personal* albums? Where are they?"

"B-but you said . . . aren't—aren't these the ones you want?"

Pike stomped over and thrust his face up into hers. "Don't ask questions," he spat. "I said, where are Hearst's personal albums?" For a moment desperation ignited the flashes of light in the dwarf's brain, and he had to force himself to take three deep breaths. "I mean, Mary," he said in a forced, low growl, "I just want to look at them a little. While I'm here."

"But . . . I have to be back upstairs soon, and—"

"Just for a moment, Mary!"

She gaped at his outburst. "I'll show you," she said.

Pike followed her skinny hips and the frizz of reddish hair. Stupid dame! he thought. She led him to the next room, much like the previous one: shelves of volumes. He snatched one up; these were full of photographs of people and places. There had to be thousands, maybe a million pictures here, and Pike crowed silently in triumph. Hearst takes his pictures, I take mine—but mine will finish off the old bastard! He darted a glance at Mary who stood bewildered and scared in the doorway. If I have to use the camera in my heel, what'll I tell her?

But Mary counted for nothing now; he could handle her.

Feverishly he began sorting through the albums. Five minutes passed. Ten.

"Otis, shouldn't we—"

"Shut up!"

The soft, rapid tick of pages continued. Moaning, Mary O'Grady pressed white knuckles to her mouth.

❧ 38 ❧

"THANK you, Mr. Tashman." Joe Willicombe rose from the sofa opposite Vinny. "From an orphanage in Chicago you have become a successful screenwriter, and Mr. Otis Pike has become a successful insurance salesman. Mr. Hearst will be glad to hear it. A tribute to America, how a man can pull himself up from nothing."

"Hearst didn't pull himself up from nothing, did he?" Vinny asked standing.

Willicombe smiled coolly. "He *did* have some advantages."

"Like a father who gave him a newspaper."

"It's a tribute to Mr. Hearst that he's made the most of what he was given." Willicombe shrugged into his raincoat. "I confess I'm a little disappointed. For a friend, you don't know much about Mr. Pike. Not even the insurance company he works for."

"He must've told me, but I forgot. We haven't seen one another in years."

"He just turned up?"

"Like I told you."

"And you asked Miss Davies to invite him. Was that your idea or his?"

"I can't quite remember."

Willicombe made a regretful little twitch of hands. "Well, perhaps Mr. Pike will. By the way, his leg—how did that happen?"

"It was like that in the orphanage. We never knew."

170

"Mm." Willicombe turned to go.

"Wait." Vinny crushed out his cigarette. Should I do this, take the chance? He felt desperate. "You've been asking questions. I have one. I sent a letter to your boss a few days ago, about a screenplay I wrote for Marion." He took a step forward. "Do you know if he got it, if he's read it?"

"A letter? No, but—" Willicombe regarded Vinny for a moment, his bland smile wavering. The smile gelled. "I'll be glad to look into it for you. Let's help one another, shall we? If you recall anything more about your old friend, or learn anything"—the secretary bobbed his head at Pike's closed bedroom door—"you *will* tell me, won't you?" His glasses glinted.

Vinny swallowed hard. "I'll be sure to."

A nod. "Then we understand one another." Willicombe stepped out into the hiss of rain and Vinny shut the door behind him. He shuddered. What the hell? Grabbing another cigarette from a fancy cloisonné box, he furiously lit up. I could have told him Pike's real name, but—Vinny's thin lips twisted beneath the William Powell mustache—maybe that's my ace in the hole. He narrowed his eyes at the dwarf's door. Willicombe wants help, does he?

Pausing only an instant, Vinny Tashman hurried to Otis Pike's room.

❧ 39 ❧

IN deep thought, Willicombe splashed across Casa del Monte's courtyard, Casa Grande looming above him veiled in long sweeps of rain. Something is very wrong, Willicombe thought—and stopped dead. He started up again right away, hoping the person in the yellow slicker whom he had glimpsed watching among rhododendron bushes had not noticed his hesitation. The person

171

had been furtive, ducking quickly out of sight, obviously not wanting to be seen. Willicombe cursed the voluminous yellow coats and broad-brimmed hats that made everyone look alike.

Who is spying? Willicombe wondered.

And on whom?

❧ **40** ❧

"O-O-OH, Charlie . . ." Gloria moaned.

Suddenly her body jerked, and she half sat up. "What's wrong?"

"I thought I saw a face. At that window."

Chaplin glanced out too, but saw only whipping branches and gray sheets of rain. "Not to worry if we have an audience," he murmured soothingly. "You're giving a ripping performance!"

Gloria giggled as she sank back on very rumpled sheets. "I really did think I saw somebody. In a yellow rain hat."

"Who?"

"Dunno." Her frown dissolved to a coy smile, and she locked her fingers in his thick hair. "Maybe I'm just crazy—crazy over you."

"This will make you crazier."

"O-oh, yes!" the dimpled brunette cried.

O TIS Pike fidgeted and cursed. Photographs, photographs, and more photographs, in hundreds of albums. The albums had dates on the spines, but so what? It would take days to go through every page of every one. Mary O'Grady snuffled in the doorway, as, kneeling on cold stone in the creaking silence beneath Casa Grande, the little man scrambled through William Randolph Hearst's long life. He could only take samples for now, an album here, an album there. Recent pictures showed European trips with Marion Davies and gay weekend parties at San Simeon, famous people dressed as cowboys and clowns and acrobats. There were also pictures of Hearst's wife and five sons. Older albums showed Hearst before he was married, wearing loud checked suits and looking like a monkey in spite of all his dough. Frustration nipped at Pike, but he began to get glimmers, a prickling at the back of his neck: there was something here. He turned to older albums, the 1870s. Hearst was a kid of twelve in Europe with his mother, holding up collections of the junk he had bought, the start of his greedy career. Later, in an auction, he had grabbed up two toys glass globes with little Alpine villages and snow inside from Wiesbaden, were there pictures somewhere of Wiesbaden? Further back, the 1860s albums displayed Hearst as a spoiled brat in Little Lord Fauntleroy duds showing off his puppets, sledding in the snow, cuddling on his mama's lap. Then he was a baby. Then he wasn't even born, and rich, bearded George Hearst in a stiff collar and Phoebe Apperson Hearst in a stiff black gown stared out from their wedding picture as if they thought life was easy street.

Pike slammed the album shut. At least Hearst had a father and mother to bring him up, the son of a bitch.

He peered at his watch. Four P.M. Got to come back later. The dwarf glanced past Mary. In the room on the other side of the corridor a polka dot rocking horse grinned at him. "Please, Otis," Mary whimpered among the shadows, but he brushed past her into the other room. It was larger, furnished with the kind of junk people kept in attics. As well as the wooden horse there were a puppet theater with a dusty Punch draped like a dead man over the proscenium, and a sled with one runner missing. Didn't Hearst ever throw anything away? Pike's eyes darted quickly along shelves: a stuffed alligator, a big white chamber pot, a photograph of a woman. The picture was brown and faded, but it had a fancy frame. The little man picked it up. All the other pictures are in albums; how come this one isn't? His game leg throbbed as he examined the young, pretty face. Her lips were curled in a shy smile, and memory nudged him; he seemed to hear echoes, a voice.

He turned the picture over.

On the back in a looping, feminine hand was written, *For Billy, from your sweetie. Love.*

Billy . . . William. William Randolph Hearst.

Pike turned to Mary, who watched out of scared, blinking eyes. He showed her the picture. "Who's this?" he asked.

"I don't know. Please, let's go."

"Keep quiet; lemme think." Pike kept hearing the soft, tantalizing echoes. How old was the picture? The dame's hair was in a Gibson girl style. One of Hearst's kept women, before his wife? before Marion Davies? An idea ate at him. *Your sweetie.* Tugging at a tuft of whitish hair, Pike thought about Rose Ellen Forrest, dead, whose identity had been stolen. To cover something up?

Murder?

The dwarf's hand tightened on the frame. Was this Rose Ellen Forrest? Had Hearst murdered this former girlfriend in a fit of jealousy? Hold it, slow down, the little man warned himself. If that was true, why would he leave her picture sitting around? But it wasn't sitting around. It was hidden down here where only Hearst would pay attention to it, where only he would remember. Pike felt himself on shaky ground. There was still lots to explain, but he clung to his idea. For one thing, it fit the bastard: Hearst's rages were famous—that Thomas Ince story . . . For another, murder was a secret

174

worth hiding; murder could ruin a man. Pike leered; he felt close to bedrock truth, ugly, bloody; it would make Hearst squirm, all right, and he imagined it in big black headlines across the front pages of Bart Rawlston's newspapers: MURDERER HEARST. It would be bigger than the Fatty Arbuckle scandal, the Lindbergh kidnapping; it would finish the old bastard, all right.

Pike narrowed his eyes at Mary. "Is Hearst the jealous type?"

"He's kicked men out for flirting with Miss Davies. He has a gun."

"A gun?"

"I've seen it. Everybody knows he has an awful temper. All the servants."

"They'd swear before a judge?" The little man laughed. "You'd swear too, wouldn't you?" Pike's mind raced: Harry McGuffin, who had died falling off a train—murder too?

But he knew he was going too fast; there was no real proof. The woman in this picture might be nobody, and Harry McGuffin might have just fallen off that train.

But Harry McGuffin had been trying to organize Hearst's reporters. He was pushed, damn it, by some thug paid by Hearst!

Pike tore the picture from the frame and tucked it inside his jacket. What was its connection with the glass globe?

"But that's Mr. Hearst's," Mary protested.

"He took things from me; I can take things from him." Pike stepped near her; his leg didn't ache anymore. "I wouldn't tell anyone we were down here if I were you. You're an accomplice now."

"Accom—" Her eyes spilled tears. "You don't l-love me, do you?" she wailed.

"Love?" Pike laughed again. Another mouse scurried across the floor. The dwarf grabbed Mary's freckled arm. "Let's get the hell out of here."

❦ 42 ❧

LIGHTNING crackled, and Vinny Tashman jumped. Jesus! he thought, gaping out Otis Pike's bedroom window. Under the gloom of the lowering clouds the flash had been visible even in daylight, and thunder tumbled on its heels. Vinny peered at his watch: it was after four. Where's the damn dwarf? Back soon?

Got to do this quick, he thought; got to find out what the son of a bitch is up to.

The bedrooms in Casa del Monte locked from the inside but not the outside, probably so maids could work easily when the guests were away at play. Vinny didn't care about the reason; he was just glad sneaking in had only been a matter of opening the door. There was not much in the closet: two miniature suits that looked like they belonged to a kid; the white fedora on a hook; four shirts; two pairs of shoes, one brown and one black, both with a four-inch built-up left heel. Pathetic. I shouldn't have picked on him in that orphanage, Vinny thought. Hell, I was a kid; I didn't know any better. Pike hadn't forgotten any of it though, and that made him dangerous. He was not the forgiving type.

But what's he got against Hearst?

Vinny didn't find anything in the suit pockets. He hurried to the dresser. His worst fear was that Pike would do something to queer his chances with the publisher. I've gotta head that off! Pausing, he pictured his target pistols in their velvet-lined case. Use them? He scraped at his jaw. Maybe, damn it, just maybe—if it comes to saving my skin.

Christ, I need a drink!

There was not much in the dresser. Some underwear, socks, a belt. Dark green suspenders. Three handkerchiefs, no monogram. Two pair of cheap brass cuff links. Nothing to breathe a clue.

176

Vinny did not know what he was looking for, that was the problem. Something about Chicago?

He crossed the red-figured oriental carpet to the carved Florentine bed; he knelt and peered under the bed.

He almost did not see it; then he glimpsed something: a small flat briefcase wedged up under the springs. A tug dislodged it, and with a glance at the door and a prayer he tried the catch. Locked, damn it. Insurance papers for Pike's so-called salesman's job? Not likely. Vinny felt gleeful. Gotcha, little man! he thought, glancing about. Metal edging lined a marble-topped nightstand, and he lifted the case, swung, and smashed the catch against the metal. It tore completely off, and the case sprang open, spewing papers.

Vinny tossed the case aside. Scooping up the papers, he dumped them onto the brocade bedspread and began scrambling through them. Most were big folded blueprints of the hill: Casa Grande and the three guesthouses, all with official county stamps. Vinny was more bewildered than ever. Pike had done careful homework. Why?

At the edges of the maps were little doodles, all the same: airy little explosions of pencil lines. Funny what you remember, Vinny thought, flinching at another flicker of lightning. Pike did doodles just like this when he was a kid.

There were letters too, in a packet held by a rubber band. Vinny scanned them. They were all signed B.R., reports on people he didn't know: a Harry and Rose McGuffin and their son Eddie, and Rose Ellen Forrest who had died of flu at twenty-two. Vinny frowned; he ran his fingers through his wavy hair. There were birth certificates for the McGuffin family, and Rose Ellen Forrest seemed to be Rose McGuffin, but that did not make sense, because she had given birth to the kid when she was thirty-four, but she had died when she was twenty-two.

Vinny chewed his lip. Was Pike some sort of detective? What did the McGuffins have to do with William Randolph Hearst?

There were photographs too, of the inside of a big house. Whose? Where? No clue. They showed rooms and closets and open drawers, a half finished jigsaw puzzle on a dining room table. An anxious-looking older woman appeared in some of them, but only at the edges, like she had been snapped accidentally. Accidentally on purpose? Three photos showed a mantel, on it one of those glass globes with a little scene inside, along with a picture of Hearst next to some boys and a cake. The bottom photo showed a bare-looking room containing hardly more than a bed and a dresser with a few books on it. Vinny peered closely. *Das Kapital* was one of the titles, and Gloria Deere's sap of a brother sprang immediately to mind. Eddie Deere's room? Vinny softly cursed. What the hell's Pike's game?

Lightning crackled even nearer, and he quickly stuffed everything back in the briefcase, shut it and tucked it under the bed. He took a last fast glance around but did not see the face framed by a yellow rain hat that ducked out of sight at the window.

Pike'll know someone's been here; just don't let him know it was me.

Feeling stymied but with plenty to think about, Vinny darted from the room.

❧ 43 ❧

LOUELLA'S yellow slicker dripped water on the Tabriz carpet of Eddie Deere's room. Louella had no intention of staying long, so she did not take the raincoat off. She had meant to peek into Otis Pike's room, but it had been occupied—and not by Pike. Louella's lipsticked mouth flattened in frustration. What was Vinny Tashman up to? It was a laugh that he wanted to peddle a screenplay to Mr. Hearst. Anne Boleyn? Louella snorted. Marion was more the chambermaid type. But was that all? If Vinny was Pike's friend, why had he been pawing through his things? Louella longed to get a peek at the papers in the dwarf's briefcase. Maybe later, she thought. For now: Eddie Deere.

Brazenly she marched to his dresser. Two books sat on top, bolshie books in plain sight. He's a Red and doesn't even hide it.

What nerve! Louella jerked open the top dresser drawer. Nothing but a dog-eared photograph of a middle-aged man standing by some sort of printing machines. The man held a newspaper: the Chicago *Evening American*. He worked for the Chief? In Chicago? So did I. Louella wondered if she might've run across the man. What was he to Eddie Deere? A relative? The photograph was fuzzy; Louella couldn't see any resemblance.

She put the photograph back and opened the second drawer. Letters lay in a bundle. Private, Louella thought, and grinned. That won't stop *me*. Her red-painted nails snatched the envelopes. They all had Chicago postmarks. Her brow bunched: Vinny and Otis Pike and Eddie Deere, all from Chicago. Did it mean anything? She emitted a little whistle as her eyes focused on the name on the letters: Eddie McGuffin, not Eddie Deere; the lines furrowing her brow deepened. Deere might be a movie name Gloria had adopted, but why would her brother use it too?

Louella tapped the letters.

Maybe he's not her brother.

She sniffed. That idea didn't help; it still didn't make sense for him to take Gloria's movie name—unless he had something to hide.

Her fingers itched for her notepad. She opened the top letter. It was from a man named Swann. He had a tight, curly signature like a pig's tail, but that was all she had time to see. A muffled sound made her jump; someone was in the sitting room.

Eddie returning?

In a panic Louella tossed the letters back in the drawer and trotted to the window. Frantically she wound the brass handle and chambered up onto a chair. She launched herself out. Omigod! she thought as she sailed into rain and sticky mud.

❧ 44 ❧

I T was getting dark. Already the lamps on the heads of the statues that sprouted everywhere in the gardens like enormous mushrooms were glowing in the rain. The statues' eyes seemed to peer accusingly, and Otis Pike did not like that.

Will Mary O'Grady keep her mouth shut? She better.

Crossing Casa del Monte's courtyard, the dwarf glimpsed a flicker of bright color and turned in time to see a squat figure in a yellow slicker stagger down some steps and carom off a huge marble urn. The figure vanished in the brownish, rain-swept dusk. Somebody's in a hurry, Pike thought, narrowing his eyes at Eddie Deere's half open window. Who?

The faded old photograph was protected from the rain under the dwarf's own yellow slicker.

He entered the east wing of Casa del Monte.

❧ 45 ❧

E DDIE stepped into his room. He had glimpsed Pike stumping along behind him from the direction of the big main house. Following me? But Eddie was too full of Marion to pay attention to that. He and the soft, dimpled blonde had huddled together in that little hidden gazebo for an hour, watching the storm lash the hills, watching the lightning march closer but feeling safe, protected from the world and prying eyes. They had held hands;

180

they had talked. Marion had poured out her heart, and Eddie had longed to pour out his—but how could he tell her what he planned? He wrung his hands. Alone—I've got to do it alone!

The old shaking overwhelmed him, and he sank onto the huge antique bed, rocking and moaning. He loved her, yes. How had it happened? She was a star, famous, a pampered doll; she was not a proletarian girl, not the kind he should want. He should hate her, but he couldn't; what would his feeling do to his plans? I've got to finish what I came for! For myself! For the country! For struggling people everywhere!

He noticed the water spots on the carpet. His startled blue eyes followed their trail to the open dresser drawer.

Then he saw the open window.

Rushing to the dresser, he discovered his letters loose in the second drawer. Strangled with terror, he dashed to see if his pistol was safe under the mattress.

46

AS he entered the east sitting room Pike heard the click of Vinny Tashmar's door. What's the mug up to? He better keep his yap shut too.

Pike went into his room.

He knew at once that something was wrong; he smelled it in the air. Pike went to the bed. Kneeling, he pulled the briefcase from its hiding place.

It fell open. The lock was smashed, the papers in a mess, and the little man's face became a rigid, icy mask. He sniffed, recognizing a sweetish odor—Vinny's fancy French after-shave—and his mouth twisted into a snarl. Vinny stuck his nose in? In spite of what I said?

Fury exploded in the dwarf. The bastard'll be sorry!

❧ 47 ❧

E VENING crept on. The storm continued to pelt the terraces, the guesthouses, Casa Grande's looming white facade. It smashed against the palms and oaks and cypresses, bending strong branches, while guests huddled in their rooms or played cards or fussed at the big jigsaw puzzle in the Assembly Hall. In the zoo the animals moved restlessly. The baboons were wilder than ever, and the elephant trumpeted long mournful blasts.

An angry man from Oklahoma struggled uphill.

Ambrose the mouse dug deeper, undermining the road.

❧ 48 ❧

M ARION Davies headed from the elevator toward her third-floor room in the Gothic Suite. All at once a lean, florid-faced man came barreling out of Popsy's study: John Francis Neylan.

"Pigheaded bastard!" he muttered.

"I'll b-be glad to t-tell'm you think so," Marion said.

Neylan met her mocking gaze. "Stay out of this," he snapped, brushing past into the elevator.

"Don't stop till you r-reach hell," Marion shot after him as the doors slid shut. She laughed; she always liked to give Popsy's smartass lawyer what for. In her bedroom she shut her curtains against the dismal afternoon. Popsy didn't hear me come in—good.

I'm in no mood to get chewed out. He gave Eddie the bad eye out by the pool; now he'll be in one of his jealous snits for days. Just let him try something, I'll let him have it. Marry me, you old fart, or lemme do what I want!

Marion wrinkled her nose at her room. Goddamn antiques! I'd like something modern for a change, not all this dead stuff. Slipping out of her blouse, she kicked her slacks across the floor. She examined herself in the long oval mirror. I can't help liking good-looking guys, especially Eddie. There's something about him that . . . But she couldn't figure out what. Blowing a curl off her brow, she unfastened her bra and stepped out of her silk panties. She stroked her hips, her breasts. Not bad. Sagging a bit? Not yet, but I won't see twenty-nine again, and how much longer will the young guys want me? The idea of growing old made her afraid. She bit her knuckles. Oh, to hell with this storm!

Rushing into her white marble bathroom, she jerked the Booth's gin from its hiding place in the toilet tank.

Tilting her head back, she swigged long burning gulps straight from the bottle.

❧ 49 ❧

JOE Willicombe stared glumly at the bank of phones in his office. He had worked fast—or, rather, the Hearst research department had—and come up with almost nothing. No Otis Pike had lived in the Illinois Home for Little Wayfarers twenty years ago. Not ever. Vinny Tashman was on the list—Vincent P. Tashman, not Vincent X. He had entered at age two and left at fourteen; but no Otis Pike. Massaging his aching brow—it had been a long day—Willicombe ran his eyes down the roll call of names the Chicago bureau had wired. Little Jacks and Bobbies and Sams, lost boys.

Willicombe had to feel sorry for them. How come no relative or samaritan had ever claimed them?

The secretary adjusted his round glasses. He reread the list. There was no Otis Pike, but something he could not quite put his finger on rang a bell.

❧ 50 ❧

IN the study in the Gothic Suite William Randolph Hearst paced under vaulted wooden arches. That son-of-a-bitch lawyer, Neylan! They had wound up their so-called business meeting yelling—he had actually kicked Neylan out—but he knew he had to face it. I'm in big financial trouble. Can't buy any more art? Might even have to sell Saint Donat's?

No!

And then there was Marion and that young whippersnapper Eddie.

And those damn warning notes with the queer little doodles.

It was turning into a helluva weekend. Hearst stared out the window, but all he saw was a drowned, cheerless dusk. Lightning flickered jaggedly and he shuddered, feeling every bit of seventy. The dusk was like death coming on, lifting over him like black wings, suffocating.

He pounded the long central table. Don't let me die before my time! Don't take the things I love!

The old man's fingers curled and uncurled at his sides as he entertained murderous thoughts.

The baboons gibbered like banshees in the zoo. Rain hissed. Six P.M. on Hearst's enchanted hill, with evening and night to come.

V

Death in the Night

❧ 1 ❧

ETTA Kitt was back at the switchboard after only a two-hour break. The communications office was usually staffed in three eight-hour shifts but one of the girls was down with the monthlies, and Etta had jumped at the chance to fill in. Ordinarily a double shift would have made her spit, but not on a party night. Etta liked to be in on the high jinks at Mr. Hearst's.

Switching off the light, she settled back. She knew the switchboard by feel, and the darkness gave her an advantage: she had a clear view up two long flights of red tile steps to the broad terrace that fronted Casa Grande. People going in and out of the big house, people sneaking from guesthouse to guesthouse—most of them would have to cross her line of sight. She grinned in the dark. I'll write my memoirs for sure some day, and will I put the big shots on the hot seat!

Lighting a cigarette, she thought idly about that funny call for help this morning.

Just as idly she dismissed it.

❧ 2 ❧

I N his bedroom in Casa del Monte Eddie McGuffin's hands shook as he fumbled with the black and white striped tie he had bought just a few days ago. At last he strangled it into a lumpy knot. Staring at himself in the mirror, he hardly recognized the gaunt, scared face under the mop of brown hair. His Adam's apple wouldn't stop jumping, and he saw a kid, not a man—a kid William Randolph Hearst had handed a toy for being a good little capitalist, damn him!

Who snuck into my room? Who went through my things?

Eddie shrugged into his cheap blue Sears Roebuck suit coat. Somebody's on to me; so what. I'm ready, I've got a gun.

The Colt lay right in front of him on the polished wood of the dresser, small, snub-nosed, ugly. Eddie snatched it, and jamming it into his inside breast pocket above his heart, he arranged a handkerchief in the outside pocket over the bulge. He examined the effect. If anybody notices, if anybody tries to mess with me, I'll just shoot it out. He laughed hysterically as a *whoosh* of rain beat at his window. Dillinger, Baby-Face Nelson. I'm an outlaw too; I fight capitalism. At the thought Eddie seemed to hear gunfire, and a smile tightened his lips. Death. The idea called to him and he closed his eyes and swayed, and for a moment death's voice was Marion's, soft, sweet, beckoning him to make love, to lose himself in her arms. "Yes . . ." he murmured, "yes . . ." But his eyes popped open on reality. Thunder rolled in a big slow wave over the hill. Got to kill a man, he thought; I'm nothing if I don't.

Eddie hurried out to the sitting room to escort his "sister" to dinner.

3

GLORIA was ecstatic. Standing before the gold-rimmed mirror in her bathroom, she hummed as she added the last touches to her short brunette curls. She tilted her head. A Joan Crawford look, would Charlie like that? Pleased with her baby blue gown, even more pleased with her passionate afternoon and the glamorous night to come, she slipped into a long coat to protect the gown from the rain and snatched up the little black sequined clutch containing comb and makeup.

In the sitting room Eddie was waiting, pacing like a cat and looking as sour as ever. Gloria made a face. I just can't let him spoil things! She started across the room to give him a piece of her mind, but at that moment Vinny Tashman dashed in out of the rain wearing a trim black tuxedo. He offered his arm. "May I have the pleasure?"

"Uh . . . you don't mind?" Gloria said to Eddie, almost hoping he would punch Vinny and they would have a big brawl and she would be rid of them both.

"Why should I?" Eddie kept his hands jammed in his pockets. "It's a free country."

"You're not free to go to dinner looking like that." Vinny went over to him. "Here, let me fix that awful tie." Before Eddie could protest, deft fingers were adjusting and patting the lumpy knot into submission. But Vinny was not thinking about ties. The kid's got a helluva funny bulge in that cheap jacket. Finishing with the tie, Vinny let his right hand tap the breast pocket that Eddie had crammed with the handkerchief. I'll be damned! "That's better," Vinny said, forcing a sleek grin as he turned to Gloria, but he was shaken. The kid's packing a gun? "Shall we go?" She nodded, not

189

very enthusiastically, and they fit themselves under one of the big black umbrellas and ducked out into the wet.

Eddie's eyes narrowed. Was it that joker Tashman who went through my room? Gloria? Under his own umbrella he trudged out after them.

❧ 4 ❧

NEEDLES of rain hissed through the trees, and wind moaned a frigid ostinato. Tugging thoughtfully at an earlobe, the dwarf stood hidden in the east entrance of Casa del Monte, watching the trio scurry up the puddled terraces toward the big house blazing with lights. You didn't wait for poor little Otis Pike? Pike sneered. Hell, I'm used to getting left behind; I can take care of myself.

Grabbing up an umbrella from the stand by the door, he ducked into the storm. He wore the black shoes with the miniature camera in the built-up heel. In his breast pocket was a small flash kit, just in case. He had chosen his darkest suit deliberately: it would hide him in the night.

His leg ached, but that was nothing. Purposefully the little man climbed the terraces to the lair of his enemy.

5

T HEY were all there in the vast Assembly Hall, glittering
under its antique carved ceiling: Dick Powell, Jean Harlow,
Gloria Swanson, Basil Rathbone, Joel McCrea, Carole
Lombard, Bette Davis, Clark Gable, Harpo, Leslie Howard, Charlie
Chaplin, Cary Grant, Louella Parsons on the arm of pipe-smoking
Docky. Adolphe Menjou wore a red carnation and spats. Marie
Dressler trundled about in something like a Bedouin's tent. Arthur
Brisbane made lofty pronouncements on life, while the writers Adela
Rogers St. Johns and Damon Runyon and Herman Mankiewicz
cracked dipsomaniac jokes. Walter Winchell and the dour Chicago
editor, Walter Howey, argued in a corner, but almost everyone else
appeared in high spirits. Wonder of wonders, Mr. Hearst allowed
cocktails before dinner; he even supplied the booze! Two butlers
were working overtime mixing drinks at a gleaming bar cart, while
the women in their long silken gowns and the men in suits and
tuxedoes reveled in the privilege of being rich and famous in the
most rich and famous grand house in America. It was like a movie set
for an all-star extravaganza. The storm crashed outside, but the show
went on, the huge fireplace blazing with flames. Carole Lombard
smiled her slow, sexy smile at Clark Gable. Dick Powell plopped
himself down at the Steinway and began warbling "We're in the
Money." Louella spewed compliments like a geyser: "So lovely
. . . so pretty . . . my, my!" Tucked into a huge red leather
grandfather chair, tiny Julia Morgan sipped sherry and watched out
of eyes as dry as desert air. Charlie Chaplin did a Rudolph Valentino
imitation. Hedda Hopper tried to disapprove: "Valentino's dead!
You're just awful!" but she laughed her head off anyway.

"Don't you just *love* it?" Gloria trilled to Vinny as they relinquished their umbrella to the butler in the entranceway and were swept into the gaiety.

"Right out of De Mille," Vinny muttered from the corner of his mouth. "Bring on the Egyptians."

But not everyone was loving it. At the far end of the long room Mary O'Grady stood stiff as a stick by the silver hors d'oeuvres platters. Ashen under her freckles, she twisted her hands. Mr. Pike . . . could she face him? If he so much as glanced her way, she would just die!

Should I tell Mr. Hearst what he got me to do? But then I'll lose the only job I've ever had!

Joe Willicombe stood not far from her, squirming with his own nasty dilemma. Tip my hand? Confront the damn dwarf and ask him who the hell he is? The bellicose lawyer Jack Neylan was not making things easier. He had cornered Willicombe and was putting on the pressure. "We'll *all* go under if W.R. doesn't pull in the reins," Neylan insisted in his peppery brogue, poking Willicombe's chest. "He's got to stop spending like a kid. This depression'll sink him like the *Lusitania!*"

❧ 6 ❧

TWO more people were not enjoying themselves, although faint sounds of the gaiety drifted up the front of Casa Grande though sheeting rain and into their third-story windows: host and hostess, Hearst and Marion Davies.

Marion was charging about, waving her arms. "He's just a k-kid, a harmless k-kid. Whattaya wanta d-do, set your d-damn d-detectives on him? So what if he's a l-little funny? He's unhappy, that's wh-why, and there's more'n one person around here that's n-not too happy herself, so lay off."

Hearst stood glumly in his huge dark suit, his pouchy eyes following her. "You feel sorry for him?" he asked.

"Course I d-do."

"You don't . . . love him?" He could hardly get out the words.

Marion wore a clinging white evening dress. Stopping abruptly, she jammed her hands on her hips. "I l-like him, and who I l-like's m-my b-business. You want to tell me what p-parts I can p-play, and you wanta tell me who to h-hang around with too. Well, I won't p-put up with it. In fact, I think I'm g-gonna p-play Anne Boleyn, and I d-don't give a sh-shit if you l-like it or not. Vinny Tashman has a script for me, a g-good one, and—"

"Tashman? Metro fired him."

"S-so what?"

"He punched a director."

"That just shows he's a m-man."

"I won't hire him, Marion."

"Oh, yeah?" She came close, and he could smell the liquor on her breath. "Well, I have p-plenty of money of my own, and m-maybe I'll hire him myself. How d'you l-like that, Mr. Big Shot?"

"I don't like it one bit."

Her grin glowed incandescent with triumph. "Know what?" She shook her finger under his nose. "I don't g-give a d-damn. Now"—she flounced to the door—"I'm g-gonna go down and have a g-good time, and you just b-better not make a scene, old Droopy Drawers!"

She slammed out. Hearst wanted to rush after her in spite of the insults, the infidelities, but he made himself stand where he was, rooted in pain in the middle of the luxurious sitting room that separated their bedrooms, alone except for Helena, who whined at his heels. Lightning spurted outside. "Good dog, faithful dog." The bulky old man bent to pat her but, wheezing, he had a hard time getting up and had to lean on a chair, his ticker fluttering in his chest. Marion's fault? He moaned with fury. I spoiled her and made her a star, and she torments me for thanks!

The fury sank to self-pity. I even created a movie company, Cosmopolitan Pictures, all for her, but she doesn't appreciate the toy. Toys.

The old man frowned. Was there someone somewhere who appreciated what he had so freely given?

All at once the threatening notes with their odd little symbol leapt into his mind, and for an instant he seemed to grasp what the feathery asterisk of pencil lines meant before the idea bled into the jumble of his past.

William Randolph Hearst drew his sloping shoulders up as far as he could and headed down to face his guests.

7

MARION pranced into the Assembly Hall, her eyes glittering with the glazed brightness of half a bottle of Booth's gin. She flew from person to person, hugging the women and pecking the cheeks of the men. "Oh, my, aren't w-we d-dandy!" she cooed, sniffing Adolphe Menjou's red carnation before hurtling off.

"You look just *lovely!*" Louella gushed as Marion paused in flight. "But where's W.R.?"

"Oh, the old p-poop is in one of his m-moods! But he'll b-be down. What happened to your ch-cheek?"

Louella touched the scratches she had gotten leaping out the window of Casa del Monte. She gave a crooked smile. "Silly me, I bumped into a tree."

"B-bad tree. Les-ums!" Marion hugged Leslie Howard, then flitted to Cary Grant.

Watching her wobbling progression, Louella clucked her tongue to Docky. "Tipsy again! That girl's going to *ruin* the wonderful career Mr. Hearst has worked so hard to give her."

Docky's bland gaze stayed fixed longingly on the card tables. "Hm?" he said, puffing pipe smoke.

Louella poked his arm. "You old silly!" Her shrewd eyes fastened on Vinny Tashman. She had seen him escort Gloria Deere in. Tomcat! Her face got a pinched, sly look. Wonder what he'd say if I

194

told him I saw him going through his so-called friend's suitcase this afternoon? Look at him give the Deere girl the eye, but she only has eyes for Charlie Chaplin. Louella smiled nastily. Want to know, Vinny, what those two were up to under the sheets about three? Her smile smoked with vitriol. Damn it, she thought, I'll never get to print a word!

And then there was a little pause of anticipation as the hands of half a dozen antique clocks reached seven-thirty at precisely the same instant, and soft bongs filled the room.

William Randolph Hearst emerged from his secret door.

Conversation ceased; all eyes turned toward him, the snap of logs in the huge fireplace punctuating the moment. The jacket of his dark suit was like a tent. His long jowly head looked more ponderously prehistoric, more gray, more formidable, somehow sadder than ever. His fingers fidgeted at his sides as his cold blue gaze flicked about the room until it found Marion. Tossing her head, she turned away, and the old man shuddered. The room itself seemed to shudder. A moment passed; two. Someone coughed and a log spat sparks. At last a forced smile split the old man's face, and his teeth gleamed wolfishly. Waving a sour, grudging salute, he stepped heavily forward and pumped Arthur Brisbane's hand, and a gust of relief swept the Assembly Hall. Talk and laughter burst out like gunfire. Butlers' swizzle sticks clinked in cocktail glasses.

Poor W.R.! Louella thought.

Next to Gloria, Vinny scowled at Hearst. Has the old bastard already decided my fate?

Standing by the big black Steinway, his game leg throbbing, pale, seething little Otis Pike longed for the last piece of the puzzle that would make all the other pieces fit, damning William Randolph Hearst to hell.

Eddie McGuffin hugged the edge of the room, away from people. He felt lost and jittery, aching to have his task over, longing for gunfire and death to sweep it all into history. Through blazing eyes he watched Hearst trundle like a pachyderm about the room, lifting his arm like a wrinkled trunk to shake his guests' hands. Eddie was dazzled by the silken gowns and jewels; infuriated too. These people are useless! he thought. Poor starving folks could live for months for

195

what the swells pay to hang on their backs—and all these statues and paintings. Hearst is the worst of them. Now? A roaring filled his ears, and he clutched his breast pocket. Urgency screamed in his brain, and his trembling fingers itched to snatch the gun from his breast pocket and spray the room with blood.

Vinny saw Eddie's hand fumble at the pocket. Holy Christ! he thought taking three quick steps. "Have a drink, pal," he murmured, grabbing Eddie's elbow and twisting him around.

"Get your hands off me!" Eddie snapped.

"Whoa." Vinny glanced about. They were against a wall, by an ancient red-figured Greek krater on a pedestal, and no one seemed to notice—except maybe Hearst's nosy secretary Willicombe. "Calm down, kid," Vinny went on as coolly as he could, but he was jittery. Eddie's upper lip gleamed with sweat, and the pupils of his eyes were tiny, as if he were off in some screwy world where he might really start shooting. This mug could ruin everything! Vinny thought.

Gloria Swanson drifted by puffing on a cigarette in a jeweled holder, but she did not so much as glance at them. "Look, pal," Vinny said in a low voice, "I know about the gun."

"So *you're* the one who searched my room."

"Searched . . . ? I didn't search—"

"Don't feed me a line."

"It's no line. I've seen bulges like that in plenty of punks' coats before, and I know what they mean. What the hell're you up to?"

"None of your business."

Desperation drove Vinny nose to nose with him. "Well, I'm making it my business, see? I've got a big stake in things tonight, and no crazy kid with a chip on his shoulder is going to ruin it for me, understand? So, do I tackle you right now, or do you hand the gun over like a good little boy?"

Eddie darted out of reach behind a carved Chinese chest. "I'm not handing over anything," he said from the other side of it. "But don't worry your stupid head, I won't use it. Not yet. I've got things to do first. Just stay outta my way. I've got nothing to lose, and if you try to stop me I'll put a hole right between your eyes."

Vinny tried to laugh. "You've seen too many movies," he said, but he was shaking. Abruptly the kid whirled and stalked off, and Vinny

196

rubbed his mouth hard. He felt sweat on his own upper lip, felt his career crashing about him—for what?

God damn it, I *do* need a drink.

Joe Willicombe had seen it all; he watched Vinny scurry for the bar cart. A fight between him and that angry-looking young man? Willicombe searched his memory for the name. Eddie Deere. Eddie had been glaring at the Chief a long time; Willicombe had seen that too. Just the usual animosity? W.R. drew it like a sponge draws water. No, there was more than that, and Willicombe's sinking feeling plunged to new depths. He could manage any crisis if he understood it, but he didn't understand this: something was far out of control.

Louella had also seen the tiff between Vinny and Eddie, but her thoughts turned a different way. Why does Eddie Deere get letters addressed to Eddie McGuffin? she wondered. Who is Swann? Patting Docky's arm, "Be good, hon," she told him, and pushed past the gawking Willis Snipe to head off Gloria Deere, who had shaken Vinny and was making a beeline through the dozen black tuxedoes toward Charlie Chaplin. She plucked at the brunette's bare arm. "Charlie *is* cute, isn't he, dear?" she said.

Gloria halted. "Oh, I think he's just *darling!*"

"You and millions of women. By the way, do you know where he went this afternoon? I looked all over for him, but . . ."

Gloria colored. "Er, I don't know at all."

"Well, it doesn't matter. I only wanted to ask him about his new girlfriend. Very pretty. Paulette Goddard." Louella's smile was like syrup on pancakes. "I understand he's thinking about starring her in his next picture."

"I—I didn't know he had a girlfriend."

Louella savored the young brunette's shock. "Of course you couldn't." She touched her hair. "But that's not what I wanted to talk about. I'd like to put an item about you in one of my columns, and—"

"Oh, Miss Parsons!"

Louella recognized the greedy glitter in Gloria's hazel eyes; she had seen it hundreds of times, and it almost always meant the inside scoop. "Yes, dear. But I need to know *ev*-erything. I can do a lot for

197

you, but you mustn't hold anything back. For example, your name isn't really Gloria Deere, is it?"

"How'd you know?"

"Never mind. Are you by any chance Gloria McGuffin?"

"Why, no. My real name's Ella Swann."

Louella blinked hard. The girl was obviously telling the truth. "Swann?"

"Yes."

"With two ens?"

"Yes."

Louella made rapid mental calculations, but nothing added up. She forced a laugh. "How odd that your brother would change his last name too."

"Well, um, he just didn't like Swann either, I guess."

"It seems like a nice name to me. Where're you from?"

"Chicago. Well, Waukegan."

"Your brother came west with you from there?"

"Ye-es."

"You don't sound very sure."

"Oh, I'm sure. Quite sure. B-but . . . you're not going to write about him too?"

The girl's eyes had saucered—in panic? Louella peered speculatively at the tall, unhappy-looking "brother" across the room gulping a drink. She licked her lips. "Very handsome. He could be in the movies too."

"Oh, I don't think he wants to be in the movies."

Louella's gaze stabbed like an ice pick. "And what *does* he want?"

"I don't know. The ordinary things." Gloria felt miserable. Louella's brown, cow eyes seemed to bore into her heart. McGuffin—she knows his name! How'd I ever think I could get away with this? "Mr. Chaplin is waving to me," she blurted. "I've just *got* to go." With a tinfoil grin she scampered off.

Oh, yeah? Louella thought, muttering words Mr. Hearst would never allow in print. You can't get away that easy, honey.

Eddie stood by the fireplace, slurping big mouthfuls of gin. His hands would not stop shaking. I'll shoot the big shot, all right! Soon! But I'll talk to him first, face to face; I'll give him a piece of my mind!

198

Meanwhile the ponderous old man had taken up a place under one of the huge Rubens tapestries, *The Triumph of Religion.* "I liked you very much in *Of Human Bondage,*" he pronounced in his high-pitched voice to Bette Davis, who leaned on Canova's *Venus* batting long lashes up at him. "Of course, it's not the sort of part I'd want Marion to play, but you did it very well."

A butler sidled up to him.

"What is it?"

"Sorry to interrupt, sir. The storm is upsetting the animals. One of the elephants has torn up a tree."

Hearst purpled. "Don't bother me, damn it! Take care of it, will you? What do I pay you people for?"

"I'd like to go out an' tear up a few trees," Herman Mankiewicz babbled nearby, and Bette Davis laughed shrilly.

"It's going to be a bumpy night!"

At that moment Harpo dragged his famous blond wig from his coat. Jamming it on, he pulled out a horn and, rolling his eyes, made a lewd honking rush at the freckled maid by the hors d'oeuvres platters.

The maid flew out the door.

Bursts of laughter sounded like shattering glass.

The clocks struck eight. William Randolph Hearst led his guests in to dinner.

❦ 8 ❧

BILLY Buller swore.

But I gotta do it; Mr. Hearst says so. Pulling on his heavy boots and dark wool coat, he stared out his door at the dripping night. Heavy black branches creaked, and rain scattered through the leaves like buckshot. He had looked forward to a nice roll in the hay with Etta; then he'd been told she had to work, and

now they wanted him to drive one of the estate trucks downhill all
the way to San Luis Obispo to pick up some late editions that Hearst
just had to have tonight.

Couldn't the damn guy wait? No chance. And if you worked for
him you had to hop.

Grumbling, Billy trudged down the wooden steps to the garages
and swung open the big green doors. Wind shrieked among the
trees. A six-foot branch cracked off and spun through the air. He
backed a small truck out into the wet, pausing a moment to peer at
Casa Grande glimmering up the slope. Nuts! They're havin' a party,
and I gotta work; some people have all the luck!

He started out, knuckles white on the wheel; he did not look
forward to five miles of winding road, starless night, rain-slick
pavement, treacherous slopes falling away on either side.

9

AMBROSE the mouse dug away the last small clods of earth
and packed them against the tunnel wall behind him. He
could hear the rain pelting the road surface above, but he
was unaware that his exit had crumbled to mud.

He could not know that Billy Buller was coming.

Blithely he put the final touches to his cosy deathtrap home.

❧ 10 ❧

SOAKED and desperate, a lone man pulled himself by tufts of grass up the ravine to the hairpin turn. For my wife, my kids, Tom Goodall thought. For all us hardworkin' Joes that got our homes stole from us by bastards that never done a lick of honest work.

❧ 11 ❧

WILLIAM Randolph Hearst drummed his fingers. Frowning at the rain lashing the clerestory windows, he sat in his usual center seat on the north side of the long refectory table, while butlers pushed carts of beef from chair to chair. His guests chatted, clinked silverware, lifted crystal glasses of a fine '28 Bordeaux, but Hearst could not get out of his mind the terrible storms of 1932, which had cost the lives of several of his favorite animals. A spurt of lightning lit the windows, and his scowl deepened. 1934. Another bad winter coming on?

But more than a storm was wrong tonight; he could feel it like time ticking away, wired to disaster, ready to explode. He glanced along the table. Seating was preferential, those in favor nearest him. Marion was directly opposite, as always, though she kept her pert nose in the air and refused to look at him. Marion! Charlie Chaplin sat next to her doing a little pantomime with two forks stuck in dinner rolls. Louella yakked at Arthur Brisbane, while wizened, bright-eyed Julia Morgan discussed architecture with Willis Snipe. "But W.R. *is* Casa Grande," she insisted in her dust-dry voice as Snipe bobbed his head like a marionette. Harpo talked about horse racing with Louella's husband, Docky, but beyond these nearby guests conversation blended into an echoing hubbub muffled by the huge tapestries depicting Daniel and Nebuchadnezzar. Most people looked happy in spite of the storm. Damn it, this is La Cuesta Encantada, my enchanted hill; they'd better be happy! Dick Powell and Hedda Hopper snickered at a newspaper story Dorothy Parker told them, punctuated with jabs of her butter knife, and Gloria Swanson grinned like a lynx at Cary Grant, but there were sour expressions here and there. Vinny Tashman's, for instance. He looked as strangled as if he had swallowed his socks, and Hearst fidgeted with the silverware flanking his blue willow china. Give in? Buy his goddamn script? Appease Marion? He glowered at the financial advisor, John Francis Neylan, next to Vinny. Neylan was red-faced as usual, wearing his know-it-all expression, but Hearst only snorted. I'll be damned if I'll let him make me cut back too far.

The old man was startled by a strange, tiny man staring at him a dozen chairs away. Who the hell? Hearst did not recognize him, but that was not unusual; there were always new friends of Marion's, friends of friends, hangers-on. The little man's face was long and pale, the scalp showing tufts of whitish hair. His chin came just above the edge of his plate, and his slit eyes gazed over a steaming slab of beef with startling malevolence. He hates me, Hearst thought glumly. He was not surprised. Lots of people felt that way. "One of the most despised men in America," the Rawlston papers said all the time. Still, the dwarf unnerved him. Who is he? An actor? Some bum Marion felt sorry for?

The dwarf grinned suddenly; he inclined his head as if to acknowledge Hearst in some intimate and obscene way, and the old man blinked. Then the moment was past; eyes down, the dwarf sawed hard at his meat, and Hearst could not be sure it had even happened.

The old man felt a tightening about his heart; he repressed a shudder. Eddie Deere hates me too. His eyes found the lean young man far down the table, by one of the tall silver candlesticks. Eddie glowered, and Hearst returned the look. Hands off Marion, she's mine; I paid for her! He flushed with shame at the thought. You shouldn't buy and sell people—though he had done it once, hadn't he? How come I can't hate the poor kid back? Something about his unhappy face prevented that.

Suddenly, without knowing why, Hearst pictured snow on steep village roofs, a small German town.

As he reached for his glass of Bordeaux the whole room shook.

🎕 12 🎕

AMBROSE sensed it first, a tensing of the massive hill under him. He scurried and found mud where escape had been. He saw his own death.

🎕 13 🎕

SOAKED and desperate, Tom Goodall pulled himself up onto the road just above Ambrose. Wind moaned; the storm lashed him. Wiping streaming rain from his eyes, he got his first good look at the mansion that had seemed so unreal from the coast. It glimmered on its storm-lashed hilltop half a mile away, and he hated and feared those lights and the big walls meant to shut him out even though he was only a poor farmer who needed food for his wife and kids. I just wanta work for it, Tom thought, and his fingers caressed the butt of his gun. They gotta help!

Headlights suddenly veered around the bend, stabbing at him, blinding him, and he held up a hand in front of his eyes. My legs're shakin' why? Then he knew it was the road, the hairpin turn, the whole earth, that was shaking.

Sweet Jesus! he thought.

The car was coming for him, the lights like knife blades. Instinctively he jerked out his gun. No! He struggled to keep from tumbling back down the steep ravine, but his foot broke through the crust of asphalt, which was riddled by the burrows of the fox and the squirrel and the mouse who had done the final digging, making the road a veneer over disaster.

Christ! Billy Buller thought at sight of the scarecrow shape that leapt up in his headlights. Some joker with a gun? Then his spine turned to ice. What the hell's wrong? He clutched the suddenly twisting wheel, and terror grabbed him by the throat. He could not control the truck; it was wiggling all over, and the road seemed to have gone nuts, jumping around. Holy cow, the turn! Billy pictured the ravine at the jutting edge of the Santa Lucias, the truck hurtling into it, him plunging toward death, and he began to scream.

He jerked the wheel.

The truck swerved left; it struck an oak on the safe side of the road. The oak struck back, twisted the truck, lifted it and sent it tumbling.

The goldarn ground is swallowin' my leg! Tom Goodall struggled to pull free, but the road was like quicksand, tugging his leg as it folded inward, down, sucking him with it as it slid toward the ravine. A mouse leapt up at his face from the hole his foot had made.

Then Tom saw the truck hit the oak and begin bounding end over end toward him. For an instant the world stopped shaking, the road let him be; the asphalt seemed to sigh. But the truck lifted, tumbled one last time. It struck the hairpin turn and tore the road and tons of rock and mud downward in a hellish nightmare slide.

❦ 14 ❧

"**O**H!" Gloria squeaked, and grabbed the thick wooden arms of her chair. Loaded forks stopped on the way to mouths; Herman Mankiewicz dropped his in his plate—*crash!*—and stared at his jiggling wineglass. "I'm going on th' wagon!"

Instinctively all eyes turned upward to the massive curved ceiling, ominously creaking, and Carole Lombard began to whimper. "Oh, Docky!" Louella moaned, clutching his arm.

"Crikey . . ." Cary Grant murmured.

"There goes my career," Jean Harlow groaned, while Adela Rogers St. Johns looked like slapping her. Gloria glanced at sweet Charlie Chaplin next to Marion and longed for his arms to comfort her. There was a low, steady roar; it seemed to surround the room, to shake the very air. Silverware jiggled, and the condiment bottles, reminders of the good old days, wobbled and tipped. Catsup reddened the table. The silver candelabra clattered; one tipped and crashed, spilling wax and fire. The huge Daniel tapestries rippled like water on the walls, and the hammered brass chandeliers swayed and clinked.

Eddie felt all three stories of mansion above them. For the first time in days he was not afraid: he exulted. Concrete and stone, tons of weight. Fall, he prayed; crush us all!

Otis Pike was not afraid either; his little legs kicked in fury under the table. I don't want Hearst to die now; he's got to suffer too!

All at once Julia Morgan was on her feet, holding on to her chair. She glanced right, then left. "There is no need to worry," she announced in a piping voice that shrilled above the roar, and all eyes swung to the flinty, birdlike little woman. "It is true," she said, each word deliberate, "that the San Andreas Fault bisects the mountains

205

nearby, and it is obviously also true that the dear little thing is acting up. But Casa Grande will not fall. I built it to stand, and it will stand. Its shell is thick reinforced concrete, and the ceiling is swaying because I designed it to sway; it is suspended from strong copper cables that will absorb any shock. Now"—she flashed a granite smile at the Chief—"shall we have dessert?"

Hearst blinked once. "Damn right." He thumped the table. "Clear these plates!" he snarled at the blanching, cowering butlers. "Bring dessert!"

At that, as if he had ordered it, the roaring and shaking ceased. With crooked grins and sheepish titters, forty guests gingerly settled back in their Dante chairs. The steady grinding of the storm, audible again, was positively reassuring.

Marion beamed at Hearst. "Isn't m-my old b-bear *w-wonderful?*" Stretching across the table, she planted a smacking kiss on his forehead. "We're s-safe—hurrah!"

Charlie Chaplin led a round of applause, and butlers scurried out with peach melba.

But death had occurred down the road.

15

HEARST still felt something wrong, something creeping up on him. In spite of what Julia Morgan had said, had there been any damage? At ten P.M. he rose and led his guests through the morning room and the billiard room toward the movie theater. Sly glances expressed longings for more intimate recreations, tête-à-têtes, small drinking parties, but everyone knew the rule: fall asleep if you must, but attend the nightly film!

Louella made sure she was at the Chief's side. "What will it be tonight?"

"Blondie of the Follies."

"Co-starring Bob Montgomery and Jimmy Durante? Oh, Marion was never lovelier than in that one!"

Hearst gave her a bleak half-smile. Is Marion already kicking up her heels? Louella wondered. With whom?

The theater was small but sumptuous, with seats for over a hundred. Red velvet covered the walls, and gilt caryatids held sprays of tiny metal flowers sparkling with lights. People jockeyed for places. Gloria was glad to see Marion snuggle next to Hearst in the front row; that left dear Charlie free, and just as she had hoped he gallantly swept her into a seat on the left aisle. Vinny was desperate to talk to Hearst. He made a beeline for the publisher, only to feel Otis Pike nipping past him into the strategic seat he had aimed for. "Move, damn you," Vinny ordered furiously under his breath.

The dwarf's long horseface lifted, the wide mouth smiled; the soft voice was more terrifyingly insinuating than ever. "Hello, Vinny. You didn't wait when you came up for dinner. Avoiding me? Sit next to me now. There's plenty of room. I'm afraid I can't move; if I don't stay right here I can't see."

Vinny wanted to wring Pike's neck, but he had no choice. I drank too much, he thought, flinging himself down behind Marion. "Uh, Mr. Hearst," he said, leaning across Pike.

Hearst's massive head swiveled "Hello, Tashman."

Most people had found seats; there was a lull in the conversation, and Vinny hated the way his voice carried. "I wondered, sir, if . . . if Marion had talked to you about that script idea of mine."

Hearst looked displeased. "She has, but—"

Through a dull echo in his brain, Vinny listened to himself as if it were someone else, some begging toady. "It's a *terrific* idea for her, sir. Just the thing. I heard about the trouble with Thalberg over the Marie Antoinette part. A shame. Marion should've had it. But this is even better: Anne Boleyn. I'd like to tell you about it, if we could talk. Maybe later this evening? It's tailored for her, and . . ." Vinny rattled on, afraid to stop for fear Hearst would cut him off. He felt miserable, idiotic. I *did* drink too much, he thought, I'm naked, making a fool of myself in front of all these people. He sensed that dope Eddie Deere close by, staring. Hedda Hopper, Basil Rathbone, Bette Davis, Louella Parsons—they all hear how much I need this.

I'm killing my chances, spoiling it all! Flushed, feeling hot and cold at the same time, he hated Pike the most, the damned leering little dwarf wheezing gleefully at his side.

"Maybe it is a good idea."

"Er . . . what?"

"I said, maybe it's a good idea."

Hearst's voice, Hearst's mouth forming the words. Vinny stared into the lined, gray face, hardly able to believe his luck.

And then Pike giggled. "Marion Davies as Anne Boleyn?" The little man's words whined with derision.

Hearst's heavy body turned. He stared down. "I don't think I know you," he rumbled.

"Otis Pike. I'm an old friend of Vinny's. Sorry for laughing, but—"

"But what?"

"Shut up, you bastard," Vinny screeched.

Hearst's blue eyes glinted ice. "Let him speak his piece. But what?"

Pike leaned forward. "Well, I'm a great fan of Miss Davies. It's such a privilege to be here. You're a terrific comedienne," he said to Marion, who dimpled and fluffed her hair, "but . . . Anne Boleyn? I'm just afraid people would laugh."

Hearst looked like thunder. "Marion is a *fine* actress. She can play *any* part."

"Of course she can," Vinny snapped.

Pike merely shrugged. "Mm, yes, she's good, very good. But is *this* the part you want?" His voice became insinuating. "Anne Boleyn was a—let's say a woman who was no better than she should be. She had affairs. The king of England accused her of sleeping around, then he chopped off her head. You want your star to get her head chopped off for loose morals at the end of a picture?"

Hearst glared at Vinny. "Is this true?" he demanded.

Vinny smallowed hard. "Nothing was proved against her," he jabbered. "It's a tragedy, a great tragedy. You want Marion to have great roles, and—"

"I don't want her to play a prostitute, and I certainly don't want her to have her head cut off."

"But—"

"No. It's out of the question," Hearst said, turning away.

Marion gave Vinny a helpless little shrug and turned away too, snuggling her blond head against the old man's sloping shoulder, and Vinny felt as if a trapdoor had suddenly gaped under him and he had plunged through into an abyss. "You bastard!" he hissed softly at Pike. "You filthy son of a bitch!"

The dwarf also kept his voice low. "You went through my things, Vinny. I told you to mind your business, but you didn't. Now you have to pay."

"I'll fix you for this."

"Don't get any wise ideas. You fix me, I fix you worse. Remember Chicago and that little accident with the gun?" The lights dimmed. "You didn't get tossed in the clinker; be thankful for that. Now, just sit back and watch the movie. Mr. Hearst won't like it if you don't."

Hands opening and closing helplessly at his sides, Vinny slumped back, while nearby Louella frowned. She hadn't heard the words, but she had seen their faces, and Vinny Tashman and Otis Pike were definitely not friends.

At the end of the third aisle Charlie Chaplin slid his hand onto Gloria Deere's thigh.

The darkness wrapped Eddie in its cloak. Images flickered brightly on the screen, but he was not cheered by them. Marion. She was pretty and funny and heartbreaking up there; she was heartbreaking here too, her head on Hearst's shoulder. Love? Eddie wanted to spit. Love didn't count in this world; it was money that mattered—and that was wrong, all wrong.

The old corrupt world had to die!

Hearst still felt uneasy; he could not watch the movie. Ordinarily he loved Marion's pictures, but tonight old voices whispered inside him, a gathering of ghosts moaning regrets, demanding reparations. I'm one of the richest men in the world, he thought. Why am I unhappy? Because someone in this room is kicking up the past?

Helena had curled up on the old man's lap. Putting the dachshund down, he slipped from beside Marion and headed up the aisle.

Eddie McGuffin watched him. Hearst—my chance.

His own voices screaming inside his head, Eddie followed the old man.

🎋 16 🎋

T HE sumptuousness that characterized the rest of Casa
Grande was absent in its huge kitchen, replaced by the
bright clean efficiency of big gas stoves and gleaming metal-
topped worktables. William Randolph Hearst was glad to find the
long room empty, the leftovers of the banquet disposed of. The staff
of six had washed and put away the dishes and gone to bed. Rain
flung itself at high, dark windows; wind howled but could not get in.
Hearst hesitated only a moment. Dr. Dilworth says I eat too much—
but I won't give up my food! He often cooked late at night;
whipping up dishes had a simple, honest purpose that soothed him.
Pulling mustard, Worcestershire sauce, and cayenne pepper from a
cupboard, laying out milk, butter, and cheddar cheese from the cold
storage locker, the old man set about making a Welsh rarebit.

He tied a white apron about his dark-jacketed girth; he even
hummed as he worked. He was stirring milk in a copper pan when
he felt someone nearby.

He looked up. A lean young man with fierce blue eyes and an
unruly shock of brown hair stood six paces away: Eddie Deere.

Hearst gave Eddie a dark look. His revery was spoiled—he had
been dreaming about good times up here with his father in the
1870s, roughing it, camping, enjoying a simpler world of horseback
riding and clean blue skies—and he was annoyed. "Everyone is
supposed to be watching the movie," he grumped.

"Oh, yeah? Well, I have things to say."

Hearst stopped stirring. Eddie wore a cheap, ill-fitting suit and
pinched-looking shoes, and in spite of himself Hearst felt sorry for
the gawky scarecrow of a kid; his thoughts surprised him. What if I
had started like him, with nothing? "You can say them another time,"
he said. "Get back to the movie."

210

Eddie took a step forward. "You bastard."

Hearst's shaggy brows lifted. "What?"

"You heard me."

The spoon dropped in the pan. "Now look here, young man—"

"No. You look here."

Another step, and Hearst could see the tension jumping in the kid's face, rippling the jaw muscles. Those notes that've been coming for months, he thought. Is this . . . ?

"I've waited a long time for this," Eddie snarled, "and now that I've got you alone you're gonna listen. The world is going to hell, and you're the reason for it, you and your kind. Rich bosses who think they own people and can step on them and murder them and—"

"Murder? Who do you think you're talking to?"

"I know who I'm talking to. William Randolph Hearst, who owns all those papers that never tell the truth, that lie and make people think it's their fault the country is in a mess, when all the time it's really you behind it, building big houses and having fancy parties with that—that woman of yours, when people are starving and dying, and you don't lift a finger to help them."

"Do you have any idea how much money I donate to charities? All the breadlines I support? All the jobs I provide? How dare you—"

"That's a load of crap. Bandages on a festering wound. But you're the guy who made the wound in the first place."

Hearst's eyes flashed. "You're a Red, are you?"

Eddie laughed hollowly. "You bet. I'm a member of the American Communist Party—American, that's right, and proud of it, and we Americans are gonna wipe the country clean of you and your kind; we're gonna make it a decent place to live."

"Decent? You?" Enraged, Hearst wiped his hands on the apron. "Now you look here, I'm an American too, and a good one. I was an American long before you were born. What makes you think you people have a monopoly on citizenship?"

"You've acted like you had a monopoly on it for years, and just look where that's got us."

"You're crazy."

"*Don't call me that!*" Eddie's yell rattled around the room. "You're the one who's crazy, if you think you can go on getting away with stepping all over the little guy."

Hearst opened his mouth, closed it. The anger would not stay. His voices hummed again, wailing, warning. Rain kept lashing the windows, while intuitions stirred in a muddy current that would not wash clear. "Do I know you?" the old man asked.

Eddie faltered. "Whattaya mean?"

Hearst took a step toward him, peering, searching. "We've met before, haven't we?"

Eddie looked afraid. "Sure. Once, a long time ago, when I was a dumb kid that didn't know any better." He drew himself up. "So what? That's not what counts. What counts is that maybe you and my pa met, too—or maybe he was just a guy who got in your way that had to be rubbed out."

"What are you talking about?"

"I'll show you what." Eddie's hand leapt toward his chest.

At that moment the milk boiled over. Hearst jerked around to switch off the gas. When he looked back Eddie's blue eyes were wild and his hand was inside his jacket.

"So, *here* you are!" Louella Parsons exclaimed, and Eddie's hand stiffened and slid limply to his side. Bustling in her floral-print dress, Louella fixed motherly cow eyes on Hearst. "What are you doing in that apron? Cooking? How precious! But you've let the milk boil over. You shouldn't be doing this, it's woman's work, and I'm just the woman for it. Let me fix something for you, anything; I'd be glad to." Grabbing a dishrag, she stepped between the men and began busily sopping up milk. "Welsh rarebit, I'll bet. It's one of Mr. Hearst's favorites," she said cosily to Eddie. She looked brightly from one to the other. "Were you two having a nice talk?" Neither answered, and she chattered on as if nothing was wrong, though she had heard every word from her hiding place behind the big six-burner stove.

Eddie jammed his hands in his pockets. "You'll see, you'll see!" He spun around and strode out.

Louella's eyes followed him. "What an odd young man," she said as she began to grate cheese.

"I think I know him," Hearst murmured.

"Really?" Louella blinked at her boss. "I had the same idea."

They held each other's eyes for a moment, and Louella suddenly thought she knew why she had recognized Eddie, but she could not believe it. Nervously she tittered.

Hearst turned away, staring in a funk out the window at the wet dark. Then the hair at the nape of his neck prickled, and he knew there was someone else in the room. Glimpsing a flicker of shadow, he hurried breathlessly to the door, but whoever had watched, listened—for how long?—was gone, and he bunched his fists in fury. My home is as riddled with holes as a cheese! Wheeling, he found Louella staring at him, but his thoughts remained on Eddie. I ought to give orders to have that arrogant pup kicked off the hill right now! he thought angrily, stroking his jaw. His pa, rubbed out? We met a long time ago? The voices screamed in Hearst's brain, and he knew he would not kick Eddie out, not yet. We have to finish our talk, he thought, stalking out without a word.

"Well!" Louella exclaimed to the empty room.

Back in the theater Hearst slumped into his seat. On the screen Marion was tussling with Billy Dove, yanking her hair, while Zasu Pitts comically knotted and unknotted her hands. The audience laughed, but Hearst could not. Gloomily he noted that the two seats behind his—Vinny Tashman's and the dwarf's—were vacant.

🙿 17 🙾

AN hour later the movie ended. The lights came up to applause, and people stood and began filing out. Vinny Tashman and the dwarf were back, but Hearst was not sure when they had returned. He watched Eddie Deere speculatively.

Louella scurried to Marion. "You were simply *terrific* as Blondie. It's one of my favorites."

"Th-thanks, dearie."

Louella tugged Docky's elbow. "I'm just exhausted; let's get right to bed."

Marion turned to Vinny. "Sorry Popsy d-doesn't go for your idea," she said.

Vinny was seething. "Sorry? What good does sorry do? I *need* that job!" He knew he was talking too loudly, jabbering again, making a public fool of himself, but the liquor was coursing through him like lava, hot and bubbling, making him crazy, and the worst of it was he wanted—needed—more booze, and he knew just where he was going to get it.

"P-poor Vinny," Marion said, touching his arm, but her sympathy only made him flinch. It was nearly midnight, everyone drifting toward the morning room, from which they would disperse to bed, and she hurried ahead to join Hearst.

Joe Willicombe was waiting for the Chief by the carillon keyboard in the hallway. "Sir," he whispered, "I'm afraid I have some bad news." He had not meant for anyone else to hear, but three people did: Joel McCrea, Damon Runyon, Walter Howey. They stopped, ears pricked, and suddenly there was a small traffic jam, people sensing something; in another moment a dozen guests were waiting to hear it all. Willicombe cursed silently, but his boss was glowering, waiting, hands fidgeting, and it was too late to back out. "We sent a driver down to pick up those late editions," he said as evenly as he could, "but they called from San Luis Obispo to say he hasn't shown up."

"Why not? Our drivers are reliable."

"I thought something might have happened to him in the storm. I sent another driver, but he couldn't get more than a mile. Sorry, sir, but . . . the road is washed out."

"Fix it, then." Hearst pushed past. "I want those newspapers."

Willicombe followed him. "It can't be fixed, sir. At least, not now."

Hearst swiveled. "Why not?"

"It's at that hairpin curve about half a mile down. The whole cliff gave way. Tumbled into the ravine. The earthquake, we guess. Repairing it will be a major undertaking."

"Major?"

"Days of work."

"You mean we're trapped up here?" Jean Harlow burst out.

"Delicious!" Hedda Hopper exclaimed.

214

"Oh, no," Gloria Deere quavered, sinking against Charlie Chaplin.

Hearst looked around. Good Christ. His eyes landed on Otis Pike's waxen face. The dwarf looked gleeful—why? Most expressions were worried. The last thing I need is panic, Hearst thought, forcing a smile. "Now, there's plenty of food and plenty of things to do," he said in his best grandfatherly voice. "You'll see how fast we get it taken care of. Days to fix? Nonsense. We'll have it as right as rain in hours. All of you go to bed now; we'll probably be done by dawn. Go on, go on." He shooed them away, and they moved off buzzing, Herman Mankiewicz's voice the last to be heard: "Is there 'nough booze, thass what I wanna know . . ."

Rain slapped the morning room windows. Hearst felt Marion's languorous weight against his side. Had she drunk too much? "God damn it, Joe," he said to his secretary. "We don't need this now."

"There's more," Willicombe went on, now that only Hearst and Marion would hear the worst, "A man is dead."

𝕾 18 𝕾

TEN minutes later the morning room, the Refectory, the Assembly Hall were silent and empty. Lights burned in a few sconces but lit only solitude. Everyone had vanished into the labyrinth of Casa Grande or had scurried under big black umbrellas to the guesthouses that sat like obedient children at the feet of the huge main house. In the rain, on the heads of solemn, staring statues, the round garden globes shone on drenched paths and black, wet leaves. The clouds continued to pour as if they had siphoned up the sea, while the wind beat at the temple facades and Corinthian columns of the Neptune Pool as if it were a conspirator in a plan to tear down an arrogant man's folly. The baboons rattled their cage.

Who could sleep on a night like this?

VI

Murder at San Simeon

🎋 1 🎋

"A T least we *think* Billy Buller is dead," Willicombe said as he and the Chief rose in the small paneled elevator. "Our man shone a light into the ravine. He said he could see the truck about sixty feet down, pretty badly smashed; he said he didn't see how anybody could have survived."

Grim-faced, Hearst had sent Marion up ahead of them. "None of the guests are to hear about this," he snapped.

"No, sir."

"Get to Buller as fast as you can. If he's alive . . ."

"It's difficult. Mud and rock and rain. We're not sure how stable the cliff is. There could be aftershocks, and more of the road might give way, and—"

"Too dangerous for men to climb down?"

"I'd say so."

"How about coming at it from below?"

"That's what I thought. It will take some time; a crew will have to circle around. Shall I send them?"

"Right away." The elevator stopped at the Gothic Suite and Hearst stalked out. "Damn this storm! Damn this night!"

❧ 2 ❧

IN the darkened telephone office Etta Kitt smoked her eighth
cigarette. Dinner and the movie were over; now the interesting
calls ought to begin, and tomorrow in the servants' dining room
she would be the gossip queen of the hill.

There were sudden stabs of light through the oaks, and the thin,
sharp-browed woman stiffened. A moment later three men holding
big rubber-insulated flashlights scurried past her window. Etta
glimpsed ropes, picks, shovels in the swaying beams. One man
carried a kit with a big red cross. She got a gander at his face,
looking as glum, as if he was trooping off to have his teeth yanked
out. The men headed downhill in the whipping rain, but not by the
road and, frowning, Etta crushed out her cigarette. Something had
happened—what? Not knowing annoyed her, and in a funk she
began to hope Billy Buller might sneak into the telephone office
tonight, make a little whoopie on Mr. Hearst's time. She grinned at
that.

"Goody," she yelped as the switchboard began to rasp.

🎗 3 🎗

LOUELLA listened to Docky's rattling snore. A buzz saw, she thought, the dear silly man. How's he get to sleep so fast? No conscience—or just nothing to feel guilty about? Louella pooh-pooed the idea; everybody, even Docky, had something in his past. She got down to business. Carefully she switched off the bedside lamps made from priceless Chinese vases and, fully dressed—she had stayed in the bathroom until Docky's snores started up; no need to worry him with what she planned—she crept to sit in deep shadow by the leaded-glass window of their big room in Casa del Mar. It was the southernmost of the three guesthouses, but the window faced Casa Grande squarely, and Louella had a nearly unobstructed view up the terraces. Massed black trees rose and fell in windblown waves; garden lights shone drowned gleams in the downpour. I can see, but no one will see me—perfect. Furthermore Louella had things to mull over, and she had every intention of sitting here a good long while.

Murder: Eddie Deere had seemed to accuse the Chief of murder.

Louella's brow puckered; she thought very hard. Her instinct worked well when the mystery was obvious—what director had bedded which starlet? which marriage was on the rocks?—but when things got complicated, when they didn't follow the patterns that shaped most scandals, she got stuck. Eddie's father; was that the idea, that he was the one the Chief had done in? Louella shivered. It just couldn't be! But that ugly Thomas Ince business a dozen years ago that had had to be hushed up . . . all those other dark rumors about her boss . . .

None of them shook Louella's bedrock confidence in William Randolph Hearst. He simply could do no wrong. Yet what if there was real scandal behind the latest dark cloud? Louella actually began

221

to hope for a gleam of truth behind Eddie Deere's implications, because then she could pay back Mr. Hearst for saving her life: she could protect him.

Louella glowed at the prospect. After all, if W.R. had stepped outside the law it must have been for good reason. *I just want to be his heroine.*

She perked up. Who's that? Someone, a shadow against the storm-washed lights, flitted across the upper terrace.

Time for work! Louella decided.

Her notepad and pencil were already in her voluminous skirt pocket. Quietly, so as not to interrupt Docky's steady snores, she pulled on her boots.

❧ 4 ❧

IN low lamplight Otis Pike sat on the edge of his bed, little legs dangling. Holding the photograph he had stolen from Casa Grande's vaults, he scowled. A dame with a Gibson girl hairdo. Sixteen? Eighteen? Jailbait, but obviously the old-fashioned type, nothing like the whores running around the hill today. A whipping branch scraped at the window as Pike's lips curled. *For Billy from your sweetie.* Damn Hearst! His stubby fingers tightened on the picture. He just knew it was important. How? Hating having nearly all, maybe all of the pieces yet unable to see how they fit together, he angrily jammed the photo back in his jacket pocket and thought about what he had overheard in the kitchen. That was a close call—good thing Hearst didn't catch me. Why in hell'd that nosy Parsons broad have to stick her face in just when things were getting interesting? *You rubbed out my pa,* Eddie Deere had seemed to say, and Pike slowly scratched his long pale jaw as Rose McGuffin's words replayed in his brain: *He was a reporter and he died falling off a train . . . he was a reporter and . . .*

222

Eddie McGuffin? Couldn't be, just couldn't, Pike thought. Too coincidental.

Unless the coincidence had an explanation.

Suddenly twitching with shivery excitement, the little man switched off the lamp and slid down from the bed. Rain oiled the windows to a black sheen, and far downhill the sea shone with a strange burnished glitter. Pike considered. The road washed out—just fine; that'll prevent any outside meddling. He winced. His leg ached like hell, but he had to see this through.

He pulled on his yellow slicker. It was too big, dragging about the thick awkward heels of his shoes, but there was nothing he could do about that.

The little man crept out into the storm.

🎜 5 🎜

VINNY Tashman was furious. Drunk too, and wobbling. His eyes kept going in and out of focus. Haven't been this soused since Chicago, he thought in a brief lucid moment. Well, I jus' don' care! His drunken state only increased his fury, at Hearst, at Marion, who didn't really give a damn—especially at that son-of-a-bitch dwarf who had opened his ugly yap and smashed everything. Thunder rumbled; the lights in his room in Casa del Monte flickered, but Vinny ignored them. Thrashing about from baroque Spanish bed to Italian Renaissance chair, moaning, he did not stop to think that Hearst might have rejected his script anyway, that the publisher would decide on his own that Marion shouldn't play Anne Boleyn, that in fact the Anne Boleyn idea had been bum from the start. Vinny wanted, needed, a fall guy, and his spite focused on Otis Pike.

So-called Otis Pike, Vinny thought, knocking back the latest hefty gulp from the whiskey bottle that had been wrapped in a shirt in one of his bags. Leaning against a heavy carved chair, he began to sob with self-pity. The whiskey was supposed to've celebrated my triumph, when ol' Hearst said yes. But Pike queered that for me. Hearst said no, and I even lost that bitch Gloria. Charlie Chaplin stole her—the bastard is probably screwing her right now— and . . . and now I'm up shit creek without a paddle. Peering at the bottle, Vinny made a face. Christ. Empty! Flinging it across the room, he yowled at the injustice of the universe. Nothin' I can do to get back at Pike? His expression set in a grim, acid mask. I know the dwarf's *real* name. The dirty louse thinks he can make a chump out of me and get away with it?

Lurching, Vinny jerked a dresser drawer onto the floor and began flinging shirts, ties, underwear into the air. At the bottom were hidden the target pistols in their red-velvet-lined box. He lifted one and pointed it at the window, where night returned his bleared, staggering reflection. "Bang, bang!" He cackled. It would be only a little death, just a little man. A goddamn dwarf.

"Bang, bang!"

Vinny jammed the gun in his pants. Grinning, he struggled into his tuxedo jacket: formal wear for death.

Easy. It'll be like wiping the scum off my shoe.

6

"POPSY th-thinks I went upstairs. B-but I didn't." Marion's voice was a husky whisper, promising. Behind her, streaks of rain silvered the morning room's French doors. Feeling unreal, weightless, Eddie inhaled a vaporous gin smell mixed with perfume and Marion's own musky scent. Swaying, the slender blonde draped her arms around his neck. "I s-snuck off to m-meet you," she said, eyes unfocused, but the bright blue irises seemed to sparkle, and Eddie wanted to drown in them.

They stood in the shadowed corner where he had waited to meet Marion, as they had planned. About them the silence was so intense that the whole big house seemed to be leaning over them, listening. Someone had died, a man named Buller. Hidden, Eddie had listened to Joe Willicombe deliver his message. Now the knowledge that accidental deaths *did* happen filled him with a prickling terror, a sense of being swept by an irresistible undertow toward a yawning sea.

Marion molded herself to him. "Gee, s-something about you gets to me. Are we g-gonna have a little f-fun?" She pressed soft lips against his. "I've gotta go up, say g'night to the old bear, but I'll c-come to your room just as soon's I c-can." Giggling, she tapped his chin. "Don't be 'fraid. I know which one it is."

🎀 7 🎀

CHARLIE Chaplin peered cautiously from under his dripping yellow rain hat. The storm beat at Casa Grande's ghostly white facade, but no one seemed to be in sight. Avoiding the floodlights stabbing up at the big house like garish pointing fingers, Chaplin splashed across the broad main terrace, past the Baroque fishpond that overflowed onto the tiles. Suddenly his heart jumped, and he ducked behind a marble Aphrodite on a plinth. Close call! He grinned under his black umbrella. Guess I'm not the only bloke on an errand of love. He had glimpsed someone on one of the lower terraces. Waiting a moment, he poked his head out, preparing to head on, but a second figure, also in a yellow slicker, popped up at almost the same place, and he ducked back again. Gorblimey, it's Trafalgar Square! The sheeting rain prevented him from telling who it was. One of the old man's bloody watchdogs?

Chaplin waited. The second figure crept off, and glancing about, he made a cautious but rapid beeline for Casa del Monte, unaware that he too was watched by more than one pair of baleful eyes.

8

A long, pale face lifted above the damp sill of Eddie Deere's window. Otis Pike's whitish brows wiggled under a black umbrella. The kid's scrammed? Where to? The dwarf didn't waste much time on the question. He wanted the whole truth and nothing but about Eddie Deere, and he was glad to take advantage of his absence.

Scurrying around to the front of Casa del Monte, Pike slipped in the west entrance. The sitting room was empty, but a trail of damp led toward that hot little brunette's door. Somebody just came in, Pike thought; he also thought he knew who and leered. They'll be busy.

Careful to make no sound, he tucked his slicker and umbrella in a side closet and wiped his shoes; he never left a trail if he could help it.

He crept into Eddie's room.

Drawing the heavy brocade curtains, he began. He had searched many places before, and knew just where to start.

🎔 9 🎔

CHARLIE Chaplin squinted through a crack in Gloria Deere's curtains. He frowned. Hearst's mansion stood on the top of the hill like a stern guardian; he did not like that. The rain poured endlessly, but through its lashing veils the garden lights glimmered watchfully. Chaplin felt restless, wicked. He wanted to shock old Hearst.

Then he recalled the marble Aphrodite, naked on the upper terrace, and all at once he grinned and flashed Gloria a broad lewd wink. "I've got a bright idea, love. Want some larks?" Slyly he patted her behind. "Before we take up where we left off this afternoon, that is?"

Gloria clapped her hands. "Ooo, name it!"

"Righto." Charlie chucked her chin. "Now just nip out of that bra like a good little chap."

"You *wicked* man!" but Gloria did not have to be told twice.

🎔 10 🎔

EDDIE trudged downhill, his umbrella pouring waterfalls. He could still taste Marion's lips, hot and eager, and he felt powerless to resist her. He panicked. How could I have said she could come to my room? I've got a job to do.

But can I really murder the man she loves?

227

Eddie burned with shame. I should've shot Hearst in the kitchen! If only that Parsons dame hadn't poked her nose in.

The young man paused. But would I have done it? he asked himself. I met him, I faced him, I said my piece, and I oughta hate his goddamn guts. It should be easy. But . . . but . . .

Eddie was finding it hard to hate the old man. Hearst's trenched, ravaged face was real, and almost sad. So was the wheezing breath that said he was near death already. Those breadlines, the jobs Hearst gave . . . Eddie despaired, because it was so easy to hate his own confusion and fear.

Coward, making excuses! What good are you?

His hands balled into fists. I've gotta kill the son of a bitch!

Moving on, he kicked at an oily puddle. Just downhill the Neptune Pool looked more fantastic than ever through curtains of rain, an exaggerated movie dream of wealth. He was alone on a curving path. The wind whipped fiercely. Leaves and twigs flew about, and all at once it seemed as if Hearst's big floodlit house was a ghost house, its gay company all dead; and Eddie longed for the storm to whirl him up into the air, carry him off, smash him, so it would all be over and he could be in ghostland, too, where the struggles of life didn't crush you. Giant palms rattled in the wind. Eddie stopped short. Red-roofed Casa del Monte lay just below. A figure wearing a yellow slicker was creeping suspiciously from the west to the east entrance. A little guy. Otis Pike? Eddie stood in a grove of oleanders. Their long narrow leaves rustled oddly, and he had the sense that something other than the wind shook them.

He shuddered.

Hurrying to his room, he found everything as it had been. Then a chill shot through his body. The photograph of his father had been slipped into the wrong page of *Das Kapital*.

Pike!

Eddie's hand flew to his gun.

❧ 11 ❧

THE dwarf sat at the heavy, marble-topped desk in his room, not fifty feet from Eddie McGuffin. He felt torn between gloating and snarling.

He was staring at the photograph of the picture on the mantel in Rose McGuffin's house Hearst and the Chicago newsboys, Eddie among them with Hearst's hand on his shoulder. He could see now what he should've been sure of when he met the kid in the Glendale station: Eddie Deere was Eddie McGuffin. The letters from Chicago, which he had just discovered where the kid had clumsily hidden them under the sink in his bathroom, confirmed that; so did the kid's books. The problem was, how did this new piece of the puzzle fit? Why was Eddie McGuffin here now? Why did he pretend to be Gloria Deere's brother? The breath whooshed in frustration. For that matter, why had the dame let him pretend it? Was she in on something with him?

It was more of a goddamn mess than ever!

Pike's stubby fingers drummed. There's gotta be some juicy, nasty connection between Rose Ellen Forrest McGuffin and Hearst, but unless the old man is slicker than I think, he really doesn't know her kid. I don't get it. There had been a photograph of a man in Eddie's *Das Kapital*, a man in a newspaper press room, holding a copy of the Chicago *Evening American*. Had to be Eddie's father, Rose McGuffin's husband.

Died falling off a train . . .

Pike yanked at his whitish tufts of hair. Time was against him; tomorrow they were all supposed to head back downhill, if the washed-out road let them. He forced his mind on. So the kid thinks what I think: that Hearst bumped off his poor old pa. Is that what'll

229

finish Hearst? Pike almost laughed. In that case Eddie Deere's on my side; we oughta get together.

But something was wrong with this particular idea, and the dwarf squirmed, trying to figure out what. Wind hit the window as if pounding to get in, rain writhed down the glass like tiny snakes. For the hundredth time he dragged out the packet Rawlston had sent: birth certificates, reports, a half dozen letters. Old news. Rose Ellen Forrest had died of influenza when she was twenty-two. That meant that the woman in Chicago, Rose McGuffin, was not Rose Ellen Forrest.

Who then?

It all seemed to hinge on that.

Pike shifted the papers about on the cold marble desktop until they became a blur. There had always seemed to be something in them, a clue he could not pin down, but he had pored over them so long that his eyes ached; he could hardly see. His eyes, aching. He rubbed his aching eyes.

Eyes. Eyes? *Eyes!*

Frantically he scrambled through the papers, found—Harry McGuffin; Rose McGuffin; Eddie McGuffin.

Their eyes!

Pike jumped up; he forgot the pain in his leg. That meant . . . it meant—and suddenly the thing took on a whole new twist, and Pike felt almost dizzy: suddenly he knew, really, why he recognized Eddie McGuffin.

Ha!

And then he was afraid—Will the kid spoil it all?—because in his room there had also been a box of pistol cartridges, not quite full; that meant there had to be a gun.

Don't shoot Hearst! Lightning flashed, and the dwarf yelped and cowered, and the old explosions began to go off in his brain, bright searing flickers that could make him crazy. No! Sweating, he grabbed the edge of the desk, held on, made himself think. Proof, I need proof for Bart Rawlston, to make him smear the dirty story across all his newspapers. There was only one place to find it, but there was not much time. Throwing on the yellow slicker, jamming the rain hat on his head, Otis Pike rushed out.

❧ 12 ❧

EDDIE McGuffin was waiting, watching. He followed the little man into the crashing night.

❧ 13 ❧

THE liquor Vinny Tashman had drunk had reached its flash point, the point of blind, mad action. Dragging the pistol from his belt, he flung open his door, staggered across the sitting room, and smashed into Otis Pike's room. "Now we'll see who's boss!" His heart sank. Gaping, he flailed about; he even peered under the bed.

But Pike was not there.

Vinny gulped air. Thinks he can get away from me?

He pulled on a yellow slicker and charged out to find the dwarf.

❧ 14 ❧

IN their yellow slickers Charlie Chaplin and Gloria Deere snuck out of Casa del Monte. Giggling, they raced uphill.

❧ 15 ❧

CROUCHED behind a dripping oak, Louella Parsons cursed the wind that found every vulnerable gap in her clothing. Phooey to the night and the rain! She also hated her hiding place. There were swarms of people chasing frantically around the hill as if it were mating season. She longed to know who; she wanted to be able to use the knowledge later, if only for blackmail, but they all wore those darn yellow slickers, and she was too far away from the main action to be able to identify any faces.

Then Louella glimpsed someone who was not wearing a slicker, a figure that was suddenly just on the other side of the oak, as if it had jumped up out of the earth. Immediately it crashed off wildly into some bushes. It had been only a blur, and Louella was momentarily shaken, unnerved. Did he—she—see me?

Louella shivered. Hugging herself, she gazed up the front of Casa Grande to that special private room above the soaring entrance: The Chief's bedroom. How she admired him! How she—but she would not let her thoughts go that far. Yet they had been through such a lot. In New York, Chicago, Hollywood. She would be nobody without Mr. Hearst, and her cow eyes swam again with dreams of being his heroine.

You're safe, you old sweetie! Louella is here!

16

WILLICOMBE watched too, from the fourth-story Celestial Bridge above the Gothic Suite. He shook his head. People were sneaking about far below, unaware someone peered down on them. But a fat lot of good that does me, Willicombe thought. He wiped rain from his glasses. From up here the figures were mere small yellowish blurs picked out briefly by lamps before they were swallowed up in wind-whipped shadows, harmless-seeming. Just out after a little hanky-panky—or bent on deadly errands? The secretary's domed head corrugated. Wish I hadn't had to send three men downhill to see about that truck and Buller. That leaves only two security men.

Let them be alert!

"Oh, here you are, Mr. Willicombe," a butler's voice said.

Willicombe turned to the shape in the doorway.

"Sorry, sir. Mr. Dix, the zookeeper, says there's heap big trouble."

🎜 17 🎝

MARVIN Orr fidgeted in his black slicker. He screwed up his features at the storm. Lookit them cats and dogs! Marvin was squat and burly, with a face like a bulldog. He had been a security guard at Metro before Colonel Joe, as he thought of Joe Willicombe, had hired him to keep an eye on things up here on the hill. He had worked for Mr. Hearst two years. Marvin was loyal but lazy; the new job paid pretty good, but he liked it mostly because there was hardly ever anything to do but walk around and smell the flowers. But, tonight! Marvin stamped his boots in wet leaves. He hated cold and rain, hated to be out watching—for what? Colonel Joe had not been very strong on that; he'd snapped at the men, "Just report anything suspicious!" Marvin stamped again. Shoot, when those Hollywood folks were here there was always something suspicious! His lookout near the telephone and telegraph offices let him see quite a bit without being seen, and there was a helluva lot of scurrying around out there. What to do? Marvin decided he'd just follow one of them; Colonel Joe sure couldn't say he'd sat on his duff.

Dreaming of warm spring weather, Marvin Orr picked someone at random and set out on his tail.

He was very careful not to be seen, but Marvin had not had much practice at not being seen.

꧁ 18 ꧂

IN the telephone office Etta Kitt lit her eleventh cigarette. She was gleefully happy: the phone lines had been hot as a pistol, and her ears were burning. Leslie Howard had made a very interesting proposition to Bette Davis; there was a huge drinking party, almost a brawl, in Dorothy Parker's room in Casa del Sol; and Carole Lombard kept making anonymous obscene calls to Clark Gable. There was lots to see, too. There: someone in a yellow slicker. And someone else—and someone else. It's like hide-and-seek, Etta thought, grinning. Swell! Leaning back, exhaling smoke into the dark, she hoped Billy Buller would show up soon. Why should the big shots have all the fun?

꧁ 19 ꧂

LOUELLA just had to know what was going on; she had to take a chance. Creeping from her hiding place, she joined the yellow-slickered night dancers.

Eyes watched her, inflamed with hate. They had watched Charlie Chaplin too.

More than one pair of eyes.

235

❧ 20 ❧

"**S**IR," Joe Willicombe said.

Hearst didn't answer right away, though his shoulders twitched to show he had heard. Lightning flickered at the windows of the study in the Gothic Suite, but Casa Grande's thick walls muffled its thunder. Hearst stood with his back turned, staring at the painting of himself at the end of the vaulted room. It had been done when he was thirty by his old friend from Harvard days, Orrin Peck, now dead. The young man in the painting burned with confidence, ambition, idealism. *Have I betrayed my ideals?* Hearst thought. *I used to fight the bosses; have I become one of them?*

He hated the way the painting reminded him of Eddie Deere's accusations.

It seemed to remind him worryingly of something else.

"What is it, Joe?" he said at last, turning.

"Sorry. More bad news. The earthquake hasn't done any damage to the main house or guesthouses—at least, no one's reported any—but Waldo Dix, the head zookeeper, says the concrete foundation of one of the monkey cages was cracked. There was a break in the bars; the baboons have all escaped."

"It's Buller I want to know about."

"Too soon for that. Three men are on their way down. About the baboons—Dix thinks they'll come back at feeding time, but meanwhile—"

"But meanwhile they're out there, and they could be dangerous?"

A nod, "The storm riled them up, Dix says. That's why I came to you. They're mean at the best of times. Should we warn the guests?"

"No. Who would be fool enough to be wandering around in a storm so late at night?" Willicombe said nothing to this. "Let the security men know, of course. And send someone around to the

236

guest rooms early." Hearst shook his head. "Road washed out . . . escaped baboons . . ."

"And those warning notes," Willicombe added. "Sir, I've been looking into that."

A sharp glance. "And?"

"The man, Otis Pike—"

"The dwarf?"

"Yes."

Hearst looked glum. "He hates me, Joe. He gave me a look at dinner that . . . And the boy hates me too."

"Eddie Deere?"

Hearst peered at his secretary. "What do you make of him?"

"He doesn't look very happy. I've hardly spoken to him, but—"

"He's an arrogant pup!" Hearst exploded, jowls shaking. He controlled his fury. "What about Pike? You think he wrote those notes?"

"I don't know." Willicombe described his suspicions. "He was supposed to have been in an orphanage in Chicago with Vinny Tashman. I got hold of the orphanage records." Pulling the list of names from his clipboard, Willicombe handed it over. "Tashman's name is there, but there's no Otis Pike."

"Maybe he changed his name."

"Could be. There's no crime in that, only—"

"Only you don't trust him?"

"Something's wrong about the man. I caught him in your room during lunch."

Hearst's massive chin lifted. "My room?"

"I'm afraid so. He had that glass globe with the little village inside that you keep on your dresser. He said he was just looking around, but I don't believe it. He's up to something."

"The nerve of the man." Hearst ran his eyes down the orphanage list. Something seemed to click, but he couldn't identify it, and he stuffed the paper in his jacket pocket. "Are we keeping a good eye on him?"

"As much as possible." Willicombe hated not having a more secure answer. The snap of the elevator sounded; then a light, gay woman's hum came from the sitting room: Marion. Willicombe glanced at his boss in time to catch a dark look. Where's she been? it demanded; Willicombe wondered the same. A log sighed, sinking deeper into the flames. Uneasily the secretary poked at his glasses. Too many unanswered questions tonight. "I brought up the latest telegrams and letters." He slid the pile onto the long central table. "Er, shall we do some work now?"

The old man's ponderous gaze was fastened in the direction from which Marion's hum had come. "No. It's no night for it, Joe," he muttered distractedly, and strode out.

Willicombe stared at the door. Alone, he clutched his clipboard tighter, darting his gaze about, as if someone, something might hide among the deep shadows. Silly, he thought, but his wide jaw set. With a last sweeping glance, he headed out. I won't sleep well, that's for sure.

The letters and telegrams remained on the thick polished mahogany.

The top letter bore a Chicago postmark.

❧ 21 ❧

MARY O'Grady trembled under the bedclothes in her little room on the first floor of the servants' wing. She could not sleep. She disliked the storm—the lightning and thunder was unusual for California, and it frightened her—but it was not that that kept her awake. It was Mr. Pike. She hated herself for being taken in by him, for allowing herself to believe that . . .

She shook with sobs for the fourth time in an hour; she wailed; she beat at her pillow. Washed clean of self-pity, she found a new feeling: anger. Sitting up straight, thin and stiff as a stick, she stared into the night, her fingers laced tightly together. Lightning flickered at the edges of her drawn shade, but she could ignore it now.

That terrible little man is up to something, she thought, and I *will* tell Mr. Hearst, even if it means losing my job!

Sinking back, the freckled young woman sighed like a deflating tire. Her lips hardened in a righteous smile. Tomorrow morning first thing I'll tell him.

Mary sank into sleep.

🙢 22 🙠

HUGE wet leaves framed the bower where Aphrodite hid from the wind-whipped night. Charlie Chaplin beamed at the statue; he kissed her rigid marble lips. "Smashing!" he pronounced. Gloria Deere stood behind him. Hearing what he thought was her happy cry of delight, he threw his head back and crowed, letting the rain splash his face. But when he climbed down from the plinth and turned, the pretty brunette was not laughing with him.

She was nowhere in sight.

Chaplin frowned. "Crikey." He peered into the drenched night. "Gloria?" he called softly, then more loudly, "Gloria, love!"

The crashing hiss of rain drowned her answer—if she made any.

Nearby a thin gaunt form raised its head.

🙢 23 🙠

T HE elevator whined to a stop. Otis Pike opened the door and stepped into the dimly lit vaults below Casa Grande. He shivered. It was colder than a witch's tit down here, and it smelled like death, but at least no one had tried to stop him.

Just let me remember the way, he thought.

Wearing a knife-edge smile, he headed with his hobbling, wounded walk toward what he hoped was the end of his long, long quest. I see how the pieces fit now; I just need the last one. The elevator buzzed to life behind him; someone had called it up, but he paid no attention to that.

🙢 24 🙠

W ITH barely a glance at the empty mouse cage, William Randolph Hearst crossed to Marion Davies' bedroom. Her door was half open, and he paused there. He felt faintly queasy, strange. His heart? But as usual, it was his job to smooth the ruffled waters. I'm her slave, he thought.

Marion was humming and dancing about the room, holding out a new peach-pink dress. She stopped. "Oh, it's you." Her brow furrowed. "I h-hate this room. It looks like a . . . a m-museum! Why do I have to have all th-these old antiques around?"

Hearst warily stepped in. "They're art. I saved some of my best

240

pieces for you. That's a Watteau, and that was painted by Vermeer. They're worth a lot of money."

"To you, not to m-me."

He took another step. "Please, Marion. Can't we be friends?"

"Oh . . . I g-guess so." But she shrugged off the bulky arms that reached for her. "L-leave me alone now, P-Popsy. I want to g-go to bed."

"Why're you trying on that dress?"

"I c-can do what I want."

"You're not going someplace, are you?"

"And what if I am?" Her tone was warning.

"Where?"

She giggled. "Just thought I'd take a little w-walk down to the ocean for a s-swim. D-don't b-be an old p-poop." She turned her back. "J-just go 'way."

Hearst's heart thudded. Her slender white neck, the half oval of pale flesh above her blouse—so tender, so beautiful. He had met her when he was fifty-four—oh, to be even that young again! "You *do* understand about Tashman's script?" he said.

Her shoulders wriggled with indifference. "I don't c-care about that old thing."

"I couldn't have you play a . . . a—"

"*I told you, I don't c-care!*" Her blue eyes flashed. "Play a what? Why c-can't you say it? A *whore*, that's what. Well, what's wrong with a whore? At least she m-makes her own m-money—and m-maybe she has a good time doing it."

"Marion!"

"Oh . . . oh, shit!" She stamped her foot.

Hearst felt his heart racing, and his fingers opened and closed at his sides. "Don't use four-letter words. You know how I—"

Her alcohol breath hit his face. "You h-hate 'em, yeah, and d-don't I know it. Well, as f-far as l-little Marion is concerned the only b-bad four-letter word is 'dull,' got that? Who d'you th-think you are, my d-daddy? Well," she thrust her chin at him, "you're old enough to be."

He blinked, too shocked to be angry.

"Get out of here!" she yelled.

He slapped her.

"Ow!" She tumbled onto the bed, one shoe clattering to the floor. "P-Popsy!" she yelped, holding her jaw.

Lightning licked at the windows.

Hearst stared. "Marion . . ." he said, feeling dizzy and stupid, holding out a hand, wanting only to stroke and soothe her and make it all right.

She pushed his hand aside and jumped up. "Oh, I hate this r-rain and I . . . I hate this house, and I hate *you*. I'm young!" She quavered near tears. "How much longer w-will I be young? I want to have fun while I'm young, and you're not g-gonna st-stop me!"

"You can't—"

She crawled on the floor, scrambling for her shoe. "I'm g-getting out of here." She pulled the shoe on, "and d-don't try to say I'm not."

"The road is washed out."

She thrust her face into his. "I d-don't p-plan on going that f-far, b-buster."

"Stay away from Eddie Deere!" he called.

Marion turned on him, her pretty face a furious blue. "You're a married man, remember that—only not m-married to m-me!" She ran from the room.

Hearst started to follow, but he felt dizzy again, as if huge waves tossed him about. He heard their roar. No, that was only the thunder: God's roar. Help me, God! He found himself on Marion's bed, though he did not remember slumping there. Soft satin sheets. Marion's perfume. Her dachshund's brown eyes stared at him from a pillow; her lingering scent drove him crazy. Eddie Deere, that kid who hates me—she's going to sleep with him, damn her! I love her, I tried to get a divorce. He pushed himself up with a grunt, tottered, found a shaky balance. Rain slammed at the windows. How dare she! This is *my* house, *my* land. He staggered to a chair, leaned heavily, chest heaving.

Well, I won't let her.

The dizziness stopped; rage took its place. Hearst had had rages before. He knew they led to no good; he broke and destroyed valuable things—and people—but he could not stop this one and did not want to.

He charged to his room. His eyes fell on the glass globe on his dresser, and he blinked in momentary confusion. Snow . . . Wiesbaden . . . Otis Pike. No, not now. He jerked open the top drawer, pulled out the pistol, and shoved it in his jacket pocket on top of the orphanage list.

Marion!

No young bolshie bastard can poach on my territory.

The massive old man rushed to the elevator.

🎋 25 🎋

LOUELLA crept higher uphill in the rain. Glimpsing movement at Casa Grande's arching portal, she ducked behind a marble baluster just as Marion Davies dashed out into the storm. Louella chewed her lip: what's little Marion up to now? The slender blonde wore nothing to protect her from the lashing rain, and in seconds her champagne-colored silk blouse and slacks were plastered to her like a second skin, revealing every curve. Her hair went limp. She flung out her arms and pirouetted, then leapt into the fishpond and began to frolic and dance, uttering shrieks. Laughter? Sobs? She grasped a gin bottle in her hand.

The wild dance stopped. Marion lifted the bottle, drank. Then, sleek with wet, she dashed off in the direction of Casa del Monte.

Uh-oh, Louella thought. She hesitated. Chase after her, or . . . ? The hill seemed suddenly deserted. Where'd all those people go?

The Chief lumbered out of Casa Grande. The storm hit him, flattening his lank grey hair against his brow. He too wore no raincoat, and he looked like a volcano about to explode. He glowered right, then left. Looking for Marion? That floozie isn't fit to pour your coffee, you poor dear man! Louella was about to reveal herself—she longed to rush and comfort her Chief—but all at once she realized what he waved in his right hand and stayed crouched where she was. Shaking, she recalled that awful Thomas Ince business a dozen years ago; being a good reporter could be dangerous.

Good grief, do *I* need a gun?

❧ 26 ❧

GULPING hoarse agitated breaths of excitement, Otis Pike knelt on the cold cement floor of a vault deep under Casa Grande. He flipped through page after page.

Near, so near . . .

The pale little man could not hear the storm, which was muffled by the massive weight of the big house. A rustling stilliness enveloped him. Mice scampered nearby; he ignored them. His bad leg ached worse than ever, but he pushed pain aside and kept at his task amidst the discarded jumble of photo albums he had already rifled. They had not been the right ones, and he had simply tossed them aside—he sat encircled by a hill of them, like a bulwark—rushing on to the next: Hearst's past, preserved.

The old bastard's ruin preserved, I hope, Pike thought.

He cursed the dim light cast by the single bare bulb, but his stubby fingers continued to flick album pages, and faces, places fled by. It had been a revelation, those last moments in Casa del Monte. *Eyes.* Ha! And now, and now . . .

The album spines were labeled, and he knew approximately, out of Hearst's long ugly life of seventy years of stepping on people, of snapping pictures as if he was proud of it all, which years to search through: 1890–1910. But it was still not easy. Those years had spawned hundreds of the thick volumes, and Hearst's hated face gazed at the dwarf seemingly endlessly, over and over: the long nose, the sly, sloppy grin, the steely eyes. He was younger then, but

244

he was the same Mr. High and Mighty. There were pictures of Hearst and his mother, political meetings, the newspaper crowd. Who were all those mugs? Bet lots of 'em are dead by now. Dead. The idea ate at Pike—the ones I loved and who loved me are dead!—and he moaned, and the horrible muted flashes threatened to overwhelm him again.

Pike swore; he kept on turning pages.

And then he found it. One of Hearst's summer jaunts, a bunch of his stupid toadies trailing him like sheep through foreign cities, where they didn't do anything but hang around and eat swell food and stay in swell hotels because Big Shot Hearst was paying the bills. White captions identified the places: Monte Carlo, Como, Wiesbaden.

Wiesbaden.

Pike cackled. There were plenty of pictures—enough. One face in particular. The resemblance was sure.

He knew exactly where Rose Ellen Forrest's death fit in.

Still chortling, almost singing, he began ripping the pages from the album. Maybe he wouldn't expose the old bastard right away. Why not a little blackmail to make him sweat before tossing him to the wolves?

"What're you doing?"

Ice surged through the little man's veins, and he scrambled up, spilling torn album pages. Photographs fluttered like big flakes of snow about his feet.

Someone stood in the shadows.

The figure stepped into the light.

Pike's whitish brows lifted. "I shoulda known." His laughter was like the eager yipping of a dog.

27

MARVIN Orr had followed someone, then lost him—or her.

At least Colonel Joe can't say I didn't move my tail, the security man thought, inching his baggy raincoat back, fingering the pistol on his lumpy hip. Feeling jumpy, he wiped his brow. Never had to use this thing yet; don't want to use it now.

Then he heard a strange, sliding sound. His hand tightened on the gun. He stopped, waited; the sound ceased abruptly.

He took a cautious step into the light.

Something struck him. There was no pain, only the shock of the blow. In his last instant of consciousness he felt a strange dizzy relief. See, Colonel Joe, I *did* do my job. . . .

28

BLOOD, Charlie Chaplin thought, quaking.

But I made it back to my room.

Feeling stinging pain, Chaplin slipped out of the yellow slicker and eased off his coat. The torn left shoulder of his white shirt was stained red, and when he peeled it off he saw on the deltoid muscle the long gash oozing. The blood had seeped down his arm, run between his fingers.

I shouldn't have done it, Chaplin thought. He thought too of scandal. The newspapers, that Parsons woman, damn her—they already say I'm a skirt chasher and a Red.

Teeth clenched, he pictured the Tramp on trial; beloved Charlie in the dock.

Don't panic.

In his bathroom in the Doges Suite he washed the wound in cold water and splashed on after-shave as antiseptic, wincing at the sting. Tearing a clean strip from the bloodied shirt, he managed a clumsy bandage.

Carefully he packed the rest of the shirt and the coat at the bottom of a suitcase, piled clothes on top. The slicker with the two holes in it? That was harder. He peered out his door; no one was in the long corridor that led to the maze of the house. His shoulder was beginning to throb but he could stand the pain; he wouldn't faint. He made his way unseen up to the second floor, where two rows of windows faced north and south onto side terraces. The storm beat against the windows, and beyond their thin fragile shell the night seemed cavernous.

He tossed the incriminating slicker out one of the windows into the rain, then crept back to his room and slumped into a big claw-footed chair. He struggled to sort things through. His face flamed. I left that little bird, Gloria, out there, but what could I do? She ran off. Where?

What in bloody hell happened? Chaplin thought.

🎔 29 🎔

ETTA Kitt was bored. She had been sitting by the switchboard in the dark for over six hours. She had glimpsed plenty of yellow slickers flitting to and fro in the storm; that had been fun. But, she thought, tearing open her second pack of Luckies, the problem was that those darn coats made everyone anonymous. Who were they? She pictured tomorrow's daily gossip session at the servants' breakfast: Queen Etta, who knows all. They'll expect names. I'll make up names, she thought, blowing smoke through sputtering laughter. Who'll ever know the diff?

She thought about Billy Buller. Why'd the big lug stand me up? Suddenly stiffening, she forgot Billy. She had not seen anyone for at least fifteen minutes; now a person in a yellow slicker, rain hat pulled low, was creeping down a curving tile path from the upper terrace. Something was funny about this one, and she wished the drooping oak branches did not block her view quite so much. The figure seemed to be carrying something—what? Etta held her breath. He was heading toward her!

Etta did not like that at all. She jumped up. I'm alone, she thought, shivering at the sneaky way the figure slithered along. Etta dropped her cigarette; she squinted. That thing it carried . . . something metal that caught glints from the garden lights.

The figure entered the oaks.

It came straight for her window.

Etta saw what it was carrying: long sharp shrubbery shears. Moaning, she leapt at her switchboard to send a call for help to Joe Willicombe. Let him be awake!

Pulling, flailing at the phone cords, which seemed suddenly to be a nest of snakes, fighting her, Etta began to sob. All the lines were dead.

❧ 30 ❧

AS if to hide—as if hiding could help—Gloria Deere pulled the heavy covers of the huge Renaissance bed in Casa del Monte right over her head. She kicked her feet in anger and disgust.

What a horrible thing to happen! Horrible!

Shaking, fighting to calm herself, she stuck her thumb in her mouth and sucked hard. Charlie. The worst of it was that he had deserted her. All those stories about him were true: he was a beast! But she couldn't be mad at him, only at what had happened. Tears dampened the soft brown lashes from which she had not bothered to remove the mascara. After all, maybe it wasn't Charlie's fault.

Gloria beat her fists on her pillow. Oh, she *hated* Mr. William Randolph Hearst!

🐾 31 🐾

VINNY Tashman sat on the edge of his bed gaping at the pistol in his limp hand.

The gun stank of cordite: a shot—shots—had been fired. Did I kill someone out there?

Oh, Christ!

Vinny held his head. He thought of the orphanage in Chicago. Why didn't I die there?

"Drunk, I'm still drunk," he moaned and realized that he had not even removed the yellow slicker, that water from it was soaking into the fine brocade bedspread. The price of the spread would probably pay a year's rent at the Alto Nido. Damn Hearst! Clumsily pulling off the slicker, reeling, Vinny flung it across the room.

Not fair! Not fair! He laughed wildly. Maybe *I* ought to become a Red, he thought. He stopped laughing as despair slammed into him. I'm finished—and who gives a good goddamn?

Vinny stared at his gun. Stick it in my mouth? Blow out my brains?

🦋 32 🦋

LOUELLA huddled against her husband in the dark.

"Oh, Docky . . . Docky . . ." He woke, reeking of pipe smoke. I hate that smell, Louella thought.

"Wha . . . what?" Docky flopped an arm over her. "Why, you're freezing, Lollipops."

"I've been up."

"Shouldn't be up," he mumbled.

"I'm *so* scared!"

"There, there." A hand limply patted her; shortly there were snores.

Louella felt lost. He's not awake, he doesn't care, she thought, shaking, and even if he were I couldn't tell him. The night gathered about her like the end of the world. She chewed on her nails.

Oh, what have I done?

🦋 33 🦋

THE storm continued to pour over the Enchanted Hill, drenching—but its flailing attempts grew fitful, as if it had given up the battle against Hearst's strong walls; there was even a ghostly glimpse of moon through shredded clouds. The zoo animals ceased shifting and grumbling in their shelters. Yellow slickers no longer fled along the curving, rain-slick paths.

Marion Davies had dried her hair as best she could with the

towels in Eddie Deere's bathroom. Naked, she lay in his bed. Naked, too, shivering, he crawled in next to her. "What time is it?"

She woke, peering in low lamplight at the only thing she had on, the thin gold watch Popsie had given her on her thirtieth. "After two," she murmured languidly and, gazing at the blue eyes that didn't quite meet hers, smiled. She touched his cute, cute nose. "And where's my b-baby boy b-been?"

"Hang on to me."

"Why, you're sh-shaking." A giggle. "D-do I d-do that to you?"

"Yes. It's you."

He tried to hide his face, but she held it so she could search its sharp angles, so bewilderingly familiar. "Well, I just d-don't believe you."

"It's you! You!" he said almost angrily and turned his head, burying his wet hair against her.

"Me. Yes it's m-me," she said, giving in, squeezing tight. His urgency surprised her, and she laughed. "Oh, my shy b-boy isn't shy anym-more!" He stretched an arm to turn out the light, but she stopped him. "No, I l-l ke to see." Purring, she began to lick his ear. "It's always b-better to s-see—especially with a h-handsome b-boy like you."

🎴 34 🎴

J OE Willicombe woke to a pounding on his door. Switching on the lamp on his bedside table, he peered at the round clock dial: almost three. Just got to sleep, he thought, planting his feet on cold tile and rubbing his eyes. His sleep had been marked by uneasy dreams, dwarfs firing pistols in a blinding snow. Unwillingly he recalled the moment just before retiring, his glimpse of the Chief trundling through the Assembly hall in a fury. The Chief hadn't seen him. That bulge in his jacket pocket—the pistol he usually kept in his dresser? Willicombe did not like to think about that.

The pounding got more frantic. A woman was shouting. He plucked up his glasses from the nightstand and shrugged into his long maroon robe. In slippers he padded to the door.

Soaking wet, the telephone girl Etta Kitt practically leapt into the room.

"Oh, Mr. Willicombe!" she moaned, holding her head as if it might fly off.

"What's wrong?"

"Someone's cut the telephone lines—the telegraph lines too. Some *crazy* person!" Clutching his lapels, she blew her shrill breath in his face. "Oh, Mr. Willicombe, I was so scared, it was so awful. He came at me through the trees. With clippers! I thought I was going to get killed, and I tried to call you, but I couldn't; everything was dead. And I just screamed, and then—"

"He? Who?"

"Or she." Etta's brow furrowed. "Yes, I s'pose it could have been a she. I couldn't see the person's face. Oh, didn't you hear? The telephone lines are cut."

Willicombe fought the ropy vestiges of sleep. "Try to calm yourself," he said thickly. "Sit here." Leading her to a big overstuffed chair by the dresser, he shut the door. Got to keep this private, he thought. "Here's some water," he said, bringing a glass from the bathroom. His head was clearing. "Now, just start at the beginning."

She gulped the water. It was as she had said, and she knew little more. She had cowered in the telephone building until Mavis Penny, her replacement, had popped in just past two. The two women had worked up the nerve to explore outside, and that's when they had discovered the cut lines. "But they weren't cut so they could be patched back together," Etta said. "Whole big pieces've been chopped away and made off with. Now, who would do a thing like that?"

"Mr. Hearst's guests get a little rambunctious at times," Willicombe said, but his smile was weak, and Etta's sharp glance told him she didn't believe in unicorns or Hollywood virgins either. She's no dope, Willicombe thought, rubbing his temples; his head had begun to pound.

There was another knock at the door. Willicombe glanced at Etta. Now she was safe, she looked eager to be in on things, but he did not like that; he knew her reputation for gossip. Can't just chase her away, he thought, sighing inwardly.

He opened the door.

It was Al Bushmiller, one of the workmen he had sent downhill. Bushmiller was a big looming man, tough and dependable. In khaki work clothes he looked exhausted, and he was wet and dirty. His grim face prepared Willicombe for the worst.

He spread his hands. "Like we expected, sir. The poor joker's dead. Got thrown out of the truck, and it crushed him like a bug. That hillside's pretty bad too. Don't think we should fool with it until the rain stops. we ought to call up help from San Luis Obispo, I guess."

Call? How? Willicombe thought. Hearing a small sharp gasp, he turned.

Etta Kitt was on her feet. "Who's . . . dead?" she gulped.

"Billy Buller," Bushmiller said before Willicombe could stop him.

"Billy?" Etta's hands flew to her mouth. "No!"

Willicombe saw at once how it was. She staggered, and he helped her to sit down. "You can go," he said to Bushmiller over his shoulder. "Bring the body up here—but I don't want any of this to go beyond you and your men. And don't risk anyone trying to fix anything."

Bushmiller's eyes were on Etta. "No kidding." His gaze flew to Willicombe, and he stiffened. "Yes, sir." He backed quickly out.

"I'm sorry," Willicombe said to Etta, who was rocking and moaning.

"Billy," she blubbered wetly.

"Willicombe!" A new voice.

Willicombe turned. Bushmiller had left the door open, and Waldo Dix, the small wiry head zookeeper, stood just in the room clutching a dripping rain hat. Dix was touchy at the best of times, he looked particularly nasty now, and Willicombe silently cursed. "What is it?" he said.

Dix came in like thunder. "What the hell's going on up here, that's what I want to know. I'm so mad I could pop—and when Mr. Hearst hears it, he'll be mad too, you bet!" The quivering man hardly glanced at Etta. "Most of the baboons've come back on their own, that's somethin'; but God damn it, one of em's been shot."

"Shot?"

"Dead as a doornail. *Blam*, right through the noggin, and I wanta know what you're gonna do about it."

Willicombe stared at Dix's taut, outraged face, but he could feel no surprise, only a numbness. This weekend had been mad from the start, and the latest insanity fit. "All right," he said at last.

"All right?" Dix looked like he was about to throw his dripping hat in Willicombe's face. He shook his finger. "It sure as hell's *not* all right!"

"I mean," Willicombe said in sudden fury, "you've made your report; now go!"

Dix stiffened. "I'll be damned," he said, "I'll be good goddamned." He shook his finger again. "Wait'll Mr. Hearst hears about this! Just wait!" He stomped out, fuming.

Willicombe sank onto his bed. There's one I'll have to patch up, he thought. Staring at Etta, hunched and sobbing, he pitied her. How much of what had gone on between her and Buller goes on among other servants up here? he wondered. But he could not spend time consoling her. Buller was dead; that could not be helped, and he needed to concentrate on making sense of things.

A baboon shot through the head?

He got Etta to her feet, glad she had waited until Mavis Penny replaced her. Wait. the lines were cut; we don't need an operator. He almost laughed, until he thought, We can't even call for help.

When Etta was gone, Willicombe took two aspirins and forced himself to think. Tell the Chief now, or wait till dawn? He paced. That bulge in the Chief's pocket—could he have shot the baboon? Not likely; he loves animals almost better than people. Yet he had looked crazy. Marion again. Willicombe winced at the memory of his boss's past destructive rages, but Hearst had never to his knowledge done anything criminal.

Of course, I've only worked for him ten years, and there can always be a first time.

Willicombe went to his closet. Got to face the Chief now, he decided. Tell him about Buller, the cut phone lines, the baboon. And ask some questions of my own.

He dressed quickly and headed out into the first-floor corridor. The big house lay hushed about him, dozing. Suits of armor stood stiff as mummies, and a mouse scurried under a bow-fronted Regency commode. He reached the Assembly Hall, deserted and echoing. Lights burned dimly in sconces. The hearth was cold; the storm seemed to be dying against the north and south windows. He opened the hidden choir panel—and stopped right there. Beyond it the elevator door was not shut as it should be. A leg held it open.

A short leg, ending in a foot wearing a thick-heeled built-up shoe.

Willicombe opened the elevator door all the way. He looked down.

He had thought he could not be shocked more tonight, but he had been wrong. An acid taste burned his mouth, and for a moment he could not get his breath.

All he could think was, Right through the head, like the baboon.

At that moment he heard a woman singing. He turned.

Marion was dancing toward him across the Assembly Hall, twirling, dipping, pirouetting as if a handsome young partner held her tight in his arms. Seeing him, she halted in the midst of a tipsy turn. "Oh, Joe-sy!" Getting her balance, she laughed and pinched his cheek. "You should b-be in b-bed. G-got a g-girlfriend stashed someplace? Goodness!" Her eyes saucered at the body on the elevator floor. "Is he d-dead?" Her slender fingers flew to her lips. "Why I *d-do* believe he's d-dead."

VII

Detective Hearst

🎕 1 🎕

HEARST looked up. "Buller's dead?"

"There's more." Hearst stirred irritably, and Willicombe did not like the way his boss's expression said he expected that there was more; he did not like the washed-out, beaten look. It was 3:30 A.M. He had found Hearst in his bedroom. A single lamp cast a muted spidery light; it barely touched the photograph of Hearst's mother on the wall by the canopied bed, but her pinched, shrewd eyes seemed to watch everything. In a silk robe, the bulky old man sat by the mullioned window at an antique Italian writing desk drumming his fingers on its marble top. Willicombe recalled when Hearst had picked up the desk at an auction in Verona four years ago in a fever of bidding. He paid too much, the secretary thought—he's always paid too much. He's paying now—and he pitied the misunderstood old man to whom he was devoting his life.

The rain seemed gentle now, almost kind, as it flicked against the window.

"Have they brought Buller's body up?"

"Yes."

"What've you done with it?"

"Put it in the cold storage locker." With the meat, Willicombe thought.

Hearst barked an ugly laugh. "It's grotesque, isn't it? Death. Is someone else dead, Joe?"

Willicombe started. "You knew?"

"You're acting like someone else is dead." Hearst suddenly pressed his fingers against the desktop, and his webbed old eyes flared with terror. "Not . . . not Marion?"

"No. She's all right. We found the body together."

Hearst sank back. "Together?"

259

"She was . . . coming in. I was heading up to tell you about Buller."

Hearst rubbed the smooth marble. "Coming in. From where? Never mind. Where is she now?"

"I saw her to her room."

"She's all right?"

"Shaken. She's . . ."

"Drunk? You can say it."

"Tipsy. It softened the shock."

"Liquor softens a lot for Marion—too much. I love her, Joe. You think I'm crazy to love her?"

"Marion is a charming young woman." Willicombe wished he had left out the *young*.

Hearst sighed. "All right. Who's dead besides Buller?"

"The dwarf, Otis Pike. Someone shot him in the forehead."

The wind sang against the eaves. Hearst shook his head. "I can't work up a good goddamn about him, Joe. But in *my house!*" The idea glavanized the publisher; he pushed himself up out of his chair, and Willicombe was not happy to see what was revealed on the desk: the glass globe with the alpine scene in it, and next to it, Hearst's small black pistol.

Hearst caught his stare. He smiled oddly, and for a moment he seemed far away, in some distant place. He picked up the gun. "Yes, I fired it. Here, smell. It's a nasty smell, isn't it?" His expression darkened. "But I didn't kill anyone, Joe."

"Of course not."

"Put the idea out of your mind."

"I will."

Hearst gripped his secretary's arm hard. "I need you now, Joe, as my ally, on my side. We have to decide what to do."

Willicombe gazed into the age-blotched face. The pinpoint blue eyes seemed to spin; the nostrils flared, and there were dots of spit at the corners of the drooping mouth. Hearst gazed back. He seemed surprised at himself, then ashamed; his hand fell, his look went elsewhere.

Willicombe shifted his feet. "There are complications," he said. From the zoo an elephant's trumpet rose above the soft hiss of rain as the secretary explained about the cut telephone and telegraph lines. "And someone shot one of the baboons."

"Shot one of the . . . Why?"

"Waldo Dix reported it. Who knows why?"

"An innocent animal. Damn him for doing it!"

"Or her. We don't know that it wasn't a woman."

A sharp look. "You sound like a policeman. But then," Hearst said, pouchy eyes sparking, "we *will* have to play police, won't we? Because the road is out, and the lines are cut, and—"

"We could send men downhill."

"No. Too treacherous for that." Jerking the belt of his robe tight, the old man began to lumber back and forth across the room. "The cliffs, the wet and mud," he murmured. "Who knows what else that quake might have loosened and left ready to slide? The men would have to cross at least three miles of animal compound, and some of the animals can be dangerous, especially if this damn storm and quake have riled them up. No, for now we'll just have to do what we can by ourselves."

Hearst stopped at the window, staring out, rising on his toes, settling, hands in robe pockets. He *wants* to play policeman, Willicombe thought, unable to shake disloyal ideas. *Could* he have cut those lines? The secretary poked at his glasses. If only the real police were here! If only everyone could be sent off the hill, safe! "I'll help however I can," he said. At least the Chief had his old energy back. If there was one thing that always roused him it was deciding things, giving orders.

Why did it have to take murder to do it this time?

Hearst turned from the window. "Where did you find Pike?"

"In your elevator. First floor. His game leg was propping the door open."

"He's still there?"

"Yes. I got one of the security men, Donovan, to stand guard, to prevent anyone else finding out."

"Good for you, Joe; you're on top of things. Of course, someone else knows, besides us. That's who we've got to smoke out, isn't it? A murderer."

"Sir, he's killed once, and—"

"Or she."

A nod. "Yes. Or she. The point is, could it happen again?"

Hearst's mouth clamped in a hard thin line. "It's something we have to think about, isn't it?" He rubbed his hands, as if he had at last found a fire to warm them. "Let's see the body."

2

JAKE Donovan was a balding, stocky Irishman whose broad flat face ordinarily glowed ruddy red, but he looked shaken and pale as he shuffled aside to give Hearst and Willicombe room. Because the body prevented their using the elevator, they had trudged down the concrete stairs that spiraled around its shaft. Hearst still wore his silk robe. "Good man, Donovan," he said, patting the guard's shoulder. There was little space between the hidden door to the Assembly Hall and the elevator. Hearst gazed down. "This is how you found him?"

Willicombe did not like to look again, but he made himself, feeling queasy. "Just like that, except the door was closed on his leg."

Hearst nodded. "Wait in the Assembly Hall," he said to Donovan, and the Irishman looked glad to leave.

When he was gone Hearst said, "It's ugly, Joe, isn't it?" It was. Otis Pike lay face up, his good leg twisted under the short one sticking out the door. One arm was flung above his head; the other was bent in an L, wrist curled, hand twisted like a claw. The unnatural awkwardness of the pose made him look like a stuffed doll thoughtlessly tossed aside by a child. Worse was the face, even paler than in life, as if modeled in wax. The mouth was open, upper lip curled. Yellowish teeth seemed to snarl, but the snarl was frozen, rigid, and even more horrible for it. The nostrils flared. The eyes that had peered so narrowly were for once open wide, staring, and they seemed to scream *No!* Then there was the wound, centered just

262

above the eyes, a small, black, bruised hole, from which remarkably little blood had seeped, though there was a reddish smudge on the elevator floor under the dwarf's odd, tufted scalp. There was a smell too, of the sphincter letting go in the death agony.

Willicombe wanted to push the body in and wall up the elevator.

"How *dare* someone do this in my house," Hearst snapped. Grunting, he stepped over the body and began peering around the wood-paneled elevator. He squinted at walls and ceiling. At last he turned. "He wasn't shot here, Joe. No bullet holes."

"Where, then?"

"Why? is the more important question. But, yes, where? Well, there are a lot of rooms in this house."

"Plenty of places outside too. The bottom of his pants and his shoes are wet."

"But not the rest of him. So he was wearing a raincoat. Where is it?"

"Where he was shot?"

"Maybe. He was a peculiar little man, wasn't he?"

"You said he hated you."

"Yes . . . that look he gave me at dinner. A lot of men hate me, don't they, Joe?"

Willicombe didn't answer. He hated himself for wondering if the bullet that had plowed through Otis Pike's brain were the same caliber as the ones in his boss's gun upstairs.

"First things first," Hearst said, stepping out of the elevator. "Discretion is number one. None of our guests are to hear about this. They know the road is caved in; they'll know soon enough that they can't phone out. We're cut off, and if they discover someone's been shot we'll have one hell of a panic. That's one reason."

"The other?"

Hearst gazed into the dimness of the curving concrete stairs. "It's almost," he murmured, "as if whoever cut the lines was . . . helping." His gaze returned to his secretary's face. "So, we have time to figure this out ourselves, before the police and reporters come barging in. I don't want a scandal. Frankly, I'd rather this never came to light."

"But it has to."

Hearst's eyes turned to flint. "Not necessarily. Official reports don't have to be made. Don't look so shocked, Joe. They will be, of course, if it's unavoidable, but . . . murder? In this house? It would blacken all our names for the rest of our lives. The Ince affair was a dozen years ago, and people still haven't forgotten it. No. I can't afford more of the same; my reputation as a newsman can't afford it; neither can Marion's career. We'll bring in the police if we have to, but for now we have a perfect excuse to delay."

Willicombe didn't like it. He nodded nonetheless.

"I want the body out of here."

"But if the police *do* have to be brought in—"

"I know: you're not supposed to move bodies. But I won't be inconvenienced, damn it. And we can't leave him here for someone to trip over. Besides," Hearst said, wrinkling his nose, "the smell will only get worse. We'll put him in cold storage under the house, with Buller. But first we'll take pictures; we can show the police those if we have to, to prove we tried our best. We have plenty of cameras. Go up and get that big Rolleiflex flash. Take plenty of shots, from all angles. We're our own police now, Joe; let's do it right."

In spite of misgivings, Willicombe had to admire his boss's decisiveness. "Uh, you'll stay with the body while I get the camera?"

"No. Donovan can keep watch." Hearst massaged his brow. "I hate to let somebody else know about this, but we need a doctor, and I'm going to get one."

❧ 3 ❧

L OUELLA had not gotten to sleep; she huddled next to Docky in the unfriendly night. Darn his snores! But she had other things on her mind: things she had seen, done. Shock and horror. Decision. Foolishness?

She gripped the sheets with fists like claws. What a stupid woman I am!

There was a knock on the door, soft but firm, and Louella panicked. Have they come to get me? she wondered in terror. Quaking, she slipped from bed and put on her robe. The click of the lamp barely interrupted Docky's placid snores. She gazed down at the round lax face of the man who loved her, and tears squeezed from her eyes. Oh, how can I ever explain to him?

Braced for martyrdom, she flung open the door.

Mr. Hearst stood there in a yellow slicker and rain hat. Louella was surprised—and then she was not surprised at all. Of course. She took a breath. Forgive me, she was about to plead, but she did not get the chance.

"Very sorry to wake you, Louella," Mr. Hearst said solemnly, "but I need to speak to your husband."

❧ 4 ❧

DOCKY lit his pipe in the narrow space just behind the hidden door to the Assembly Hall. The elevator still contained its gruesome contents, and his hands had trouble with the match. "Not used to dead bodies," he got out, "especially shot ones. Pregnancy is more my line—or preventing it." His laugh was shaky.

"Dead bodies aren't my line either," Hearst grumbled, "and I damn well didn't ask for this one. But I'm stuck with it. Dr. Dilworth is off in Pasadena this weekend, so you're on call. Can you tell us anything that might help determine who shot him?"

"Only that he was shot close up and hasn't been dead long." Docky shuddered. "But shouldn't the police be asking that? They *will* be here soon?"

Hearst glanced at Willicombe, who held a large press camera with which he had just taken a dozen photographs. "Listen carefully," he said to Docky. "The storm has temporarily, ah . . . interfered with our phone and telegraph lines, and with the road out we can't get to the police just yet. I refuse to leave the body here for an indefinite time."

Docky pulled out his pipe. "You're going to move it? Oh, that's not a good idea; I can't be a party to that."

"I'm not asking you to. It's my decision, and I have plenty of reasons for it. I wanted you to look at him only in case later on there's some help you could give the police, some clue; I want to do the right thing as far as I can. But I *am* going to move him, and I need your cooperation: you're not to tell anyone there's been a murder."

Docky sputtered laughter. "Impossible," he blurted. "Louella finds out everything!"

Hearst did not laugh. He jabbed Docky's lapel with a hard, gnarled finger. "This is no joke, and you'll just have to see that she doesn't find out about this."

"Um . . . ah . . ." Docky swallowed his grin.

"You can go back to bed now. Tell Louella one of the servants was ill, that's why I needed you."

"Y-yes," Docky said. Looking chastened, he hurried out through the hidden door.

Hearst turned to Willicombe as thunder muttered faintly through the old wood. "This isn't going to be easy, Joe."

"No, sir."

"But we have to face it. Can you and Donovan manage to get . . ."—he bobbed his head at the body—"downstairs with Buller?"

"He's a small man, sir. And he's already in the elevator."

Hearst's face was a jowly, brooding mask. "I still want to know why."

"Why he was shot?"

"More than that. Why he's in the elevator. Why he was moved. Never mind for now. I'll take the camera; I'm going to see Marion. When you've got Pike put away, clean up that spot on the elevator floor; then meet me in the study."

❧ 5 ❧

MARION Davies' hair was strewn across her pillow in thick honey waves. She wore a lacy peach-colored nighty. Her breasts rose and fell evenly. Hearst pulled the covers up to her throat, gently tucking them in, and she sighed but did not wake. At her bedroom window the rain was steady, quiet, a soft susurration. Muted light flowed from a bedside lamp. Hearst sat on the edge of the big bed and gazed at his love, while her dachshund, Gandhi, blinked at him from a chair. He fingered a blond curl. Dear Marion. I would give up everything for you—almost. Hearst hated his *almost*. But I *love* my statues and pictures and tapestries! I *love* my strong stone walls! I want them *and* Marion; I want it all! He cursed. Damn weekend; it had been wrong from the start. The storm, and Jack Neylan pressuring him to cut back; Marion flirting with Eddie Deere; then that earthquake, the road washing out, the driver killed, the dwarf murdered; the cut lines, the shot baboon.

Those notes that've been coming for months—did they start it all?

Hearst quivered; he raised his heavy head, filled with the sudden prickling sensation that each event connected. Why can't I see it? Because I don't want to? Snuffling, Gandhi drooped into sleep, and Hearst heaved himself up from the bed. He would talk to Marion later. Where the hell had she been for two hours?

Crossing the sitting room, he glanced only briefly at the cage where Ambrose the mouse had scampered on his little wire wheel. Clipboard at the ready, Willicombe was waiting stolidly in the Study; he adjusted his glasses as his boss strode in.

Hearst glanced at the antique clock. "Almost five," he said, sinking into his red leather chair at the head of the long central table and running his hands through his bone gray hair. He pushed aside the pile of letters that still sat on the gleaming mahogany. "Pike's taken care of?"

"Locked in cold storage. I swore Donovan to secrecy. He's patrolling, keeping an eye open, but—"

"But?"

"It's probably nothing. . . . I can't locate Marvin Orr."

"Orr?"

"One of our security men."

"Mm. Could this Orr have gotten overzealous? Could he have shot Pike and run away in panic?"

"Not Marvin Orr."

Hearst shook his head. "Not one body but *two*, damn it. Buller would be bad enough, but Pike had to get himself murdered. We need clues; isn't that what the police go after?"

"And witnesses."

Hearst bit down hard. "Somehow I think there's only one witness to this."

"Could someone have heard the shot?"

"Depends where it was fired. The storm was making a hell of a racket. If the dwarf was killed outside, I'll bet no one heard it. But I don't think he was killed outside. He would have fallen down, gotten wetter, muddier. It's hard to believe he was shot in one of the guesthouses either. Why would someone drag him up the hill and stick him in the elevator? No, I think he was murdered right here in Casa Grande." The big house seemed to stir, shake. Somewhere a shutter banged. "Look, Joe, it's almost morning. No sense waking people and questioning them; that'd just cause an uproar. We've got to be smarter than that, play our cards close to our chests. I want you to keep your eyes and ears open at breakfast. Everybody up here loves to gossip. Ordinarily I hate that, but maybe someone will play into our hands; maybe they'll let something slip, something they heard or saw. Meanwhile I've got another idea: tell the morning maids that a guest has reported something missing—an expensive watch, let's say—and that we think there's a thief around. Tell them to keep an eye out for anything unusual when they do the rooms and to report to you right away."

"Good idea, sir. But won't Pike be missed? How will we explain that?"

Hearst rubbed his temples. Otis Pike. The name had not been on the orphanage list, but . . . "He didn't seem to know many guests. Most of them probably won't even notice he isn't around, but it might be helpful to pay attention to who asks about him."

"And when someone does?"

"Say he probably slept in, or isn't feeling well. Pretend it doesn't matter. If we make up a story, the killer will know we're trying to hide something. Act like nothing happened; that'll unsettle him."

There was a momentary silence, and Willicombe took his chance. "Sir?" The clock softly bonged five A.M. as he shifted his clipboard from one hand to the other. "You said you had fired your gun."

Hearst gave him a warning look. "Several times."

"Several—?"

The old man stood. "I was mad as a hornet, and I shot it off, and that's all there is to it!"

Willicombe flushed pink. "Sorry. I only . . . that is, well, if the police are brought in—"

"All right, Joe. I get your point. Of course you'll have to tell them all you know; I would expect you to. I've got nothing to hide, but let's wait to face that when—if—the time comes. Damn it, why in hell would someone shoot one of my baboons?"

"Self-defense?"

"Or did the killer mistake it for the dwarf? Pike was small, and in the dark . . . See what I mean?" Hearst ground his hands together. "It's farfetched, I know. This detective game is new to me; I'm just trying to look at all the possibilities."

"You think it all ties together?"

"I'll tell you one thing: I think the threatening notes are part of it."

"You think Pike's killer might've cut the telephone and telegraph lines?"

"Or his—or her—accomplice. I just can't believe they don't have something to do with one another." Hearst came around the table. "Joe, I know you must be tired, but there's one more thing I need, before people are up and about."

269

"Anything, sir."

"Look for a trail: blood, heel marks. Whatever might show where Pike was shot."

"Of course." Willicombe hesitated. "Sir, about his being small . . ."

"Mm?"

"That really does mean a woman could have done it, doesn't it? Could have moved the body pretty easily?"

"I guess it does," Hearst said.

❧ 6 ❧

G LORIA Deere stepped out Casa del Monte's west entrance into a fresh rainless morning. Lifting the button nose which Miss Pilgrim of the Waukegan School of Thespian Arts had assured her was simply *made* for movies, she sniffed the sweet brisk air. Clouds still stitched the sky, but sunshine beamed through, glimmering in the puddles on the red tile terraces. She peered up. Casa Grande looked as romantic as ever, white and clean-washed, but a marble Pan leering from rhododendron leaves nearby seemed to mock her, and Gloria's button nose wrinkled with ill-ease. It was nine A.M. After what she had experienced last night, she was wary. If only it had all been just a bad dream! But it hadn't been, she couldn't kid herself. Still, she was determined to make the best of the rest of her weekend.

She heard a woman's voice saying a name she couldn't quite make out and another word, which she could: *dead.* Her carefully penciled eyebrows puckered. *Dead.* That had been the word all right, and she peeked out Casa del Monte's courtyard to see Clark Gable and Carole Lombard heading up some steps nearby. Gable, Lombard. Gazing into one another's eyes. The couple seemed to float on a cloud, and Gloria loved her little secret, but its champagne fizz was flattened by that word. Someone's dead? Gloria shuddered. She needed company. Now.

She started to chase after the pair.

"G'morning."

Gloria turned to find Vinny Tashman peering at her from the shade of the east doorway. "Oh. Good morning." He looked like something the cat had dragged in, and she frowned. His skin was waxy, his eyes dark smudges; he looked strangely guilty, as if the morning might accuse him of something. Gloria's nose elevated ten degrees in disdain. "I was just going to breakfast," she announced with icy politeness.

"Yeah? I'll tag along."

"If you like."

As they headed up, Gloria gave him a sly once-over. He wore a sporty blue blazer, but his white shirt was rumpled and his tie was so balled up it might have been knotted by Eddie. The brunette smirked. What'd he do, try to strangle himself with it?

"A bad night?" she asked.

"Whaddaya mean?"

"Well, don't jump down my throat. You just don't look terrific, that's all."

He jammed his hands in his pockets. "Too much booze."

Gloria beamed him a spotlight smile. "I drank *lots* too, but I feel tip-top."

Vinny's mind raced as they started up the steps. He focused on her pert, firm breasts under thin green organdy. So what if Chaplin had her last night in place of me? There're lots more dames around. Lots more chances to make good, too. Blow out my brains? Don't make me laugh. I'm not down for the count, I'll make my comeback. But he could not help asking, "Er, anything funny happen last night?"

Gloria gave him a sharp look. "Just what d'you mean?"

"Now who's jumping down whose throat? I just mean, you sleep okay?"

"You said 'something funny.'"

"So what?" Then Vinny glanced past her, and his mouth fell open.

"Well, boil me for an egg!" Staring at the marble Aphrodite at the top of the steps, he felt wild laughter bubble in his throat.

Gloria looked too. She knew just what she'd see, but she flushed as red as could be all the same.

She did not laugh.

※ 7 ※

IN the Refectory the waiters stood by the steam tables at the far end of the room as they had yesterday morning, making sure the eggs, toast, bacon, and chops were plentiful and hot. People drifted in and helped themselves as they had yesterday, chatting, choosing places at the long central table under the bright Siennese banners, but there was a new undertone: someone had died, and a shadow darkened the conversation. Not much however; it had only been an employee, no one important. One of the workmen who had gone down to see about the washed-out road had whispered it to a maid, who had conveyed it to Walter Winchell, or maybe Basil Rathbone. Anyway, the news was out: one of Mr. Hearst's drivers was dead, and people tsk-tsked about it.

"But if the road's out what've they done with him?" Hedda Hopper asked.

"Put him on ice," Herman Mankiewicz murmured. "Speaking of which, I need an ice pack for this head." He wobbled off.

Cary Grant slid into one of the big Dante chairs next to Hedda Hopper. "Anybody get a gander at Venus on the way up?"

Next to him Bette Davis choked back laughter. "I *said* it'd be a bumpy night."

Two chairs down Harpo bugged his eyes lewdly.

"Discussing Venus?" Dick Powell chirped, joining them. "My theory is, it's the long arm of the Hays Office." Sitting, he showed

272

his dimples. "Me, I prefer my dames on the half shell, as raw as oysters."

"I'm at my best on the half shell, sweety," Jean Harlow crooned, leaning so far toward him that her breasts threatened to tumble from her blouse.

"You're raw all right," Hedda put in.

"Well, I just don't care to spend *my* weekend with a dead man, that's all," Gloria Swanson intoned as she stalked past.

Harlow sniffed over her shoulder. "What're you gonna do about it, honey, hike out past the wild animals?" She sprayed laughter at Swanson's back. "I'd love to see it! All that'd be left is your shoes."

Harpo popped a sausage into his mouth. "The animals up here are wild enough for me."

Harlow chucked him under the chin. "And, honey, am I wild!" She swiveled in her chair "Say, what's eating you, Charlie? You look like you swallowed a buffalo."

Chaplin had been sitting silently to her left, poking at two fried eggs. His smile was strained. "Just a bit under the weather, love."

Harlow hugged him, rattlingly. "Cheer up, the storm's over."

That's what you think, Chaplin thought, suppressing a grimace. Her hug had made his wounded shoulder scream. At that moment Gloria Deere walked in with Vinny Tashsman, and Chaplin followed her gloomily with his eyes. Got to talk to that bird.

The Hearst reporter Adela Rogers St. Johns watched it all from a few seats down. What's up with Charlie? she wondered. And what's up with Uncle Joe? St. Johns thoughtfully tapped a tooth. She had been keeping an eye on Joe Willicombe, whose large dignified form loomed to her right. Looks like a stuffed penguin, she thought, smirking, with a microphone wired in his feathers. "Hiya, Joe," she purred. "Snooping on the rich and famous?"

His whole frame quivered. "Snooping?" She had never seen him blush.

"Sure." She poked him. "It takes an old newshound like me to know that look."

A pained smile. "Oh, I'm just enjoying your delightful conversation, Miss St. Johns." He hurried off.

Adela Rogers St. Johns drummed her red-painted nails on her plate.

Gloria paused near the big fireplace, blazing with logs. Oh that darn Charlie—I wouldn't bait a hook with him! She couldn't help glancing his way nonetheless. He gazed back. He looked as sad as a basset, and her heart nearly melted, but she hardened it. He's just *not* a gentleman! He leads poor defenseless girls on, then leaves them in the lurch. Lifting her nose for the second time that morning, Gloria roasted him with the stare Bette Davis had given Leslie Howard in *Of Human Bondage*, before pointedly trailing Vinny to the steam tables.

Louella and Docky came in. Docky gave Willicombe a brief nod. Meaning, Willicombe hoped amid his swamp of gloom, that he's kept his mouth shut about the murder. Louella was pale, droop-shouldered, hollow-eyed, with none of her usual pushy ebullience. She's a wreck. Why? Willicombe's gaze shifted to Eddie Deere, who had trudged in after them. He looked just as hangdog, and Willicombe sighed. You'd think a few hours with Marion would cheer anyone up.

Had Marion been with Eddie?

When will the dwarf show up? Willicombe wondered before he recalled with a sickening twinge that the mysterious little man would not, could not, show up anywhere ever again. He was in heaven by now—or hell. Willicombe frankly hoped it was hell.

Louella and Docky carried plates to an unoccupied section of the table. Louella, who usually ate three eggs and half a dozen sausages, had nothing but a single slice of dry toast. Willicombe strolled casually to a position six feet behind them; avoiding looking at them, he listened intently.

"It was just a sick maid?" he heard Louella hiss.

"Like I told you, Lollipops."

"Which one?"

"Which . . . I don't remember her name. What does it matter? It was only a tummyache. Gastritis."

"You're lying."

"Lollipops, why should I lie?" Out of the corner of his eye Willicombe saw Docky lean near his wife. "*You* went out in the rain last night, didn't you?"

Louella's flacid face quivered near tears.

"Didn't you?" Docky persisted. "I woke up, and you were gone—you weren't in the bathroom. Where did you go?"

"I . . . I needed some fresh air."

"An hour's worth?"

"I was only out a few minutes."

Docky shook his head. "I smoked a pipe. Two pipes, sitting there in the dark. I was worried, Lollipops. I'm worried now." Suddenly he caught sight of Willicombe and began busily sawing at bacon, though he looked like he wanted to throw his plate across the room.

Gloria sat next to Vinny, near Marie Dressler and Damon Runyon and that stuffy old dome-headed Arthur Brisbane. I want *fun!* she thought, but it's all going wrong. She looked at Eddie, all alone, with some scraps of food on his plate that he wasn't even touching, and she felt sorry for him. What a sucker I am. She felt angry too: he was supposed to be her brother, wasn't he? Didn't brothers take care of their kid sisters?

At that moment a man with a bloody head staggered into the room.

"Oh!" Gloria piped. Eddie dropped his fork with a crash, and Louella jumped up, shrieking.

8

WILLIAM Randolph Hearst slipped quietly into Otis Pike's room in Casa del Monte. He fussed and fumed. What's the dwarf's real name?

He was convinced it was not Otis Pike.

Watching from the Gothic Suite, the publisher had waited until most of his guests had gone up to breakfast; then, descending in the elevator, he had slipped out the north side entrance and crept by a little-used path down the terraces under the cloud-smudged sky. Shutting Pike's heavy door, he wrinkled his nose in distaste. The guest room smelled alien, and he hardly recognized the expensive antiques with which he had decorated it: the Della Robbia Madonna with the sweet placid smile, the glowing Turkish carpet, the carved oak bed from an Italian villa. I bought every one, he thought, rubbing his fingertips over a Carrara marble bust of a hawk-nosed Florentine patrician; Once each of them meant the world to me. Goddamn Pike.

Hearst had managed only two hours sleep, but he felt no weariness. Old age had not diminished his capacity for working around the clock when there was a problem to be solved.

He began to search the room.

The dresser contained only odds and ends of clothing.

A second pair of the dwarf's special shoes stood pathetically in a corner, leaning against one another as if in grief.

And then the briefcase. It did not take Hearst long to discover it, hidden at the back of a high closet shelf. A maid would not have noticed it, but Hearst was tall. Feeling about, his fingertips easily found the leather handle, and he pulled it down.

He set it on the bed. He did not have to break the lock; someone had done it for him. Who?

He opened the case.

It was almost empty, though what it held told a kind of story— and solved a mystery. With a sense of personal violation, as if he had discovered secret photographs of himself, Hearst unfolded big architectural drawings of Casa Grande and the guesthouses, copies of the ones that had been filed with the county years ago as a matter of course. They were public record, available to anyone, and Hearst shuddered to discover how easy it was to get what amounted to a road map of his home. The dwarf had planned well. For what? The doodles at the edges of the sheets were what interested him most: little sprays of lines identical to those scrawled on the threatening notes. The old man stared into space. So Pike had sent those notes. He clenched his fists. Am I supposed to know what the damn things stand for? A star? Marion's star. Something to do with Marion? He hated that idea.

The only other things in the case were two large rubber bands. What had they been wrapped around? Hearst was about to toss the architectural plans back when something fluttered from a fold in one of them, a three-by-five photograph. Had the rubber bands held packets of photographs? Possible, then, that someone—Pike's killer?—had gone through the case and removed them but missed this one? It showed a large, well-appointed dining room. The focus was on a cabinet open to display glassware and knickknacks. Hearst's sloping shoulders twitched in frustration. Why would Pike take a picture of a cabinet? A corner of the dining table stuck into the left edge of the picture, on it some pieces of a jigsaw puzzle; on the right, part of a woman: her hip, a glimpse of arm, a slender hand. None of it meant anything to Hearst, yet the picture seemed to whisper to him, to hint, and he tucked it away in his coat.

Putting the briefcase back, he began to go through the dwarf's clothes. His breath wheezed. Wish I were younger; wish I could move faster. His search turned up only one thing, buried in lint deep in the pocket of a gray suit: a brass button about two inches in diameter with LCP embossed on it. It was the kind of button you pinned to your coat, though the fastener was broken off. It was dented, tarnished, obviously old. LCP: Pike's real initials, or something else, some organization? The letters also struck a chord, but nothing more than a vague irritating buzz rose at the back of Hearst's mind.

He went over the room once more. Not a checkbook or business card or set of keys.

Who got here before me?

The old man did not want so much as one of the maids to know he had been snooping here. Annoyed at how well even in death the dwarf covered his tracks, he thrust the brass button in the pocket with the photograph and peeked out the front door of Casa del Monte. No one in sight. Ducking through bushes, he trudged uphill. My hill, my estate! But he hated the way the weekend had seemed to tarnish everything: the Neptune Pool's graceful columns, the heady ocean vista down the long green slopes. A chilly wind blew up from the Pacific, and the clouds seemed to be closing in once more, nibbling at the sunlight. On the upper terrace Aphrodite stood with a last glimmer of morning gold glinting off her graceful marble limbs—but there was violation there too, and Hearst halted, staring.

"Son of a bitch," he growled.

9

MARY O'Grady did not believe Mr. Willicombe.

I just know they've found out! she thought.

Wrapped in misery, the thin, red-haired maid huddled alone at a small wooden table in the maroon-linoleumed servant's dining room at the back of the south wing. Blue checked curtains were at the windows, the morning light slanting past them with a bleached-bone look. Mary had meant to tell Mr. Willicombe everything, but now? Desolate, isolated more than ever from the other maids and butlers by her shameful secret, she hardly tasted the cream of wheat she dribbled into her mouth. She could still see Mr. Willicombe rocking on his heels an hour ago, informing them that there might be a thief and that they were to keep their eyes peeled when they did the rooms and come straight to him if they ran across anything suspicious. But Mary was sure the story about the missing watch was a lie: the jumpy way Mr. Willicombe had fiddled with his glasses told her so. *It's more than that; I just know they're after me!*

Getting up, she earned a frown from the Filipino dishwasher by almost breaking her plate as she clattered it onto the pile waiting to be scrubbed. She didn't care. She plunged outside wrapped in gloom. She and Binnie Fitch were supposed to make up Casa del Monte, but she paled at the thought of doing Mr. Pike's room. *How can I set foot in there again?*

Confess everything? A mental image of the Virgin, patiently smiling, urged her to tell all, and in her confused mind Mr. Hearst got mixed up with God.

She bit her lip. *What a terrible sin!*

People were drifting out from breakfast. They looked serious. Gathered in close-knit murmuring groups, they seemed to be clucking over something that had just happened. *What now?* Mary

278

began to cry, helpless wracking whoops; not wanting to be noticed, she wobbled out of sight into a cluster of rhododendrons. Suddenly Charlie Chaplin popped into view not ten feet away, grasping the shoulder of a small, pretty brunette who seemed to be trying to escape from him. Mary cowered deeper among the leaves. "Where'd you run off to?" Chaplin said urgently. "I looked all over in the rain."

Mary watched through a green tunnel. The brunette seemed to waver but fastened on anger. "Well, you didn't look very hard, that's all I can say. Where did you go, you . . . you *cad*?" Nose in the air, she pulled free. "Just let me alone!" She flounced off.

Chaplin vanished after her, and the voices of the other guests grew faint. It's safe now, Mary thought, her tears drying. She blew her nose. She was about to step from hiding when a glimpse of yellow stopped her. Bending, she scooped up one of Mr. Hearst's slickers. They were provided for the guests; she herself had delivered several to the rooms when the rain started. How had this one gotten here?

Her fingers found two small holes in the left shoulder.

"Oh!" Her fingers came away sticky with blood.

❧ 10 ❧

GLORIA breezed into the west sitting room of Casa del Monte. Is Charlie still following? Oh, let him be!

At her bedroom door she heard a sound and turned, words of forgiveness on her lips, but it was just Eddie, tromping in in his glum heavy-footed way.

Gloria composed herself. "Oh, it's you. Are you all right?"

He shot her a glazed, furious look. "If that bastard William Randolph Hearst is still stepping on people, then I'm not all right, and neither is anybody else!"

Gloria stared. "Oh, you make me so . . . tired!" she said with Norman Shearer hauteur, slamming her door.

SOFTLY: "Marion."

Marion Davies stirred, stretching under the pink satin spread, blond hair rippling. Her lids fluttered open. "Popsy." A dimpled, unfocused smile.

"How are you, dear?"

"Jus' l-lemme sleep." She tried to roll onto her stomach, but Hearst held her, and she was warm, soft, as yielding as a child. "What does P-Popsy want?"

The old man touched her hair with a liver-spotted hand. So fragrant, so golden. "You remember last night? I'm sorry we fought."

"S-skip it." Her eyes drifted shut. "Now just go 'way. M-Marion needs her b-beauty rest."

"Do you remember the dead man?"

The blue eyes opened, but they looked driftingly vague, as if his words were just lines in a movie script. She kept her little smile. "Dead?" Then she stiffened and sat up straight. "Oh, my! There w-was a b-body, wasn't there? In the elevator. That l-little m-man with the f-funny leg. Oh, Popsy!"

Holding her shoulders, he made her look at him. "You've got to listen to me. Carefully."

She jiggled her head yes.

"He was shot. You saw that. The phone lines are down, so we can't call the police just yet. I'm doing what I can to find out who did it, but in the meantime our guests are not to know. We don't want to frighten them, understand? We can't afford a scandal."

"N-no scandal."

"That's right. Your career—"

A numb nod. "My career. Y-yes, we have to p-protect my career."

Hearst soothed, reassured her. He stood. "I have to go now, to see to things, make arrangements. You'll be all right?"

"I'm s-scared."

Hearst remembered how easily Pike had gotten into his room. "Lock your door," he said.

When he was gone Marion slumped back, chewing on a nail and staring bleakly into the morning while her dachshund dozed at her side. That little man, dead. Awful! I don't like *dead*. Mommy and daddy are dead, and just last year my favorite niece Pepi . . . She moaned, thinking about Pepi's suicide. Now all at once death was an ugly little man who had wriggled his way up here where she was supposed to be safe. Wrapped in peach-colored silk she curled into a knot. Yes, she had seen it: that horrid hole in the little man's head. Coming back from Eddie, that's what she'd been doing. Eddie. Such a funny kid—why did she like him so much? He was more her age than Popsy, that was one thing. And? She couldn't think of why else, but she remembered how it had been with Eddie—delicious, a little crazy, like she liked it—but afterward kinda funny. He had stared at her "You and me together!" he had exclaimed. "And Hearst is your Popsy?" He had laughed wildly at that, and Marion shivered at the sound echoing in her head: it gave her goose bumps. She remembered, too that sad boy Eddie had a gun. But he promised to put it right away; he wouldn't break a promise to me.

Would he?

Marion cuddled Gandhi for comfort. Oh, how can I tell Popsy about the gun? He'd know for sure I was with Eddie.

❦ 12 ❦

JOE Willicombe's polished black shoes crunched the gravel at the side of the road a quarter mile down from Casa Grande. A raw, cold wind swayed the creaking oak branches over his head. There they were, in plain sight: the sharp, wooden-handled garden shears, looking as if they'd just been tossed there. In graying light he bent to pick them up with gloved hands, though he bet there would be no fingerprints. Still, the shears had to be saved for the police—if there were police. Willicombe's mouth set grimly. In spite of his loyalty to his boss, he liked to do things by the book, and he hated not being able to leave this to the people who were supposed to solve murders best.

A murderer loose on the hill? Willicombe frowned out to sea, and its iron gray surface seemed to ripple frantic warnings. A thin line of road twisted along the coast only five miles away, but they were five miles of cliffs and mud, inhabited by wild animals, and they might as well be a mile-high wall. Willicombe sighed. The Santa Lucias made another wall behind them. We're cut off, he thought, in a box, and not a damn thing we can do about it.

Ducking under gnarled branches, he took a shortcut to the wooden communications building. Behind glass panes the office where Etta Kitt and the other operators usually worked around the clock was deserted. Etta and Billy Buller; liaisons did happen up here. Between whom else? For a moment Willicombe regretted his long celibacy, a monk devoted to his god.

The operator had a good vantage point; could she have seen more that night than she told? he wondered. He found the cut lines at the side of the building, just as Etta had described them, severed in two places: where they emerged from the building and many yards further on where they dived underground. The chief had insisted on underground lines, but that caused problems when they needed fixing. Grumbling, Willicombe searched among the wet leaves and dripping bushes for fifteen minutes, but he could not find the thick twenty-foot-long electrical cables that would reestablish the hill's link with the world. So whoever had cut them had carried them off, hidden them. Clever. Why? The killer's accomplice, as W.R. had suggested? As for fixing the damage, there was surely no more of the special heavy cable up here; it had been installed long ago. Furthermore, the hill didn't have any official electrician; if things went wrong they usually sent for help. Could one of the regular workman do a makeshift repair? Maybe, though it would take time. Puffing, Willicombe scrambled from the oaks back to the road. I don't dare authorize the work, he thought; the Chief has to do that. He poked at his glasses. The Chief wants to keep scandal at bay: does he have any other reasons to be so glad the lines were cut?

Knotted with unease, Willicombe headed back toward Casa Grande. Around a bend he came across Louella and Docky trooping down to Casa del Mar. Louella still looked puffy and gray, but her eyes had regained some of their old ferrety gleam.

Docky poked his pipe at the shears Willicombe held. "Going to cut some flowers?"

"Er, no. One of the gardeners seems to have left these out in the rain. I'm just taking them back. Did you have a good night? The storm didn't keep you up?"

Louella frowned at the shears. "Oh, no. A good night." Wearing an artifical smile, she nudged Docky so hard he winced. "Didn't we, honeybunch?" She bloomed with gossip-hunting glitter. "Tsk, tsk, that poor wounded man at breakfast. One of the Chief's security guards?"

"Yes. I have to be getting back." Dark coat flapping, Willicombe brushed past before Louella could ask more questions about Marvin Orr.

❧ 13 ❧

"ANY news, Joe?" Hearst said, looking up. The old man sat at the long table in the study, framed by the painting of himself at age thirty. Hearst old, Hearst young, Willicombe thought edgily. What could there be in that?

"I told the maids about the stolen watch," he said. "They'll keep their eyes peeled."

"They're good at that, aren't they?"

Willicombe nodded. Gossip was human nature; the servants rarely missed any juicy morsel.

Hearst shifted position. "I just hope to hell one of them doesn't come up with something we'd rather she didn't know. But we can't help that. What about breakfast—anything besides the security man with the bloody head?"

"Three or four people looking under the weather, but that's not unusual. No way to tell if any of it was guilt." Flames sizzled in the fireplace. "Sir, I'm doing my best to keep an eye on the guests," Willicombe said, "but could our killer have been one of the servants?"

Hearst slapped the arm of his chair. "It could have been the Man in the Moon for all we know. No, I don't think it was one of the servants, but I suppose we have to suspect everyone. That just makes things harder, doesn't it? Hell, we knew it would be hard."

"Louella Parsons was out in the storm."

"Louella?"

Willicombe related what he had overheard. "She didn't want Docky to know, but he did; he stayed up smoking his pipe waiting for her."

"Now, what could she have been doing?"

"Shall we ask her?"

284

"Ha!—and set her barking up every tree on the place? We'll have to talk to her eventually, I suppose, but I don't want to do it just yet. Speaking of being out in the storm, have you seen Aphrodite?"

"The statue? I didn't go down that way."

"She's wearing a bra and panties."

"A bra—?"

Hearst nodded. "And a rain hat. And she's got a flower in her teeth. Looks damn silly! Louella isn't the type to've done it, so someone else was busy last night. Our murderer? It's hard to imagine him—or her—dressing up a block of marble. But whoever did might have seen something."

"It's beginning to look like lots of people were out last night."

Hearst grimaced. "Hopping like fleas. D'you think you could find out who put those things on the statue?"

"I can try."

"In the meantime have someone get them off her. I don't like it; it's indecent." Hearst peered sideways at the rapidly graying sky. "I've been poking around too, Joe. I went through the dwarf's room. I hated it—it was as if his ghost might pop in any second. It turns out Pike was up to something, all right: his briefcase was full of blueprints of Casa Grande and the guesthouses. And he was the one who sent those notes."

"How do you know?"

"There were doodles like big asterisks all over the blueprints."

"They can't be just doodles."

"We both think they mean something—but what?"

"It's funny, sir. I keep thinking I already know, that it's right in front of my eyes."

"So do I. So we have two mysteries: Otis Pike, and who killed him. I found these too." Hearst placed the photograph and button on the table. "What d'you make of them?"

Willicombe bent, peering. "The photograph, nothing. It's a child's button, isn't it? A toy? Old too; look at this bit of rust. 'LCP'; I have no idea what it means."

"The dwarf's real initials? P for Pike?" Hearst pocketed them again. "Those are the shears that cut the lines?"

Willicombe had forgotten he still held them. "Yes," he said, placing them carefully on the table so the eighteen-inch blades would not scratch its dark polished surface. He described his fruitless scramble among the leaves near the communications building. "If one of the maids finds twenty feet of heavy-gauge electrical cable packed in someone's closet, we'll know who cut the lines."

"Unless it's put there to throw us off. That reminds me: I found Pike's briefcase on the top shelf in his closet. He was less than five feet tall. How'd he get it up there?"

"Climbed on a chair?"

"Or someone else hid it." Hearst thumped the tabletop. "Damn it, Joe, there's too much we don't know! Is that man Orr fit to be talked to yet?"

"He's got a gash in his head and a bad bruise. And a splitting headache. But Docky says he's okay—no fracture. I've had him lying down in one of the unused guest rooms so no one could get to him.

"Good work, Joe."

Willicombe squeezed out a smile. "All in the line of duty, sir. I'll bring Orr here." He left.

Hearst struggled up from his chair, heart fluttering. He clutched his chest. Life is all heart trouble, he thought, God damn it. The fluttering calmed, and he frowned at the shears on the table, long and ugly with glinting jaws. Dangerous. But there was danger everywhere; an enemy didn't need a gun. A man's past could be used against him, and it could pick him off as efficiently as a bullet. Swiveling suddenly, fitfully, the jowly old man stalked past his portrait to the stone-arched windows. Thousands of acres under lowering skies. Mine! he thought, rising on his toes. He thought too of Marion. Mine? He drove a fist into his palm, over and over. She also had been out. A long time. What had she seen, done? Been with that damn young bolshie, Eddie Deere? Yet inexplicably Hearst still could not feel anger at the wild-eyed kid. All his talk about oppressing the masses—could some of it be true; have I lived my life wrong?

"Sir . . ."

Hearst started and drew himself up as Willicombe led in a stocky middle-aged man clutching a gray cap. The man wore blue work pants, a tan shirt, a loose-fitting zippered jacket. A white gauze bandage encircled his head, and he looked cowed and confused.

Hearst went to him. "Sit down, Mr. Orr. You did a fine job for me."

"Wh-what?"

"A brave job." Willicombe showed the man to a high-backed leather chair near the fire. "Wounded in action, they give medals for that," Hearst said.

Orr sank down. "Do they?"

"Of course they do." Hearst sat facing him. "Now, tell us what happened."

Orr rubbed his mouth; he fidgeted with his cap. "Well, sir, I was doin' my job like Mr. Willicombe asked me to. Out in the storm. Keepin' my eyes open. It was rainin' cats and dogs, but there was lots of people around, and—"

"Lots?"

"I saw three or four in them yellow slickers."

"Who?"

"Like I said, it was rainin' and dark, and under them yellow hats, I couldn't tell. I couldn't keep an eye on 'em all, so I picked out one, a little guy I did right?" Hearst and Willicombe exchanged a glance. Hearst nodded, and Orr went on. "Well, this little guy was actin' mighty suspicious, but he musta known just where he wanted to go, 'cause he came straight to Casa Grande and walked right in like he owned the place. I was just in time to see him takin' your elevator. That surprised me. Worried me too. What was he up to? Course, it could be nothin'. You know, it could be, well . . ." Flushing, Orr licked his lips. "A man meetin' a woman. That sorta thing happens. I thought I'd wait a bit. And then there was the other people."

"Others?"

"Three of 'em. They mighta been followin' the little guy, but I ain't sure."

"Men or women?"

"Couldn't tell. If I'da got close enough to see, they woulda known I was watchin' 'em, so I figured it was better to lay low. I hid just outside the big door. Can't say what they did when they went in. They mighta took the elevator, too, might not. Anyway, after a time I got worried, 'cause Colonel Joe—Mr. Willicombe—had give me

287

special orders. What if somebody was up to no good? So I snuck in, and there was the big room in that low light and nobody to be seen. But I thought I heard the elevator. That secret door of yours was open a crack, and I went over. I was surprised to see the elevator'd gone down, not up. That was mighty funny, and I really started to sweat. I had to do somethin', but I didn't want to use the elevator—that might sound the alarm—so I headed down them circular stone stairs. And that's when I got conked." Wincing, he touched his bandage. "I guess I musta laid at the bottom a mighty long time." He ducked his head. "Sorry I scared everybody at breakfast."

"You couldn't help it. However, we don't want to frighten our guests any more, so you're not to tell anyone that someone knocked you out. Mr. Willicombe told them a branch broke off in the storm and hit you, and we've got to stick to that—except with the police, of course."

Orr's eyes got big. "The police?"

"We might have to call them, just as a matter of form—although the whole thing is probably the work of a rambunctious guest. You didn't see who hit you?"

"No, sir."

"And your gun." Hearst bobbed his head at Orr's holster. "You didn't fire it?"

"Oh, no, sir."

"By the way, where is it?"

Orr grabbed at the holster. "Why . . . it's gone."

"You don't know where?"

"No. I had it, I swear. It was in my hand when I got conked."

"Was it?" Hearst forced a smile that was miles from how he felt. "Well, it's likely to turn up at the bottom of the stairs. We've probably just overlooked it."

Orr goggled from one to the other of them. "Somethin' else happened, didn't it?" he croaked. "Somethin' you're not tellin' me?"

"We just have a little problem, that's all," Hearst said. "Someone else got hurt, but we know"—his chair creaked as he leaned forward to tap the guard's knee—"that we can count on you to not to breathe a word until we straighten it out."

When Willicombe came back from returning Orr to hiding,

288

Hearst shot him a sharp look. "There wasn't a gun anywhere near where Orr was knocked out?"

"No. I looked."

"Damn. A fully loaded gun unaccounted for."

Willicombe slowly thumbed the edge of his clipboard. "Maybe at least one of its bullets has been fired."

"But where the hell's the gun now? Joe, this whole situation is ready to explode, I feel it. Can we keep a lid on things?"

"If we keep everybody locked away from everybody else."

"Marion? Docky? Louella? We can't lock them all up."

"I agree."

Hearst began to pace. "So. It looks like Pike was shot in the vaults."

"And the killer knocked out Orr. But what would Pike have been doing under Casa Grande?"

Hearst didn't answer. He looked away, and Willicombe watched a shadow cross his face, darker than any the weekend had produced so far. "I've got to protect my guests," Hearst murmured, "but . . ." Willicombe read his mind: *I've got to protect myself too.* The secretary shifted his feet as a spattering of rain started up, ticking at the windows. "We'll have to tell them soon, Joe," Hearst said, turning, his jaw visibly tightening. "But not yet. I count on you. Get them together in groups, playing games, anything. Safety in numbers. Break out the liquor if you like. Meanwhile, I . . ." He seemed to be struggling with an idea. "Have you developed those pictures you took in the elevator?"

"They came out perfectly."

"Lock them away, with these shears. Maybe we *will* need the police. They . . . they—"

Don't have anything to hide? Willicombe offered silently. Feeling shaken, he gathered up the shears as the rain spat more insistently. He was about to go when the elevator doors clicked from the room beyond, and Mary O'Grady stumbled into the room. At sight of the two men she stopped, gaping. They stared back.

Mary clutched a bunched-up yellow rain slicker to her flat little chest.

"Bullet hole!" she cried. "B-bullet hole!"

❧ 14 ❧

D ICK Powell and Carole Lombard were playing mixed doubles with Cary Grant and Jean Harlow on the courts above the indoor pool when the rain began again, a fine gray wash. It was shortly after eleven. Below them maids could be seen hurrying linens and cleaning things to and from the guest houses. Palm leaves rattled in a whipping wind. "Last one in's a big palooka!" Harlow cried, and, giggling, they scampered like rabbits in their gleaming whites toward Casa Grande, tumbling through the grand portal into the Assembly Hall and looking about brightly for fun. Things were sober and quiet. Flames leapt in the huge fireplace. Gloria Swanson and Hedda Hopper were frowning over the jigsaw puzzle in the center of the room, while at the far end under the Rubens tapestries Harpo, Docky, Herman Mankiewicz, and Adolphe Menjou huddled under a cloud of tobacco smoke at the card table.

"Aw, just poker jockeys," Carole Lombard sniffed. "How dull!"

Harlow made a face. "Where's Charlie?" she demanded. All heads turned. "I want Charlie to make me laugh!"

Just then Joe Willicombe slipped in through the Refectory door. He glanced about. Nearly twenty guests. Safety in numbers? Any who looked like he or she had shot a man last night? John Francis Neylan sat in a corner scowling over financial reports. Marie Dressler had her nose buried in a book. Basil Rathbone and Damon Runyon played Parcheesi blithely. Jean Harlow began turning vigorous somersaults by the fireplace shouting "Whee!" Seeing Adela Rogers St. Johns leaning crisply against the grand piano, watching it all through wry eyes, Willicombe chose her as the most promising of the lot.

"Still sticking to that story that a tree branch clunked that guy,

290

Joe-sy?" she asked, winking, as he approached. "Fess up. It was W.R., wasn't it, in one of his famous pets."

Willicombe adjusted his glasses. "Of course it wasn't the Chief. You know how bad the storm was. A branch just knocked the poor man out." He gazed momentarily at his toes. "But there is an—ah, mystery; maybe you can help." He faced her. "Did you see the statue?"

"Venus in the fancy getup?"

"Yes. You don't have any idea whose, er, garments she was wearing?"

St. Johns grinned like a cat. "Not mine, honey, and you won't have a hard time proving it." She raised her arms. "Go ahead. Check if anything's missing."

Abruptly everyone turned at the sound of clinking glass: a butler wheeling in a liquor cart. Eyes goggling, Herman Mankiewicz shot out of his chair. "Booze before nightfall?" He did a mock faint. "I've died and gone to heaven!"

❦ 15 ❦

GLORIA Deere paced in her room in Casa del Monte. Are Charlie and me all washed up? Was I too hard on him? Oh, he probably thinks I'm just a little dope! In a fit she threw a pink powder puff; it ricocheted off an antique Spanish oil lamp into a big Greek vase. She glanced at her windows. "Darn!" Runnels of wet smeared them. Not rain *again*. I wanted my weekend to be so perfect. What's it doing for my career? Fussing, the brunette pulled on a yellow slicker and checked her stockings. She touched up her pouting lips. In spite of the rain, she would just march up to Casa Grande and have some fun. That Cary Grant was cute. Maybe him? Fluffing her hair, she practiced a dimpled grin in the oval gold-framed mirror. I'll show Charlie!

But first she would give that Eddie McGuffin a piece of her mind. She wanted it out with him: why'd he talked her into getting him up here?

Gloria swished across the sitting room and, without knocking, flung open Eddie's door. The thick Persian carpet muffled the sound of her entrance; so did his blubbering. He was slumped on the edge of his bed staring at a photograph. His lank brown hair hung in his eyes, and his shoulders heaved with sobs. Gloria momentarily softened. There was something so sad about him, so lost. She almost rushed to give the dumb kid a hug—until she saw the dully gleaming pistol right next to him on the brocade spread. She covered her mouth with her hand. Oh, no, I don't want to know about that; I don't want to know about any of it! I just want a good time; I want a party!

Besides, enough terrible things had happened last night.

Backing out, she quietly shut the door and rushed uphill to safety.

Eddie did not see her—but from the window Vinny Tashman watched her, clenching his fists.

❧ 16 ❧

IN the Gothic Suite high above, flames flashed lemon and garnet in the study fireplace. By their flickering light William Randolph Hearst gazed with rapidly diminishing patience at Mary O'Grady, snuffling and shaking opposite him. The red-haired maid cringed in the chair Marvin Orr had occupied, but she filled it with far more misery. She had been bawling for ten minutes, twisting the yellow slicker in her hands, fighting to talk but getting nothing out. "Go on down, Joe. See about the guests," Hearst had murmured at last. Now the study door was firmly shut, the sound of the rain a soft drumming, but it could not muffle the maid's wails. "Mary?" Hearst encouraged her for the tenth time, grinding his teeth. Get to the point, he thought, a killer is loose out there.

292

Finally she quavered, "Oh, s-sir, I . . . I've done a terrible thing. The Virgin will never forgive me!"

"I'm sure it can't be so terrible."

She raised her freckle-blotched face. "I've *slept* with him, sir." A new flood of tears.

Hearst blinked. "Who?"

"Mr. Pike, sir."

The antique clock ticked. "I see," Hearst said.

"I'm a wicked girl!"

"No, Mary. Just a human one."

"Yes, wicked! And I showed him . . . things of yours."

Hearst's gray brows bristled. "What do you mean?"

"I took him under Casa Grande, sir. I led the way. I loved him—th-thought I loved him. I thought he loved me too. He made me promise. So I did it. I knew it was wrong, but I did it. He said you were bad, said you had . . . had an heirloom of his, and that was all he wanted."

"An heirloom?"

"Y-yes."

"And you believed him?"

"I *wanted* to believe him. I wanted to do what he liked. S-so he would like me. He was only a short little man, but no one had ever . . . oh, Mr. Hearst!" More sobs.

Hearst patted her shoulder. "We all make mistakes. What kind of heirloom?"

"He n-never said. I think he was lying, because after I took him down there he treated me like dirt. It was your photographs, sir, your picture albums. That's what he really wanted to see. He went through lots of them. He even took one of the photographs. Of a woman."

"From one of the albums?"

"No. From a fancy frame on a shelf."

Hearst lifted his jowly head like an animal sniffing death. He was surprised that his heart continued to beat so steadily. He swallowed; voices clamored in his mind, laughed, screamed. The past. Secrets indeed—and had he suspected this all along, waited for it? He wiped his brow with a large white handkerchief. I've got to stay calm.

293

But none of it explained the symbols on the threatening notes. "And that's all?" he managed gruffly.

Mary sputtered the details of what had happened in the vaults. Hearst was appalled. A cruel little man, he thought; she had good reason to kill him. His expression grew stormy. Maybe I did too. Tell her he's dead? No, not yet; too many people know already, and—

"Sh-shall I pack my things?"

"Don't be silly. You're an honest girl; you've told me the truth"—all of it?—"and I'm not going to fire you. Now about that rain slicker— what did you mean about a bullet hole?"

She stared at the slicker as if she had never seen it before. She thrust it toward him. "Yes. Bullet holes. In this."

Hearst took it. There were two small holes and some brownish-red smears at the left shoulder. Rain dampness had kept the blood sticky, and he wrinkled his nose. Someone else shot? He peered at her. "Where did you find this?"

She told him. "Mr. Chaplin was asking some girl about being out last night, and she got mad at him and ran off and he ran after her, and then I looked down and there it was in the leaves."

"Out last night? What girl?"

"I don't know her name." Mary described her.

"Mm." Hearst was sure who it was. Not the name exactly: Marion had introduced them yesterday at lunch, before disaster had avalanched—Gladys? Glenda? But she was Eddie Deere's sister. "Is that all, Mary?"

"Yes, sir."

He helped her up. "You're a good girl. You've done the right thing, and you have nothing to be ashamed of. Now, you're excused from work today, but I want you to do exactly as I say: go down to your room and shut the door and stay there."

"Oh, sir, you're a saint!"

No such thing as a saint, Hearst thought when the pathetic girl was gone, and if there were I wouldn't be a candidate. Staring at the slicker, he pictured his own gun, six shots gone last night, echoing in the rain.

Did I . . . ?

But where the hell was the photograph Otis Pike had stolen, the one that told so much?

❧ 17 ❧

TEN minutes later William Randolph Hearst gazed down on Otis Pike's body in the meat locker under Casa Grande. Donovan was on guard outside; he had let the publisher in, jerking back the bolt on the massive metal door with a sharp snap. The room was ten feet by twenty. Sides of beef, pork, lamb hung from hooks. Hearst's breath rose in frosty plumes. He shivered— from the cold or the presence of gruesome death? Both, no doubt, because Buller was here, too, nearby, looking puffed, bruised, bluish, hardly human. Thank God his eyes were shut. But Pike's were not; they still stared in gelid protest that he had not accomplished his aim—or at least, had not seen its nasty end. What? I'm not out of danger, Hearst thought, bending over the stiff little body on the gleaming metal kitchen cart, preparing to do what he must. Hating the job, he lifted the coat and checked the inner pockets. Nothing. Nothing in any pocket at all. The photograph Pike had taken was not here, nor in his room.

Who had it?

Hearst surveyed the pathetic little man, now a side of meat himself. The bleak truth of death. His pouchy eyes fixed on the built-up shoe, and he frowned. Something odd about it . . . The heel seemed twisted. Then Hearst glimpsed the small hole. Puffing in the cold, he fidgeted with the thing. It unscrewed and lay in his hand discharging flakes of mud. A side piece slid down to reveal black metal and buttons. The hole was a lens; the heel was a miniature camera.

Hearst ceased to feel the cold. He seemed to hear wolves pursuing him, howling.

With one last grimace at the dwarf's grotesque death mask, Hearst pocketed the camera and stomped from the vault.

"Sir?" Donovan asked uncertainly, jumping up from his chair. Hearst scowled. "Just stay where you are!"

The old man wound his way unerringly through dimly lit passages to the concrete rooms where his past was stored, where playthings of his childhood and misspent young manhood at Harvard crowded together on floor-to-ceiling shelves. *What good are they? They'll only be packed up when I die, or sold, or shoveled into a big furnace to be eaten by flames.* Slumped against a doorjamb, Hearst paused to catch his breath. *I should have tossed them out years ago. No, they're part of me, they're my memories; I love them even though some of them give me pain. Will they trip me up? Send me crashing?* Hearst thought about Eddie Deere's accusations. *Has my life meant anything at all?* Warily he looked about, as if specters hid in the shadows. There were stacks of the yellowing German comics he had picked up on his first trip to Europe, age eleven, with his mother; the Katzenjammer Kids had been modeled after them. Further on, dusty but still leering, Champagne Charlie, his stuffed crocodile, crouched on a shelf as if waiting to pounce. And there was the polka-dot hobbyhorse, his puppet theater, the sled mama bought for his first winter in the Sierras.

Snow. The old man pictured a small German town.

He shook his head; Pike could not have been interested in that.

Hearst came to the room with the volumes of photographs.

The room was a disaster. Albums had been dragged from shelves and scattered about the cold concrete floor; pictures had been ripped out and flung like confetti. Hearst shook with rage. *My pictures!* An empty space lay at the center of the mess. Grunting, Hearst crouched and stretched reluctant fingers to touch a sienna stain. *Blood; Otis Pike's, no doubt. This was where the dwarf was murdered, therefore, where his vicious search had come an end.*

Who had trailed him here?

Grimly Hearst noted the dates on the scattered albums: the turn of the century. *So the dwarf had zeroed in; he had known. Looking for proof? Was he a blackmailer?* A wave of fear swept over the old man, and feeling dizzy, he wobbled to a shelf. His eyes focused on the ornate brass frame; the photograph, as Mary O'Grady had said, was missing.

296

Hearst passed a trembling hand over his eyes. *For Billy from your sweetie.* He recalled joyous, youthful days.

Wiesbaden.

And a girl.

And a girl, dead.

And a plan that could not fail.

He beat on the shelf with his fists. *I'm an arrogant bastard to've thought I could get away with it!*

Feeling drained, he stumbled back through the murky corridors. *Who can I count on? Loyal Joe!* He can put back the albums, scour out the bloodstain. No one need ever know where the snooping little monster Pike was killed.

But someone knew. Hearst's fingers curled at his sides. Someone who had to be stopped.

❦ 18 ❧

TEN minutes later in his study in the Gothic Suite the publisher slumped at the big mahogany table from which he controlled his empire. A whirlpool seemed to be sucking him under, and he struggled against its strong magnetic wash. The stack of letters and telegrams still waited, but he could not face them. He pulled the muddy heel from his pocket. *Film in it? Pictures?* Hearst almost laughed. *What if the dwarf had photographed his own killer? What if the answer lay here?* He took out the orphanage list, thirty-seven names, none of them Otis Pike's; furthermore there were no descriptions, no indication whether one of the boys had been small and lame. But something still rang a bell, mockingly: *find me!* It eluded him, and his wide amber thumbnail dug a deep crease by one name: Vincent Tashman. *I'll talk to Tashman, I'll wring something out of him.*

There was a knock, and Willicombe came in, clipboard in hand.

He halted at his usual respectful distance, looking solid and dependable in his neat dark suit. He looked worried too. The steel rims of his glasses glinted in the firelight. "All the guests accounted for, sir. I recruited two more men from Nigel Keep's gardening staff. They're in strategic positions, keeping watch on the paths. I said a couple of baboons were still loose, and people should stay indoors as much as possible. Two or three guests are a little jumpy, but most of them seem to think it's some sort of adventure. In fact, a lot of them are overjoyed to have airtight excuse not to report to their movie sets Monday morning. Most are entertaining themselves—Harpo's even swimming in the rain—but no one's admitting to dressing up Aphrodite." The secretary's brow wrinkled. "What's that, sir?"

"A heel, Otis Pike's. But it's a camera too." Hearst showed him.

Willicombe's smooth pink cheeks quivered. "It's crazy."

"Just the opposite. It makes a damn lot of sense. You know how many people would like to get something on me. Take the thing, Joe, If there's film inside, develop it. I can trust you."

Willicombe pocketed the heel. "Sir, I've taken the liberty of bringing someone up. The telephone girl, Etta Kitt. She's the one who told us the lines had been cut. I didn't mention it before, but she seems to've been—well, having an affair with Billy Buller." A pause. "I think you ought to talk to her."

Hearst scowled, then sighed and nodded, and Willicombe led in a small sharp-browed woman with a frizz of blackish hair.

"Etta Kitt, sir," he said.

Getting up, Hearst forced his voice into a pleasant purr. "How are you, Etta?"

The flicker of a drained smile. "I'm . . . I'm all right. Is it true? Is Billy Buller really dead?"

"I'm afraid so."

She shuddered but managed to control herself. "I remembered something. Because of the person who cut the lines. I wanted to tell you." Her voice was as dry as a leaf. She described the man on the telephone calling for help. "I meant to tell Mr. Willicombe before, but I couldn't get him, and then last night happened, and—"

"You have no idea whose voice it was?"

"No."

"And there's nothing more?"

"I . . . guess not."

Hearst glanced at Willicombe. "Thank you then, Etta," he said, and walked her to the door.

She turned suddenly. "There *is* something. Can I see Billy?"

Hearst pictured the battered body along with Pike and the hanging sides of meat. "It's best that you don't," he said. "You'll remember him better f . . ."

A bleak nod. "Sure, I get it." Her eyes glittered fiercely for an instant. "I didn't *really* love him, don't think I did!" Helplessly she backed from the room.

Wind buffeted the leaded-glass windows. "It happens up here, doesn't it, Joe?" Hearst said.

"It happens everywhere," Willicombe said. His lips made a flat line. "Sir, does this mean that someone from outside murdered Pike?"

"Climbed all the way up the hill just to get him? If he did, damn it, where is he?" Stalking around the table, Hearst pulled the yellow slicker with the bullet holes from a locked cabinet and tossed it to his secretary. "Just in case you think things aren't in enough of a mess." He repeated Mary O'Grady's story. "Among other things, it means Chaplin and that brunette, Gloria Deere, were out last night. Louella too. Also Marion, Pike, and who the hell else?"

"You were, sir," Willicombe reminded with careful neutrality. "You don't recall seeing anything that—"

"I *didn't* see anything, Joe. If I had I would have told you."

Would you? Willicombe thought, ashamed again.

"Whose slicker is this?" Hearst demanded.

"You mean, which guest house was it delivered to when the rain started up? No way of telling. They're all pretty much alike."

There was a quick rapping on the door. "Now what?" Hearst snapped, but he grunted assent, and Willicombe opened the door. A plump, broad-faced girl in a crisp black maid's uniform marched in as if she owned the room. She had an eager, polished-apple glow.

"I just *had* to tell you, sir," she exclaimed breathlessly to Willicombe. "I knew it shouldn't wait. You told us all to keep an eye out for anything funny." Her voice lowered to a conspiratorial warble. "Well, I ran across something funny, all right. I was straightening Mr. Chaplin's room, and one of his suitcases fell off a chair and popped open, and I was putting the clothes back in when I saw his coat. It must've been stuffed right at the bottom, under everything else. And there were two holes in the shoulder. I wouldn't have noticed them except for the stain. It had rubbed off on a white shirt, too. And whatta ya think, Mr. Willicombe? Blood—I'm just sure it's blood."

Hearst came around the table. "Where is this coat?"

Large brown eyes gleamed at him. "I'm no dummy. I put it back. Put the suitcase back too." The young woman lowered her voice even more. "Don't want to rouse suspicion." She gazed eagerly from one to the other of them. "Well, what're we gonna do?"

Willicombe glanced at the Chief. "This is Miss Ivy Dixon." To the girl he said, "Mr. Chaplin just seems to have, er, injured himself. He changed shirts and coats, that's all. Now, you've been very conscientious, Ivy, however—"

"But they were bullet holes!"

"Are you positive?" Hearst's rumble made her start, but she did not back down.

"Say, I wasn't born yesterday. I know blood when I see it, and—"

Hearst's big hand firmly encircled her arm. He turned her around and marched her toward the door. "Thank you so much, Ivy. I'll speak to Mr. Chaplin about the matter, you can be sure. After all, he is *my* guest. You, Ivy, are my servant, and you will speak to no one about it. Do you understand?"

Sparks leapt in the fireplace. The girl looked at her arm pinched in his meaty hand, then up at him. She flashed a grin. "I get it." She poked him. "Heap big mystery, huh?" He let her go. "Well," she said smoothing her skirt, "there ain't no flies on me." She touched a finger to her lips. "Mum's the word, right? You can count on me, boss." She scampered out, smirking.

"Saucy," Willicombe observed when she was gone.

"I like her spirit," Hearst said. "And I think she'll do just as I said—unlike certain other people with well-oiled jaws."

"Louella?"

"Among others, damn it. I don't suppose any of the maids has reported twenty feet of heavy electric cable falling out of a suitcase?"

"No, but some of the guests are complaining about not being able to telephone or telegraph out. Especially Jack Neylan."

"To hell with Neylan.' Hearst strode to the windows and peered into the steady fall of rain. "I'm beginning to see how things fit together, Joe," he said.

"Sir?"

He turned. "You wouldn't think any the less of me if you found out something because of all this? Something . . . disgraceful."

Willicombe blinked. His boss was watching, waiting, "I . . . hope not, sir," he said at last.

Hearst's eyes narrowed. "Ver good, Joe. Very politic." He stared out the window once more. "Well, I hope not too." The rain made a whispering sound. The antique clock softly bonged noon. "A man makes mistakes. He does his best to fix them. . . ."

"Yes, sir.'

Whirling, stalking tc the long central table, the old man slammed the polished wood. "We're wasting time. Get Charlie Chaplin up here now.'

🙖 19 🙖

JEAN Harlow dragged Charlie Chaplin to the very center of the long Assembly Hall. "C'mon, honey, let's show 'em how to dance!"

Chaplin forced himself not to wince at the throbbing in his left shoulder as he allowed himself to be led to the space where Harlow and Bette Davis had jerked back a scarlet and blue Turkoman carpet. He felt trapped. Harlow had spied him creeping down from his room. He had come only to search for Gloria, but there was no wiggling out of Harlow's clutches. Dick Powell's white teeth gleamed from the grand piano, while at least two dozen people drew into a tight knot, grinning, eager for diversion this rainy noon in a hilltop castle with the only road washed out and a man dead. Not everyone goggled in greedy expectation: Louella Parsons looked strangled, and the screenwriter Vinny Tashman might've swallowed ground glass. Gloria? Chaplin spied her. She was practically glued to Cary Grant, but when Chaplin tried to catch her eye she turned up her nose. Dick Powell began to warble "Life Is Just a Bowl of Cherries." Bloody hell, Chaplin thought, I've got to go through with it. Gritting his teeth into a smile, he lunged into a cakewalk with Harlow.

They kicked up their heels. After five minutes Powell segued into "We're in the Money," and Chaplin managed to pass the platinum blonde to Clark Gable. "Last one in is fish bait!" Carole Lombard shrieked and jumped onto the floor with Harpo, and in a moment half a dozen couples were giggling and bumping hips. Docky swayed with Louella, who looked dazed, Joel McCrea manipulated Marie Dressler, Leslie Howard and Bette Davis glided like oil, and Herman Mankiewicz worked Gloria Swanson's long arm as if it were the handle of a pump. "H'v you seen the snakes in the Neptune Pool, m'dear?" he mumbled. "The camels are nibbling the hollyhocks."

Chaplin ducked outside the circle. How to get Gloria alone? He had to find out what she knew about last night.

"Arm bothering you, Mr. Chaplin?"

Starting, Chaplin turned to find Joe Willicombe at his elbow. Cool and solemn, the secretary peered down at him, and Chaplin felt an unpleasant jangle of anticipation. "Arm? Why, ah no."

"You were rubbing it. No pain?"

"Why should there be?"

Willicombe's steel rims glinted. His breath smelled of mint. "If I had been shot, I would feel pain. Mr. Hearst would like a word with you, sir. Right now, if you please."

❧ 20 ❧

"**S**HOT?" Chaplin exclaimed. "I haven't been shot."

"May we see your shoulder, then?" said William Randolph Hearst.

Chaplin feigned indignation, but he felt more trapped than ever. He drew himself up. "I'll keep my clothes on, if you don't mind."

Old Hearst sat in a red-leather chair at a long table. His ominous change of expression reminded Chaplin of a rhino about to charge. "Have it your way, but if you don't show us your shoulder, we'll have to tell the police what one of our maids discovered this morning in your suitcase. That might prove embarrassing—but of course it's up to you."

Chaplin stared around the study: strong stone walls, no escape. A painful shrug. "You win." Carefully he peeled off his jacket. A bulge showed under the crisp white shirt. "I bandaged it with some torn cloth. You don't actually have to see it, do you?"

"Would you like Docky to look at it?"

"Good Lord, no!"

"Why not?"

"It's only a graze. Besides, that bloodsucker Louella Parsons is his wife. Sorry. I know she works for you. But I don't care, I don't want her to get wind of it. The press is hot on my heels as it is—women, communism. I just can't afford this."

"Afford what?" Hearst leaned forward. The log fire was smouldering ruins, but no servant had been let in to revive it. Rain tapped steadily at the high arched windows, and Willicombe stood like a dour palace enunch by the firmly closed door.

Chaplin paced, dragging his fingers through his thick white hair. "Damn me for an Irishman if I know. I was out in the storm last night, and somebody simply shot me."

303

"For no reason? That sounds pretty lame. What were you doing out?"

"It wasn't just me. I and that little brunette Gloria Deere were putting a bra on your statue."

"And panties? And a rain hat?"

"Don't blame Gloria. The flower in the teeth was my idea. All of it was."

"Proud of it, are you? Aphrodite's never seemed to need dressing up to me. But it was a good joke; I can laugh too. But not now, not since— So you were just having a little fun when someone shot you? Who?"

"I haven't the foggiest. I had climbed up on the pedestal to top it all off with the hat—the crowning touch, don't you know. I heard a sound; I thought it was Gloria laughing. But when I climbed down I couldn't find her. She had been right there, but she'd simply gone up in smoke. I looked for her; I even called her name, several times. Then it felt like someone punched me in the arm, hard; I didn't know at first what had happened, but there was a popping sound in the storm."

"Just one pop?"

"I think so."

Hearst nodded.

"At any rate," Chaplin went on, "I just sat down in the rain, in a daze. I must've sat there two minutes, woozy. In shock. Then my shoulder began to ache like the devil, and I put my hand on it, and there was blood oozing out of the yellow slicker."

Hearst reached down. "This yellow slicker?" He slid the raincoat across the table.

Chaplin fingered it. "Two holes, yes. One in, one out. Where'd you find it?"

"You tell me."

Sheepishly: "Er, the north side of Casa Grande?"

"You tossed it there? That's disposing of evidence. Why, if you're not guilty of anything?"

Chaplin threw up his hands. "'Tramp Shot at Wild Party'—you can imagine the headlines. I told you, I can't afford scandal."

Hearst's brow knitted. "None of us can, damn it. I want to avoid it as much as you, but hiding things won't help. Did you bring a gun up here?"

"Me? That's bloody absurd—I hate the things. There was no shoot-out, if that's what you're driving at. I really have no idea who did this."

"Or why?"

"Or why."

"And there's nothing else you saw, or heard?"

"Just . . . there were other people out last night, of course."

"People?"

"I saw two, but I don't know who they were. It was after I was shot. No idea if one of them pulled the trigger on me. Don't know if they even saw one another. They were up near Casa Grande."

"Was one of them short?"

"The dwarf? No. Where's he got to, by the way?" Chaplin eased his coat back on. "The only thing I'm sure of is that one of them wore a yellow slicker and the other one didn't."

🐾 21 🐾

T HE white porcelain clock on the mantel of the guestroom in Casa del Mar chimed one P.M. "We didn't have to come back so you could change for lunch, Lollipops," Docky protested, taking his pipe from his jacket. "That purple dress of yours is very pretty; I've always liked it."

Louella stood shaking by the window. She wrung her hands. "I just *had* to get out of that house!"

Docky poked tobacco carefully into the pipe. He watched her from under his brows. "Why? I thought we were having fun."

"*I* wasn't having fun."

"But you love to dance."

"Not today." She screwed up her face at him. "You *still* claim it was a sick maid that W.R. wanted you to see last night?"

Docky patted his pockets for matches. His eyes lifted to his wife's unhappy face. "Something *is* wrong, isn't it? You didn't just stroll around in the rain for over an hour last night. What happened out there? Something did, didn't it?" Crossing the room, he stroked her trembling chin. "Tell Docky-Wocky."

"Oh . . . oh!" Tearing away, she rushed into the bathroom, and Docky heard sobs and splashing water. He frowned at the bathroom door. His wife's relationship with William Randolph Hearst was a headache at the best of times—she worshipped the damn old walrus; her beloved Chief could do no wrong—but there were some new twists being knotted in the rope this weekend. Murder? Docky shuddered. Ever since Hearst had shown him the dwarf in the elevator, he had felt balanced on a high wire between the publisher's wrath at one end and Louella's suspicions at the other, with a murderer waiting right underneath for any false move. Grumbling, Docky felt in his nightstand drawer. A maid usually put matches there, but it was empty. Trying Louella's side of the bed, he found a blue matchbook with the Hearst Ranch monogram. Lighting up, he tossed the matches back. He was about to close her drawer when he glimpsed something at the back of it. He took it out: a photograph of a young woman, old-fashioned-looking, pretty. Puffing smoke, he turned it over; *For Billy, from your sweetie,* written on the back.

"Look what I found," Docky said, carrying the photograph into the lavish marble and brass bathroom. "I wonder who she is?"

Wet-mouthed, Louella gaped at the picture. She burst into tears.

22

WILLIAM Randolph Hearst was alone. Charlie Chaplin had gone down to lunch, and Joe Willicombe had slipped out to see about developing the roll of film that had been found in Otis Pike's heel. Hearst had retreated to his bedroom. There he stood gazing at the glass globe and the pistol on his marble-topped desk. Sitting, he placed next to them four other items: the brass button embossed LCP; the photograph showing an open cabinet, a jigsaw puzzle, a woman's arm; the orphanage list; Otis Pike's last threatening note with its askerisk-shaped jotting of lines. Kneading his heavy cheeks, the old man frowned at the collection as wind pulsed through the sodden afternoon. He knew more than he had told Willicombe: he knew that five of these objects were linked. The sixth, the gun—it stood for death. There had been another death, hadn't there? No—two deaths, long ago. Convenient deaths.

I'm innocent! the old man thought.

But he was not innocent. No man was innocent, only more or less flawed, culpable.

The button lay on top of the orphanage list.

And then Hearst saw it: what had rung a bell about the list. He snatched up the paper. LCP. Lester Crane Penworthy was the nineteenth name on the list, between Jerry Moriarty and Bobby James Profitt.

Otis Pike's real name was Lester Crane Penworthy.

Hearst almost laughed. Stupid, pompous name! The laugh choked off. The name belonged to a dangerous little man who had come frighteningly close to unearthing something Hearst had believed was buried long ago. The old man's lips curled. *Buried*; damn right word. Did the dwarf know the secret hidden in photograph albums and fake snow in an old glass globe? Wiesbaden. Hearst squinted at the paper. There was more right in front of him, if only he could grasp it. LCP: Lester Crane Penworthy. Where had he seen that name before?

Then he knew, and he stared at the gray, drizzling afternoon sky. He knew, too, the secret of the doodles, which were not doodles at all.

"My God," he muttered, and almost laughed again.

He rang for a maid to search out Joe Willicombe.

❧ 23 ❧

"FIREWORKS?" Willicombe said, poking at his glasses.

"That's got to be it," Hearst said.

The two men stood in front of the cold hearth in the study. Hearst held out the last note: HEARST, I'M HERE. Willicombe looked at the circular spray of lines decorating its upper right corner. His imagination had rung many changes on the symbol over the past months: it had been a porcupine, a cocklebur, a dandelion, a star. But in the light of his almost dead certainty that Otis Pike's real name was Lester C. Penworthy, the drawing had to represent a fireworks explosion—not an explosion in the sky but one on the ground, an accident that had killed many people and blown off a policeman's head in Chicago in 1902 at a Hearst sponsored rally.

"So *he* was the Lester C. Penworthy we couldn't find to pay his settlement," Willicombe murmured.

"He wanted a different sort of settlement," Hearst said grimly. "Did you bring the files?"

"Yes." Thumbing through a manila folder, Willicombe nodded. "The details fit. Mr. and Mrs. Albert Penworthy, killed, but not instantly. Their little boy was walking between them, holding their hands. Three years old. They found him hugging his bleeding, dying mother." Willicombe shuddered. "The explosion injured his leg. No relatives except an aunt. She took him, and"—he looked up—"that's the last we know, except that the aunt lived in Chicago."

"We know more than that. We know she died or didn't want him, and he ended up in the Illinois Home for Little Wayfarers."

Willicombe shut the folder. "Penworthy held a grudge all these years?"

"Can you blame him? Look at it from his point of view. He thought I had murdered his parents, crippled him. But it wasn't my fault, Joe. Not my fault."

"Of course not, sir. An accident. These things happen. But why should he send threatening notes? Wouldn't they tip you off?"

"But they didn't, did they? It took us a long time to figure them out. Penworthy probably guessed it would, and he got a kick out of tweaking me. He was an arrogant little man; he wanted to make me sweat."

Willicombe had the frustrated sense of peering into a murky sea in which some shape darkly moved, but he still could not see what it was. "I still don't understand. Those blueprints of Casa Grande, that camera in his shoe—what was on his mind?"

Hearst stared into the dead ashes. "Blackmail? No. Something tells me he wasn't after money. He wanted revenge; he wanted to ruin me."

"But how?"

Hearst's gaze rose slowly. "There are things a man has to keep to himself, Joe. The point now is that someone stopped him—dead. Who? A friend to me, or another enemy? I need to talk to that girl, Gloria Deere. Louella too." The publisher's cold blue eyes glittered. "But first Vinny Tashman. He knew Lester C. Penworthy in Chicago. Get him up here, on the double."

I must've been crazy last night! The booze made me do it.

A hand touched Vinny Tashman's arm—"Pass the salt"—and he jumped. But Louella Parsons hardly glanced at him as he handed her the silver shaker. She looked a mess, her face chalky, her mascara smudged. At least she's off my back about Otis Pike. In misery Vinny gazed down the long refectory table. Julia Morgan and Willis Snipe discussed architecture. Hedda Hopper and Basil Rathbone chattered back-lot gossip. Dorothy Parker and Herman Mankiewicz speculated with dipsomaniac glee over Hearst's mysterious lifting of the customary daytime booze prohibition. "Nev'r mind." Mankiewicz patted Parker's hand. "After lunch le's go see th'snakes in the Neptune Pool—Mr. Hearst's fav'rit pets!" Farther down Gloria Deere flirted with Cary Grant, while her loony brother stared at his plate. Charlie Chaplin looked lousy, and Vinny knew why.

Under the table his hands with their carefully manicured nails began to shake.

After lunch he attempted to creep unnoticed back to Casa del Monte.

He didn't make it.

Joe Willicombe caught him in the entrance hall, by the big brass cowbell that called people to lunch. He gripped Vinny's arm firmly. "Mr Hearst would like a word with you, sir."

Vinny gazed longingly past Willicombe's dark suit into the rain and freedom. "I . . . I'm not feeling absolutely tip-top. Couldn't it wait?"

"As a matter of fact, no," Willicombe said.

The sudden rising of the private elevator made Vinny dizzy. "What's this about?" he asked unsteadily.

Willicombe remained granite. "Mr. Hearst would prefer to tell you himself."

On the third floor the big carved door to the study in the Gothic Suite was pushed open and Vinny went in. Willicombe did not follow, and Vinny jumped as the door banged shut behind him. Swallowing, he peered about. The inquisition chamber? Where were the instruments of torture? He saw a long, arched, richly furnished room, like a medieval chapel, the head monk, Hearst, sitting at a heavy table, stroking his dachshund. Stumbling toward him, sweating, Vinny fumbled with a smile, but Hearst was not smiling; the old man's eyes were tiny waiting slits. Vinny halted an uncertain six feet away and tried to find something to do with his hands. They would not stop twitching. "Mr., uh, Hearst?" A screaming silence. "You, uh, want to talk about my script after all?"

"No."

Vinny made the corners of his mouth lift in a fawning grin. "I could write something else for you. Anything you like," he begged. "I'd be *glad* to."

Hearst stopped stroking the dog. "I don't want to talk about movies; I want you to tell me about your friend, Otis Pike."

"He's not my friend," Vinny blurted.

"Really? My social secretary Ella Williams tells me you got him his invitation up here. Through Marion."

"Yeah, I guess I did, but—"

"Then why, if he's not a friend?"

"I owed him a favor."

"For what?"

"Look, Mr. Hearst, that's personal, and—"

"Don't tell me if you don't want to." Hearst resumed stroking the dog's head. "Of course, you may have to tell other people. The police, for example.

Oh God, Vinny thought, and his knees became rubber.

"However, the police might be left out of it, *if* you agree to tell me all you can about Otis Pike." The slit-eyes glinted. "Yes or no?"

Vinny felt defeat rise about him like floodwater. He sagged. "You win."

"You and the dwarf grew up in the same orphanage?"

"Y-yes."

"In Chicago?"

"Yeah."

"But then he was Lester Penworthy."

Vinny blinked. "How'd you know?"

"Lester C. Penworthy?"

A nod.

"Let's call him by his real name, then. That was twenty-five years ago. Did Penworthy tell you why he was orphaned, what had happened to his parents?"

"No one talked much about that. Most of us didn't know who our parents were. I didn't."

Hearst's hand kept stroking the dog. "You and Penworthy kept up with one another over the years?"

"Not really."

"Then how could you have owed him a favor?"

"It wasn't exactly a favor. He, um . . ." Vinny fidgeted, "Okay, I confess: he had something on me."

"What?"

"Don't make me tell," Vinny whined.

Hearst's half-smile was livid with contempt. "That serious? Murder?" He pursed his lips. "You worked for one of my papers in Chicago, didn't you? Whatever Penworthy had on you"—his hand lifted from the dog—"did it have anything to do with me?"

"No, I swear."

Hearst visibly relaxed. "Then keep your secret; I understand about secrets." He leaned forward, eyes sparking dangerously. "But I need the rest. Why did Penworthy want an invitation up here?"

"I don't know."

"The truth, Tashman!"

"That *is* the truth!"

Hearst peered hard at him. "All right," he said, "let's say it is. He didn't drop any hints?"

"He hated you, that's all I know."

"Lots of men hate me. But they don't wangle their way into my home."

312

Vinny giggled. "I'll be damned—he had something on you, too, didn't he?" Instantly, he regretted saying it.

"I'm asking the questions," Hearst barked. "Keep your unfounded ideas to yourself. You ransacked his room?"

"I went through it. I wouldn't say ransacked, but—"

"You broke into his briefcase?"

"Yes."

"What did you find?"

"Not much. Some blueprints of the buildings up here. Some letters and photographs."

"Letters?"

Vinny described them. "They were signed B.R., talked about a McGuffin family. And about some girl named Rose Ellen Forrest who died a long time ago."

Hearst's pouchy old eyes seemed to flay Vinny's skin. "Forget those letters. Every line. If you ever breathe a word of them to anyone besides me, you won't be able to get a job mopping floors, much less writing for the movies, understand?"

Vinny wobbled his head yes.

"And the photographs?"

"There were lots, at least three dozen. They all showed a house. Big. Nice. I don't know where. There was a dame in some of them, about sixty. Three or four showed a mantel with a picture of you on it, standing next to some boys and a cake. Oh, yeah—one of those glass globes with snow in it was next to the picture."

A sound escaped Hearst's lips. He quivered, and Vinny felt more than ever that he was in over his head, drowning. The dachshund stirred, whimpered, and the liver-spotted hand absently soothed her. It was a moment before Hearst's eyes focused again. "I want those letters and photographs," he said flatly.

"I haven't got them."

Hearst rose ominously, still holding the dog. "Don't lie to me."

"Honest," Vinny gasped, "I really haven't got them."

"You didn't take them last night?"

"Last night? I wasn't in his room last night. I went there yesterday afternoon. I hated being under the little bastard's thumb. He was acting funny; I wanted to get something on him. I broke open his briefcase, just like I told you. But I put everything back in and stuffed it under the bed."

"The bed?"

"Where I found it, jammed up under the springs."

Hearst gazed away for a moment. "So," he said, and Vinny's face burned; he felt suffocated. The rain sounded miles away, but he longed to escape into it, to run and splash like a kid.

At least he doesn't know the worst, Vinny thought.

That didn't last long. Willicombe came back, the executioner's assistant bringing the rope. Shutting the door behind him, he placed a box on the table in front of Hearst, and Vinny moaned. "I found it in his room," Willicombe intoned. "One of them's been fired recently. You can smell it."

Hearst frowned at the gleaming target pistols nestled in purple velvet. His eyes glittered in triumph. "So. *You* murdered the dwarf."

Vinny's jaw fell. "Murdered . . . ? He's *dead?*"

"You know damn well he is."

Vinny's lips worked, but he could make no sense come out of his mouth. "But . . . but—"

"He had the motive: blackmail," Hearst said to Willicombe. "Call Donovan. He can lock Tashman in one of the guest rooms until we can get the police up here."

"No!" Rushing forward, Vinny slammed his palms on the tabletop in front of Hearst. "I *didn't* kill him!" he gibbered. "I didn't even know he'd been murdered!"

Hearst glowered pitilessly. "You brought not one but two pistols into my home. You fired one of them last night. Now a man is dead. Explain your way out of that."

Vinny shook all over. "Yes, they're my pistols. And, yeah, I shot one last night. I was a little crazy. I haven't got a dime—I hocked things to buy the cigarettes I'm smoking. I need a job, and I counted on that Anne Boleyn script, but you nixed it. And then Penworthy, who called himself Otis Pike, was on my neck. And Charlie Chaplin stole my girl, and—"

"Your girl?"

"The brunette, Gloria Deere. I brought liquor up, two bottles. Everybody does it; don't tell me you don't know. I was boozing yesterday afternoon and all last night. Alky makes me crazy. That Chicago business the dwarf had on me? it had to do with shooting somebody when I was snookered. I didn't kill the guy, and the police never found out who did it, but Penworthy found out somehow, he had proof too. I should've cut out the boozing—I knew I was going off the deep end—but I didn't care after you said you wouldn't buy my script. I hated you, the dwarf, Chaplin, Gloria. She was treating me like dirt. I charged out in the rain meaning to shoot somebody, maybe even myself. Chaplin just happened to be the first guy I got my sights on. He and Gloria were whooping it up, having fun. Then she sort of . . . ran off, and I . . . and I . . ."

"You shot him?"

"I thought I did; at first I thought I'd killed him, because he went down like a duck in a shooting gallery. But he was sitting and moving. And then he got up and walked away. I must've just nicked him."

"And the girl?"

"I don't know where she went. All of a sudden I was scared out of my wits. I hightailed it back to my room."

Hearst looked at Willicombe.

"You've got to believe me!" Vinny pleaded.

Hearst took a deep breath. "Get out of here," he rumbled. "Go down to your room and stay there and don't come out for any reason. I shouldn't believe you—I don't yet—but you just might be telling the truth. Don't forget, you're not off the hook yet."

Vinny wanted to kiss the old man's shoes. "Thank you, thank you," Dazed, he headed for the door, but stopped and turned back. "Uh, something about those pictures—one of them showed a room with a couple of books, bolshie stuff. I dunno if it means anything, but Gloria Deere's dopy brother Eddie is always spouting commie crap." He flailed out the door, and a whoop of hysterical laughter burst from the sitting room. The sound of the elevator was followed by silence.

Willicombe cleared his throat. He closed the box of pistols. "I'll put these away. If he's telling the truth, we know why and how Mr. Chaplin got shot. But what was that about pictures and Eddie Deere?"

Hearst didn't answer. Eddie, he thought, staring at the portrait of himself when he was young.

🦋 25 🦋

CHARLIE Chaplin stood on the Pompeiian mosaic gazing out the front of Casa Grande. Rain fell steadily. Last night's rain had seemed vicious, vindictive; this afternoon's was resigned, glum, monotonous, a straight-down drizzle, and at three o'clock the light felt limp and wan. Someone bumped Chaplin's shoulder. The comedian turned. "I say, watch your step, old man."

Vinny Tashman halted. He peered at Chaplin as if he had never seen him before; then his face split in a crooked grin. He looked as gray as a corpse, but there were bright red spots in his cheeks, and his tiny dark pupils seemed to vibrate. "You're alive, I'm alive!" He giggled. "Know what? Life *is* just a bowl of cherries!" Hatless, coatless, he strode humming into the rain, leaping up halfway across the terrace and clicking his heels before vanishing with joyous yelps.

Chaplin shook his head: it had been a mad weekend—mysterious too, and he needed to solve the mystery. Getting into one of the yellow slickers hanging on pegs by the tall front portal, he headed out too. He half expected a Hearst minion to collar him—the publisher's last words had been to stay in his room—but no one stopped him.

Hearst or no Hearst, I'm going to find out where Gloria popped off to last night.

Splashing through puddles he made for Casa del Monte.

Its roof came into view. Above the red tiles the palm trees looked bedraggled, beaten by the storm, and the sea below the rain-washed slopes was a rippling, pewter gray sheet. Chaplin entered the guesthouse—and at once something felt wrong. He paused. The sitting room was deserted. A battered old hat lay on the floor by a spindly-legged table. Some workman's, accidentally left behind? Chaplin shook his unease; he rapped on Gloria's door, and she opened it almost at once, wearing a fetching pale green frock. She seemed to have been crying. "Oh!" she cooed, wiping her damp cheeks, and Chaplin was encouraged by her melting look and trembling mascaraed lashes. Her soft young breasts heaved. Jolly good, he thought, grinning, perhaps an hour's reconciliation in that nice big bed old Hearst conveniently provided—

A fierce roar erupted behind him.

He whirled.

A beast stood snarling at them both.

No, not a beast. A man. But so mud-encrusted, with clothes so torn and hair so smeared, wearing an expression so wild, that he looked like a crazed ape.

"What in bloody hell?" Chaplin sputtered. This crazed ape waved a pistol.

Gloria shrieked.

"Goldarn you all! Goldarn you!" The man's pistol exploded, spitting fire, and a two-hundred-year-old Chinese celadon by Chaplin's elbow shattered to dust.

Instinct galvanized the comedian; he had been shot once—he did not want to be shot again. Coiling, arching, in an acrobatic leap he had not used since his days with the Fred Karno troupe in England, he lashed out. His right toe nicked the pistol, and it flew into the air to clatter at the feet of Eddie Deere, who had darted from his door at the other end of the sitting room ruffling his shag of brown hair.

Staring at the pistol, then at the skinny, grimy intruder, who cowered, moaning, Eddie yammered laughter. *"The forgotten man, the forgotten man!"* he crowed, pointing, as Joe Willicombe rushed into the room.

317

𝕏 26 𝕏

"CALM yourself, Mr. Goodall," said William Randolph Hearst.

Tom Goodall's lean jaw set. "Calm? How c'n I be calm when my wife and babies is starvin'?"

"Starving." Hearst could only nod, gazing down into Goodall's weary, angry face with its tight-drawn leathery skin and burning eyes. I've seen photographs of faces like this in my newspapers, he thought, passing a hand across his brow, but this is the real thing, right at my doorstep.

Wrapped in a blue quilted comforter, Goodall shivered in the wing chair in front of a newly rebuilt fire in Hearst's study. "Don't git me wrong," he said in his dust-dry voice, gripping the chair arms. "I ain't sayin' you big bosses owe us little guys nothin', but you've got the goods, and we ain't, and we deserve a decent chance t'work for 'em."

"Of course you do."

"My wife and kids." A bony finger pointed. "They're down yonder in my Ford. A man's got to help another man. I'll work it off, but you got to get 'em food and blankets now."

"The storm washed out our road."

Fiercely: *"I got up the hill without no road."*

"You did indeed," Hearst said. He did not bother to explain about dangerous animals. Animals were animals, people were people, and it was time to do the right thing, no matter how hard it was. "Joe," he said to Willicombe, who stood at a discreet distance.

"Sir?"

"Get a party of men together. Give them ropes—and guns, in case any of the animals act up. Tell them to be damn careful, but tell them to get through. They're to take plenty of milk and food to Mr.

318

Goodall's family, and then they're to hitch a ride to the nearest telephone and call for help."

"The police too?"

Hearst glanced at Tom Goodall. "The police too."

"Oh, Lord," Goodall whimpered and clamped his face in his weathered hands.

"Do it, Joe," Hearst said. When Willicombe was gone, he pulled up a chair near Goodall. He pitied the man, even if he might be a murderer; he searched for the right words. "You say you didn't mean to harm Mr. Chaplin and Miss Deere?"

Goodall's Adam's apple bobbed. "Th-that wuz really Charlie Chaplin? I saw him in a movie once. Course not; I wouldn't shoot nobody, not even you, mad as I wuz. The gun just went off. Guess I didn't know what I wuz doin'." He shuddered. Willicombe had led him up and on the way had gotten his story haltingly from him. Goodall had nearly gone over the cliff in the accident that had killed Billy Buller. He had scrambled the rest of the way up the hill. Cold, wet, exhausted, he had fallen asleep on one of the sofas in Casa del Monte's sitting room. The sofa faced away from the door; no one had seen him. Chaplin's knock had startled him awake, and mingled confusion, anger, and fear had caused him to wave the gun, which had gone off accidentally.

They had fed him hot broth. A steaming cup of coffee sat at his elbow.

There was a long silence. "B-but I *did* shoot somebody," Goodall stammered, looking like a condemned man being strapped into the electric chair.

"A little man?"

"Yep. Guess I'll just have to face the p'lice when they get here."

"Why did you shoot him?"

"Him and his friends jumped me."

Hearst leaned forward. "His friends?"

"Yep. Bunch o' midgets. I thought a goldarn circus'd broke loose. I'd got to the top, headin' for your big house, lookin' for help for my family. I wuz in some bushes when a whole tribe of 'em jumped me."

"A tribe? . . . Was it very dark in those bushes?"

319

"Like the inside of a cow."

"You didn't see these little men very well, then?"

"Nope, but they screeched and grabbed at me—even bit. See this blood?" Goodall showed a crusted-over gash on his thumb. "I had my gun in my hand. I shot one, and t'others run away. I meant t'stop and help the one I'd hit, honest I did, but like you say, it wuz so dark and I got so mixed up and so turned around I couldn't find 'im. I wuz mighty scared though. Guess I wuz dizzy too, from climbin' and not eatin', so I just run in the first house I come to, the one you found me in. I didn't mean t'fall asleep, but I did. Couldn't help myself."

Hearst stood. He felt like laughing, but there was nothing funny. "You shot a baboon, Mr. Goodall."

"A baboon?"

"A sort of a monkey. I have a zoo up here. The earthquake damaged some cages, and the baboons escaped. You shot one of them."

Goodall stared. "I'll be goldarned! And . . . and the p'lice?"

"You didn't harm Mr. Chaplin or Miss Deere, only scared them. And I don't think it's illegal to kill a baboon in self-defense."

Goodall's deep-set eyes narrowed. "You say you run a newspaper?"

"I own a few."

"Well I just bet they tell the truth about things. You ain't half bad."

"Thank you, Mr. Goodall." The compliment didn't make Hearst feel proud. He turned to the fire. Why couldn't it warm him? The forgotten man, that's what Joe had said Eddie Deere had called Tom Goodall, and it was true: Goodall was one of the forgotten men from the dust bowl, the whirlwind at the heart of the nation, one of the people reeling under the blows of closed banks and buried farms and gangsters shooting up the land. Truth, real truth, sat in the leather wing chair, as if some larger plan had led Tom Goodall here to make Hearst see. Eddie had seen it instinctively. The kid knows more, Hearst thought. How much? Did Pike-Penworthy tell him before Eddie shot him?

Hearst's shoulders twitched. *If* Eddie shot him.

He turned back. Tom Goodall must have been the person without a yellow slicker whom Charlie Chaplin had glimpsed near Casa

320

Grande, but who had the other person been? "You didn't cut my phone lines, did you?" Hearst asked.

Goodall's weathered brow furrowed. "Now why would I do a thing like that?"

The old man rubbed his jaw. Why, indeed, he thought.

❧ 27 ❧

A T four forty-eight Louella Parsons charged into the study. "Oh, W.R.!" she moaned, and burst into tears.

Tom Goodall had been led to a guest room in the north wing, and Hearst once more had been alone at the long mahogany table drumming his fingers and brooding over motives for killing Pike-Penworthy. Some people had them, that was for sure, but some people also would have good reason for cheering on the dwarf if they knew what he was up to. Not all of my friends are friends, Hearst reflected glumly as Louella stumbled in like something coughed up by the storm. He rose and she wobbled across to him to paw like a dog at his shirtfront. "Now, now, get hold of yourself," he said, unnerved, patting her lumpy shoulders. The damn woman has perfect timing! he thought. Outside the third-floor windows, daylight was thinning, crowded by the rain and the impending end of afternoon. Hearst scowled at the looming dusk. Too convenient for a killer. Damn it, I want this over, the truth!

Murmuring reassurances, he manuevered the sobbing Louella to the wing chair that was seeing so much traffic. The columnist flopped into it like something boneless and broken. Her lipstick was as crooked as if a child had smeared it on, and at least two inches of white slip hung lopsidedly below the hem of a purple dress that bloomed with lurid scarlet poppies. Wailing, she plunged a hand into her bosom.

Spare me, Hearst thought.

She pulled out a bent photograph and thrust it toward him—"There!"—and sank into weeping once more. "Awful! It was so awful! But I did it"—she sniffed—"for *you!*"

Hearst gripped the photo as if it might fly off of its own accord and vanish once more. The girl: demure eyes and a soft dimpled smile. Unswept hair with curls at the neck and shell-like ears. His heart ached. He did not have to turn it over to know what had been written on the back in the looping feminine hand nearly three decades ago: *For Billy from your sweetie.*

Pain stabbed him. My sweetie . . . Tessie. Tessie Powers. But Tessie had long since ceased to exist.

"Where did you get this?" he asked.

"I took it off that nasty little man's body. P-Pike."

Hearst stared gravely. Louella?

"Why did you shoot him?"

Louella's mascara ran in spidery rivulets down her cheeks. Her puffy face lifted. She blinked, her mouth worked wetly. "Shoot him? I didn't shoot him." Louella dragged a gun from her purse. "*You* did." She pointed the gun at Hearst. "With this."

❦ 28 ❧

"L OUELLA cut our lines?" Willicombe goggled in disbelief. "Louella Parsons?"

"She says she did. Her story is easy to check; she says she dragged them downhill and threw them in the Neptune Pool."

"Snakes!" Willicombe exclaimed, poking at his glasses.

"What?"

"Herman Mankiewicz has been going on about snakes in the pool. I thought he was drunk, seeing things, but it must be the cut lines. So Louella *did* tell you the truth. But why did she cut them?"

The two men stood in the alcove at the east end of the study. Blotches of long deep shadows stretched into the hundred-mile wilderness of the Santa Lucias, and the last fragments of daylight seemed to flee into the vastness. "To protect me," Hearst said.

"Protect . . . ?"

Hearst curled his fingers in the pockets of his maroon velvet robe. "It turns out you weren't the first person to discover the dwarf's body in the elevator. She was. She had seen me with that gun; then she stumbled on the body and put two and two together—the wrong way. She thought I had shot him, and she went a little crazy. She even searched him, took a photograph off him that she thought might have been evidence against me. She knew the road was out. She thought if she cut the lines it would keep the police away, give me time."

"But that doesn't make sense."

A gloomy nod. "It doesn't, does it? Time for what? How could I escape, if I needed to? But it made sense to her. She sees herself as a kind of heroine, performing valiant deeds for me."

"It's remarkable loyalty," Willicombe said after a troubled pause.

"Of course, there was a story there, a real scoop. Maybe she thought she could print it one day." Rain spat against the wide windows. Hearst sighed. "In any case, she did lift the picture and she did cut the lines. She took this too." He pulled a revolver from his robe pocket.

Willicombe narrowed his eyes at it. "Marvin Orr's?"

"The same."

"Has it been fired?"

"There are bullets in only three chambers. "Orr's negligence, or . . . ?"

"Too many hours since yesterday night to smell it and tell?"

"Yes, Joe, too many hours."

"Where did she get it?"

Hearst crossed the room and placed it on the mahogany table. "She says she found it in the elevator with the dwarf. She thought it was mine; that's why she didn't leave it there."

"If I ever kill someone I want her on my side! Sorry, sir; it's no joking matter. We *do* need the police, don't we? Their lab men could tell whether a bullet from this gun—"

"Matches the bullet that killed Penworthy? But we don't have that bullet."

"I forgot. You said Louella thought the photographs Penworthy stole might be evidence against you. Why would she think that?"

Hearst seemed to debate inwardly. "Let's leave that for now," he said at last. "I'll tell you this much, Joe: Louella may have done me a favor after all."

"I see." But Willicombe did not see at all. "What in the world was she doing out last night?" he asked.

"Following a lead. People make fun of Louella, but she's a good newspaperwoman, of her kind. She has an instinct for a story, and she knew all along there was something funny about the dwarf."

Willicombe followed Hearst to the table. "Did she see anything else? Does she know who killed him?"

"No. At least she says she doesn't. She's very upset. I sent her back to her room and asked Docky to give her a sedative. Speaking of upset, how are the other guests?"

"This rain isn't helping. They're jumpy, all right. People want to know why Marion doesn't come down. She will, won't she? She always cheers things up."

"It would help, wouldn't it?" Hearst toyed with the letters on the desk without seeing them. "I'll talk to her. She doesn't like the idea of death any more than I do. But I've got to face it. Damn it, I hate the night! You sent men downhill to help Goodall's family?"

"An hour ago. They have heavy-duty flashlights and food, but it will take a long time to work their way around the collapsed section of road, especially in the dark. And then it's another four miles to the coast highway."

"Get those telephone and telegraph lines out of the pool. Then get a workman started fixing them."

"That will take time too."

Hearst stared into the rain-filled dusk. "Time's a goddamn tyrant, Joe. Lunchtime, dinnertime, deathtime." He turned. "Death is creeping up on me."

"Don't say that, sir. You have lots of years left."

"Not if whoever killed Pike is after me too."

Or if there *is* some scandal that might finish you, Willicombe thought. "You think—"

"Forget I said that, Joe. I want to speak to that young woman, Gloria Deere. Get her up here right away. And without causing a fuss."

When Willicombe had gone Hearst sank into the big old armchair by the fire. The study was well insulated, but he could feel the massive house stirring as if it were alive, pumping blood. Downstairs the Filipino cooks would be preparing dinner, butlers would be setting the long wooden table in the refectory, maids would bustle about making final preparations for the night. Night . . . death. Hearst almost longed for death. Then he trembled in fear. No! Stay away for a few more years! I'm not ready yet! He made his heart calm. Ready . . . the readiness is all. His thick fingers drummed. He had not told Willicombe everything. Louella had searched Eddie Deere's room; she had found letters from Chicago, from a man named Swann.

The letters were addressed to Eddie McGuffin.

So it's true. Hearst faced it: Eddie McGuffin, Rose McGuffin's son.

There had also been a photograph, of a man in a linotype room holding a copy of the Chicago *Evening American*. My paper, Hearst thought, and he was sure he knew the man: Harry McGuffin, who so many years ago had died falling off a train.

Oh, God, Hearst thought.

Listening to rain and fire, he waited for Gloria Deere.

❦ 29 ❦

"Y OU'RE very pretty, Miss Deere."

A fetching blush bloomed in her round, fresh cheeks.

"Gee, thanks, Mr. Hearst."

"Don't be shy. I just want a friendly chat. Sit down?"

"Oh, sure." Gloria Deere had been led in by Willicombe, who had then discreetly departed. The large-eyed young woman settled in the leather armchair. She wore a black lacy dress, long white gloves, pearls she had obviously put on for dinner. Hearst examined her: brunette curls, creamy skin, dimples and a ripe young body. A thousand girls like her, he thought, all fighting for parts in the movies. She was obviously nervous. Guilty? Bosom heaving, she perched right on the edge of the chair, hands on her knees, fluttering her lashes up at him and waiting.

"You were in one of Marion's pictures, I understand," he began.

"Oh, yes sir," she said. "*Going Hollywood*. With Bing Crosby and Fifi D'Orsay. Only a little part, but it was just *thrilling*. To work with Marion, I mean. She's such a great actress."

"I'm sure she'd be glad to hear you say so." He bent toward her. "Have you ever worked with Charlie Chaplin?"

"Charlie—?"

"Chaplin. Here? Outside? At night?"

The girl's eyes saucered, and her lower lip trembled. "Oh, gee . . . oh, dear . . ." Her hands fluttered. "Oh, I just *knew* you'd find out, and now my career's sunk; I'll never get a part again."

Hearst had to smile. "You overestimate my power—and you underestimate my sense of humor. It was a good joke; I like to have young people have fun up here. So you did help Mr. Chaplin dress up Aphrodite?"

"He told you?"

"Let's just say I found out. I don't mind; guests have played far worse pranks. I don't want to ask you about the statue so much as where you disappeared to in the rain."

"Oh, you're aces, Mr. Hearst! Well . . . the reason I ran off—" Her bare white shoulders twitched at the memory. "it was just awful! *Monkeys* chased me."

Hearst blinked. "And that was all?"

"All? I was scared out of my pants. I mean . . . you know. And Charlie didn't lift a finger to save me; I just hate him for that!"

He was occupied being shot, Hearst thought. He felt relief: Gloria's story tied in with what Tom Goodall had said. "Don't be too hard on Mr. Chaplin. He probably didn't realize what had happened to you. My baboons didn't hurt you, I hope. They're all back in their cages now."

"One tore my dress, but I'm all right. You really think Charlie didn't know?"

"I'm sure of it. But let me give you some advice: don't count too much on him. Those stories about him and women—lots of them are true."

"Oh, I know that; I wasn't born yesterday. I know that Charlie and me . . . it's just a fling. I just think that a girl has to have flings, before she's too old, and, well, I'll be honest: a girl who comes to Hollywood has to take care of herself, because no one else is going to. She has to keep her eyes open and grab every chance. I like Charlie and all—gee, I'm even a little cuckoo about him—but maybe he can do something for my career, too, I've gotta think of that. You see what I mean?"

Hearst nodded. He liked Gloria's frankness; she reminded him of Marion at her age. "Perhaps I can find you a part in my next production," he said.

"Oh, *could* you?" She leapt up and pecked his cheek.

Gravely he held her at arm's length. "We're with not through with this little talk, however. Tell me about your brother."

"Eddie? Oh, gee!" The young woman sank back into the chair.

"I thought so."

"Now you'll want to kick me right out of your house!" she wailed, her hands in the white gloves twisting and fidgeting. "Okay, here goes. He . . . he's not my brother." Eyes down, cheeks flaming, she told him how her real brother had written asking her to get Eddie a job at Metro.

"Your real brother?"

"Frank Swann. My true name's Ella Swann—Gloria Deere is just for the movies."

"I see." Hearst saw more than Gloria knew; he decided to take a chance. "Is your real brother a Communist?"

"Why, how'd you guess?"

"It doesn't matter."

Gloria described how Eddie had begged her to get him an invitation for the weekend.

"Why did he want to come here?"

"Wouldn't anyone want to?"

327

"But you don't know if he had any reasons other than the usual ones?"

Her pink tongue licked red lips. "You know, I *think* he does, but I don't know what."

"Why did you agree to lend him your name?"

"It was dumb, wasn't it? But I thought he was awfully cute. And sad." She looked up desperately. "I guess I'm just a sucker for men!" Then her eyes opened wide. "Omigosh, I just remembered: he has a gun! I saw it, this afternoon." She jumped up again. "Is that it, is that why you're asking?"

Hearst did not answer. Of course he has a gun, he thought; he has to have a gun.

❦ 30 ❧

FROM his window in Casa del Monte Eddie McGuffin gazed uphill toward the big floodlit house glimmering through its veil of rain. I hate that pile! It was built by sucking the life's blood out of the poor folks of this country. The bodies of the proletariat seemed to writhe as if buried alive beneath its stones, and Eddie seemed to hear their voices crying out to him *Help us!* He wiped a trembling hand across his brow. No. There aren't any voices, it's only the rain. Anyway, he didn't need anything to get him going. He had come here to help, to *do* something, hadn't he? Couldn't back down now. But things had changed. Marion; old man Hearst—and Eddie's awful guilt, which he had not felt before. Guilt for something he had not known yet and could never escape: blood.

His own blood.

He glanced at his cheap watch; nearly dinnertime. He pictured all the swells who never had to worry about their next meal stuffing their faces in the Refectory and making smart wisecracks while the world went down the drain. Would anyone miss him? No. If he jumped off the face of the earth not a single person would shed a

328

tear. He shook his head. Wrong again. Ma would miss me—the lying bitch!

Eddie stood; he jammed the gun in his coat pocket. His upper lip glistened with sweat. Time for murder, he thought, but not the man I planned.

❧ 31 ❧

"DEAREST." William Randolph Hearst paused in Marion Davies' bedroom door.

Marion sat before her dressing table mirror, staring at herself. She turned amid a rustle of orchid crepe de chine. She looked frail and lost, and Hearst could not help thinking of her niece who had killed herself. Did a penchant for self-destruction run in the family? "Am I g-getting old, P-Popsy?" she asked.

Hearst stepped into the room. He chose his words carefully. "We're all getting older."

"Old, I said, n-not older!" Peering into the mirror, leaning close as if it were a crystal ball that could answer any question, she caressed her face. "There are l-lines around my eyes. J-Just l-little ones, but . . . lines."

Crossing to her, Hearst placed his hands on her soft shoulders. "I don't see any lines. I'll never see any lines, and you have beautiful eyes. Are you okay now? Can you go down to dinner? Everybody's asking for you."

"To h-hell with them! . . . Oh . . . all right." Abruptly she turned and grabbed his hand, staring up in sudden fear. "What'd you d-do about that d-dead man?"

"Don't worry. I've hushed it up. For now. Our guests don't know anything about his being killed, so you mustn't mention it."

She searched his face, then jumped up and flung a pink boa about her shoulders. "It won't be like that Ince thing? The c-cops'll take care of it?"

I'll take care of it, Hearst thought.

Marion cosied up to him, pressing her body close. "L-let's go down together. I'm awfully sorry for being s-so b-bitchy this weekend." She breathed seductively in his face. "I'll m-make it up to you."

"You don't have to make up for anything." He clasped her hand hard. "Marion . . . I have to tell you something. I was so mad at you last night that I chased after you. With a gun."

Her blue eyes flickered with panic. "You didn't *sh-shoot* that little guy?"

"Of course not. But I wanted to shoot someone. I did shoot, too. Six shots, into the air. I was just letting off steam. I'm telling you this in case . . . in case—"

"Popsy! You l-love me so much you went after me with a g-gun?" She put her fingers on his lips. "No, d-don't s-say one word more. I don't want to know. You're s-silly, but you're s-sweet, and I just *adore* you for it! Now, it's dinnertime. L-let's go eat."

He let go of her hand. "Not quite yet. I have things to do."

She smacked a kiss on his chin. "Work, work, work. B-but you're c-cute anyway, P-Popsy. Come down s-soon as you c-can." A flashing grin, and she was gone.

Why do I let her charm me? Hearst thought. He felt a chill, an aching void where her slender, perfumed form had pressed against him. Because I can't help it, came the answer, and because I know she really needs me. He crossed the sitting room, where the mouse cage still sat empty. He was glad he had told her about shooting the gun last night. I *do* love her enough to kill for her, and I want her to know it. In his dressing room he pulled a dark waterproof coat on over his pin-striped suit, Helena whining at his heels. "No, girl," he told the dog. Grimly he descended in the paneled elevator, where less than twenty-four hours ago Willicombe had shown him the gruesomely dead body of Lester C. Penworthy, alias Otis Pike. Any other aliases? Hearst made a face: the sad little man must have been after me for years. On the ground floor he heard laughter from the Assembly Hall, but he turned away from the hidden door.

Opening an unobtrusive side exit, he slipped out into the softly raining night.

330

❧ 32 ❧

T HE north wing of Casa del Monte felt deserted. They're all up at the big house, eating my food, making jokes, Hearst thought as he passed from the entranceway into the sitting room—though he bet not all his guests were laughing. A battered old hat lay almost out of sight by an end table. Tom Goodall's. That hat is important to Goodall; I'll take it up when I go back.

The massive old man slipped into Eddie McGuffin's room.

Low lamplight illuminated it in a soft orange glow. The windows were shiny black, slick with rain, and to avoid being observed Hearst quickly drew the curtains.

He turned and peered about. The room was as antique-laden as his hundred other guest rooms: oriental carpets, dully gleaming old wood. A Della Robbia Madonna smiled gently from a niche above the fireplace, and a small Cranach, *The Sacrifice of Isaac*, hung by the door. Only the faintest *whoosh* of rain could be heard from outside.

Hearst found the letters from the man named Swann under a shirt in a dresser drawer. He did not spend much time with them, just enough to see that Swann had used the kid. The damn bolshie exhorted Eddie, put ideas in his brain, nutty ideas about wiping out the ruling class by violence, but the letters were carefully couched; Swann was so slippery that no court of law could convict him of complicity if Eddie happened to run out and shoot somebody. In disgust Hearst tossed the packet back. The other letters were more important.

They weren't hidden, sitting in plain sight on the oak nightstand. The bed's brocade coverlet showed an indentation. The old man touched the spread. Was it his imagination that he could still feel warmth? Eddie had sat there: how many moments ago? thinking what? Poor confused kid. Grumbling under his breath the old man

331

scooped up the second bundle of letters and went through them. There were only seven, all ending with a typed *B.R.* Bart Rawlston, had to be; the bastard Rawlston always knew just what to do with scandal! Feeling balanced on disaster, Hearst read each one. Though at the opposite end of the political spectrum from Swann, Rawlston proved to be just as canny: he had used cheap paper and allowed no hint of his true identity to peek through. Hearst stared unseeing at the curtained room. Eddie must have stolen Swann's letters from the dwarf's room. Was it Eddie who had shoved the briefcase on that high closet shelf? Hearst's hands shook. No doubt: Rawlston was in collusion with the dwarf to smear me. What if Rawlston had succeeded? Worse, could he still do it? The letters said he knew about Rose Ellen Forrest, so he must have guessed her father was bribed to come west to work for my papers in a nice secure job where he would keep his mouth shut. Thank God old Forrest is senile; he couldn't reveal the truth about his daughter's death even if someone got to him. Hearst crammed the letters in an inside coat pocket, shuddering as the wind rattled a window, as if the plan he had hatched decades ago had taken human form and clawed the pane, seeking revenge.

It *had* taken human form, hadn't it? Eddie McGuffin.

Impelled by a sense that there was little time left, the old man searched on with wheezing breath. In the nightstand drawer he found the packet of photographs Vinny Tashman had described, and a box of pistol cartridges. Several cartridges were gone; Hearst let the remainder dribble through his fingers. Had one of the missing ones plowed through Penworthy's brain? And the rest? Were they in the pistol Eddie carried now, waiting to finish what he had started? Eddie had ransacked the dwarf's room, so he must know it all—had to, because he himself was the final link Penworthy had been searching for when he was killed. So Eddie must have shot him. But why? Wouldn't Eddie want to help the dwarf?

Unless . . .

Still frowning, Hearst examined the photographs. Rose's house in Chicago. There was no doubt about that either. He was glad to see that it was so obviously a nice big comfortable house; the woman deserved that. She appeared in several pictures, and though he had not seen her in decades she was unmistakable, still pretty in a soft, girlish way. And there was the mantel; on it, the photo of him and the newsboys, his hand on Eddie's shoulder—and he saw that it *was* Eddie, Eddie Deere—Eddie McGuffin—and his soul ached with pain and guilt. Damn the dwarf! He had gotten these pictures by some ruse; he had tricked poor Rose. Had Penworthy recognized that the nine-year-old kid in that photo had grown up into the glum young man who said he was Gloria Deere's brother? Likely only at the end. How could Penworthy imagine Eddie would arrive on the hill at the same time, with the same purpose: to get at William Randolph Hearst? There too on the mantel was the glass globe with the Alpine scene inside, the twin of the one in his bedroom upstairs. Hearst peered years back, into memory: Europe; Verona; Wiesbaden. Tessie. Eyes swimming, he clutched his chest. She kept the picture and the toy in a position of honor, he thought, and he trembled, crying out in rage and self-loathing. I don't deserve any honor, none at all, even if I tried to do the honorable thing, to fix the awful mess.

Or was I just a coward?

Hearst could not find the picture of Harry McGuffin; the kid must have it on him. He grunted ironic laughter. Of course. A boy's father is important to him, someone to look up to.

Even when the father is a son of a bitch.

Will Eddie shoot me? Hearst thought, tramping out into black night and rain.

Maybe I deserve to be shot!

If so . . .

Clutching the forgotten man's battered old hat, he headed up to face what must be.

❧ 33 ❧

HEARST paused in shadow near the elevator, his old head lifted, listening. A volley of cheer burst from behind the closed doors of the Refectory, but the gaiety could not thaw the gnawing chill about his heart. They were like voices wishing him bon voyage. He paled. I complain, but I like to have people here, he thought. I need them. To show off to, to make Marion happy.

Marion. Tessie.

I've loved two women in my life.

Entering the elevator, he rose to the indifferent hum of the cables. The elevator stopped at the third floor, and, exiting, he paused. Not a sound except for the muffled hiss of rain, but he sensed he was not alone. He glanced in Marion's room. Empty except for her dachshund asleep on silk sheets. Good, she was safe downstairs, in company. The study in the Gothic suite was empty too, gloomy and more cloisterlike than ever in the light of a single parchment-shaded lamp. The sitting room: deserted. That left only his bedroom.

He stepped into it.

The man sat at Hearst's desk, very still, head bowed, shoulders hunched.

Slowly he turned; his cheeks ran with tears.

Eddie. Of course.

Eddie, who, when you knew what to look for, uncannily resembled the portrait of William Randolph Hearst as a young man that hung above the fireplace in the study.

Hearst took a deep breath, let it out. Time, his whole life, seemed to gather to this moment. Pulling off his damp raincoat, he tossed it over a chair. He slid his hands in his jacket pockets. "Well, Eddie."

"You bastard." Eddie's voice was choked, strained, and Hearst thought his own heart would crack. Pathetic boy! His hair hung in a mop over his brow. My hair used to be thick like that, it used to hang like that, Hearst thought. And there's the long nose, like mine. The eyes blue, like mine. Eddie had been staring at the glass globe containing the ingeniously carved Alpine village. Knuckles white, he lifted it, shook it furiously at Hearst while the snow swirled in an obscuring cloud. "What is this?" he cried.

"I bought it in Wiesbaden. In Germany."

"You bought two of them, didn't you?"

"Yes."

"With my ma?"

Hearst nodded. "She picked them out. She never liked big things, only little ones, pretty ones. For sentimental value."

"It was on one of your summer trips, wasn't it? Your famous summer trips?" the young man said contemptuously.

"Many years ago."

"Before your wife? Before Marion Davies?"

"Before Marion."

"You *are* an old bastard. I s'pose you were happy with yourself? But I came along. You weren't married to my ma—a kid wouldn't do. So you had to cover it all up. What was wrong with marrying my ma? Not good enough for you?" Eddie slammed the globe onto the marble desktop so hard Hearst thought it would shatter. Dragging a dog-eared photograph from a pocket, he thrust it out accusingly. "My father! M-my father . . ."

Hearst recognized the picture Louella had described, the blur of a man by the Linotype machine. "Not your blood father. But Harry McGuffin was a good man; he was your father, more than I ever was. He loved your mother. He believed she was Rose Ellen Forrest, a young girl who had gotten in trouble and had a baby boy, but he loved her just the same, enough to marry her. He loved you too, I know he did. It's too bad he died in that accident, but—"

"Accident? You killed him!"

Hearst lifted his hands from his pockets in shock. He stared at Eddie's working face. "You must hate me very much to believe that. Killed him? Why would I want to do that? I paid for the best medical care to try to save him, and—"

335

A terrible uncertainty flooded Eddie's eyes. He stood slowly. "B-but he was fighting your papers, organizing, trying to start a union."

Hearst drew himself up. "I *fight* my enemies; I don't assassinate them."

Eddie gasped. "Oh, God."

Hearst peered at him. "You really thought I had Harry McGuffin murdered? Is that why you came up here? Because you believed I had him pushed off that train?"

"And . . . and you didn't?"

"Of course not. Your mother had grown to love him. I would never do anything more to hurt her."

Eddie swallowed, an audible gulp, as if he were swallowing a thick, bitter lump of truth. But his expression still raged. He plowed a hand through his hair. "Forget about that, then; you've committed enough crimes without that." He jerked a blunt-nosed pistol from his pocket. "Besides, I didn't come up here for me, I came because you're a capitalist oppressor, and you and your kind have got to be stopped."

"You got those words from a man named Swann."

"You searched my room, huh? Think you're smart? Think you know it all? Well, maybe you don't kill your enemies, but I *do* kill mine." Eddie pointed the gun at Hearst's face.

Hearst stared into the round black hole of the barrel. "I'm not your enemy," he said.

"You're the enemy of the little man. You're the enemy of this country."

"I love this country."

"You don't have any right to love it."

"Why? Because I have money?" Hearst took a step closer. He wanted to comfort the boy, save him, but Eddie also had to hear the truth. "The poor aren't better than other people, Eddie, just poorer. You really want to do something about what's wrong with this crazy country? Maybe I can give you a chance. Only put away that gun."

Eddie sneered. "Scared?"

To his surprise Hearst found that he was not.

Eddie saw it. A bleak wash of confusion swept over his face, and

336

his voice became small, a child's. His gun arm sagged. "Wh-what's my mother's real name?"

"Powers. Tessie Powers."

"P-Powers . . ." He tasted the name on trembling lips. "You've sent her money all these years?"

"Yes."

A self-mocking laugh. 'I thought it was insurance, from my father's death. That's how dumb I was."

"Not dumb. You had every reason to believe it."

"And . . . he wasn't even my father." Eddie stared helplessly at Hearst.

"He was a brave, idealistic man. He loved you."

Bitterly: "And you? Do you love me?"

Hearst looked directly into the young man's face. "I want to."

Rain tapped the windows. The honesty of the response seemed to stun Eddie, and he recoiled as if he had been punched. He shook his head again and again. "Well, I don't care, I don't care!" He seemed lost, frantic, wavering at the edge of a deep abyss. "You're still a bastard! The dwarf told me. Before I shot him. Told me . . . everything. How you stole a dead girl's identity for my mother, bought her father out by giving him a job."

"The girl was already dead," Hearst said, "of natural causes; I had nothing to do with that. Abel Forrest needed a job. And your mother needed a new life. We made a fair exchange."

"To protect you."

"I admit I didn't want to face a scandal—not that your mother ever would have said a word. But it was to give *you* a chance too."

Eddie spread his arms, scarecrowlike, mouth working. "And look how I turned out."

"What do you mean? You look okay to me; you're a fine young man." Hearst took another pleading step forward. Only two feet separated them, and he was shocked at the hopelessness that swam in Eddie's eyes. "You're young, strong. Idealistic, like Harry McGuffin."

Eddie pressed the pistol barrel to the old man's chest. "Don't try to soft-soap me. It's too late. The dwarf told me how you ruined

337

everything for him too. You smashed his life, his leg; you killed his parents."

"That was an accident?"

"Like me? Don't feed me that malarkey! But he was smarter than me. He knew, and he came after you. He told me a lot. Those little marks on the notes he sent? They were his joke; he said you'd never guess until he'd nailed you. Well, he mighta been wrong about your killing my—Harry McGuffin, but he figured out the rest. He said he finally knew it by the eyes. He had papers that some man had sent him, about us. Harry McGuffin's eyes were brown. So were my mother's. But mine—mine are blue, like yours. So we're alike, aren't we, just stupid bums who make big mistakes?"

"You're not stupid, Eddie. . . . You shot him in the vaults; why did you move his body?"

"Because it was there, where the evidence was. I had to get it out. I was going to put him in the rain, but a guard came along, and I had to hit him; and then, just as the elevator got to the main floor, someone else showed up—that snooping Parsons woman, and I couldn't hit her, couldn't do any more . . . any more hurt . . . and I . . . I ducked out of sight and just ran back to my room."

To meet Marion? Hearst did not speak the painful thought. Marvin Orr's gun must've tumbled into the elevator when Eddie hit him; that was where Louella had found it.

"I meant to go back to the vaults," Eddie jabbered on, "to clean up the mess the dwarf had made. I didn't want anyone to know."

"About you and me? Is that why you shot him?"

Eddie's upper lip curled. "He was a slimy little rat. Shooting him— it was like shooting myself. Yes, I didn't want anyone to know. The dwarf was going to publish it, ruin you."

"You didn't want to ruin me?"

"It would ruin Ma too. Why did she lie? Oh, God, I hate her! I hate you both, but . . . but . . ."

Hearst saw in Eddie's face that he loved his mother. Could he love me? Could I really make it up to him?

Eddie blinked. His face seemed to dissolve. "Don't you see? Nothing else would have stopped him. It was all too late, too late for—"

Hearst held out his hand. "It's not too late, Eddie. I made a mistake, lots of them. But I can make it up. I—"

Eddie stepped back. "I came here to shoot you, know that? But I can't. How can I shoot the man who . . . who's my . . ." Something changed in his face. "There *is* something I can do though. Something that will fix everything. You know what that is? Do you?"

"No," Hearst said; then the lost glint in Eddie's squinting blue eyes told him, and he lunged for the gun—but not in time. With one last horrified stare at an imperfect world, the young man swung the pistol up, jammed it under his chin, fired. The crack of the shot echoed flatly, absorbed by the thick walls, and a stink of cordite flooded the room. Eddie twisted, slumped; Hearst caught him. The gun struck the crystal globe; there was the sound of breaking glass. Hearst lowered Eddie to the scarlet carpet, felt frantically, vainly for a pulse.

Cradling the form, Hearst moaned as his hands grew sticky with the dead boy's blood.

Casa Grande's clocks struck nine.

🎜 34 🎝

FLAMES leapt in the fireplace in the Assembly Hall. The vast room was deserted, all the guests were gone, led in a chattering string along an arduously constructed quarter-mile detour around the collapsed road and ferried downhill by rented limousine. They had dispersed, to be swallowed up by Hollywood, New York, Chicago, and not a trace of high spirits remained. Cold, so cold. Shivering, alone, surrounded by the tokens of a life— antique lamps, crystal boxes, life-size marble statues that stared without sympathy—a bulky old man knelt before the fire like a suppliant, seeking warmth, feeding scraps of paper into its dancing flames. William Randolph Hearst. His damp gaze drifted to windows north and south, where rain tapped steadily, gently, before he fed in in another scrap, a photograph of a room in a house in Chicago: an open cabinet, a table with a jigsaw puzzle, a glimpse of a woman's slender arm and small, mottled hand. Hearst's gut wrenched.

Eddie! We tried to save you, Eddie! To make up for our mistake!

He heard footsteps, and Joe Willicombe's shiny black shoes came into view. Hearst slid another paper into the fire. He raised his eyes.

Willicombe poked at his glasses. "You're . . . all right, sir?"

"Yes, thank you, Joe."

"I thought you'd want to know about Tom Goodall and his family."

"I do want to know."

"Randolph Apperson has taken them in hand, as you instructed. Their bellies are full, and they've been settled into a little house on the ranch. Goodall will be a useful addition, Apperson says."

Hearst passed a shaky hand before his eyes. "And the other forgotten men?"

"The other—?"

"Who will save them?" the old man demanded fiercely.

Willicombe touched his glasses again. "I . . . don't know, sir."

"God damn it, Joe, who will save *me*?" Hearst ducked his head. "Sorry . . . sorry . . ."

A veil of sparks danced in the fire. Willicombe looked like saying many things, but all that came out was, "Jack Neylan asked me to give you this." He pulled an envelope from his clipboard.

Hearst ripped it open. Inside, columns of figures spelled disaster for the Hearst Corporation if drastic cutbacks were not made. "To hell with Neylan," he muttered, crumpling the message and tossing it in the flames. "There's something I forgot: Vinny Tashman. Get him a job at Warners. They owe me. Jack Warner says the latest Jimmy Cagney needs a rewrite; Tashman can surely handle that. And that little brunette, Gloria Deere—sign her for our next picture; I promised her."

"Yes, sir." A shifting of feet. "Sir, Donovan knows to keep his mouth shut, but—just in case—I'd like to transfer him to Wyntoon."

Wyntoon was Hearst's northern California estate, isolated among redwoods. "Good idea."

"And, er, will Docky and Louella—?"

"Will they keep quiet too? Oh, yes." Hearst sighed. "People say Louella knows where all the bodies are buried, but they overestimate her. She's certainly not going to know how we've disposed of Penworthy, but she knows she can count on a dead end with my papers if she ever leaks a word of what she found in the elevator. That isn't the reason she'll shut up, though. She'll do it for me; it's payment for the time I saved her life. Docky will follow suit." The old man ground his hands together. "Speaking of the dwarf, how are arrangements proceeding?"

"We're managing. He's already off the hill. He'll be found in Los Angeles, in a small hotel on La Cienega, with enough identification so they'll know who he is if not how or why he died. An unsolved crime. There are plenty of those. We'll pull strings: he'll be buried with his parents in New York, as you wanted."

Hearst stirred. "It's some sort of justice."

"Yes, sir."

"Buller went downhill too?"

"To his family, in Paso Robles."

"Family," Hearst said. He swallowed hard. "And . . . the boy?"

"The Santa Lucias have him, sir."

Hearst pictured the spot he himself had chosen, pristine, windswept, under a huge, lone bay laurel, with a view of the sea. A secret grave, but inviolable. Near. A place he could visit, among sweet grasses. Honorable? His hands clenched. It's the best I can do to honor you, Eddie! Looking up, he saw worry on his secretary's face; questions too. "The boy was my fault, Joe," he said, "but it's not a matter for the police, believe me."

"Not necessary to say so, sir."

"I can't tell you more."

"Your word is good enough. Is there anything else?"

"No. Wait, I forgot—that roll of film in Penworthy's heel: you developed it?"

"Blank. He never got around to photographing whatever he wanted pictures of."

"Thank you, Joe."

More sparks shot up. Wind beat at the old leaded panes. "If you need anything more, sir . . ." But the Chief had turned silently back to the fire, and Willicombe slipped away. Hearst stared into the flames. He had fed them almost everything: photographs, the letters from Swann and B.R., even the plans of Casa Grande with their cryptic marginal doodles; the fire had eaten the evidence. Only two things remained. A photograph of a pretty young woman with an old-fashioned hairdo, and a letter Hearst had discovered on the table in the study upstairs. *To Billy from your sweetie,* said the back of the photo. Not my sweetie, the old man thought, not for a long time, and he hated what he must tell her today when he called Chicago. He could not send her money to make up for that; money bought only a big empty house and lifeless antiques. Bitterly Hearst thought of the piles of photographs in his vaults downstairs. Useless, and I must give this up too. Tenderly he placed Tessie's picture on the flames. She smiled at him one last time; the edges curled, crisped, and the girl was gone, ashes drifting up. Hearst squeezed back tears. He reread the letter. "Dear Mr. Hearst," it began (that she could call him mister!).

> I know we agreed long ago that we must stop seeing one another, because of your position, because of Eddie. But I am terribly worried. Eddie is a very mixed up boy, always has been, and now he's taken up with the godless Communists, and he hates the church and me. Dear Mr. Hearst, he hates you too. If only he could know what you've done for him! He's run off to California, to Hollywood. He said he means to get a job in the movies, but I think he means to do something else. I don't know why, I just do. Please try to find him and befriend him. I know this goes against all we decided years ago, but after all you are his . . .

Hearst choked; his eyes swam, and he bunched the paper into a ball. It had to go too, the last scrap. He thrust it in the fire, and in seconds it was carbon.

"Popsy?"

Marion had come up silently; she hovered at his side in a pink chiffon robe.

"What're you d-doing, Popsy?"

He peered up. "Keeping warm."

Kneeling beside him, she shivered. "It's c-cold, isn't it? I *hate* it when p-people have to go away. I w-wish we could have a h-houseful all the time."

"We'll have another party soon."

Draping an arm around his shoulder, she snuggled close. Her scent filled his nose, and his heart ached. "I w-wanted to t-tell you something."

"What?"

"You know that g-guy Eddie you were so m-mad at?"

"Yes."

"Well . . . I *d-did* kinda l-like him. I admit it. B-but I figured out why: 'cause he m-made me think of you." A giggle. "Can you b-beat that? I don't know why, but he d-did." Her ivory brow furrowed. "That reminds me—where'd he g-go? I d-didn't see him leave with everybody else."

"He decided to leave early."

"Gosh, I h-hope he was careful down that w-washed-out road!"

Hearst said nothing.

She poked him. "Well, that p-proves something, doesn't it?"

"What does?"

"My l-liking him 'cause of you. It p-proves that it's only my old bear that I r-really l-love." She nibbled his ear, then jumped up. "I just h-had to tell you." Impatiently, Marion pushed aside her blond curls. "Oh, d-damn this rain! Let's have that n-next party real soon."

She floated out. Up to the booze?

I love you, Marion!

Hearst's right hand rested on the stone hearth. Feeling a soft warm something, he looked down. A mouse was sniffing his index finger, a mouse with one white paw. Hearst lifted the tiny creature, and it made no attempt to get away; it seemed to want to be back. The old man found a smile as he stroked its head. "Decided which side your bread was buttered on, eh?" He could even chuckle. "Damn mouse." Rousing his ancient body, he carried his pet upstairs.